Lonely Hearts
TRAVEL CLUB

DESTINATION:

CHILE

Praise for
KATY COLINS

'As well as being a sensory tour of a stunning country, this is a story with real heart. We absolutely loved it.'

– Heat on *Destination India*

'Katy writes with humour and heart. *The Lonely Hearts Travel Club* is like Bridget Jones goes backpacking.'

– Holly Martin, author of *The White Cliff Bay* series

'The perfect first-sunny-afternoon in the garden book!'

– Kathleen Gray on *Destination India*

'I cannot recommend this book enough. It is beautifully written with a brilliant plot and fantastic characters. READ IT!!'

– Blabbering About Books on *Destination Thailand*

'Imaginative, fascinating, and funny!'

– What's Better Than Books? on *Destination India*

'If you're looking for an escape from the cold, winter nights, the drudgery of day to day life and love to read about exotic locations then Katy Colins's debut novel is the book for you.'

– Ellen Faith on *Destination Thailand*

'A great book to pop in your holiday/weekend bag that will make you just want more.'

– The Reading Shed on *Destination India*

'*Destination Thailand* had me hooked from the very first page and kept me up 'til 2:30 a.m. as I was dying to know what happened next.'

– Books and Boardies

'I loved this book.'

– For the Love of Books on *Destination Thailand*

DESTINATION: CHILE

Katy Colins

CARINA™

This edition is published by arrangement with Harlequin Books S.A. CARINA is a trademark of Harlequin Enterprises Limited, used under licence.

First Published in Great Britain 2016
By Carina, an imprint of HarperCollins*Publishers*
1 London Bridge Street, London, SE1 9GF

© 2016 Katy Colins

ISBN 9780263923704

Our policy is to use papers that are natural, renewable and recyclable products and made from wood grown in sustainable forests.
The logging and manufacturing processes conform to the legal environmental regulations of the country of origin.

Printed and bound by
CPI Group (UK) Ltd, Croydon, CR0 4YY

KATY COLINS

Katy sold all she owned, filled a backpack and booked a one-way ticket to south east Asia after her wedding was called off – and never looked back.

The acclaimed travel blogger's experiences inspired her to pen The Lonely Travel Hearts Club and even saw her labelled the 'Backpacking Bridget Jones'.

When she's not globe-trotting, writing about her adventures and telling anyone who'll listen to grab life by the horns, Katy loves catching up with family and friends and convincing herself that her cake addiction isn't out of control – just yet.

You can find out more about Katy, her writing and her travels on her blog www.notwedordead.com or via social media @notwedordead

Available from
KATY COLINS

The Lonely Hearts Travel Club

The most inspiring people are the ones who don't even know they're doing it.

Charlotte, this is for you.

CHAPTER 1

Glean (v.) – To find out

'Do you *really* need another candle?' Ben asked, pushing our overflowing trolley through the winding aisles of Ikea.

I'd stopped to sniff the warming scent of a pale green, stumpy candle and stared at him as if he'd just asked me if I ever got tired of eating chocolate. 'You can *never* have too many candles; everyone knows that.'

'Well if it makes you happy, I guess. I just don't see the point in buying things to then set fire to; it's like you are literally burning money.' He laughed, shaking his head. 'Although the question is, are they called Grönkulla or Färdfull or even Knutstorp? I mean that could change *everything*.' He put on a terrible Scandinavian accent, like he had for most of the last hour, making me giggle.

'Actually, they're called Fyrkantig, but, oh my God, you're like fluent!' I teased.

He pushed out his chest proudly. 'Yup. Oh wait should that be "ja"? Come on, though, I'm starving and you promised me meatballs.'

I dropped a couple more gorgeously smelly candles in amongst the fluffy white cushions, photo frames and other practical and pretty household goods and linked my arm around his waist. 'Okay, one plate of meatballs coming right up.' I then bit my lip and looked at our stash. 'Do you reckon we've got everything we need?'

'We literally have got *everything*.' He let out a long groan, which I knew was hiding how much he'd actually enjoyed our jaunt through the huge warehouse that was so enormous it could be its own nation state.

I, on the other hand, had been stupidly nervous about our first couple's trip here. After all, shopping for joint furniture in Ikea was a rite of passage in any relationship, especially as the last time I'd been here with my ex, Alex, in this 'Swedish hellhole', as he'd called it, and we'd left with a Billy bookcase and a blazing row. We didn't speak for two hours after the shopping trip that I'd previously imagined to be full of excitement at building our home together and not the fraught nightmare of bickering arguments – and that was before we'd even got to the tricky part of assembling the damn things.

This time, everything was different. Ben and I had meandered through the vast shop on our first official visit; we weren't squabbling over who did the most cooking as we walked through the kitchen showroom, or awkwardly quickening our pace through the kids' section. It was, well, actually fun. It was everything I'd imagined it would be before that disastrous trip with Alex.

But now, two hours after first stepping foot in here, I realised that Ben's enjoyment levels were waning. The only time that we could both make it to come here was a Saturday and it felt like the rest of Manchester had had the exact same idea. We shuffled along, behind harassed DIY-ers, screaming children and couples having heated rows under their breath over who had the better taste in curtain patterns, all diligently following the maze of yellow arrows to the exit.

'I reckon they need to move away from each other before these tiny weeny pencils find themselves wedged some place they shouldn't be,' Ben had said, nodding at one older married couple who were glaring at each other with looks so vicious it seemed they might start divorce proceedings amongst the Jeff chairs and Ektorp sofas. For many people, stepping foot in here makes you suddenly realise that your partner's awful taste in soft furnishings represents all the things you despise about them and that, really, you can't actually stand each other.

I'd let out a little laugh and pulled him through one of the mystery *Scooby Doo* doors, a hidden passageway to skip over the bathroom showroom completely, a trick I'd remembered the last time I'd been here when I'd marched off in a huff after Alex had called my choice in bath mats 'too common'. The rat maze they force you to follow is why coming here is so full of potential pitfalls for any relationship whether new or well established: you can't easily leave. They lie to you about the exits – well they don't lie, but in my pissed off state I'd felt like I was stomping around in circles, passing the same bunch of equally harassed people clutching their bright yellow carrier bags like comfort blankets. But this time I was prepared. This time I knew the shortcuts.

'Let's never become like them. Promise me,' I'd whispered clutching Ben's hand.

We'd found ourselves, quite aptly, in the bedroom section. Ben playfully pulled me onto the nearest perfectly made up king-sized bed, with a duvet cover that would actually quite suit our bedroom, and lay me down on the soft surface.

'I promise.' He leant over and kissed me hard.

The tutting of an Indian man examining the nearby hypoallergenic pillows made me blush so I pulled us back to our feet to finish the shopping and get back home, to our own bed. Ikea is not a place for idle browsing and I may have strayed somewhat from the list I'd scrawled out as we'd had breakfast earlier. It was time to call it a day.

'Oooh, wait. I forgot we need cereal bowls!' I exclaimed as we moved onto the next section, remembering that the ones we currently had were chipped and, well, just not deep enough for my liking.

'Okay. Cereal bowls and *then* let's get out of here.'

'Deal.'

Ben's eyes had narrowed as if he was a character in a video game, some sniper assassin that had been trained to keep their focus on the target, refusing to be drawn in by my 'oh look, isn't that gorgeous!' or 'we need one of these' lines as I shuffled through the Market Hall getting carried away by the funky coloured spatulas.

I imagined that in a moment he would take my hand and break into a run just to tear me away from ALL OF THE PRETTY THINGS, called Rort or Skedstorn or even a word with no apparent vowels in, that I couldn't help but chuck into the crispy, oversized blue bags. I could feel Ben's amused eyes flick to me as I snuck in another couple of tea towels.

'Really, babe?' he asked with a wry smile, faking a yawn.

'I know, but they are so cheap!' I took a deep breath. 'Okay, please get me out of here. I don't know what's happened to my self-control!' I wailed as he laughed and took my hand.

We made it to the self-service checkout section of the shop pretty disgustingly smugly if you ask me, especially with relationship apocalypse exploding around us. We sauntered through to the right aisle (I'd been meticulous about scribbling down where the dining table was located that we'd both liked) holding hands and coming up with how many famous Swedish people we could think of. Ulrika

Jonsson and ABBA topped the poll after some obscure football players Ben suggested. It was all going rather swimmingly, maybe too swimmingly, until we saw the oblong-shaped thick cardboard box on section A shelf 39.

'Oh.'

'Balls.'

'It's enormous!' I gasped. Not only did I worry about us getting it into the car, I also didn't know how it would fit in our already cosy flat. This was the main reason we'd come here as we were having a dinner party in a few days, a posh house-warming, and I'd panicked that our guests would have to eat from their laps.

'I'm sure it's all just packaging. I don't remember it being that big in the showroom,' he said, scratching his head.

I nodded even though I wasn't convinced. 'You did do the measurements before we came out, didn't you?'

'Yep, come on. It'll be fine,' he said, through a heavy wheeze as he awkwardly hoisted the giant box onto the flat trolley, ignoring my narrowed eyes.

We were both exhausted and as fun and relatively painless as this shopping trip had been I was ready to get home, put the kettle on and brew up in my new matching mugs. *Of course he had the sizes worked out in his head – just trust him, Georgia.* But the meatballs and lingonberry sauce were soon forgotten as we struggled to just get the damn thing into Ben's car. We drove the whole way back to our flat with my seat pulled as far forward as it would go. I told Ben to be careful not to brake suddenly or else my neck would be sliced open by the sharp corner of the box that was precariously close to decapitating me.

We eventually both fell onto the sofa trying to catch our breath from lugging the enormous box through the front door. My smugness at surviving Ikea was starting to fade, but our spirits were still relatively high as we found a way to laugh at the experience, a pretty impressive feat considering how stilted the car journey had been – although I did smile to myself at Ben's cautious grandma-style driving.

'Well, it's in!' He smiled, wiping his damp forehead. 'How about I crack on with putting it up and you clear some room in the bedroom for all these candles you've collected?'

'You sure you don't want a hand?' I asked, looking at the mess he was making tearing his way into the giant box, pulling out the surprisingly thick instruction manual, bubble wrap and screws that were soon littering the floor.

'Nope. If I can't put up a simple table for my woman, then I basically fail at being a man.' He grinned, looking unfazed by the debris around him and popping the lid off a cold bottle of lager, ready for the challenge.

'Okay then, if you're sure…' I leant down and pecked him on his mop of dark brown curls. 'Good luck.'

I made my way around the boxes that lined the hallway, the ones we still had to unpack, trying to ignore the possible fire risk they posed, and dragged the full, blue Ikea sack into the bedroom. This was already my favourite room in the flat. It was a larger than average size with wide sash windows that let in so much light it made the calming space seem even bigger. I was still amazed that after moving out of the house I'd shared with my ex, Alex, and then going backpacking, I'd amassed so much stuff. Since moving in a month ago, Ben and I had been dancing around each other, finding places for both of our life possessions and bringing a touch of homely charm to the previously blank canvas.

It had been only a matter of time before Ben had moved out of the flat he'd shared with his best mate Jimmy and we got a place of our own. The decision to live together had been such an obvious one, especially as we spent all of our time in each other's company at work anyway and our relationship was going so well. The times I did find myself apart from him I'd hated.

I artistically arranged my new candle collection on top of the chest of drawers, next to the framed photo of us taken when we'd first met on a sun-drenched Thai beach. So much had changed since that moment I sometimes forgot where it had all started. Since then we'd launched our own joint business, The Lonely Hearts Travel Club, fallen in love and were now living together. I never could have predicted any of this back then when this hot stranger had placed his arm around my waist as I grinned at the camera lens.

I pulled myself back to the moment and smiled at hearing Ben whistling along to the radio from the lounge. I couldn't remember feeling this happy and excited about the future before; it was such a special, precious feeling that I never wanted to end. It had made sense to move in together. Both of our diaries were always full of short breaks, taken separately, to promote The Lonely Hearts Travel Club – just in the last few months I'd been to Spain, Greece and Morocco. But sadly, the most I got to see of the fascinating destinations was the airport and a variety of nondescript hotel rooms. It also meant that when I wasn't away from the office then Ben was, both of us taking it in turns to keep in personal contact with our travel guides and excursions, as well as trying to bring in new clients.

This was all so exciting, but it meant we had to manage our downtime carefully, with planned date nights and time together booked into our diaries weeks or months in advance. I wouldn't say I ever really got homesick but I had found myself feeling sick of not having a home – with

Ben. Somewhere we could both at least wake up and fall asleep together whenever we were in the same country.

Not wanting to get in the way of his furniture assembly techniques, I decided to make a start on unpacking those boxes littering the hallway. They were labelled *Ben's Clothes* so I ungracefully dragged them into the bedroom and pulled open the floor-to-ceiling, built-in wardrobes, wincing at how cluttered it was already looking in here.

I closed my eyes and inhaled the comforting and familiar scent of my boyfriend as I pulled out soft T-shirts and piled them in the drawers on his side of the wardrobe. Lost in heady memories that his smell caused my brain and my lady parts, I almost missed it. In amongst neatly folded winter jumpers, my hand touched upon a solid object. Digging further into the cardboard box I felt my stomach clench and my heart skipped a beat as everything around me froze.

Tucked – almost hidden – in the pocket of a thick woollen jacket was a small, maroon-coloured, velvet box.

CHAPTER 2

Qualm (n.) – A sudden feeling of doubt, fear or uneasiness, especially in not following one's conscience or better judgement

For a few seconds I just stared at the golden trimmed little box as it sat in my trembling hands, as if holding an injured bird or an unexploded landmine. I was too nervous to move a muscle or even catch up on the breath that had caught in my dry throat.

'Ah, bollocks!' I could hear Ben swearing as he got on with assembling the dining-room table, unaware of the momentous discovery that his girlfriend had just made in the very next room.

'*Open it, open it,*' my subconscious urged. '*No!*' my brain shrieked. '*Once you do, everything will change.*'

I rubbed my index finger slowly over the lid as I battled with whether to look inside or not. What if it was hideous? What if it wasn't even an engagement ring but a nice set of earrings instead? *Screw it, there's only one way to find out.*

I gingerly lifted the lid and heard myself take a sharp breath. The sunlight streaming through the bedroom windows caught the diamond that was proudly set on a simple but elegant platinum band, forcing me to blink. It was gorgeous. And, it was most definitely an engagement ring.

Unanswered questions, thoughts and emotions suddenly flooded my shocked mind, which is probably why I did what I did next. It was as if I had come out of my body, lost all of my common sense and had shoved my fingers in my ears singing *'la la la, I'm not listening'* to my brain, which was currently having a panic attack. Checking the bedroom door was firmly closed and hearing Ben muttering to himself over the music from the radio, I lifted the sparkling diamond out of the plush box and put the ring on.

It slid down my ring finger effortlessly. Like Cinderella trying on the glass slipper, it fit like it had been made for me. I couldn't hide my bright smile as I admired the gleaming rock glinting on my hand, making my usually quite stubby fingers and gnawed cuticles appear as smooth and pretty as a hand model's.

I didn't even stop to think about what finding this hidden box would mean for our relationship, if I was even ready to get married to Ben, if I wanted to be someone's fiancée again after the disaster I'd made of it the last time. All that mattered was me and this ring, which was so obviously meant to be mine. I'd become blinded by its beauty, causing all rational thoughts to exit the building. It had left me curled up on the floor, Gollum-like, stroking *my precious*.

I don't know how long I sat like that, with my back leaning on the edge of our bed and my open mouth gaping at the beauty of the piece of jewellery, but in my admiration I hadn't realised that the radio Ben had been badly humming along to had been turned off.

'Babe, I think you might want to come out here,' Ben's voice sounded louder in the stillness, floating through the flat and shocking me back into the moment.

'Oh right, erm, yep, give me a sec,' I cried, hurriedly pulling at the ring to get it off, tuck it back in the box and hide it away before he came into the room and found me like this.

I didn't know if the room had heated up or it was karma coming back to bite me for opening the box, but the ring wouldn't come back up past my joint. Shit! I tugged it, pulled at it and even spat on my own stubby, stupid finger to prise the thing off. But it remained stubbornly jammed on.

'You know we were a little concerned about the table being too big?' Ben asked nervously, right outside the bedroom door.

'Mmm?' I replied, only half-listening. *Come off, just come off!* I was sweating and wincing at the pain of trying to force this damn ring over my finger without snapping a bone, just as the handle turned. I launched myself to the bedroom door and blockaded it using my body weight to keep Ben from getting in, all the while twisting and tugging at my hand that was now red and swelling up in pain.

'You okay in there? I can't get in!' he called out through the wood.

'Yeah, fine, just got boxes everywhere. I'll be out in a sec,' I called back, my voice strangely high-pitched and strangled.

I could hear him standing on the other side of the door for a few seconds longer, my head throbbing as much as my hand in fear at him coming in.

'Oh right. I'll pop the kettle on shall I?'

'Yep, great, fine, thanks!'

Eventually, as I heard his footsteps on the wooden floors head back towards the kitchen, I let out a sigh of relief. My hand had now turned a strange shade of yellow with angry-looking red blotches from the force of me fighting with this damn ring. With one final tug, and a female tennis player style grunt, it flew off and skittered over to the other corner of the room. I leant my head against the door and tried to control my breathing. I wiped the sweat from my forehead, wincing at my sore finger. I quickly pulled myself together and shoved the ring back in its box, stuffing it back in the pocket where I'd found it.

A moment later the bedroom door opened. Ben was stood there holding out a steaming mug for me. 'Here you go.' I was sure his eyes widened at the mess I'd made in the bedroom. 'You okay, babe?'

'Ah thanks, yeah, all good. Right, let's see your masterpiece!' I said, pecking him on the cheek and shooing him out of the stuffy room, rubbing my sore hand behind my back.

'Well, like I said, you might need to manage your expectations.' He coughed. 'It is a *little* larger than I'd… well, you'll see…' Ben trailed off.

I stopped still as I walked into the lounge. All thoughts of rings and wedding plans vanishing from my mind as I saw what he'd assembled. 'A *little* larger?' I gasped.

The dining-room table that had seemed so stylish in the showroom was now taking up pretty much all of our floor space. It looked ridiculous. I couldn't concentrate on what he was sheepishly explaining. As he rambled on about measurements, sizes and dimensions, I zoned out and self-consciously rubbed my sore ring finger. Was this an omen? A sign of things to come? Our first proper adult purchase as a couple and it didn't fit, just like the engagement ring? If that was the case then what the hell did that mean for us?

CHAPTER 3

Equanimity (n.) – Evenness of mind, especially under stress

You know how sometimes they say that when things are going well it is as if the stars are aligned and everything in the universe is exactly how it should be? But, the thing they don't tell you is how precarious this configuration is, how it can all fall out of alignment at any second. Imagine a steel tightrope with everything perfectly balanced on this sturdy, but still pretty vulnerable wire; this was how my life seemed to me. Maybe I had been too smug, too content, but with the gift of hindsight I could see how a gust of wind, a heavy bird plonking its feathered butt on the high line, or even a slip of the tongue and a secret that was never meant to be shared, could cause all the elements that had previously been so perfectly positioned to tumble and free-fall from a dizzying height to the ground. How could I have known that the laws of physics – or whatever it was that had caused this chain of events – would be the start of the stars falling out of alignment, the start of everything going so very very wrong? How naïve I was.

*

Of course, these thoughts were far from my mind as I went to meet my best friend the next day to fill her in on the drama of discovering the ring, the upcoming proposal and the monstrous dining table taking over my lounge. With all that had happened yesterday – including Ben and me having a silly, bickering row over the sodding table and its elephantine dimensions, ending with me telling him that size does matter – I hadn't given much thought to what discovering this engagement ring actually meant for us.

Of course, I'd be lying if I told you that I hadn't, at various times since we met, imagined the wedding day that Ben and I might have. Him in a cool linen suit with his freckled nose, me in a simple but stunning long, floaty dress, both promising our vows as we stared adoringly at each other on an exotic, cashmere-soft, sandy beach. I'd imagined how he would be as a father: kind but fair, hands-on but not smothering.

As fun as these daydreams were – strangely I was always a slimmer, swishy-haired version of myself – we'd never really had deep discussions about babies and weddings. There had been light-hearted jokes at unusual baby names – Ben was on a one-man mission to bring back the name Roy, and I had laughed, but secretly hoped he'd been joking, just in case. But having children and marrying each other wasn't completely outside the realm of possibility. I mean, we had successfully navigated working together as we ran our ever-growing travel and tour agency for broken-hearted singles, and so far living together had been a sickeningly easy breeze; but neither of us had spoken about marriage being on the cards. At least, not yet.

In a way I was grateful that I'd made the shocking ring discovery, to give me some time to get my head around the idea and figure out if I thought we were in the place Ben so obviously thought we were. Not that I didn't want to marry my clever, kind, good-looking, amazing-in-the-bedroom boyfriend, of course, but because I'd been so badly burned after ending up a jilted bride before. I was meant to have married my ex, Alex; we'd had everything planned, paid for and organised but just before the big day he had revealed that he had been cheating on me and called the whole thing off. Him uttering those painful words *'I can't marry you'*, had brought about the biggest change in my life.

I had gone backpacking, met Ben, fallen in love, started my own business and truly found that travel did heal a broken heart. I now believed that what Alex did was the best thing that ever happened to me. Not that it wasn't heartbreaking and difficult – I mean, what girl wants to be told by someone they love and trust that actually they weren't worthy enough to become their wife? But, over time, I felt like I'd healed myself and I had discovered that all those irritating clichés people harp on about, like time being the best healer, actually were true.

My life was so much better now than it had ever been, thanks in a large part to Ben and the success we'd made of our joint business. Maybe the non-wedding with Alex was all part of the plan – the rehearsal, if you will – for what would be the wedding of the year with Ben?

'Will you take over pushing the buggy for a minute?' Marie asked, breaking me from my bonkers bridal thoughts. 'I've got cramp, *another* wonderful side effect of *being with child*,' she grumbled.

We were slowly meandering around the local park – and I mean slowly; even the ducks were waddling faster than us. Marie was on her 'get this baby out of me' mission, and I'd completely forgotten that I'd agreed to support her until she called me this morning. Her due date was still weeks away but she was determined to deliver precisely on time. She'd been exactly the same with her toddler, Cole, her firstborn. Marie was having this baby on her due date, come hell or high water.

'I don't feel like I did with Cole, so I need to be upping my game to get this baby out of me,' she said, as I took over wheeling his pushchair for a while over fallen branches and skirted round piles of dog poo. Marie had a crazed look in her eyes as she spoke. It was a look I remembered seeing when we were both eighteen and she was determined to finish the line of shots in Waverley's bar in order to win a free T-shirt. Those luminous shooters never stood a chance.

'Marie, it's a baby. I know I'm not a world expert on the subject matter but don't they kind of come when they're ready?'

She glared at me. The mood swings were clearly still going strong. 'Georgia Green, I may have developed haemorrhoids, darker nipples, and lost the ability to hold in my pee when I sneeze or cough or laugh, but this, this is something I *know* I can control.' She looked like a determined Michelin Man under the many layers swaddling her neat bump as she waddled around.

'I still can't believe that you haven't found out what you're having.'

'We're having a baby, Georgia. Did no one tell you?' She stuck her tongue out playfully.

'Ha, bloody, ha. I mean, how have you not been desperate to know if it's a girl or a boy? I'd certainly need to know if a teeny, weeny penis was currently growing inside me.' I shuddered.

'Well, we all know there have been enough of them inside me.' She laughed, blushing at the carefree memories of her single days. 'Nah, seriously though, I don't want to ruin the surprise. It will make it even more *magical* when he or she does finally make an appearance.' She put on that drowsy hippy voice that she used to use to imitate Lorraine with the lazy eye. Lazy-Eye Lorraine. She was an earth-mother-type woman who ran the antenatal classes and got right on Marie's nerves by implying that basically she'd been a lousy mum to Cole and that nowadays they did things differently. Everything was *magical* in Lorraine's world.

Marie didn't do '*magical*'; she did practical, and right now the most practical thing she could do was try her hardest to get her baby safely into the world on her due date. It was a mini achievement but still one way to show bog-eyed Lorraine that mummy Marie wasn't a failure.

'If you don't know what you're having then what have you been buying for it? Isn't there some unwritten code of motherhood that you go all out and splash the cash on anything and everything pink for a girl or blue for a boy?'

Marie rolled her eyes and sighed. 'It's all about gender-neutral clothes for babies nowadays, so he or she is going to have a wardrobe filled with yellows, greens and whites. I just hope people will be able to tell what sex it is by the look of him, or her.'

I scoffed. 'Well, if it was me I'd dress my baby only in teeny tiny Halloween costumes. That's one way to do the gender-neutral look.'

She let out a burst of laughter. 'Thank the Lord you're not expecting then. I'm not sure how the baby would like to look back at their first year of life to realise they were dressed as a pumpkin or a bat for most of it.'

'Yeah, maybe, but how cute! God, Marie, it's just mad to think that soon he or she will be here sharing this buggy with Cole.' I felt this strange tingle in my chest as I said it. Everything was changing. My best friend's life would never be the same again. When she was pregnant with Cole we had spent ages imagining what he would be like, how he would grow into an actual person with a personality, and what becoming a mum, rather than just being Marie, would be like. I guess a small and selfish part of me had worried that I'd be sidelined from our friendship once she had this other human who was the complete centre of her world. How could her best friend ever compete with that?

They say a mother's love is like no other, but not having a child I could only understand that from a rational perspective. Now we were on the edge of her life changing again, but this time I was less concerned with how I was going to fit in, and instead focused on the fact that my life was about to change, too.

'I know.' She smiled tiredly. 'And then Operation Skinny Jeans is back on.'

I frowned at her.

'Don't give me that look! I'm not going to be going all A-List celeb and ping straight back but I am desperate to feel like my body is my own again. Plus, if I'm going to meet my five-year plan then I need to be getting trim for the big day.'

'This big day that Mike knows nothing about,' I teased, then let out a deep sigh. 'It's amazing to think that a few years ago we were both in such different places – and yet somehow exactly the same – as where we are now. What with you popping out sproglets and me…about to get engaged…'

It took a few moments for this to click in.

'Oh my God! What? You're getting married!' Marie's squeals made a lone dog walker jump from the other side of the lake. My ring finger throbbed in memory of the torture it had been under as she mentioned the M word.

'Shush! You're going to wake Cole!' I glanced down at her toddler son, wrapped up in blankets in his buggy. He remained fast asleep with just his pink nose and angel-bud lips peeking out of the many covers she had piled on him earlier.

'Tell me *everything*!' She'd stopped in her tracks and snatched up my hand to hunt for any sign of bling. 'Wait – where's the ring?'

'Well, okay, so I'm not engaged yet. But I will be…'

She stared at me, blank faced, as if I'd totally lost the plot. 'You what?'

I sighed and told her about the trip to Ikea, the unpacking, finding the ring and damaging the nerves in my finger from the force of trying to get it off before Ben caught me.

'Wow, so what was it like?'

'Dreamy.' I hugged myself without realising it.

'Better than the last one you got?' She raised an eyebrow.

I pulled myself together. 'Yes, actually.'

She nodded slowly, thinking of how to word the next question. 'Are you ready to do all of that again? You know, with what happened last time?' she eventually asked, leaving a whisper of breath hanging in the air.

'Yeah, course. I mean, I think so.' She gave me a look. I stared back. 'I love Ben, and this time it already feels so different to how I felt with Alex. It's like I've grown up and realised what's actually important in a relationship. Plus, I just know myself so much better – I know what I want now. I am so different from old Georgia, it's like I finally know who I am. At least, I think so. It has come as a bit of a surprise.'

'You *think* so? Georgia, this is a big deal. You need to be sure.' She paused. 'I'm only asking because I was the one who saw how everything collapsed the last time. I never ever want that to happen to you again.' She visibly shuddered.

I stuck my chest out. 'It won't. Ben loves me, and he obviously thinks we're ready for this otherwise he wouldn't have gone to the trouble of buying the ring –'

'I just worry about you that's all.'

I looked down at her swollen tummy. 'Well, that makes two of us.'

'You know I love Ben, and I think it's great that you're living together, but don't you want to, I don't know, just enjoy that part rather than dive headfirst into the crazy world of weddings?' She must have caught my expression as she hastily added, 'I'm thrilled for you – well I will be when it actually happens – it's just I don't want you to feel like you're being rushed into big decisions all because you've seen a lovely shiny ring.'

'He does have very good taste in jewellery,' I mused. 'I'm joking – it's not just about the ring. I understand what you're saying, it was a shock for me too. Of course, *someday* I could see us taking that big step, I just hadn't realised that Ben's someday was now.'

'I also think you need to consider how this might affect Lonely Hearts, how your team will feel working for a husband and wife and the marital dramas that could spill over into your business decisions…'

I'd spoken to Marie many a time about how even though business-wise we were as thick as thieves, in terms of our relationship I sometimes struggled making it less about work and more about us. It was a hard balance made even harder when Ben was the type of person who kept his cards close to his chest, especially where his family were concerned. I still hadn't even met any of the Stevens clan, something that would surely have to change before our big day.

I blew on my fingertips for warmth. A puff of breath, like smoke from a Heston Blumenthal recipe, escaped. 'I guess it's something we need to consider. I know we're both focused on making sure we don't only talk about work but it's easier said than done, especially with him being so keen on us expanding to London.'

'You not a fan of cockneys?'

I laughed. 'It's not that! It's nothing against London or Londoners, it's just a big decision and one I don't think we're ready for just yet. Yes, it could bring about a lot of money and new opportunities, but as much as the business is growing and making a healthy profit with the Manchester store, I don't know if it would pay off taking on the stress and risk of having another venue in another city. Ben's a dreamer, and he's adamant it will work, whereas I'm trying to be more rational before making a call on it. It's been hard recently, as this is the one area we don't see eye to eye on.'

'Bigger doesn't always mean better,' she said, then clapped her hand to her mouth. 'Unless you're pregnant!'

'Yeah.' I smiled and shook my head, also thinking about the gigantic dining-room table that had taken over our flat. 'I don't know. This London move is one decision, and a blooming big one at that, where we're not singing from the same hymn sheet.'

'I don't know what the hell that means, but it sounds like you're not exactly ready to be getting married to Ben if you can't even agree on the direction you take your business.' She raised her eyebrows and pulled her coat tighter. 'It sounds to me like you need a plan. I know how much you love them!'

'What, a plan to get my boyfriend to open up more and convince him the London move is not a good idea, well not any time soon anyway?'

Marie shrugged. 'Maybe you need to get away from things for a bit? I don't know, take a holiday or something before you make any big decisions on London or on your future as a couple. That way you can get out of Manchester and maybe by having a change of scene it will be easier for you to talk about where you're going with this, and decide whether you're ready to commit to him for ever and make lots of model good-looking babies?'

I scoffed. 'I'll leave the baby making to you for the time being. Although a holiday on some exotic, sun-drenched beach sounds idyllic right now.' I nodded at the pathetic and unloved playground we'd made our way towards. A chipped and forlorn swing set wafted in the cold breeze; thankfully Cole was still in the land of nod, saving us from spending longer than needed in this depressing place. Is there anything sadder than a children's play area without children playing in it? In the dull grey light, it seemed even more unloved, especially when framed by the lake with empty crisp packets and cans of Stella bobbing on the surface of the murky waters.

'Hmm. You keep telling yourself that. I know you don't want to hear it but your biological clock will soon be saying another thing.'

'You're sounding like my parents.' I laughed and hooked my arm into hers for extra warmth. 'So, back to you, are you getting nervous for the big day?'

'What, the wedding?' She looked at me in surprise.

'No!' I slapped a gloved hand to my forehead. What was it with all this wedding talk? 'Marie, there is no wedding until you get engaged first.'

'Oh yeah.' She shrugged. 'That's just a slight bump in the road. Mike will ask me. I bet there's been some scientific tests done to prove that more couples get engaged just after they've had a baby than at any other time in a relationship. I mean, at that point, the guys are just in total awe of you for pushing out their child in one piece from your lady parts. You can do no wrong.'

'I have no doubt that he'll be putting a ring on your finger before this year is out. But no, I was talking about the actual birth. Are you not slightly cacking your pants in fear of doing all that again?' I rubbed her arms that had tensed against the bars of the pushchair. Cole's birth hadn't been easy. There had been complications and we had very nearly lost the pair of them, something that we'd long brushed under the carpet but that still sent a chill down my spine when I thought about it.

I'd never seen my best friend so distraught as when her newborn son was kept under observation for a few days after his dramatic arrival, and despite making what the doctors classed as a miraculous and speedy recovery herself, she had been in pieces that she was to blame for his terrifying entrance into the world. She'd tortured herself by staring at his tiny, fragile body attached to tubes and wires in the incubator, repeating that she hadn't taken good enough care of herself during the pregnancy, that because she didn't find out she was expecting until she was fourteen weeks gone, she had caused too much irreversible damage by drinking on a couple of nights out that we'd been on.

It was all bollocks, and the doctors could tell her until they were blue in the face that no one was to blame, it was just one of those things, but until Cole had grown strong enough to leave the sterile incubator and come home she didn't dare relax. This was why she'd been so strict with herself during this pregnancy; everything had to be done by the book. It was something Mike had lost patience with a few times, telling her to stop stressing and start enjoying the whole thing, but Marie had been steadfast that this birth was going to make up for the experience she'd had with Cole – that it was going to go to plan and be as perfect as it could be.

I couldn't tell if it was the grubby light of the park or if she had suddenly gone very pale. 'Nah.' She brushed a strand of her ruby-red hair off her face and swallowed.

'Marie? It's okay to be frightened,' I said softly.

She stopped waddling and turned to face me. Tears had pricked her tired eyes and the tip of her nose was a raspberry pink from the cold air. 'I'm shitting myself, Georgia. But I can't let myself be scared. I've done it once so I know the score, but in a way that's made it even more terrifying as I know exactly what to expect and, ignore the awful pun, but it's not a walk in the park.' She let out a laugh that I didn't recognise as hers. Suddenly my bolshie fiery redhead regressed to the skinny-legged teen desperate to be an A plus student that I knew and loved. I wrapped my arms around her, difficult to do with the many layers she had on and the large bump between us.

'It's okay to be scared. But you're going to nail it. I know you are.'

She sniffed and wiped her nose on the sleeve of her coat. 'Thanks. I hope you're right. Everyone says it's worth the pain for what you get at the end of it, and I know that's true, but at the same time it really fucking hurts! That's what I mean about my body not being my own, I have no control over what's going to happen to it when I go into labour and I just have to hope that it'll do what it's biologically designed to.'

I nodded fervently. 'You will be amazing. Mike will probably propose to you right then and there at seeing what an awesome gift you've given him.'

Her lips curled into a slow smile. 'It will get me out of doing the chores for a good couple of months, at the very least.'

I shook my head. 'I seriously don't know how you're going to do it with two children under the age of four! I mean, I find just being in charge of me exhausting.' I wished that I was half joking about this. 'Stop laughing, I'm being serious! I still get spots, I use Google to find the answers to things way more than I probably should, and I don't know how to correctly pronounce quinoa or what the hell it even is. Then here's you totally nailing the yummy mummy thing. Soon you'll be all National Trust memberships, Saabs and Waitrose cards!'

She laughed and patted my arm. 'I doubt it! Anyway, your life is great, you know it is. It makes me jealous to remember being able to book a last-minute holiday, head out for drinks on a weeknight or even leave the house without some military-style plan. Just don't leave it too long till you join my club. I mean maybe Lazy-Eye Lorraine is right. This whole birth thing is just so bloody *magical*.'

We both broke into peals of laughter and picked up our pace to head back to hers for a steaming mug of tea and some chocolate Hobnobs. As we trudged down the muddy path to the main road I just wasn't sure why I felt niggling doubts creeping in. I loved hanging out with my best friend but she did have a habit of speaking the truth; at times this dose of reality was hard to swallow. Maybe Marie was right, maybe I shouldn't think about marrying Ben when there were so many unanswered questions between us.

All the talk of babies made me feel itchy, a feeling that made me realise I wasn't ready for children, not just yet, but marriage wasn't a complete no-no. Although maybe Marie was right: as loved up as I felt we had only just moved in together and were still discovering things about each other. Maybe I needed to silence the ding dong of wedding bells in my head and think rationally about what this engagement would mean for us and the changes it would cause. When things were going so well why did any of it have to change?

CHAPTER 4

Callow (adj.) – Immature or lacking adult sophistication

'I still can't believe you're getting engaged!' Shelley squealed.

I gave Marie a look.

'What? I couldn't *not* tell her.' She put her arms up in defence.

'Well, I'm not engaged yet,' I said straightening my work skirt. 'And please, please don't mention it to Jimmy. I can't have Ben finding out that I know and ruin the proposal he has planned.' I winced.

Shelley placed my hands in hers and nodded firmly. 'Scout's honour. Ah, this is so exciting though! Where do you think you'll get married? Ah, I know! What about Thailand? Where you met? I could just see the pair of you walking hand in hand down the white shores of Koh Lanta to tie the knot, then heading back to the Blue Butterfly for a knees-up after. I'm sure Dara would be thrilled to help out, plus Chef would make a fantastic wedding cake. Oh and then we could let off lanterns into the sky as you two have your first dance.' She glanced at mine and Marie's faces as if she'd missed the memo. 'What? You don't think it's exciting?'

'Yeah, course it is. I'm just a little wary after what happened last time.' Since I'd left Marie's I'd been thinking about what she'd said. She was right to be concerned. I did need to think with my heart *and* my head, rather than be blinded by the gorgeous ring that Ben was soon going to present to me.

'Ah yeah, sure. But you two are made for each other. You can't let the past rule your heart.'

I smiled at my Australian friend; we'd met when backpacking in Thailand and I couldn't imagine my life without her in it. 'I know; I am pretty disgustingly loved up at the minute.'

'Living together is going well then?' Shelley winked. 'Well, apart from your giant dining-room table.'

I rolled my eyes. 'Yeah, apart from that, it's great!'

I still pinched myself that I had this amazing man as my boyfriend, plus I soon learned that Ben was well house-trained. This came as a shock as Alex had never used a vacuum cleaner or an iron before. He was spoilt by his mum who did everything and expected that his future wife would pick up the baton, which foolishly I did. Ben was so self-sufficient: cooking, doing the food shop without a list and detailed aisle plan of the supermarket, and even cleaning the bathroom without me pestering.

'Wow, Jimmy can be such a slob, always leaving the loo seat up and used teabags near the bin. I sometimes threaten to not put out, which usually makes him slap on a pair of Marigolds!' Shelley laughed. 'Okay, so if Ben is thinking about marriage and you're not totally averse to the idea then maybe you need to think of what's missing to work out how you can get to the same level as him?' Shelley suggested.

'Yeah, like is there anything you want to know about him but don't?'

'Well, I haven't met his dad yet, but it's just because of logistics and finding the time, I think.'

'Oh yeah, didn't his mum abandon him?' Marie remembered and clutched her chest at the thought.

'Yeah.' I shook my head sadly. 'She left when he was little but I've never been able to get any more out of him than that.'

'Well then, that's something that needs to happen. You can tell so much about someone from what their parents are like, and what kind of relationship they have.'

'Oh God, yeah! Remember when I was seeing that Shane?' Marie asked me. Memories of being the third wheel as they sat snogging in a booth in a naff nightclub came rushing back.

'Eurgh, I never liked him. Always thought he was a bit needy.' I shuddered.

Marie raised her finger in the air. 'Well, you were spot on, and it all stemmed from how he was with his mum. Seriously it was as if she was waiting to clamp him back on her breast whenever we went to his parents' house. He was a complete mummy's boy, and I don't know about you, but that is such a turn-off. I swear he still kissed on the lips.'

'Ewww!' Shelley and I cried.

'So that is why meeting your potential in-laws is so important.'

'Okay, so after you've met his dad, then what?'

I scrunched my eyes up to think. 'Well, I guess apart from meeting in Thailand we haven't actually travelled anywhere together; all of our trips with work have been taken separately so we could cover the office.'

'You have to do that! Anyway, you've got Conrad now – isn't that what he's there for, to watch the office whilst you two gallivant across the globe?'

I nodded slowly. Conrad was a blunt, brash Yorkshireman who we'd hired as office manager but seemed to turn his hand to anything that came his way, from consoling sobbing, heartbroken customers to standing his ground with surly maintenance men. He came highly recommended from another travel agency, had travelled the world in a previous life as cabin crew – which was something that I still couldn't get my head round, especially how someone with his build could nip down the aisles without taking people's eyes out. Plus, he loved to swear, made lewd and hilarious comments, which kept the team's spirits high, and he called a spade a spade. He was the perfect addition to the 'Lonely Hearts squad', as Kelli called us.

Marie rearranged herself on the cushion she was sprawled across. 'They say you never really know someone until you travel with them – he could be full of airport anxieties or one of those sunbed hoggers.'

I laughed. 'I doubt Ben would be getting up at 4 a.m. to bagsy the best spot with his towel.'

'Yeah, but you don't know…'

Shelley began telling us about her friend whose holiday with her boyfriend ended in them breaking up over his wandering eye as he was more obsessed with the travel rep than his girlfriend. She had found them in bed together on the third day of the trip and had to spend the rest of the week eating with a kind, middle-aged Swedish couple who took her under their wing.

'It can be a minefield. People think that when you go on holiday it will be this unrealistic romantic trip and all of the problems they had at home will disappear. The truth is, you bring them thousands of miles with you and they become even more magnified in this strange, unusual environment.'

'But, if you can't get along on some idyllic tropical beach when the only thing you have to worry about is applying more sun cream and which book to read next, then you won't be able to get along anywhere. It is the *ultimate* test.'

I scoffed. 'Yeah maybe, but Ben and I work together, we live together and we talk about travel all day, every day, so I honestly don't think there will be any issues with us going on holiday.'

'It could be good for you to get some time away to properly talk through all the London stuff that's niggling you,' Marie suggested.

I nodded. 'Yeah, you're both right. Our first couple's holiday needs to be a priority on my to-do list. Oh, pass us a slice will you?'

I nodded to the pizza box on Shelley's lap. Marie, Shelley and I were having a girly night in at Marie's house. It was an impromptu night as I'd actually hoped I would be doing something with Ben. We'd hardly seen each other outside of work since dining-room-table-gate. We'd called a truce on it and both become skilled at literally – and figuratively – skirting around the thing.

'So, where's lover boy tonight?' Shelley asked as if reading my mind. She was mid mouthful of pizza, the grease from the stuffed crust base glistening on her chin.

'Out with a friend, I'm not sure where.' I shrugged, picking off a rogue olive that had found its way onto my slice.

'A friend?' Shelley raised an eyebrow. 'Well it's not Jimmy as he's taking some body blitz class in the gay village, which I know wouldn't interest Ben in the slightest.'

'He didn't tell me where he was going, only that he was meeting up with an old friend as she's just moved to Manchester.'

'A she?' Marie's eyebrows were now at the same raised height as Shelley's, both threatening to merge into their hairline. I nodded. 'Your boyfriend, sorry, your soon-to-be fiancé has gone on a date with a girl you don't know to a place you don't know, and you're okay with this?'

I rolled my eyes at the pair of them. 'I trust him.' Even after what had happened with Alex, I did trust Ben. It had taken a lot for me to get to this point, but we shared the most important thing in my life – our business – as well as our bedroom, and we wouldn't have got this far without trust. 'And it's not a date. God, you two are so melodramatic sometimes!'

'Yeah you might trust him, but are you not a little bit curious about her?' Shelley had now finished off her slice and picked up my phone, like a woman on a mission. 'Right, what's her name?'

I laughed at the absurdity. 'I'm not Facebook stalking her. I told you, I trust him.'

'*You're* not Facebook stalking, *we* are,' Marie said, with her eyes alight at the prospect of some real-life gossip that wasn't baby related. 'Okay, name?'

They weren't letting this go. They'd even paused an old episode of *Sex and the City* that had been on in the background to focus on the task in hand.

I sighed and closed my eyes, thinking. He'd only mentioned heading out in a passing comment, giving it as much thought as it probably deserved. But apparently, according to these two, these were things I was meant to get all psycho, bunny boiler on his ass about. This whole playing games thing was not something I was interested in; having a relationship and everything that comes with it in discovering each other's boundaries was hard enough at times, let alone adding in this sort of crap.

'You weren't even a teensy bit intrigued to know more?' Shelley pushed.

'I honestly didn't give it much thought. He mentioned it as we were both in-between speaking with clients, so I didn't sit and analyse what he meant, no.'

'I would have found out the girl's bra size by the time he'd finished speaking,' Marie said, without a hint of humour.

Maybe I should be more concerned, I began to think. Looking at their faces it seemed I should be taking this more seriously.

'I don't want to worry you or anything, but you did say that he'd been even quieter than usual recently,' Marie piped up.

Damn, why did she have to have such an elephant memory? That was true, but I'd just put it down to him sulking over not being able to use a tape measure correctly or even that he had been silently plotting my elaborate proposal. Now I was worried.

'Alice something,' I said, suddenly remembering that when he had told me I'd thought it sounded like a pretty name.

'Right, I'm on it,' Shelley cried, automatically knowing my phone code and heading to the Facebook app, as Marie bit her bottom lip and rubbed her belly.

'This is silly though, I mean, yeah he's been a bit quieter recently –'

'And you've been fighting about whether to open a London office or not,' Marie called out.

'Well, no, we haven't been *fighting*.' I turned to face her. 'It's just been a slight sticking point, that's all, but it doesn't mean he's off having sex with old friends –'

'Found her!' Shelley grinned, forgetting that she wasn't playing some TV quiz show but was actually digging up dirt on my own life. 'Ah. Shit.'

'What?' I asked, craning my neck to see the phone screen. Marie gasped loudly and blocked my view as she leant forward to see what Shelley was pointing at. 'What?!'

She slowly passed me my phone. Oh God. Alice was utterly gorgeous.

'Whoa.' Shelley gasped. 'Stunner McStunnerson alert.' She turned and gave me a sympathetic look at the shock on my face at realising that this potential Victoria's Secret model whose face currently filled my phone screen was the 'old friend' my boyfriend was hanging out with. 'But it's fine, yes she may be the most attractive woman in the world without a Kardashian surname but you trust Ben, so it's fine.'

'Is this defo her?' I asked slowly.

'She's the only Alice listed as Ben's friend.' Shelley winced.

Alice Sherman was stood leaning against a balcony railing with some exotic beach behind her. She had her head tilted back and what looked like a natural laugh escaping from her plump lips. Her eyes were scrunched up, lost in some joke between her and the photographer and her glossy brown hair was dancing in the breeze around her tanned shoulders. She was flawless and had curves in all the right places that were accentuated by the classy but not slutty peach-coloured chiffon dress she was wearing. She looked like the kind of girl you would take home to your mum but who would also be filth in the bedroom. Great.

I stared at her profile picture for longer than was necessary, mentally beating myself up as I compared my own body with hers. I already knew which one I'd prefer to be hanging out with if I had a penis.

'Maybe that's just a really good angle – everyone always puts their best shot as their profile picture.' Marie tried to look on the positive side.

'Check out her other photo albums!' Shelley said, as I scrolled my finger across the page. 'Thank the Lord for people who don't set their accounts to the highest privacy settings.'

Alice's other albums were a collection of tagged images, old holiday shots and nights out with her friends where she looked more natural but still disgustingly gorgeous.

'Yep, she may be the person I would want to swap my face with if I ever had a horrific car crash,' I admitted. 'But it still doesn't mean that anything dodgy is going on with her and Ben.'

Not wanting to look at any more photos and send my self-esteem plummeting even further, I put my phone on the coffee table. Marie instantly snatched it back up and began scrolling as Shelley topped up my glass and listened to me going on about how much I trusted my boyfriend.

'Wait!' Marie cried, interrupting me.

Shelley and I both snapped our heads up in unison to look at her.

'What?' I asked, feeling a strange tingling rush up my arms as she passed my phone back.

'Alice isn't just an old friend…' she paused dramatically '…she's his ex-girlfriend.'

I waited for the page to upload as fast as I was scrolling down and saw what she'd been looking at. Right at the bottom were a couple of much older albums with a younger, grinning Alice wrapped around a clean-shaven and youthful Ben. My Ben. In other images they were holding hands and kissing as a friend with spiked-up hair did the peace sign as he photobombed the young couple. I felt a funny, sinking feeling in the pit of my stomach. Why was my boyfriend meeting up with his ex, and why hadn't he told me?

'Oh,' Shelley said, a tiny bit relieved that her boyfriend was working out with a bunch of gay men rather than reminiscing about old times with this worldie.

'Oh crap!' I yelped.

'What?' Marie leant forward and knocked my glass with her tummy, sloshing wine onto my legs.

'I accidently pressed *like* on the photo of her at an elephant sanctuary!' I panicked.

'Quick! Click unlike. Click UNLIKE!' Marie gasped.

'I am,' I wailed, but the screen had frozen and now I wasn't sure what I'd done. 'Oh God, can she see that I liked it?' I felt woozy at the thought.

Shelley grabbed my phone off me to check. 'It's fine, you haven't liked it. Well you did, but it isn't showing now and she'll only know if she was online right then. But as you're not friends with her we won't know for certain. She probably won't have been though.'

'Probably…' That didn't fill me with much confidence. She *probably* won't be online as she will *probably* be making out with my boyfriend for old time's sake, my subconscious whispered.

'Don't worry, here have some more wine,' Shelley said, topping up my glass. 'Just try not to think about it. He's going to propose to you for goodness' sake!'

I nodded and wanted to change the conversation. 'Yep, you're right. So, erm, how are things with you?' I asked Shelley, trying to get Ben out of my head. Since when had I turned into this jealous, anxious girlfriend? It was not a look that fitted well.

She scrunched her face up. 'Well, I actually have some news of my own…'

There was a silence as she trailed out, pulled her hand away, and began busying with unscrewing the wine top. Marie was suddenly engrossed in picking off a piece of skin around her nail bed as if she knew something I didn't. Shelley turned to face me and took a deep breath. 'I wasn't sure how to tell you this.'

When anyone utters those words you know the next part of the sentence ain't going to be pretty. A chill danced along my spine as she glanced over at Marie and swallowed.

'Shel? You're both freaking me out. What's going on?'

'Georgia. I'm going to be moving back to Australia. To live. Permanently.'

The world stopped still for a second.

'What?! You're leaving? You and Jimmy?' My eyes flickered across her face, desperate for her to break into her signature grin and tell me she was joking. But her expression remained sober and slightly pale.

'Yep. I've been offered a job back home and Jimmy can head over on a visa. He's already got interviews lined up for some personal trainer work so we can look at making it permanent, or possibly we get married ourselves…'

'Oh wow. Erm, that's great news.' I paused to let this all sink in.

She winced and picked up her wine glass. 'The other thing is, because of these jobs we're going to be going soon. Like, in a month.'

'No! A MONTH! Did you know?' I turned to Marie who blatantly did judging by her pinched expression.

Shelley jumped in to save Marie from answering. 'I was worried at how you'd take it. I wanted to ask Marie for her advice before I told you as she's known you for so long,' Shelley blustered.

I sat back in my chair feeling disappointed that my two best friends had had to confide in each other on about how to handle me taking big, stupid, life-changing news like this.

'Right. I mean…wow. Shel, I'm chuffed for you!' I said a few moments later, probably taking longer to say it than I should have done. 'This is SO exciting!'

'You sure?' she asked, pulling out of the hug I'd grabbed her in as I tried to pretend I was embracing her when really I needed a moment to gather my thoughts on her shoulder.

'Course. I mean, this is great news. Who wouldn't want to go and live in Australia? Wow. How exciting, really, this is great.' I then let out this strangled laugh that matched my high-pitched voice. 'This is great. We should have champagne!' I announced, getting to my feet and suddenly wanting to get some fresh air. 'I'll head to the shop right now!'

'Georgia. Are you sure you're okay?'

'Positive! We need to celebrate! Ha ha, look at you two. You don't have to worry about me. I'm fine. More than fine,' I babbled, rummaging through my handbag for my purse. Where the hell was it? For fuck's sake.

'Georgia,' Marie said firmly, placing a hand on the arm that was desperately tearing through my bag. 'Just chill out a moment.'

'I'm fine. Why wouldn't I be? I mean, look at you all blossoming and yummy mummy and then look at Shel going to live thousands of miles away and then look at me and…and…' It was too late. The tears were falling as the enormity of the situation hit me. I was losing my two best friends to real life when I still wasn't sure of the direction mine was heading.

'Aww, hon, come here.' Shelley tried to put her arm round me but I shrugged it off and roughly wiped my eyes.

'I'm fine. Fine. Honestly. Although have we got any more wine?' I said, a little softer. 'I'm just being silly.'

'You're clearly not fine.' Marie shook her head. 'There might be a bottle in the drinks cupboard in the kitchen. I've no idea how long it's been there as I've not had nice booze in the house since being pregnant.'

I glanced at the almost empty wine bottle we'd brought with us. 'Oh, okay. Well then, who fancies one of Georgia's special cocktails?' I asked, jumping to my feet. Neither of them joined in.

Soon I was back in the lounge holding a glass of Georgia's Special Cocktail that I'd rustled up in super quick time, which was basically a concoction of the dregs of a Baileys bottle and some green alcoholic syrup I'd found in the back of Marie's cupboard. It was the best of what was available, you know the stuff you accumulate over the years after parties, for recipes, or over the festive season but never get through – as who the hell ever finds themselves craving a glass of Advocaat? But I didn't care. Judging by the time those bottles had been in that dusty drinks cupboard, the alcohol must have tripled in strength, as it was strooooonnnggg and *exactly* what I needed.

'You're both missing out!' I said taking a long gulp. It did not taste good. 'So, Australia, wow, tell me *all*!' I managed, wanting to make conversation and purposefully ignoring their sceptical faces that I clearly wasn't as fine as I was insisting that I was.

'Well, I was originally just going to head there myself and Jimmy would join me when he could, but then we thought, well why not just go together. I've already handed my notice in and Jimmy is winding down his contracts as we get things sorted.'

'Ben will be crushed,' I breathed. Jimmy had been his best friend for years. It wasn't just me who was losing out. 'When is he telling him?'

Shelley ran her finger over the rim of her now empty wine glass. 'He's already told him.'

'Wait – Ben knows and didn't think to tell me?!' Well this news had just got a whole lot shittier.

'I think Jimmy asked Ben not to tell you until I'd had the chance to speak with you. I didn't want you to hear it from anyone else.' Her cheeks had flushed as she spoke. Marie shifted in her seat. I wasn't sure if it was the baby pressing against her bladder or this uncomfortable atmosphere.

'Oh. Right.' We weren't celebrating. We should be commiserating the end of an era. 'Well, at least it shows Ben is good at keeping secrets, ha!' A bark of fake laughter escaped.

'All men have some secrets, just like us women. The point is that as long as they don't hurt each other then it's okay. I mean, you do love Ben, don't you?' Marie asked out of the blue.

'What is love?' I asked stretching my arms out and sloshing some of my special cocktail on the sofa cushion. 'Baby, don't hurt me!' I finished Haddaway's 90s' song lyrics with a dramatic flourish and cracked myself up.

'You do need to speak to him about it all though, babe,' Marie said, ignoring the signs that my cocktail was kicking in.

'I know, just not right now,' I muttered sticking my tongue as far as it would go into my glass.

My best friend was soon to give life to another human being, my other best friend was starting a new life down under with her doting boyfriend, whereas mine was currently on a date with his stunning ex-girlfriend. Plus, he knew Shelley's Australian bombshell and hadn't prewarned me. But then again I'd found the ring he was going to propose to me with, so why did this matter? Even in my happiest moments, when I knew I had achieved and experienced things not a lot of people would do in a lifetime, I would still feel those crushing dark thoughts tap at my mind that I was missing out on what others had. That I had been left behind in some way. I always thought that – if things had previously gone to plan – by now I would have had a baby with Alex, that we would have celebrated

our wedding anniversary and maybe even added an en-suite
bathroom to our house.

When he'd called it off I'd been faced with an
alternative to what I guess is the 'pre-packaged' idea of
how you are *supposed* to live your life with the husband,
children and mortgage. My life was now focused on
growing my business, getting to see the world, building
a future with Ben and doing the things that made me
happy. I fluctuated between feeling unsure that I wanted
to follow the traditional path, as it hurt me so much
last time, yet eager not to miss out on what deep down
I desperately wanted – a loving husband, a healthy child
and a place to call home. I guess settling down doesn't
mean you have to settle. I felt an excitable tickle in my
stomach when I thought about the upcoming proposal
from Ben and how honoured I would feel at him getting
down on one knee. So then why was I suddenly so
unsure? And how could he be on a date with his ex if he
was about to ask me to marry him? What was he playing
at? It was all so confusing, and my strong cocktail wasn't
helping me think straight.

Once I'd drank all the booze, including two more special
Georgia cocktails, and decided it would be hilarious to
use Marie's birthing ball as a prop in my version of Miley
Cyrus's *Wrecking Ball* video, it was time to call it a night.
Shelley was meeting Jimmy at his gym once he'd finished
his late night class so I left Marie's in a fug of hugs and
cocktail breath, and ordered an Uber to take me home.

'All right, love? Good night?' The shaven-headed, plump
driver asked as I slipped into the back of his Corsa.

'No. Not really. I've just found out that my best friend is
moving ten thousand miles away and my other friend knew
and didn't warn me. Plus, my boyfriend has been hanging

out with his ex-girlfriend on the sly and I drank some nasty cocktails and now have heartburn to go with my heartache.'

'Oh.' He drew in a breath and sucked his teeth; he turned down the radio station he'd been listening to. 'That's going to hurt.'

Realising that I had an impartial and sympathetic listener I then proceeded to tell him everything that had happened over the past few hours in drunken, inane detail. By the time he pulled up at my flat I felt like that old woman from *Titanic* who'd taken a four-hour film to explain one life event.

'And that is why, even with all this going on,' I slurred, waving my hand into thin air and whacking my wrist into his headrest by accident. 'Even with this, I'm still going to be fine. Fine.'

He flashed me a look of relief as I stumbled out of his car. I eventually made it inside my flat after struggling to get my key in my front door and turn the handle at the same time. But when I realised Ben wasn't home yet, I felt a heavy weight press on my shoulders.

I was going to be fine, but today, today was not that day.

CHAPTER 5

Auspicious (adj.) – Attended by good fortune; prosperous

I was battling through storm Bertha, or whatever the weather presenters had named this one, as I made my way from the warmth of our shop to go to a lunch meeting. Luckily, I knew the person I was meeting quite well, otherwise they would have taken one glance at the drowned rat look I seemed to have adopted and called off any business arrangement right then and there. My umbrella was probably doing more harm than good as I gripped the handle with my icy hands, finding it hard to breathe as cold gusts choked my throat.

I'd called him earlier as I glanced out of the window at the apocalyptic street scene to see about changing the date of this meeting, but he was adamant that we had to meet today, the sooner the better he'd said. I was now rushing behind schedule to meet Rahul, the part-time tour guide who I'd met when I'd travelled to India. He was back in Manchester and had booked us a table in Rocco, a fancy Spanish restaurant that had recently opened not far from the bank, so at least I could nip in there and do some business admin and not feel so guilty about being out of the office for what would basically be a gossip session with a friend.

I half tumbled into the elegant room, which was full of white, starched-linen tablecloths, industrial steel and exposed brickwork, with splashes of deep red and blood orange. It was less quaint, Mediterranean tapas, and more hipster, Brooklyn loft. The large glass door slammed shut behind me, making the other diners turn and tut at the wild-haired woman with watering eyes and wind-slapped cheeks who'd stumbled in with all the grace of a charging rhino.

'Good afternoon, do you have a reservation?' The *maître d'* asked, able to hide his look of disgust on his Botoxed features.

'Georgia!'

I was saved from having to reply as Rahul strode over and pulled me into an enveloping hug, filling my nose with citrus aftershave.

'You made it! Come in and let's get you warmed up.' He nodded his thanks to the *maître d'* whose face lit up like the Blackpool Illuminations at being so close to this demi god. *Subtle, mate, real subtle.* Although, to be fair, Rahul was a hottie. There was no denying it. Wearing a tight but perfectly fitted pale grey suit and white shirt that could have been starched along with the tablecloths, he was a sight for sore eyes. His head of thick, dark hair only offset his tanned complexion and made his light-olive eyes appear even brighter. He did not look like he had been out in the same weather that I just had, more like he had teleported himself in, as not a hair was out of place.

'Sit down, sit down.' He pulled out a chair for me as I flinched at the heat coming back to my frozen body. My fingertips started to tingle and I felt the colour rush to my glacial cheeks. 'So, how are you?'

'Cold, windswept, but happy to see you again! It's been ages,' I said, winding my scarf from around my neck, managing to almost choke myself in the process. *Classy, Georgia, really classy.*

'I know I know, but better late than never, hey?' He flashed a pearly white smile. 'So how's everything going at work?

The last time I saw you was when that article about you and what happened with the Indian tour had just come out.' He shook his head in disbelief at how much time had passed since then. 'What was it? Farting during a yoga class?'

'Yeah, my "unusual management technique",' I said, indicating air quotes with my fingers and laughing. 'Although it seems to have paid off, as we're doing really well, thanks.'

I still couldn't believe just how much our profits had risen since that, and subsequent, media coverage. The power of the press. At the time I had been beside myself, preparing for the absolute worst, thinking the stinging poison pen of journalist Chris Kennings would damage our brand beyond recognition and put us out of business. I mean, I did fart on the poor fella; what else did I expect from a ruthless national journalist to get his own back?

Thankfully, the review was mostly positive and had since led to increased bookings in nearly all of our tours. If I was honest, it really had been the catalyst for our sudden growth, allowing us to take on Conrad and, seeing our healthy bank balance, had planted the seed of the potential London expansion in Ben's mind.

'Crazy how things work out. The moments you dread the most can turn out to be the ones that make you,' I mused, shaking my head.

'Well, however it came about, it is still amazing news!' He chinked his glass to mine.

We ordered from an eager young waitress, who was nailing the fishtail-plait look and was as unsubtle as the *maître d'* in swooning over Rahul. As soon as the braided beauty had simpered away to give the chef our order, Rahul unbuttoned his suit jacket and leant forward.

'How about Ben? How's he?'

I spluttered on my drink, causing the liquid to go down the wrong hole, and coughed ungracefully. 'Excuse me. Erm, yeah, he's fine. Great.' I thought back to the last few days; he'd never mentioned his evening out with his ex, Amazing Alice, and I hadn't known how to bring it up without him knowing that I'd been snooping.

Rahul began telling me about this model named Marli he had started seeing. 'Hence I wanted to meet you for lunch. I'm desperate to go out for a meal with a girl who actually enjoys decent scran.' His eyes creased up.

'I guess I'll take that as a compliment,' I said, taking a bite of crusty bread weighed down with salty butter, suddenly very aware of how many glorious calories I was about to ingest.

He laughed. 'You should, seriously. Marli is great and we're having a lot of fun.' He winked. 'But, man, dating a model is tough.'

'Oh, poor you,' I said, with my mouth full on purpose. 'Excuse me while I get out my violin.'

He let out a deep roar of a laugh. 'Yeah, yeah, I know, woe is me. I hadn't realised just how much work it takes to look that good. I keep telling her that eating carbs after 4 p.m. won't mean she'll wake up like the Nutty Professor – not that she listens.' He wiped his mouth with a napkin and took a sip of water before continuing. 'Obviously, being able to stuff my face with the finest Argentinian steak was only part one of my plan in meeting you today. I also have a very exciting proposal for you,' he said, baring his perfectly straight, white teeth.

'Don't tell me it involves sadhus?' I smiled, thinking back to when we were in India together and he'd encouraged us to ask three wise men wearing hardly any clothes for a blessing for our future. Instead of bestowing their years of knowledge and imparting their wisdom on me, one of the long-haired dudes had hacked up a load of phlegm at my feet. I guess actions do speak louder than words sometimes.

'Hey, that was a blessing in disguise!' Rahul let out a heavy laugh. 'I mean, maybe that was the key to you becoming so successful, all because of a holy sadhu clearing his throat.'

'Er, yeah, maybe.' I rolled my eyes. 'So, go on. What's this "project" that was so urgent for you to see me about?'

Rahul leaned closer and lowered his voice. 'So, you know that as well as giving tours in Mumbai I also live the glamorous life of a TV producer…?'

'Yeah.' I'd picked up another piece of bread and dipped it into the dish of glassy oil that dribbled down my chin after I'd taken a bite. Bugger.

'Well, as part of this I get to attend pitch meetings for new television shows that are hoping to be commissioned.'

'Mmhmm…' I was struggling to see what point he was trying to get to here, as I was too busy dabbing the greasy oil stain from the front of my blouse with the napkin I'd sloshed with water.

'One programme that has been the talk of the boardroom is called *Wanderlust Warriors*.' He paused, presumably to build drama. 'This show that's got everyone buzzing in the office is actually inspired by you and Ben.'

'Wait, what?' I looked up from the growing wet patch I'd created, causing more damage than good, to catch his eyes that had creased into a genuine smile while waiting for my reaction. Rahul laughed at what must have been the most idiotic, blank expression I was rocking on my face.

'I may have told you a little white lie earlier. I've known how well Lonely Hearts is doing because my team have been watching you grow, especially since that piece in the *Daily Times*.'

'What are you on about, watching us?'

He held his palms up. 'Don't look at me like that! Not in a weird sense. Just that because of your success story there has been talk of putting together a show that documents couples who work together in or around the travel industry who are poised to become the next big thing in the industry. A sort of inspirational piece that looks at the highs and lows of managing a business and a relationship at the same time, mixed with globetrotting.' He took a long sip of his drink. 'And you and Ben were the reason for this idea, the spark that started it all.'

'Oh, right, okay, cool.' I felt myself blushing. I'd never been called inspirational before.

'The show will not only be about mixing work and pleasure but also about how travel has impacted these couples' lives, as the contributors all work in the travel industry or use travel a lot for work reasons.' He paused to flash a genuine smile to the waitress who placed our plates in front of us and shimmied off, obviously for Rahul's benefit but it had been lost as he was currently making love with his eyes to the hunk of red meat on his plate.

'Sounds exciting!' I smiled at him. 'Wow, this food looks amazing.'

'I know! Right, let me get to my point.' He pulled his eyes away from the delicious-smelling dead cow and back to my face. 'So, where was I? Oh yeah, the show will also follow this travel theme as the filming is going to take place in South America, Chile specifically, I think.'

'Ooh wow. When will it be on? I hardly ever watch telly these days but that sounds right up my street.'

Rahul flicked his head back and let out a light laugh. 'Georgia. You won't just get to *watch it*; we want you and Ben to be *on it*.'

'Wait, what?' The chunky chip I'd speared on my fork paused just before my open mouth.

'They want you, along with three other couples, to take part. You get an all-expenses-paid trip just speaking to the camera about how you manage your work and relationship. Plus, there's a cash prize up for grabs at the end of it all for taking part in some fun games along the way!'

I started to laugh. 'Hahaha, funny. Oh. Wait. You're serious?'

His face had dropped as if he didn't get the joke.

'Rahul. You're serious? You want Ben and me to be on the telly?'

Rahul nodded. I stopped fanning my hands in front of my face and choked down the giggles.

'Er, I really don't know.'

'Think about the publicity this could drum up for The Lonely Hearts Travel Club! I can see the headlines now.... Wanderlust Warriors Take On The World.'

That did sound pretty good, to be fair.

'Georgia, your story is really inspiring, how you have turned a negative experience into a hugely positive one, and found love and a cracking business model along the way. Ever since that article you've been the talk of the industry and people want to know the secret to your success.'

I scoffed without thinking. 'There is no secret. Hard work, determination and sacrifice is what it's taken,' I said quietly, thinking back to when Ben and I had nearly lost everything – including each other – when Serena stole from us and the Indian tour looked like it was about to ruin us.

'Exactly. But people love to hear stories like this; sometimes good news does sell. Trust me. Plus, it means you both get to go to South America, which is such a stunning part of the world. Have you even been away as a couple yet?'

I shook my head thinking about the couple's holiday idea that Marie and Shelley had suggested. 'Hmm, well what would we need to do? Hypothetically speaking, of course.' Oh my God, was I even entertaining this idea? Ooh, I wondered if there would be a hair and make-up artist included.

'Of course, hypothetically speaking.' He pressed his hand to his broad chest and winked. 'Well, the first thing would be to get both of you to London where the head office is for pre-filming interviews. That's where you'd meet the producers in charge of the show, find out some more about the concept, get to know the other couples and decide if you're up for it or not.'

I thought this all over as I chewed on a chip. 'Do you know who the other couples are?'

He shook his head. 'Don't think they've been confirmed. I know that you and Ben are top of the list because you were the inspiration behind the show, but there's a long list of potential contributors as it's such a great premise. That's why I needed to see you today and to let you know to act fast if you think you and Ben would be up for it. Also, have you not seen the weather here? If someone was giving me the option of jetting off to the sun, all for free, with my partner, well I wouldn't have to think twice.'

He had a point. This storm Bertha was beginning to get to me. What he was proposing sounded too good to be true. An all-expenses-paid trip to South America in return for doing some interviews, probably on a white sandy beach or while taking a salsa class. Ooh, I wondered if I could wear a flamenco dress, and I could so see Ben dressed as a hunky Latino stallion. Minus the heavy gold chains and love-rug chest hair.

'Well, why don't you have a word with Ben and then let me know?'

I nodded slowly. 'Yeah, all right.'

'Ace. Right, now leave me in peace to give this meat the attention it deserves.'

After finishing our plates, both of them almost licked clean, Rahul got up from his seat and nodded to the lingering young waitress so that he could pay for our lunch. Amazingly, it seemed like big Bertha had gone for a nap as even the heavy dark clouds had floated off slightly.

'Have a think about everything and give me a call, Georgia,' he said, before gently kissing me on the cheek and filling my nose with his expensive-smelling aftershave. 'You more than anyone should know that you have to say yes to things in this life. I honestly think this would be the ideal chance to grab an opportunity that hardly anyone gets offered.'

I nodded distractedly.

'Right, I'd better be off. Call me as soon as you've decided.' With that we said our goodbyes and he headed off in the opposite direction.

I was just about to make my way back to the office when I realised that I'd left my umbrella in the restaurant. Even though the downpour had stopped, I didn't trust my chances that the heavens wouldn't open once more. I turned to head back inside when I saw that right next door was an art gallery.

Large colourful canvases hung in the windows lit by uplighters that brought to life the bright swirls of yellow and orange paint of the stunning paintings. The main three pieces of art were clearly from a collection by the same artist. One was a painting of a wrinkled and grinning old woman in Peru with a chubby arm casually slung around a gurning llama; another was a close-up of a glamorous, busty lady with an incredible afro shaking what her mother gave her at Rio Carnival, wearing a barely there but intricately beaded costume in the colours of a peacock feather; and the third and the largest was of a city scene that appeared to be made of bright and wonky Playmobil buildings, tagged in graffiti print 'Valparaíso, Chile'.

I pressed my nose closer to the glass to read the small glinting plaque attached to a stand.

'Jose Vasquez's collection has been inspired by the artist's journey through South America, where he felt compelled to replicate the colours, flavours and ambiance of this fascinating part of the world.'

I couldn't contain the smile trying to escape. This was a sign.

I rummaged in my pocket to grab my mobile and quickly dialled Ben's number. He answered in a few rings.

'Hey there, beautiful, how was your lunch? I hope you're bringing me back a doggy bag?'

'Ah sorry! No doggy bag, but I can go one better.'

'Oh yeah? Wait, why do you sound so excited?'

'Well, because I've just been offered the chance for both of us to take an all-expenses-paid trip to South America!' I squealed. Despite working in the travel industry we rarely received perks, unless you counted the stacks of branded luggage tags or passport covers piled in the bottom drawer of my desk. Somehow the *'Don't be flighty, get your life insurance plan sorted first'* fountain pen didn't have the same gravitas as this potential freebie.

'What?' He let out a confused laugh.

'Rahul works for a TV company who want to send us, along with some other couples, to Chile for some documentary they're filming on people who work together in the travel industry. He said that everything will be paid for, we get time to travel and explore, just in return for doing a short interview or something!' That was what he'd said, wasn't it? Well I'm sure that was the gist of it.

Ben started to laugh. 'Did this lunch turn into a boozy one? You want us to be stars on the small screen?'

I nodded down the line, still keeping my eyes trained on the stunning art in front of me before realising that

Ben couldn't see me. 'Yep! How amazing is this? We can promote the business *and* take our first holiday together. I'm sure from what Rahul said the filming part of it all will be so minimal we could get it done in a day or so and then head off to finally travel together!'

There was a strange silence on the phone as Ben thought it over. I could hear Conrad's booming laugh in the background at something.

'Ben? You still there?'

'Yeah, yeah, sorry, G. Erm, wow. It sounds amazing and I don't want to be a party pooper but how are we going to manage everything going on with the business if both of us are taking time off?'

My heart sank. He was right. Maybe I was getting totally carried away with Rahul's enthusiasm.

'Well, the show will be going ahead with or without us, as they have other couples lined up. If we don't take them up on it then we'll miss out,' I said. 'And now we have Conrad, I'm sure he can handle things for a couple of weeks without us. And think of the PR opportunity! They've asked us to go to London for some pre-filming meeting thing to discuss things further. We'd be under no obligation to take it any further; it's just to get some more details on it all…' I trailed out and began chewing my lip. *Come on, Ben.*

He let out a breath he'd been holding. 'Ahhh…okay. Let's at least go and hear what they've got to say, hey?'

'Eeeee! Okay!' I did a little jig.

'It's never boring with you, Georgia, that's all I can say.' He laughed. 'Right, get yourself back here before I change my mind.'

As soon as I'd hung up I hurriedly dialled Rahul's number to tell him we were in. This was going to be the start of a whole new adventure; I could just feel it.

CHAPTER 6

Vagary (n.) – An erratic, unpredictable or extravagant manifestation, action or notion

Once we had agreed to at least look into Rahul's offer by heading down to London to meet the producers of the show, I'd been unable to get the conversation I'd had with Marie and Shelley out of my head. A trip to Chile would be the perfect opportunity for us to talk, and for me to make sure I was one hundred per cent on the same page as Ben. Maybe he'd even make use of the opportunity to propose? If Ben so obviously thought we were *there*, then surely I should too? It was definitely time I met his family.

Just this morning as we'd been rushing to get ready I'd brought up the possibility of popping in to see his dad whilst we were down in London. He had met my parents enough times and they liked him as much as I did, but it was starting to feel one-sided. Previously Marie and Shelley had told me that I needed to just let him go at his own pace, that he was just a typical man and that putting off learning all about him – warts and all – for as long as possible meant the dewy-eyed shine would last longer. But finding the engagement ring had changed all of that. The other night at Marie's house had been a sort of wake-up call that I needed to get some answers to my questions before we even thought of getting married.

When I'd broached the subject of meeting his dad as I brushed my teeth this morning I'd just got a non-committal, 'yeah, maybe' answer, but I swore that as he said it his face clouded with a look of worry, or was it something more than that? Oh God, maybe I was being paranoid after having a not-so-rosy experience of Alex's family. *Ben's not going to have any potential psycho family members, trust him. You know and love his godmother, Trisha, and if she's anything to go by then you could soon be able to inherit the in-laws of your dreams!* I told myself.

We arrived in London on time and caught a cab to the production team's head office in Hoxton. I felt my tummy whirl with excitement at what the pre-show filming would involve; it already sounded so glamorous! Marie, being a part-time actress, had been giving us tips, telling us to wear something smart and business-like with no stripes or bright colours for the cameras. Hence I was now teetering down a cobbled courtyard to the head office that was in a complex of old converted stables, wearing my #girlboss black heels that gave me blisters but looked amazing with the deep green jumper dress I had on.

Ben looked super class in his thick woollen coat and the cable-knit scarf that brought out the colour of his eyes. If this went well we could soon be losing all these extra layers and feeling the heat from the sun and I could ditch the one hundred denier tights that were currently the only thing preventing me from developing frostbite.

'After you.' Ben winked, holding open the heavy barn door for me. I gave a small curtsey and laughed, before suddenly stopping at the commotion going on inside the open-plan office we'd stumbled into.

There were people everywhere; small meeting rooms seemed to shoot off down bright corridors like clavicles on a heart. Phones were ringing, people were shouting, TV screens were playing some dance music video with three very orange women gyrating in tiny string bikinis. I must have taken a step back into Ben who was gawping at this lively scene with a similarly shocked expression.

Rahul had said it was a low-budget, small TV company, so I'd expected to meet maybe one or two people in a coffee shop or something equally as chilled. I hadn't expected to be dropped in the media equivalent of the Wall Street trading floor on uppers. We were barked at to move out of the way by three harassed men in baggy black T-shirts and scuffed Converse trainers as they pushed large cameras on tracks past us, while a young woman about the same age as Kelli was concentrating on not dropping a stupidly full tray of teas and coffees, and a pack of hipsters with matching beards and spotty red bow ties were sitting at a round table typing furiously on gleaming Apple Macs.

'Erm, Ben? Is this the right place?' I whispered, wanting him to put his arms round me and reassure me that this hadn't all been a huge mistake. He didn't get the chance to do this or even answer me as a grinning, chubby man danced over and planted himself in front of us. He literally pirouetted to a standstill and put out a fleshy pink hand as he smiled at us expectantly.

'Let me guess…' He twirled a finger that had a tattoo of a moustache down one side. 'Georgia…' I nodded. His clean-shaven face broke into a bigger smile, making him look like a plump version of the Joker. 'I knew it! And that means you must be…' He pressed his fingers to his temples and closed his eyes, deep in thought. 'Ben?'

'Hi, yep, that's right,' Ben said. His voice sounded deeper and more manly than normal, in contrast to the high-pitched, camp dancer who was clapping his hands together like a hyperactive seal as if he'd just guessed which box held the £250,000 on *Deal or No Deal*.

'Awesome! Welcome, welcome. My name is Blaise; Rahul has told me SO much about you both!' He started walking off and nodded his head for us to follow him. We nervously glanced at each other and picked up our pace so as not to get separated. Blaise turned back to me and put a hand up against his mouth and said loudly. 'By the way, can Rahul, like, *be* any hotter?' He wiped his brow and pretended to faint before letting out a bark of a laugh that made me jump.

'Oh, erm, well...' I stuttered. Ben hadn't actually met Rahul yet and I may not have told him just how handsome he was. Of course, I knew that he trusted me, but there was no point rocking the boat by telling him I was having lunch with a buff Indian god. *But I hadn't forgotten to mention whether my stunning friend was an ex, unlike Ben when he went out with Alice*, I huffed inside.

Luckily Blaise didn't go on to drool over Rahul any more and just waved manically at a woman at the other end of the room who was on the phone. This didn't put him off as he yelled loudly, 'I've got Georgia and Ben here! You know, the jilted bride, and her new man!'

'Oh, well, that's not really what the story is,' I said, feeling my face grow flushed.

Blaise turned to face me with a look of surprise. 'Ah now, darlin', that is right isn't it? Your business all came about because you were *dumped* before your big day?'

He pronounced that word as if spitting out a wasp's sting.

I nodded. 'Yeah, but that's not why we're here today.' I couldn't bear to look at Ben, knowing how humiliated he must feel that he had just been referred to as my 'new man' rather than the invaluable business partner and half the brains behind The Lonely Hearts Travel Club that he really was. I felt for his wounded pride and was determined for Blaise to get this.

'My past relationship doesn't have anything to do with why we're here. Rahul told us that this show is going to focus on our business, so we can share advice with others.' I tried to say it in my most forceful way, despite Alan Carr's hyperactive younger twin manically grinning back at me.

Blaise wafted his hands and let out a giggle. 'Sure! Course. Right, come on. We need to get you both set up. Ben, if you could go with Anna here.' As if by magic, a glamorous and jaw-droppingly gorgeous woman in a clingy wrap dress, with shiny blonde swishy hair cut into a cute long bob, was by our side. She guided Ben off with one swoop of her clipboard and flick of a tanned wrist. I didn't get the chance to even say good luck or ask what was happening as Blaise then led me down a corridor and shooed me into a darker but thankfully quieter room.

'Here we go. Just in here,' he said, looking at his chunky plastic watch at the same time.

'Oh... I...' I stuttered before he winked and shut the door. What the hell was going on?

'Georgia?' A man's voice with a soft Scottish lilt startled me, making me spin round to locate the source. The voice was coming from behind a large, kidney-shaped desk, and hidden behind three ginormous computer screens was a man in his mid-fifties peering down his wiry spectacles at me. His thick beard was peppered with greys, less London hipster and more kindly grandfather, and his lips had curled into a wide smile through this bushy facial hair. 'Come and take a seat.'

He wafted his hand at the two sofas and got up to sit on one himself. 'I take it you've been offered a cup of tea?'

I shook my head and stayed planted in the same position. He sighed and rolled his eyes heavenwards. 'I am sorry about that. Those kids out there have lost the art of good manners. Unless it comes with a whizzy app or a hashtag, they're not interested.' He shook his head at the youth of today and picked up a phone on the cluttered desk.

I smiled, starting to warm to this man who looked like a funky Father Christmas in his checked shirt and Levi's.

'Hello, Dana, can we get a cup of...' He glanced up at me to get my order.

'Tea please. No sugar,' I said, finally finding my voice.

'Make that two cups of tea, no sugar. Thanks.' He replaced his phone and pointed to the sofas again. 'Please take a seat as we wait for our drinks. You can take your coat off if you like; it's bitter outside today, isn't it? Although, thank goodness that snow didn't last as long as everyone was expecting it to. Oh, I don't think I've introduced myself! My name's Jerry, by the way.' He stretched out a thick, rough palm. His hands looked like they'd actually been used to a day's hard work, unlike the soft, pudgy palms of Blaise.

'Hi. Georgia. Nice to meet you. Sorry if I seem a little lost, I've never been to a TV studio before and I didn't really have any idea of what one would be like,' I admitted, awkwardly shrugging off my coat.

Jerry laughed, reminding me of Rahul. I could see the two of them working together. 'Oh well then, let me welcome you to the head office of See Me TV. Out in the cattle yard, as I like to call it, is where you've got PR, marketing, sales, web design and all these jobs that go over my head. I've been working in TV for the past thirty years and back then it was nothing like this performance it seems today.' He rubbed his beard and sighed. 'But things change.' A knock at the door made him pause as he gratefully took two steaming mugs of tea from a woman wearing a thick fluffy jumper that had dog paw prints embroidered over each large breast. 'Thanks, Dana.'

Dana blushed and dipped her head before scurrying out into the corridor.

'So, Georgia, I'm one of the producers here and we thought it would be great if you and I got to know one another a little better. Today is about you and Ben, and informing you both about the premise of the show, and why we'd love for you to be involved. I spoke to Rahul who said he'd filled you in on some of the details but I wanted to make sure that you're comfortable with everything before you sign up.' Jerry passed me a cuppa and grabbed a notepad. 'To really make sure you're both happy we prefer to interview potential guests separately – that's why Ben was also whisked off. He'll join us shortly.'

I gave a hesitant nod; this was the one time when I could have really done with having Ben by my side. *Don't be such a baby. Where's that fearless traveller gone?* I berated myself.

'Is Rahul about today?' I asked, blowing on the steam of my cup of tea.

Jerry shook his head. 'No, he won't actually be working on this series. He's going to be away filming something else. He just acted as matchmaker.'

My face must have given away how disappointed I felt. I really got on with Rahul, and as charming as Jerry seemed to be, I had hoped that my first foray into the world of television would be with the support of people I already knew and trusted. I felt like I needed some hand-holding especially after the last time I was on camera in India it caused me so much trouble.

'Oh, okay.' I paused. 'Erm, Rahul also said that maybe we could meet the other guests?'

Jerry shook his head sadly. 'Ah, well, until contracts have been signed I can't reveal who you'll be travelling with. But I can tell you that I'm sure you will have six new friends by the end of it all.' He smiled at me.

I blushed slightly before asking the next question,
'Rahul also mentioned something about a cash prize?'

'Yes! Our sponsors for the show have agreed to give
quite a healthy sum of £25,000 to the couple who win
the most challenges, with the idea that it will go towards
investing in their business, but how the winning couple
spends it is up to them!'

'Wow!' Before he finished speaking I'd instantly banked
the money into the Lonely Hearts Foundation, the charity
fund Ben and I had set up after my trip to India, knowing
how it could help such a valuable cause as getting children
off the streets, *and maybe bringing about some decent PR*,
my business side nudged me. 'What sort of challenges are
we talking?'

'Oh simple things, just to add a bit of colour to the
show really. Between you and me, this cash prize is just
so the sponsor gets more shout-outs in the show. It's all
about building that special viewer–brand relationship.' He
rolled his eyes as if it never used to be like this in his day.
'I can't imagine they would be expecting the contestants to
go above and beyond the call of duty.' He waved his hand
dismissively and glanced at the sheets of paper on his lap.
'So, I think that's a short overview. Can you tell me about
your relationship with Ben? I know it feels weird to be
talking about something so personal but what you tell me
in this room stays in this room. It will just help shape the
interview questions that you'll be asked once you're away.'

I nodded. 'Erm, sure, okay, well Ben and I met in
Thailand –'

'Ah yes, you travelled there after being jilted, didn't
you?' he interrupted me.

I felt my hackles rise like they had with Blaise. I had
to put a stop to this angle they were clearly looking to
go down. I cleared my throat and sat upright. 'Yes I did.

But honestly, Jerry, I don't want to be known as "the jilted bride".' I made inverted commas with my fingers and cringed. 'I was dumped, and yes that was the catalyst for going away but that is all in the past now. I've made something out of what was a horrible time and I couldn't be happier.' He was nodding along and making notes as I spoke. I felt really hot all of a sudden. 'I don't want this part to be a big element of the show. Rahul told me it would be more looking at how Ben and I manage our time working on the business, and our passion for travel. Is that okay?'

'Mmm. I just have to ask these silly questions,' he said gently. 'I'm sure it won't be the main focus of things.'

'Okay, well if you could note that down please, I'd be really grateful.'

Jerry leant forward and put the papers to one side. 'Georgia, we're thrilled to have you both here today and we only want you to feel happy. Please trust me that you honestly don't have a thing to worry about when you're away, well apart from maybe applying sunscreen and mosquito repellent!' He laughed.

I smiled along with him. Jerry looked like someone my dad would hang out and have a beer with in his local. There was no way he'd stitch me up. *Stop being so dramatic, Georgia.* They just need to cover all bases to check you haven't got any nasty skeletons hiding in your cupboard, I tried to tell myself. Then a thought hit me: I wondered what Ben was talking to that glamorous woman about. What questions was she asking him? See, this is going to be great, you can finally learn more about each other without feeling like you're nagging him, my subconscious said smugly.

The next hour or so passed quickly as Jerry moved on to less interrogative questions about running a business, the skills needed and time-management difficulties, then touched on how dating and working together with Ben was. He was apologetic about asking tough questions and made me laugh as he told me about his wife and how they'd tried to work together once but it had almost ended in a divorce.

'So.' He glanced at his brown leather watch. 'I'm conscious of time so if you could sign this form and then we can get started on sorting out the travel arrangements, your passport details, dietary requirements and all of that.'

'Oh, well I wasn't actually planning on signing anything, not until I'd at least spoken to Ben about it all first, sorry.' I winced feeling very awkward.

Jerry nodded politely and got to his feet and rummaged in his desk, 'Course. I just need to get the paperwork, that I know I put in here somewhere, so you can have a read of it all.' I nodded slowly and watched him banging open drawers. 'Ah, here we go!' Just then, the phone rang.

'Hello? Excellent. I'll let her know. Yep we're nearly all done here. Great okay, bye.' Jerry hung up and flashed me a heartfelt smile before putting his thumbs up in a cheesy dad style. 'That was Anna, who was with Ben. She just wanted to let me know that he's just signed the contract and will be waiting for you in reception.'

'Oh right. Okay.' He'd signed it already?

Jerry handed me over a stack of papers that had been stapled together at the top. 'It's just your basic contract that covers things like insurance and some boring legal jargon.' I must have hesitated before taking it. 'Don't worry, Anna has run through it with Ben who must be happy with it all. It's all kosher. The reason we need to move quite quickly on all of this is that the filming is set to take place in the next few weeks. I only found out this morning that Channel 4 have let us know of an unexpected slot in their scheduling so everything has been bumped forward to give ourselves the best shot to fill it.'

I smiled weakly and took the forms. I couldn't believe that Ben had just signed it. *But isn't this what you wanted? I asked myself. You were the one who suggested taking Rahul up on his offer in the first place. Maybe Ben knew how excited you were and wanted to make you happy by showing you that he was on board with the idea?* I tried to shush the prickling feeling that I was about to sign a contract without running through it with a fine-toothed comb.

'Have you got a pen?' I looked up at Jerry. He nodded and fumbled in one of the messy drawers for a fancy ballpoint pen that glided across the pages where I scrawled my signature.

'Excellent.' Jerry beamed and took the papers from me. 'I'll get these sent off to the legal department and ask them to forward you both a copy for your records and all that stuff.' I nodded as he cleared his throat and leaned forward. 'I know that you and Ben are going to have a wonderful time, be incredible contestants, and I have no doubt that the nation will warm to you and what you're trying to achieve with your business.'

'Thanks, I hope you're right.' I gave a light laugh. *Forget about stressing that you didn't get to fully read every line of that contract. Trust Ben and remember that both lovely Rahul and Jerry here just want to make a light-hearted show. I mean, it's hardly going to be question time with Jeremy bloody Paxman, is it?* I could have laughed about how sensitive I was being. *We get a free holiday and get to promote our business. What could possibly go wrong?*

'So, Georgia, someone will be in touch regarding travel arrangements and what things you'll need to bring with you et cetera, et cetera. You will need to keep the seventeenth free. Which I know is very soon, but like

I said, everything has been shifted forward. Is this still going to be okay?'

I mentally ran through my diary. January was set to be our quietest month, Conrad and Kelli were perfectly capable of being in charge for less than a fortnight, Jimmy and Shelley didn't leave until next month and Marie still had three weeks left until her latest mini-me entered the world. 'Yep, I can't see there's going to be any problems.' I got to my feet as he suddenly seemed quite keen to get me out of the room.

'Great, well it was so lovely to meet you and I'm sure we'll see you again soon. We're thrilled to have you both on board for what's guaranteed to be a fun and memorable experience! I'm just jealous that I've not been asked to take part with my wife!' He let out a deep laugh and then picked up the phone once more and asked for Dog Lover Dana to escort me back to the main room before shaking my hand again. 'Good luck, Georgia!'

I said goodbye and followed Dana who was chatting excitedly about the fantastic concept and how lucky we were to be involved. I half tuned out, feeling like I'd emerged from some strange comforting bubble, and now that I was back in the bedlam of the hipster courtyard I had this strange sinking feeling that I'd been way too hasty.

It was all going to be fine, wasn't it? Wasn't it?

CHAPTER 7

Inveterate (adj.) – Confirmed in a habit; habitual

'Well, that was different,' Ben said smiling, as he pulled out a pair of gloves from his coat pocket. We'd left the television studios and had managed to hail a black cab. Thankfully we had snuck out without getting Blaise-d once more. *Please don't let him be part of the actual filming,* I said in silent prayer. Although nothing could put a dampener on travelling with Ben, it certainly would be a lot harder with Jazz Hands McJazz Face there.

Ben seemed in a really great mood, whereas I felt a little confused and dazed by what had just happened in that room with calm Jerry and his kind eyes.

'I was a little sceptical when you first mentioned this TV show thing, babe, but actually I've been thinking and I reckon it's going to be great for the business.'

'And us?' I pouted.

He laughed and wrapped his arm around my shoulders. 'Yeah, and us, of course. Although, I think we're pretty spot on. They say you can't beat perfection.' He let out a bark of a laugh as I pretended to fake vomit. Although inside I felt like that too.

'You did look over the contract properly?' I asked for the third time since we'd left.

He gave me a look. 'Yes. I've told you, Georgia, we have nothing to worry about. It was just your basic agreement, like I've said. Trust me, it's fine.'

I nodded and told myself to do just that.

'Where to, folks?' the cabbie interrupted us as we pulled out of the courtyard.

'We're done earlier than I thought, so we've got a bit of time to kill before our train back,' I said to Ben, glancing at the clock above the meter.

Ben leant forward to speak to the driver. 'Can you take us to Belvedere Crescent please, mate,' he asked and squeezed my knee.

'You're the boss,' the cabbie replied and turned right onto the busy London streets.

'Where's that?'

'My dad's place.'

'Really?' I blinked in surprise.

'Yeah, you mentioned it earlier and I just thought maybe it is time you met him.'

I self-consciously fidgeted with my dress and pulled at my tights that were bagging at my knees.

'You look great.' Ben planted a heavy kiss on my forehead. 'It's going to be very relaxed; you've got nothing to worry about.'

'Oh okay. But maybe we could stop off on the way so I can pick up a bottle of wine or something? I don't really want to walk in empty-handed…'

'No,' he interrupted sharply. 'Sorry, I mean, let's just go and see if he's even in first,' he said more softly.

'Sure.' I nodded and tried to stay cool, calm and collected. I settled back into my seat, enjoying the weight of Ben's arm slung over my shoulder. Inside, I felt a fizz of excitement. We were going to get to travel together *and* I was about to learn loads about my boyfriend from his dad. I bet he was just like him, but older and well, more cockney! Today was shaping up to be a very good day indeed.

However, as the journey continued and the buzzing centre of London faded away so did Ben's good mood. It was as if this strange cloud had passed over him as we crossed the ring road. I remembered Marie once telling me about letting men go off into their man cave, something she'd read in *Men Are From Mars, Women Are from Venus*. That no good can come from women trying to get a man to talk when they so obviously want to be left alone to stew on whatever it is on their minds. Luckily the driver had the radio on loud so the gravelly tones of Rod Stewart filled this strangely uncomfortable silence.

'You sure you want to do this? Have you called him? Maybe we should have met in a coffee shop? I could do with something to eat as it's been ages since we had breakfast,' I babbled ignoring Marie's relationship advice. We turned off a main road and headed down what looked to be a much rougher part of town, judging by the graffiti-scrawled street signs and the stained mattresses piled near a high-rise block of flats.

'It'll be fine,' he muttered, absently staring out of the window. Ben was fidgeting with his hands and a sheen of sweat had broken out at his temples. What was the big deal? My vision of being shown adorable baby photos of Ben and laughing at childhood stories with his loving father felt like it had faded into a clench of anticipation and nerves at what a physical reaction introducing me to him was obviously having on him.

Maybe this was a stupid idea? Maybe I should have let this meeting happen organically, without me forcing it. What if he hated me? What if he was as snooty as Alex's parents had been? Why was Ben getting so stressed? I too felt like beads of sweat were showing on my forehead.

'We can turn back if you like?' I said, in a voice that didn't sound like my own. The cabbie was oblivious to this new tension in the back of his black cab and was having an animated conversation with someone about last night's footy match via a Bluetooth headset.

Ben shook his head and gripped my knee, giving it a tight squeeze. 'No. We should just get this over with.' God, why was he making it sound so bloody torturous? He seemed as clenched with anxiety as if heading to get his first smear test.

'Oh. Okay,' I mumbled.

He finally turned to face me. 'Georgia, it might be better if you manage your expectations – my dad isn't really like your family. Or like me to be honest. He…he…' Ben trailed off and was cut short from finishing his sentence when the cab pulled up to a stop.

'Belvedere Crescent,' the driver said, clicking the meter off. This spurred Ben into action as he rummaged in his pocket to pay and then got out, letting in a cold whoosh of winter air that jolted me like a slap in the face.

We were in a large cul-de-sac of a council estate. Three teens wearing hoodies and walking like Liam Gallagher after a lengthy horse-riding session sloped past us as the taxi driver made a speedy exit. One sucked his teeth, looking me up and down, a slow leery smirk breaking out on his pale, acne-marked cheeks. I felt exposed, despite wearing so many layers, and pulled my coat even tighter. *It was the damn high-heeled shoes. It had to be.*

'Come on, let's do this.' Ben glared at the lads and took my hand, leading me up a litter-strewn path to a large set of doors outside one of the identical blocks of flats. One of the windows had been kicked through and replaced with a scratty piece of plywood on which someone had artistically daubed an angry-looking cock. Wiry pubes and all.

'Home, sweet home,' he sighed, thankfully not catching the shocked look on my face that I knew I was doing a crap job of hiding.

Oh, this was going to be interesting.

Ben took a deep breath and pressed some numbers into the sticky keypad by the graffiti-scrawled front door, clenching his jaw as an irritating ringer buzzed.

'Yeah?' a man's drowsy voice croaked through the intercom.

'Hey, Dad? It's me. Ben. I was in London for a meeting and wondered if you were free for a cuppa. I've…I've got someone here I want you to meet.' I noticed a deep red flush climb up his neck that he rubbed self-consciously.

The line went silent apart from an angry, white-noise type of buzzing. I suddenly wished we'd called ahead and not doorstepped him like this.

'Ben?' There was a millisecond pause. 'Right, well… er…yeah, come up.' The door buzzed and we made our way into the junk-mail-strewn foyer. The lift was out of service so we took the stairs. I held my breath at the stench of stale urine and pulled my sleeves over my hands so as not to touch the grimy banister. Neither of us spoke. Any attempt at forming a sentence had vanished in shock at the state of this place. This was where Ben had grown up? I was literally speechless.

'Here we are,' Ben said, after two flights of stairs and my heels twice skidding on dubious stains. The front door to his dad's flat was ajar so Ben nudged it open with his foot.

'Hello?' he called out, not looking at me.

My eyes took a moment to adjust to the gloom, even though it was a surprisingly bright winter's day outside. Smells of greasy food, fags and stale beer drifted past us, making my stomach turn.

'Dad?' Ben called out again. His voice sounded distorted and echoed off the bare walls.

'In here, son, mind how you walk. I wasn't... I wasn't really expecting visitors.'

We followed where the flustered-sounding voice was coming from and walked down the dim, narrow corridor to the closed door ahead. As Ben turned the handle I felt my stomach knot with a sense of anxiety at what was on the other side. With a heavy shove the door burst open and inside the equally dark room was the kitchen-slash-lounge. In the centre, looking as if he'd just heaved himself up from the sagging sofa, was his dad, dressed in a tatty dressing gown and little else. He had brown hair, a lighter and dustier colour than Ben's, which had tufted into strange peaks, and a lit cigarette dangling from his wrinkled lips. He was *nothing* like the father figure I'd imagined. I hoped my intake of breath was muffled by the blaring noise coming from the television.

'All right, son! I was just about to start cleaning.' His dad quickly took the three strides to the tiny kitchen and began hastily chucking empty cartons and glass bottles into an already overflowing bin. The washing up hadn't been done for a very long time. Congealed sauce marked chipped dinner plates that were piled haphazardly next to a couple of takeaway boxes near the greasy tiles.

'Hey, Dad.' Ben's voice was flat and I could tell he knew it. I suddenly wanted to be anywhere but here. I wanted his father to still be a figment in my imagination. What is it they say about men turning into their fathers? The thought seemed as alien as Katie Price becoming Prime Minister.

'Ah, sod it, before I put my Marigolds on, come here and give yer old man a hug. It's not often I get to see the brains of the family.' His dad left the pathetic attempt at a clean-up operation and walked back round the kitchen counter to embrace his only son awkwardly. 'Very fancy suit you got on there,' he said, letting out a whistle and running a grubby hand over the lapel. 'And who's this pretty lady you've got with you?' He leant forward and peered at me. A waft of uncleaned teeth and days-old sweat filled my nostrils as he spoke in a thick cockney accent.

'This is Georgia.' Ben placed a hand on my shoulder and stepped between us, protectively shielding me from him.

'Hi.' I smiled politely, trying to brush off the hurt that Ben had introduced me as Georgia, instead of *my girlfriend Georgia*. In boy world maybe this wasn't such a big thing but it just made me feel even more confused after an already confusing morning. *Don't fret, Georgia, he's probably just overwhelmed at doing the introductions,* I told myself. My thoughts were all over the place.

'Erm, I hope this isn't a bad time?' Ben flicked his eyes over the messy room.

'For my special boy, never. You know I miss seeing you more often.' His dad winked then clapped his hands together. 'Right, who's for a cuppa then?'

'Yeah, that would be nice, wouldn't it, Ben?' I said, desperate to relax us both and let him know that I was trying to be okay with this. It wasn't like I came from a family of royalty, but I could picture my mum clutching her chest taking in the surroundings before getting to work on these scuzzy surfaces. It was a world away from when I'd met Alex's parents for the first time in the restaurant of a swanky golf club. Although the posh and, well, cleaner setting didn't mean it went without a hitch; I'd spilt red wine down my top and hadn't realised I'd had spinach in my teeth until I'd got home.

Looking around at this run-down council estate I wasn't sure which introduction to future parents-in-law was worse. From one extreme to the other. I felt restless and unsure of where to put myself. I could see how uncomfortable this was for Ben, and I wanted to do whatever I could to make it easier. Tea was always the answer for awkward moments like this.

As his dad brewed up, smelling the milk to see if it was still okay to use, Ben cleared room on the sofa by kicking over empty beer cans and rum bottles with his feet. He beckoned me over to sit with him.

'I'm so sorry about this,' he said in a low voice. 'I thought he'd changed. It's…been a while since I last saw him.' He ran his hand through his hair, leaving it tufted and scarily similar to his dad's.

'It's fine,' I said, stroking his arm. I'd never felt it so tense. I glanced around the place that certainly could do with a feminine touch and realised that there wasn't a single family photograph to be seen.

'I've been quite good at keeping on top of this place; it's just you caught me on a bad day.' His dad let out a husky bellow of a laugh hiding the smidgeon of embarrassment he must feel at us being here. 'But it's women's work I say, and without a woman, what's a man to do?' He nodded at me. 'Since *she* ran out on us I've been meaning to get a cleaner in.'

'It's not like you've not had the time to do it yourself, Dad,' Ben said under his breath.

I could feel my cheeks heat at the domestic threatening to blow up. I guessed that the *'she'* his dad was referring to was Ben's mum.

'Yeah, true. But there's more important things in life, ain't there? How are you with a feather duster, love?' his dad asked me as he wandered over, spilling tea over his trembling hands, before passing me a chipped mug and pulling his dressing gown together at the front.

'Don't answer that,' Ben hurriedly said to me and rubbed his neck. The faint flush had now descended into angry-looking blotches. 'Can we keep Mum out of it today?'

'I could tell you a thing or two about his mum!' his dad chimed in, glancing at me.

'No one needs to hear *your* version of events, Dad.'

Gah, I felt like I was watching car-crash TV, desperate to find out the lie detector or DNA results, but also wanting to make what was obviously a hugely awkward situation for Ben be over as soon as possible.

'Pfft. The truth, yer mean?' His dad rolled his eyes and crossed his legs as he fell into the grubby green chair opposite us. Ben just kept his head dipped and his eyes trained on the rough carpet as if hoping a wormhole would appear and he could dive into it.

'It's fine, honestly...' I trailed off, forcing my eyes to stay above shoulder height in case his robe fell loose; by the looks of his skinny but hairy legs he wasn't wearing any PJs underneath.

'Well...' His dad took a deep breath.

'Dad. Stop,' Ben growled. I'd never seen him so tense.

'Fine. You're the boss.' His dad threw his hands in the air defensively.

'Listen, do you mind if I open a window? It just feels a little stuffy in here.' Ben didn't wait for an answer. He shot off the sofa and strode the short distance to the condensation-drenched window; opening the curtains filled the room with light, making it seem even more depressing, if that was possible.

'Ah, 'av I embarrassed yer in front of yer new lady friend?' Ben's dad let out a throaty laugh, which descended into a wheezy coughing fit. 'Sorry, Grace.'

'It's Georgia,' Ben snapped before I could answer. He thrust open a window and gasped at the fresh, cool air seeping in.

'It's fine,' I mumbled, suddenly not knowing where to put myself. Ben flashed me a tight smile for the first time since we'd arrived here – a smile that said he knew it certainly wasn't fine.

'So, have you got any plans for today?' Ben asked, obviously desperate to change the subject as his dad rummaged in one of the frayed, dressing-gown pockets for a packet of fags.

'Well, yeah, as it happens. I'm goin' to be meeting Nicky later who tells me he has some tasty tip-offs on the dogs.' He rubbed his hands with glee before pulling a cigarette out of the box and lighting it with one of the many lighters lying around the place.

'Dad, do you mind?' Ben said, his voice a low guttural growl as he nodded in my direction.

'Ben, it's fine. This is his home,' I said quietly.

'Ah, shit! Sorry, Gracie, it's been a while since I've had a lady's company. Where are my manners?' He threw his hands in the air in shock, ignoring Ben repeating that my name was Georgia, and went to pull out another cigarette and handed it to me. 'Here yer are.'

'Oh. Erm, I don't smoke.' I blushed as Ben sighed deeply and rubbed his face with his hands.

His dad looked sheepish before putting the unlit fag on the coffee table, next to an empty can of Stella. 'Sorry 'bout that.'

'You're still gambling then, Dad?' Ben asked curtly.

'Hey now, don't give me that look. I only do it now and then.'

I felt Ben bristle beside me. 'Just be careful, all right?'

'Yeah, yeah. So, tell me about your fancy life. Been ages since I saw you last. How long you two been courtin' then?'

'We work together,' Ben replied abruptly before I had the chance to say anything. My heart felt as limp as the leaves of the wilted plant that had turned brown next to the television. There was obviously no sign of him confiding in his father about the fact he was going to ask me to marry him. It was clear his dad had never heard of me.

'Arr, you dog you – the perks of a job, hey? Always liked a challenge. Just like yer old man.'

Ben gave him a tight smile that communicated how he felt about the comparison.

'Well, there ain't nuffin finer than having a lady takin' care of you. It's something I miss, I'll tell yer that for nuffin.'

'Maybe if you'd looked after her more,' Ben mumbled, loudly enough for us both to hear.

'What's that?' his dad asked.

'Nothing.' Ben forced himself to look his dad in the eye. I was desperately running through conversation starters in my head when I noticed the stifling atmosphere in the room seemed to ramp up a notch.

'Listen, we're going to have to get off soon. Sorry we couldn't stay longer,' Ben said sharply, obviously picking up on this suffocating vibe too, and practically jumped to his feet before gently taking my hand and pulling me up.

'Oh, right, okay, well, thanks for the tea.' I smiled sweetly and tried to brush off a piece of fluff from my dress without his dad noticing.

'Yeah, yeah, course. Another time, hey?' He too got to his feet and pulled his dressing gown a little tighter.

Ben didn't reply but hurriedly put his chunky scarf back on. 'Take care of yourself, Dad.'

'Don't worry about me. I'll keep ticking over.' He grinned and went to open another pack of fags but frowned when he realised they were empty. 'You haven't got a few quid spare 'av you? Before you go.' He looked down at his bare feet on the stained lino.

'Erm, yeah, sure,' Ben muttered and then quickly reached into his wallet and left a few notes on the worktop.

'Ah, there's a good lad.'

Ben awkwardly hugged him goodbye and quickly steered me out of the depressing flat before I could get a single word out.

I wasn't sure what had just happened.

'I'm not like my dad,' Ben said through gritted teeth, to no one in particular as we half raced down the stairwell and out into the fresh, crisp air. All his happiness and excitement at leaving the TV studios had disappeared. I was struggling to keep up with him in my wobbly heels as he strode down the street, an angry tension making his hunched shoulders rigid. I was pleased there was no one else around, otherwise groups of leery lads could be in for some aggro.

'Slow down a little,' I pleaded, tottering behind him unsteadily on these stupid heels. He ignored me. 'Ben, wait!' I tugged on his arm to pull him to a stop. 'Ben!'

He swung round forcefully, flinging my arm from its grip on his. I could barely recognise him from his tight scowl and the dark glare from his eyes that looked filled to the brim with hurt and untold family truths.

'Talk to me,' I panted, wincing at the blister I could feel bubbling up on the back of my heel as a result of these sodding shoes.

His wild eyes glanced around the empty street and he let out a deep sigh before pulling his phone out of his pocket. 'Let's just get the hell out of here, shall we?'

Before I could say anything else he was ordering us a taxi. His voice sounded curt and abrupt, so unlike my Ben it was painful to see. Hanging up, he ran a hand through his hair, flattening the tufts he had raised during our stressful visit with his dad. It was still some way from the smart style he had gone for this morning when we were getting ready in our flat. The excitement and anticipation of this trip seemed like a hundred years ago. I was kicking myself for being so desperate to meet his family, to get a sense of where Ben had come from. I wish I'd kept my bloody mouth shut and just waited until the time was right, when he had decided to properly introduce us rather than surprising his dad like we'd just done. Although I doubt that would have changed things.

Thankfully, a few moments later, a taxi screeched to a halt and we bundled in.

'Euston Station please, mate,' Ben ordered the driver, who nodded and put his foot down. He seemed to be as keen to leave this dubious neighbourhood as we were.

'I'm sorry if you thought I acted a little harsh in there, but you have to understand it's the same every time I go to visit him. Apologising now won't change a thing. It's too late for all that.'

'Too late for what?' I asked in a voice barely louder than a whisper. *Please open up. Please.*

I saw his Adam's apple bob up and down as he swallowed and mulled over what to say next. 'It's all in the past, Georgia. Please let's not open up raw wounds. I'm a totally different person now to who I was back then. Seeing my dad and the state he has let his life get in only makes me more determined to make something of myself. Every time he tells me he's changed, that he's got a grip on things and is sorting himself out, but the truth is he'll never change. The sooner I get my head round that the better.'

I rubbed his arm protectively, not sure what to say. I wanted to be out of this black cab, out of London, and back in our flat all those hours ago when he'd tried to make me stay wrapped up in our sheets together for longer. When none of this had happened.

He smiled sadly at the gesture and pulled his face away. 'So, what time's our train leaving?'

I rummaged in my handbag for the tickets. Conversation time was very clearly over.

CHAPTER 8

Camaraderie (n.) – A spirit of friendly good fellowship

'I cannot believe that you're doing this!' Conrad's booming voice bounced across the office. 'I better get a shout-out at the very least.'

I looked up from the mountain of papers in front of me and laughed. 'I can't believe we're doing this either! I can't bloody wait though.'

With the awful meeting with his dad that neither of us had mentioned since, the unanswered questions about Ben's past and the miserable weather outside, I was more excited than ever to be able to jet off to Chile. I'd been trying not to think about *that day*, as when I did I felt a sickening sensation of rising doubts about Ben, about what type of family I could soon be marrying into, and my stomach clenched at the thought. I felt awful as I compared his father to the prim and proper but snobby parents of my ex. I was ashamed to admit that I couldn't decide which was worse. And I hated myself for thinking these things.

Ben said himself he wasn't like his dad, but then Shelley and Marie had seemed adamant that all men turn into their fathers eventually, whether this was a conscious decision or not. I decided I must be the worst kind of girlfriend. Who cares what his family was like? Only I had to shush the thoughts that last time I'd almost inherited the family from hell and I couldn't go through that again.

'I'm expecting a personal message for your hard-working colleague with dashing good looks and a blinding personality.' Conrad, a balding, stocky chunk of a man turned round from the coffee machine he was sweating profusely over.

I laughed and pushed the hair from my face. 'If I get the chance to big you up then you know that I will.'

'I think you'll find that being the most loyal and longest-serving member of staff, if anyone gets to be mentioned on the telly, then it had better be me,' Kelli piped up.

'You'll both get shout-outs, if they'll let us!' I clapped my hands together to wake myself up. 'Any luck, Conrad?'

He wiped his glistening forehead with the back of his large hand. 'It's knackered. Totally had it.'

I sighed. This was the third coffee machine I'd bought in just as many months. 'I don't get it. Why do they keep packing in on us?'

Conrad shrugged. 'I'll get in touch with the shop and give them a piece of my mind, don't you worry. But until then how about I nip to the café over the road? I don't know about you but I'm gasping.'

'My hero.' I smiled at him as he took our orders and headed out of the shop. It was so nice having a man around, especially with Ben in London, meeting with some social media whizz-kids who were looking at ways we could maximise our digital presence. It was something Kelli had argued we could do ourselves but Ben had been adamant he needed to go and see them in person. I'd half expected him to bring up the London expansion idea when he was telling me about going to the capital city for this meeting, but he hadn't mentioned a thing. Maybe he had finally come round to my way of thinking that we just weren't ready for that, yet.

As soon as Conrad left the shop, Kelli leant over her desk to catch my attention. 'You know why the coffee machine keeps "breaking"?' she said with air quotes.

I looked at her blankly. 'Because we demand too much caffeine in this place?'

'Nope. It's because Conrad has a crush on the barista in that café he's scurried off to.'

I snorted. 'No way. Have you not heard how he goes on about how much his divorce stung him? That's why he's so good with customers as he's loving the single life and encouraging others to love it too via travelling.' He had been such a surprise hit and now I couldn't remember life without him here. It was reassuring to know that while Ben and I were away filming, the shop would be well looked after, and that was such a weight off my mind.

'I'm telling you! Have you not thought it's weird how the coffee machine never broke until Conrad joined us?'

I shook my head, smiling as Conrad wandered in with three cups in a cardboard holder and a big cheery smile on his face that looked more flushed than usual.

'See,' Kelli whispered.

'Shush,' I hissed. 'Thanks, Conrad.'

'Not a problem, I'll get onto the place where we got that last machine from and let them know in no uncertain terms how we will not be standing for their shite,' he muttered as he sat down at his desk, thankfully missing Kelli's knowing glance and the giggles she was failing to supress. 'I wonder if the coffee is any good in Chile. Don't they use yak's milk or some crazy stuff like that over there?'

'God knows, I haven't had much time to research.' I bit my lip. 'Are you guys sure you'll be okay here with us both gone?' I asked for probably the thirteenth time.

Kelli rolled her eyes. 'No, we're going to turn the shop into a high-class brothel, swapping travel tours for guaranteed good times.' She took one look at my horrified expression. 'Chill, Georgia, I'm joking. This place will be fine. We're quiet, the diaries have been cleared and you're only going for ten days. Don't worry.'

I found my breath and nodded. She was right, they were both more than capable. This must be how Marie feels when handing Cole over to the nursery staff, whispering *please look after my baby* under her breath, I thought.

'Just promise us you won't come back from Chile like a right diva,' Kelli warned.

'Although if you do come back wearing huge, bug sunglasses and have an entourage trailing behind you who pass you perfectly separated red and yellow M&Ms, or decking out this place in snow white lilies, then you know we'll bring you back down to earth with a bump.' Conrad laughed, ripping open a fresh pack of Hobnobs he had magicked out of thin air.

'I have no doubt that you'll keep me very grounded. Anyway, I think you're getting ahead of yourselves. This is just a small film crew – I'm sure Jerry said there would be just the one cameraman and producer – and with four couples to film for a one-hour show it's not like we're going to get much airtime, is it?' I said this as confidently as I could, although I was torn because the more we were on screen then the more we could raise the profile of the business.

'When they see just what a great team you and Ben make they'll surely bin off the other chumps and just make it the Ben and Georgia show,' Kelli said, spitting out some chewing gum into the wastepaper basket next to her messy desk and taking a biscuit.

'So, when do we get to watch it?' Conrad asked.

'I don't know. It must take ages to edit and fine-tune these things, mustn't it?' I said, gratefully taking a bicky myself.

'Can you not call buff Rahul to ask him?' Kelli asked, pretending to swoon.

I shook my head and quickly swallowed down a lump of chocolatey, oaty goodness that had got lodged in my throat. 'Nope. He isn't scheduled to work on this show. He just put us in touch with the people that would be.' I thought back to kind-faced Jerry; it would be fun hanging out with him during this trip too. As much as I was looking forward to alone time with Ben, surely there would also be some downtime when all the couples, as well as Jerry and some cameraman, would get to chill out together. That was one of the reasons I loved travelling so much, to get to know strangers who would become friends. 'I tried calling him after we went to London for that pre-meet thing, but he hadn't been told any more than we had as he was just the one doing the introductions. I think he's back over in India soon anyway.'

'That's a shame, as he is one tasty Indian curry. I wouldn't mind some pilau talk with him,' Kelli said, in a dreamy voice.

I could feel Conrad bristle from over here. 'You women are so bloody fickle,' he grumbled and shoved a whole biscuit into his scowling mouth.

Kelli flicked her hair back and pouted her lips together. Was she wearing clear lip gloss? Gone were the days of her heavy goth-inspired make-up; instead she had toned down her whole look and actually dressed, well, normally nowadays. 'Oh purlease, as if you men don't judge a book by its cover.'

Conrad's look changed to faux horrified at the insinuation and he sprayed crumbs as he spoke. 'I think you'll find that my conquests have only ever been based on sparkling wit and banter. How very dare you suggest otherwise!'

'And coffee,' Kelli mumbled.

At this I tried my hardest to restrain a snigger that was building in my chest. No such luck. He turned his head to me and raised an eyebrow.

'I just had some Hobnob stuck in my throat.' I coughed pathetically to try and prove the point.

He shook his head as if entertaining my pathetic excuse. 'Sure you did. Just be careful you don't choke now,' he said with a wry smile, before picking up the phone on his desk that had just started ringing. I caught Kelli's eye and suppressed a giggle.

The bell to the shop tinkled and reminded me to slap on my professional face, until I turned round to see that it was Trisha who'd popped in.

'Hello, dears!' she sang as she came and hugged us all in turn.

'Hi, Trisha, sorry I can't offer you a hot drink, we've been having *problems* with our coffee machine,' Kelli said throwing a look over to Conrad who ignored her.

'Oh don't you worry about me.' Trisha smiled warmly and took off her colourful woollen coat. 'Georgia, you're looking well! Must be from the bite of a travel bug.' She winked. 'Ben's told me about your upcoming trip.'

I laughed. 'I think you might be right!' I nodded for her to come and sit with me on the sofas near the brochure stands as Kelli stood up to help a customer who had just wandered in. 'It's great to see you. You're looking well too. It is actually good timing as I wanted to speak with you,' I said, lowering my voice and thinking back to the doubts that had clouded my mind since meeting Ben's father.

Trisha's expression grew more serious as she leant in towards me. 'Oh. Everything okay, lovey?'

Checking we were out of earshot, thanks to Conrad's booming voice and Kelli up-selling a European tour over at her desk I took a deep breath.

'I think so. I'm just after some advice. Relationship advice.' I paused. 'I met Ben's dad.'

'Oh. I see.' Trisha raised an eyebrow as if understanding why this was up for discussion. 'I wondered when he would eventually do the introductions.' She sighed and sat up straighter. 'He's a character, his father. And one that takes a little getting used to. It's the booze and gambling that's changed him and certainly not for the better.'

I winced, feeling terrible for even making such a big deal about it all. Although, I just felt like I needed to speak to someone about it all and Ben wasn't opening up any time soon.

'I was there for Ben when his mum left. His dad struggled to look after himself, let alone his young son. I'm sure you've already gathered that he comes from a rather unconventional family but then, who doesn't?' She let out a light laugh then looked at me with a serious glance. 'I'd met his family on a holiday before Ben was born. Back then his dad was nothing like the man you probably saw the other day. But what Maggie did messed him up, messed them all up.' Trisha shook her head, lost in a distant and painful memory. 'I was so honoured to be asked to be his godmother but because my Fred and I travelled so much it meant I could only watch out for Stevie, sorry Ben, from afar.' She slipped into using the nickname she'd always known him by.

'When I moved to Manchester to open my travel agency I'd always hoped he would come and settle here but by then he was travelling and working abroad. I think in a way he needed to see the world just so he could get out of that house. Every time he did come home he would be on the phone to me, struggling with the reality that whilst he had been away his dad had just got more and more into the booze. His father will never change and unfortunately Ben needs to accept that.'

'God, it's just so sad.' I shook my head thinking back to that scummy flat. 'So, you don't know where his mum is either?'

I was convinced I saw a faint look skitter across Trisha's wrinkled brow but she dipped her head and picked up her keys that had clattered to the floor. 'No. I was as shocked as everyone else. It's like she just vanished off the face of the earth. Blast, my keys have got lost under the sofa,' she said absently rummaging around on the floor with one hand.

I leant down to retrieve them.

'Thanks, dear. Please don't be stressing yourself out or overthinking too much. Ben loves you and you are about to have a wonderful time in Chile, I just know it!'

I smiled and felt that tingle of excitement in my chest. I was unsure whether to admit that I knew about the engagement ring. But I stopped myself. Maybe he'd confided in Trisha and she was as bad as I was at keeping secrets. I didn't want to ruin anything by putting her on the spot.

'I'm sure we will.'

*

The next few days were a blur of work handovers, preparing for the trip to Chile and getting really ruddy excited. We were going to be flying into the capital, Santiago, which I'd read was a buzzing metropolis filled with lively nightlife, colonial culture and surrounded by the snow-capped Andes mountains. I'd been day dreaming about five-star luxury apartments with a view of the sparkling city lights and its own wrap-around balcony where Ben and I could sit with a bottle of Chilean red wine in the evening, feeling the balmy night air lick our bare arms.

Jerry had warned me not to expect a detailed itinerary as he said they wanted to keep the element of surprise so the cameras could catch our reactions, but he had reassured me that it was all high quality accommodation and fun activities. I understood that, but as someone who loved to have control over every little detail of travel plans I was finding this secrecy tough to take. Ben had been his usual self, laid-back and chilled, pleased to just be told where to go and when. 'What's the worst that can happen?' he'd said last night as he watched me pack my bag and stress over how many bikinis and pretty summer dresses I could realistically get away with taking.

I'd smiled at him, then turned back to the mountain of clothes strewn over the bedroom floor and crossed my fingers that it was all going to be okay. I'd run through all the possible different scenarios in my mind and Ben did have a point, there was nothing we couldn't take on together, especially considering the dramas we'd already been through as a couple. My chat with Trisha had also been helpful in making me forget about Ben's sad and dysfunctional past. All that mattered was our future. Together. Surely it would be a free holiday in a cool part of the world, which only required a couple of hours to answer some work or relationship questions.

The experience of packing our suitcases, picking out toiletries to share, and laughing at each other's ghastly and dour passport photos had dispelled the strange atmosphere that had been hanging over us. I'd barely slept the night before as I'd been too excited. We had stayed up late chatting about the things we might get to see whilst we were away, and the things we, ahem, wanted to do to each other. I also couldn't stop thinking about what Marie had said to me the other day when I'd called to let her know what we were up to and promised her that I'd be back before her due date.

'What if he proposes whilst you're away? Takes you to some dreamy location and gets down on one knee. Oh my God, what if he does it on camera?' she'd gasped.

I felt my stomach lurch at the thought of such a public proposal and tried to tell her, and myself, that surely he would know that I'd hate that. Wouldn't he?

I'd been curious to look for the ring box again to see whether he'd packed it or not, but I felt like I'd tempted fate enough when I'd tried it on the other day. I told myself that it would ruin any surprise he had planned and that I needed have some willpower. It was easier said than done, but so far I had resisted the pull to sneak a peek at the diamond again. I would try to let matters take their course, to let go of my rigid grasp on everything around me, as I'd learnt on my trip to India that I could still survive without being in control of every tiny detail.

CHAPTER 9

Feign (v.) – To give a false appearance of; to induce as a false impression

I was craning my neck to see if I could spot Jerry and his bushy beard wandering around the departures hall while Ben had nipped to the loo, as this strange swirl of excitement, nerves and anticipation fizzed in my stomach. Luckily, I'd managed to bag us one of the few tables in the airport coffee shop as the place quickly filled up with excited holidaymakers, groups of lads on tour who were getting an early start on the drinking judging by the pints of lager in front of them, and tired-looking parents checking they had all their tickets and their hyperactive kids to hand. I hoped that Ben would hurry up as saving this spot was getting harder and harder with every passing moment.

'Sorry, that seat's taken,' I apologised for the second time.

The woman in her mid-forties with a curly auburn bob and large freckled nose stopped trying to drag Ben's stool away and stared at me. 'I don't see anyone sitting here.'

What a cow! 'It's for my boyfriend who will be back any second.'

The auburn-haired lady raised a thin, over-plucked eyebrow. 'Well, then it's not *currently* in use, is it?'

Eurgh, rude! I hated confrontation and silently willed Ben to hurry up from the toilet to save me. How did this woman not know the seat rule? It was like *the* most British thing ever.

'Well, no, technically it's not, but the thing is…' I trailed out. She was staring at me with a challenging glare when a short and dusty-haired man, who looked about the same age despite his jazzy-print, short-sleeved shirt and chinos, appeared from behind her broad shoulders.

'I've got us a table at the back, love,' he said to the angry chair stealer in a gentle voice that was barely audible over the din of the café.

His companion pursed her shiny, red lips and let go of the stool with a clatter. She didn't take her narrowed eyes from my face to acknowledge the man next to her. 'You know what? I think we'll head somewhere else, somewhere a lot classier.'

She turned on her heel, missing my low growl at the filthy look she gave me. It left me standing with one hand on the seat and one shaking on the table when Ben wandered over.

'God, it's not like the gents to have a queue. Must be all these lads filling their bladders with beer,' he joked before clocking my face. 'You all right, babe?'

I nodded and plastered a smile back on. 'Yeah, yeah, fine.' Nothing, not even that rude cow, was going to put a dampener on today. 'What time did it say in the email that we had to meet?'

Ben pulled out his phone and started swiping through his messages. 'We should probably finish these then head over to the information desk.'

Downing the lukewarm coffee and feeling that familiar buzz of caffeine fizz through my veins, we grabbed our bags and walked down the check-in hall to meet the others.

'Oh for God's sake,' I muttered under my breath as I realised the rude, auburn-haired snob and her sidekick were walking in the same direction. She was leaving that poor bloke to pull all their luggage, their matching leopard-print luggage, as she stuck her beaky nose in the air and strutted across the concourse.

'Wait, that's that woman who interviewed me when we went to the studios in London,' Ben called out, dragging my attention to where he was pointing. The glam blonde he'd been partnered with when I'd been in a room chatting with Jerry was leaning on the information desk tapping something on her phone. Next to her, a hunched and tired-looking man in his early fifties, with an expression of a bulldog chewing on a wasp, was faffing about with a camera tripod.

As we got nearer, the beautiful blonde glanced up and broke into a wide grin as she hugged the snooty cow from the café, like she was greeting a long-lost family member reunited by Holly Willoughby. My stomach sank as it was confirmed: the stool grabber and her sidekick must be one of the other couples taking part in the filming. Great.

I was about to tell Ben what had gone on when he was in the loo – I wanted to get him on board that we didn't like that auburn-haired-chair-stealing woman, so in no way was he to offer her his best and most genuine smile – when suddenly his name was being called out.

'Ben! Oooh!' The glam blonde was now waving and teetering over to us on her tan heels. Well, I say us, but I could have been dancing buck naked squirting red wine from my nipples and she wouldn't have noticed, if the laser-beam gaze she had fixed on my boyfriend was anything to go by. 'Here he is! We were getting worried that you'd been held up in traffic or something.' She giggled and wrapped her slim arms around his broad frame. With her neat, freckled nose, heart-shaped face, and perfectly shaped dark blonde eyebrows, she could have passed for a perky, young twenty-something. It was only the faint crow's feet lines I saw as she came closer to us that told me she was probably closer to her early thirties.

He jolted back in surprise, 'Oh hi. It's Anna, isn't it?' Ben said.

Anna pulled back and gently whacked him on his bicep. 'Ha ha, don't pretend you've forgotten.' I suddenly didn't know which of these two women who had just come into my life I hated more: the bouncy blonde who looked like she would know all the moves to 'Dontcha wish your girlfriend was hot like me?' or the sour-faced stool-stealer who was currently looking us up and down with the same level of disgust she'd used on me before.

'So, this is Georgia.' Ben rubbed his neck, embarrassed by the attention, and politely drew her focus to HIS GIRLFRIEND.

Anna shot me a smile that didn't meet her large, muddy-brown eyes – the colour of the Manchester canal, I noted in my head. 'Hi, ah yes, Georgia,' she mused, as if pretending she struggled to place me. 'So great to meet you.' There could not have been less enthusiasm in that greeting if she'd tried.

'Hi, yeah, you too.'

'Okay, well great. Come and meet the others.' She tugged on Ben's elbow and led us over to the information desk. Two other couples were currently perched on a couple of chairs that had been placed near the desk, all four people looking equally as awkward. At a simple look from the auburn-haired woman, her steadfast companion nodded and wheeled their cases to meet the rest of the group.

Anna stood in the centre and clapped for everyone's attention, jangling the rose gold bangles stacked on her slim arm. 'Great. So now you're all here let's do some introductions. My name is Anna, I'm the producer-slash-presenter for the show and I'll be the one leading the way and making sure everything goes smoothly.' Her voice was high-pitched and full of enthusiasm. I raised my hand. 'Yes, Georgia?'

'I just wondered when Jerry would be joining us?'

A look flashed across her muddy eyes. 'Jerry isn't coming on the actual trip; he was just in charge of logistics. So, as I was saying…any questions you have, please direct them to me or Clive.' She nodded her head over to the cameraman who barely looked up from the equipment he was setting up. 'You all ready, Clive?' she asked him, and he grunted in reply. 'Great! So, just to set the scene if we could have all the couples give a quick intro to the camera, some details of your business and why you're here, and that way we'll all get to know a little more about you.' Anna pointed to the couple sat nearest to us. 'Gareth and Jade, would you like to go first?'

'Sure thing.' Gareth stood up and tugged on his pale blue shirt that was tucked into his obscenely high-waisted, dark denim jeans. He confidently walked over to where Clive had set up the shot and began making weird vocal warm-up noises, like an opera singer does in their dressing room. What the actual focaccia? I guessed he was a couple of years younger than Ben and me, but he exuded the confidence of a man much older.

'When you're ready,' Clive said, looking unfazed by the bizarre sounds and neck rolling this man was making in front of him. Gareth suddenly stopped massaging his throat with his fingers and flashed an uber-cheesy smile at the camera. The gel on his slicked-back blonde hair shone in the artificial light that Clive had set up.

'Hey there! People call me Gareth but my friends call me Gaz The Postman. No, I don't work for the Royal Mail, it's because I always deliver.' Did he actually just make a smoking gun with his fingers and blow into thin air? Oh God. No one else apart from Gareth laughed.

'I am a brand re-imaginer and digital warrior for a travel-centred start-up.' He was like a reject from *The Apprentice* with his cheap estate-agent look, piggy, hazelnut-coloured eyes and jumped-up, arrogant personality.

'That has to be up there with the wankiest job title ever,' Ben whispered, making me stifle a giggle.

'My ethos is to deliver on spec, on target and on top of our game. Think of me as a virtual storyteller if you will, connecting clients and their dreams. Of course, I'm only doing this until my career as an international jet-setting playboy takes off.' Gareth pressed his fingertips together and flashed a smile full of scarily bleached white teeth. 'And this is my girlfriend, Jade.' He placed his arm around a whippet of a woman with obvious glued-in hair extensions and fiercely painted-on eyebrows, making her face appear permanently stunned. I wasn't sure if that was the look she had been aiming for, or if it was a reaction to having a camera shoved in her face.

'Hello,' Jade said in a Brummie accent and waved, making her Pandora charm bracelet jangle loudly. Her fake tan only made Gareth seem even paler and sickly-looking next to her. 'I'm dead excited about being here and can't wait to eat chilli in Chile!' She broke into a high-pitched bark of a laugh that even Gareth rolled his eyes at.

'Great! Next couple please?' Anna said, looking up from her phone.

Gareth balled his hand into a fist, kissed the garish signet ring on his middle finger and shouted, 'Nailed it,' to himself. Jade giggled and pulled him to sit back down, but not before he leant over and passed me a warm business card from his chest pocket.

'Oh. Thanks.' I turned it over and read. 'Gareth Smeethly: Man. Thinker. Creator.'

Tosser, I thought.

I flashed a weak smile and popped it into my handbag then turned to watch the next couple as they took their seats in front of the camera. I almost had to take a breath – they could have stepped from the pages of Italian *Vogue*. She had glossy, jet-black hair that fell in loose bouncy waves around her flawless, olive-skinned face and he was the epitome of an Italian stallion with strong muscular arms, a brooding, tanned face and sharp cheekbones. I noticed the Mediterranean model wasn't wearing an engagement ring to go with her salon-perfect nails, despite her being around the same age as me. I looked down at my own hand and wondered if I would be returning with an additional piece of baggage on my ring finger.

'This is Natalia and Tony,' Anna said to the rest of us, leaving her gaze on the obvious bulge in Tony's skin-tight trousers.

All the other contributors had made such an effort this morning. It hadn't even crossed my mind that we were going to be filmed before the trip even started, plus we had a twelve-hour flight coming up so I'd dressed purely for comfort in faded jogging bottoms, scuffed trainers and an oversized hoodie, a choice I now regretted. I looked at the high wedged sandals and cute mustard-coloured knitwear that Natalia was wearing, and the ripped, white skinny jeans that Jade had on.

'Hey there,' Natalia said confidently to the camera, in a voice that was more Rotherham than Rome. 'We own Vineopolis, the wine merchants you may have heard of?'

'Ah my dad's always harping on about some bottle of plonk he bought from one of your shops once,' Jade piped up, but swiftly got told off for talking as it meant they had to redo the shot. Clive shook his head and muttered under his breath, something about working with children and animals, making Gareth self-consciously wrap a thick pasty arm around his girlfriend's bare shoulders.

'We travel the world visiting vineyards and we are so lucky we get to share this with each other,' Natalia said, before rubbing the tip of her nose against Tony's, acting as if everyone else in the busy departures hall had vanished.

'Si, bella,' Tony replied in a husky tone before he tipped her chin so he could passionately kiss her. I didn't know where to put myself. I felt Ben prickle next to me at such a public display of affection as over the top PDAs had never been our thing. Jade was gawping at the pair of them and Gareth looked like he was about to start taking notes.

'Okay. Great stuff. So…moving on.' Anna raised a hand in the air as the amorous couple finally broke apart for air. 'Next up we have Dawn and Simon,' Anna said, literally pushing Natalia and Tony out of the way and jerking her head for Clive to put his tongue back in his mouth and focus his camera on the job in hand.

Dawn, as the auburn-haired woman appeared to be called, immediately rearranged her features to form a welcoming smile that certainly hadn't been there when we'd met just fifteen minutes earlier during Stool-gate.

'Right, Dawn, if you could just look straight down the lens and tell us what it is you do,' Clive ordered.

'Do I really need to tell people?' Dawn let out a chihuahua bark of a laugh. 'I invented *Last Call*, darling.' She paused, rearranging her long gold necklaces over her blouse, waiting for the rest of the group to show how impressed we were. Everyone remained silent apart from Anna who clapped her hands in glee.

'Guys…*Last Call*?' she repeated, turning to look at us and rolling her eyes as if we should have some clue what she was on about. In the time it was taking for someone to cotton on, Dawn was growing more agitated.

I was waiting for her to say, *'Do you not know who I am?'* when Ben nodded. 'Oh, yeah, I know what you mean. Wow. Last Call.'

This was enough to get Dawn going again. I looked up at him quizzically.

'I don't have a bloody clue but we'd be here all day otherwise,' he whispered as Dawn rummaged in her stiff brown handbag to show the others what it was she'd invented. I stifled a giggle at the exact same time she pulled out a garish and bulbous passport cover.

She snapped her head to face me and half growled at my reaction. 'Oh sorry, I wasn't laughing at that,' I mumbled apologetically but the damage had been done. If she hadn't hated me before, she defo hated me now.

'What is it?' Tony piped up, thankfully moving the focus of the death stare from me.

'Tell them, Simon,' Dawn barked. Simon – who I gathered was her husband judging by the presence of dull-coloured wedding rings they both wore and not just an over-friendly baggage handler trailing her around – stepped forward and cleared his throat. As he spoke, I realised that he'd definitely given this speech before about what it was his clever wife had created (possibly with a glue gun at the kitchen table judging by the naff diamantes, zebra print and strips of glittered fabric wrapped around his passport). In fact, Dawn looked like she was mouthing the exact same monotone words as he rambled on.

'Dawn invented *Last Call*. This is a never-before-seen product hitting the travel accessory market with a bang. It will change the way we travel for ever.' He paused dramatically and wiped his mole-covered forehead that had beaded with sweat droplets under Clive's hot light. '*Last Call* is a revolutionary passport holder that has a built-in alarm. Once you've checked in for your flight, you simply programme the time you have been told to be at the gate like this.'

Simon stuck his tongue to one side as he peeled back the garish passport cover that had a mini watch alarm superglued inside and proceeded to show us which tiny buttons to press. 'Once activated it will then beep, reminding you to make your way from duty free, or the bar.' He paused to let out a fake laugh. 'So that you will never miss a flight again. Oh. Well, this one appears to have broken.' He stuttered then composed himself to finish the 'pitch'. 'Dawn has since appeared on *Dragons' Den* and been a guest speaker at Romford's Women in Business at their autumn convention. This product's RRP is for –'

'Yeah all right, Simon, they get the picture,' Dawn chided.

Simon bowed his head and sat back down, scuffing his sensible dad-style trainers on the floor as he did. Natalia and Tony were too busy smooching once more and had missed the detailed and monotone explanation, Jade was on her phone and Gareth looked like he was sizing up how much he could flog this naff product for in the boardroom to impress Lord Alan Sugar.

'Great!' Anna clapped like a performing seal. 'So, now the latecomers, Georgia and Ben.' She presented us to everyone else as Dawn and Simon sat down.

I gulped and shuffled forward to where Clive was indicating. *Here goes nothing.* I hadn't had much experience of being in front of TV cameras and found my hands getting clammy and my throat strangely dry.

'Ben, if you could do the introductions and then Georgia you take over?' Anna explained.

Ben nodded and stepped forward almost as confidently as Gareth had done. 'Hey, my name is Ben and this is my girlfriend, Georgia, and together we own The Lonely Hearts Travel Club.' He flashed a genuine smile at the camera and turned to face me expectantly.

I took the cue and smiled down the camera lens, feeling the heat of Clive's light warm my already flushed cheeks.

'As Ben was saying we…' Oh shit. What did we do? What were we doing here? What am I meant to be talking about? What are words? Holy crap bags. I froze like a rabbit caught in the headlights.

'Georgia,' Anna hissed and did some strange hand signal to encourage me to carry on talking.

'Erm, so yes, we work in travel and we do nice things with people and travel is good and…' Oh for fuck's sake, what was I saying? Stop talking, stop talking! I could feel the rest of the group gawping at me. Ben had his eyebrows raised quizzically, half wanting to see where I was heading with this trail of verbal diarrhoea that I couldn't seem to stop pouring out of my mouth, and half in embarrassment at what had happened to his usually poised and in-control girlfriend.

Thankfully he must have decided that enough was enough and jumped in to save me. 'What Georgia means is that we offer fun and challenging tours to exciting destinations for those looking to go from lost to wanderlust.' This just rolled off his tongue and had the right amount of stage presence and charm. 'We're both really looking forward to discovering what Chile has to offer and exploring this wonderful part of the world.'

Just as Ben finished speaking a loud tannoy announcement rang out above our heads telling us that our flight was now open for check-in.

'Right, I think we've just been saved by the bell,' Anna huffed patting her flustered cheeks and grabbing her bags, seemingly desperate to get away from us – probably mainly me – before she lost her shit.

What had just happened? I couldn't move. My feet were rooted to the spot as everyone sprang into life, picking up their jackets, suitcases and making sure they had everything before walking across the check-in hall.

'You can't use any of that!' I wailed at Clive who gave me a non-committal shrug as he packed up his camera and made a swift exit to join the others.

Turning to Ben I felt tears prick my eyes. 'Oh my God, that was a disaster!' This was supposed to be *good* PR for the business, and so far I'd managed to make us – well, me really – look like a complete moron.

I'd hoped he would comfort me and tell me that it wasn't *that* bad. That it had seemed a million times worse in my head, that I hadn't just brain vomited and instead had made some valid and well-thought-out points. Nope.

He winced and struggled to hold my eye. 'I thought Jerry ran through camera techniques with you when we went to the studios?'

I shook my head. 'Not really. Did you?'

We hadn't actually spoken about what had happened when we met Blaise and were separated for our little chats, as the meeting with his dad had overshadowed the whole day. Judging by the way Anna had melted to a pool of lust at his feet, I was amazed that they'd got some actual work done. All I could remember from the Jerry meeting was me being firm on not wanting to talk about the whole jilted bride angle on my story – at least I think I'd been firm. Now I was questioning everything.

'Yeah, we ran through some practice interviews, and she gave me some tips on trying to act natural on camera and things like that. Don't worry we can work on it during the flight if you want…?'

I nodded sadly and followed after him to check in for the flight. From the moment I'd found that stupid ring, my world had begun to unravel with frightening speed. And the last thing I wanted was to have cameras record every excruciating moment. Chile had better be worth it, I thought.

CHAPTER 10

Oaf (n.) – A clumsy, slow-witted person

When we were about thirteen, Marie had once freaked me out with a story about a woman who got sucked down the aeroplane toilet as the flush was so powerful. She'd told me that this was why they did a cross-check when the flight was about to land, in case someone went AWOL through the toilet bowl mid-flight. I hadn't even been on a plane at that point in my life but the first flight I took, and every flight thereafter, I'd made sure that I held my bladder firmly in check. Easy to do on a short-haul trip to Europe, not so easy to do on a long-haul slog to Chile.

On both the lengthy journeys to Thailand and India I'd made sure I used the airport facilities before my flight, then tried to stay practically nil-by-mouth so I wouldn't have to experience the tiny aeroplane loos at all, something I'd accomplished by distracting myself with books and movies. But this time I had Ben as my flying buddy and all the stress of my failure to appear like a normal human being when the cameras were rolling. Before I knew what I was doing, I'd knocked back a few of the free drinks and necked half a bottle of water.

'Argh, I'm desperate for the loo,' I told Ben as we made our way into the busy baggage reclaim hall after arriving in Santiago. Other tired holidaymakers stood yawning,

slumped over the handles of the baggage trolleys they'd
wheeled into prime position by the opening of the baggage
belt, desperate for their bags to be the first to arrive so they
could grab and go.

'No worries, you head off and I'll look out for our bags.
Yours was a black case with a blue ribbon tied on it, right?'

I nodded quickly and was forced to do a little jig as my
bladder was screaming at me. 'Yep! Thanks!'

I ran off down the length of the arrivals hall to find a
bathroom, trying not to get my ankles rammed by vicious
metal trolley frames. I zipped my way past couples and
backpackers who all had that relieved look on their faces
that their bags had arrived. Is there anything so drawn out
and anxiety-ridden than waiting to see if your bag has
made it across the world in one piece?

I followed the signs to the ladies' loo and skidded to a
standstill as I saw the snaking queue coming out of the door.
Crap! I simply wasn't going to be able to hold this wee in
for the time it would take to get to the front. God damn the
glass of fizz that Ben had surprised me with. I hadn't told
him about my irrational fear of the plane toilet, as I hadn't
wanted him to think any less of me than he probably already
did after my terrible performance in front of the camera.

I glanced around to see if there was another female
bathroom further down the arrivals hall when I spotted a
sign for the disabled toilet. Bingo. I'd nip in and out within
a matter of seconds. I didn't have any other choice as my
bladder felt like it was close to exploding. I dashed over
to it, feeling smug. The disabled toilet looked a lot more
modern than the female toilets had; this one had a large
curved steel door similar to the ones you find on trains in
England, obviously wide enough for a wheelchair to enter,
with low buttons to press for access. All fine, except for the
fact that the labels were written in Spanish.

I bit my lip, squeezing my kegel muscles as tight as I could, and pressed the button at the top. Nothing happened. I tried the middle button and a slow beeping emanated from the speaker pad above the buttons before the door creaked open. I glanced around behind me, slipped in, and forcefully pressed the third button hoping to lock the door.

The beeping stopped but so did the door. Halfway between open and closed. I smiled politely at a family who wandered past with their trolley, the father looking quizzically at the mad woman with frizzed hair and the strange toilet dance moves.

'Hola!' I said as I jabbed the collection of door buttons once more. I swear I could feel my kidneys expanding. I'm sure this was something that Marie had also told me, that if you held urine in for too long you could rupture an organ and the rest of your body would fill with pee. And you DIE!

As I pulled a manic face and held my breath the beeping started up again. I could feel the eyes of everyone waiting by carousel seven trained on me in mirth. Amazingly, the door finally inched its way shut. Great. But now, which button locked it? In the embarrassment and desperation to pee I'd lost count of which button did what as I jabbed them all. Gah! I was literally seconds away from pissing myself.

Okay, think.

Abierto that sounds like A Beer Too, oh Gawd don't think about liquid. *Cerca*: isn't that like circa, which means around a time or date? Not that that helped in the slightest. *Bloquear.* Now that sounded like block and when you blocked something you clogged it up or closed it. But could that also be lock?! *Ayuda*, what the hell did this one mean?

I stomped my feet and shook my left leg, wincing at the pain and taking shallow pants of breath. I was out of time, so trusted the only method I knew in such circumstances: Ip, dip, dog shit, you are not it… I pressed *Ayuda*.

I tensed up, preparing to hear the droning buzz of an alarm indicating the door was about to reopen but nothing happened. Result! That must have locked it. Who knew I was secretly fluent in Spanish? See, learning a new language is all about using your brain and thinking logically, I thought smugly as I sat on the low toilet and began to relieve myself.

Forget orgasms, going to the toilet after you've been holding it in is *the* best feeling. I blissfully closed my eyes until a strange beeping filled the enclosed room.

What, the…?

I jigged to hurry myself up but the problem with holding your pee for as long as I had is the sheer amount of it you can store up. I kept my eye trained on the door, pleading with the powers that be for it to remain closed and for my bladder to hurry up and empty itself. Abruptly the noise stopped; strangely the door hadn't budged open even an inch. Weird. I did notice an orange light had illuminated by the panel of buttons, which was flashing intermittently, but there was nothing I could do until I had stopped peeing.

Then suddenly the disabled loo filled with a man's voice. Deep fast Spanish was coming out of some hidden speakers in the ceiling. I didn't have a clue what he was saying; he was talking way too quickly for me to catch even one single word.

I didn't have the faintest clue if there were even microphones in here picking up what I was saying, and even if there were would he understand me? 'Hello! Hello! I don't know what you're saying. Can you hear me?'

There was a split second of silence…

…Followed by the man's voice chattering away once more but this time sounding even more harassed, if that was possible. It felt like he was tripping over his own words. I may not have got the gist of what he was saying but it did feel like he was telling me something important.

'No understand. No speako Espaniol...' I yelled. Why the hell was I still not finished weeing?

All of a sudden, it happened so quickly. The droning buzz of the alarm started up once more, the Spanish man's voice grew louder and I swear the brightness of the lights was being messed around with. There was a loud click and the door unlocked itself and sprang back, faster than it had done to open and close in the first place. The damn thing literally pinged straight open revealing me crouching over the low steel toilet, knickers around my ankles, and sweat pouring down my red cheeks.

I was still peeing.

The whole of flight SA597, who were waiting to collect their baggage at carousel seven, suddenly seemed less interested in who would grab their bags first but rather what all the commotion was in the nearby disabled loo.

Mortified didn't even come close to sum up how I felt. The trickle of urine finally stopped, and I grabbed at my jogging bottoms, trying to hoist them up to protect my last shred of dignity, as two men in orange polo shirts with matching jet black curls raced through the opened toilet door holding paramedic bags and a plastic stretcher.

The one on the right babbled away in Spanish, the worried expression rapidly fading into mirth at the sight of me. They both tried so hard not to laugh, unlike the bloody passengers on flight SA597 who didn't bother to conceal their pleasure in the live show.

'Miss. You have problem?' the one on the left said in broken English pointing to the set of buttons by the door. The door of doom. 'Help, miss. Help,' he said indicating the *Ayuda* button. Great. I had unwittingly set off the alarm bells myself.

'It's okay, no help needed,' I said, shuffling to the sink and throwing my nose in the air. The only way I was going to get through this was to pretend that it wasn't a big deal, in the slightest. 'Sorry. I must be off.' Why had my northern accent suddenly changed to that of Hyacinth Bucket? I dipped my head and strode out of the toilet, willing myself not to cry or give the people at carousel seven even more of a show. I'm sure somebody started to slow clap.

I picked up my pace when I spotted that Ben and the rest of the crew were waiting for me by the exit. Judging by the mixture of boredom and irritation on their faces and the collection of suitcases around them, I'd been gone some time.

'Sorry!' I called out as I scooted over the gleaming polished floor. I'd never wanted to get out of an airport so quickly as I did now.

'Georgia. Finally,' Anna huffed with a hand on her hip and an impatient tap of her ballet pump. 'I hope we haven't lost our airport transfer because of this wait.' She threw me a dirty look and marched out of the arrivals hall. I heard some of the others sigh and push their loaded trolleys behind her.

'You okay, babe?' Ben asked with his eyebrows raised. 'You've been gone a while. Everything okay?'

I nodded and blushed. Normally I would have told him and we'd probably have had a good laugh over it, but I was already feeling like such an idiot I couldn't bear to tell him. 'Yep all good. Right, you got everything?'

He nodded. 'Come on you, we'd better catch up with the rest of them.' He pushed the trolley with our suitcases on away from the baggage belt that was forlornly chugging round an abandoned purple pushchair and a battered box marked *fragile*.

Welcome to Santiago, I thought as I flicked my hair over my shoulder and left the shame of the airport bathroom debacle behind me. New adventures awaited, and I was determined to enjoy them.

CHAPTER 11

Rankle (v.) – To feel anger and irritation

We made it through the dark but bustling streets of this capital city. Even in the dim light I was struck by how clean and European this place seemed as we drove through the different *barrios*, or neighbourhoods, that were basically scattered across a large hill. The cheerful driver was pointing out landmarks, unaware that most of his passengers had started snoozing in the back. He explained that the higher up the hill you go, the richer and safer the places were; I crossed everything that we would be staying at the summit then.

Less than half an hour later we pulled up outside a tall and crooked hotel, which, although not on the top of a hill, did look impressive. The traditional, colonial-style building was full of charm and faded grandeur.

'Now this is what I'm talking about.' Gareth whistled as we filed in. He was straining his pea-head to look around the sweeping reception full of large, gilded portraits of noblemen whose eyes followed you around the room. Anna was checking us all in and had sent for a member of staff to get all our bags out of the taxi as the rest of us enjoyed a welcoming glass of fizz.

'Ah, my darling, does this take you back?' Tony purred in Natalia's ear as he sipped at his champagne flute.

'If I'm not mistaken this is the 2004 reserve?' His girlfriend giggled, lost in some private joke.

'Whatever year it came from all I know is I like it,' Jade said, necking hers in one and looking round eagerly for a top-up.

Dawn tutted at what I guessed was Jade's lack of decorum as she took ladylike sips with her bottom pinkie sticking out; I was sure that I spotted the tips of Gareth's ears turn a slight shade of pink in embarrassment of his girlfriend. Jade was none the wiser and even let out a small belch that made Dawn visibly pale. I handed Jade my untouched glass as I couldn't stomach the bubbles after the long journey and the toilet incident. I felt dead on my feet.

I leant my head on Ben's chest while listening to Tony explain to Jade that the quicker you drink champagne, the quicker you get drunk, and closed my eyes. As lovely as this welcome was, all I could think about was having a shower and washing off aeroplane grime, then laying my head on the pillow and getting a good night's sleep.

'Right, grab your bags, guys, and take your room keys,' Anna called, making me flash open my tired eyes. 'The plan for tonight is to take it easy and catch up on some sleep as we have a busy day planned for tomorrow and will be getting you all up early.'

'Come on, little one, let's get you to bed,' Ben whispered in my ear, causing the familiar tingle I felt when he uttered those same words back at home. I gave him a drowsy nod. 'I hope you're not *too* tired.'

He told me to meet him in our room as he picked up our bags and I half skipped down the plush corridors.

The large double bed in the centre was so inviting I barely took in the rest of the room, which was decked out in a calming duck-egg blue with white, antique features, before Ben had picked me up and began kissing me.

'Wait! I'm all stinky from the flight. At least let me have a shower,' I said giggling, suddenly remembering the airport toilet incident and feeling my cheeks flame up. I was also aware of how much of that long-haul flight was ingrained on my skin.

Ben groaned. 'No, you're fine. I like it when you're a little dirty.' His hands were roaming my body and tugging at the fabric of my jogging bottoms.

I let out a little laugh and pulled back trying to ignore the sad puppy dog eyes he was giving me. 'I know you do. But this kind of dirty is more stinky than kinky. Let me grab my shower stuff and maybe you could join me?' I suggested, raising an eyebrow in what I hoped was a provocative way.

'Deal.' Ben winked and went to turn the shower on. Someone was keen.

I sighed happily to myself, enjoying the feeling you get knowing another human being wants you as much as you want them. I knelt on the raffia carpet and pulled my case towards me, hoping that I'd properly screwed the lids on my shampoo and conditioner and wasn't about to be faced with a gunky, coconutty mess.

'Babe, do you fancy getting some room service in a bit?' Ben called from the bathroom.

'Yeah, maybe,' I said, with one hand unzipping my case and the other reaching for the room service menu that had been placed on the bed.

'That aeroplane food didn't even touch the sides, but still it…' Ben walked out of the bathroom topless and stopped in his tracks. 'What the fuck?'

I was trying to use the duvet cover as leverage to pull the brown, leather-bound room service list towards me and looked up at him.

'What?'

He raised an eyebrow and creased up in laughter. 'Shit, babe. I knew you were looking forward to being away together but I didn't think we were at *this* stage of our relationship.'

I glanced down at where he was pointing and followed his wide-eyed gaze. I'd unzipped my case and without realising, as I'd been too consumed with the hunt for room service, had flung the cover open to reveal a quite threatening-looking bright green dildo, a studded dog collar with gleaming silver chains hanging off it and something that looked like a miniature boat paddle in shiny leather, all nestled on a few items of clothing.

I thrust a hand to cover my opened mouth. 'What! This isn't mine!'

He stepped back and put two hands up defensively, still laughing his head off. 'Hey, each to their own. No judgement here!'

A slow, cold chill crept up my spine. This was not funny. 'Ben, I promise. This isn't my bag.'

He had picked up the paddle and began examining it. The line of jewels glinted in the light.

'Ben, you watched me pack my bag, you know this isn't mine,' I said forcefully, rummaging through the sparse clothes that were in there, pushing my hand past a half-empty washbag and an enormous tube of lube to see if I could find some type of contact details and discover who this belonged to. Suddenly I felt very, very awake. And very sick.

'But, it's identical to your bag, blue ribbon and all,' Ben said, putting down the paddle and finally realising the seriousness of the situation.

If this was some random, sex-obsessed dude's bag, then where the hell was mine? This meant I had nothing to wear other than what I had worn on the plane as there was no way I was going touch a thing in this stranger's suitcase.

'We need to go and get Anna to help find my case, right now!' I zipped up the bag, suddenly desperate for a squirt of antibacterial gel after rifling through some stranger's dirty underwear. Taking the stairs two at a time with the offending case in one hand and a look of worry etched on my face, I flew into the hotel's reception with Ben trailing behind. The other couples had already headed to their rooms but luckily Anna and Clive were still there. He was looking at the viewfinder on his camera, probably at the footage he took at the airport, and she was on her phone.

'Anna! We've got a problem,' I cried. She looked up from the small screen, irritated at having to take a pause from trying to connect to the Wi-Fi.

'Yes?'

'Were there any other bags in the taxi?' I felt saliva rush into my mouth as I asked the question. I flashed my eyes around reception, as if someone could have hidden my suitcase behind the unusual naked statue or inside the large ceramic plant pot. I knew the answer before she shook her platinum head.

'Nope. What's happened?' She perked up as soon as she could sense some drama unfolding; although, the struggle for her to peel her eyes away from my boyfriend's naked torso and focus on me looked like it took all the effort in the world.

'Ben picked up the wrong bag. I don't have any of my stuff!' I panted and chucked the stupid sex-stash case to the floor.

'It was an innocent mistake to make,' Ben said under his breath, walking over to the bag to begin looking for a luggage label.

Okay, I admit, I may have become slightly hysterical but I blamed the jet lag and stress of the previous week, as usually I was quite a sane and rational human being. It wasn't even like I was some kind of style icon, but I still felt completely lost at the thought of some pervert going through my bag. And then there was the problem that I had nothing to wear. Nothing!

'Does this look innocent to you?' I wailed as I unzipped the bag and grabbed the rubbery dildo, brandishing it in his face.

'Whoa. Kinky,' Clive chirped. I growled at him and realised he was filming this whole crazy-lady banshee act that I was totally nailing. I didn't have the energy to care.

'How am I supposed to wear *this*?' I tried to let out the breath I hadn't realised I'd been holding.

'Look, Georgia.' Ben had crouched down and managed to find a luggage tag that I'd not spotted before.

I pushed past him to see what he was looking at. 'Mr J D Rathborne. Great.'

'Well then this dude must have your bag. Simple,' Ben said, trying to put a positive spin on this mess that he'd caused.

'Why did you not think to check my name was on the label when we were in the airport?' I hissed as Anna was explaining the problem to the receptionist and poorly concealing her enjoyment in the drama.

'If you hadn't taken so long in the loo then maybe you would have been there to pick up your own bloody bag,' he replied, through gritted teeth.

Whoa. I physically took a step back. This was suddenly my fault?

Anna came over just as I was about to launch into the reasons that his ineptitude had caused this problem.

'So, we've just called the airport and no one has contacted them about picking up the wrong bag. They had a look in lost property but nothing with your contact details or matching your bag's description has been handed in.'

She stopped talking and let out a long yawn. A yawn? As if my bag drama wasn't exciting enough for her! She wasn't the one who was going to have to appear on TV in the same sweaty flight clothes that I had travelled here in. There was a stain on my right breast that I hadn't noticed before, and the matter of my lack of fresh knickers.

'We need to take this back to the airport and wait to see if the man who picked up your bag will do the same.'

'What am I going to do until then? What if he hasn't realised his mistake? Or has a connecting flight?' I felt like I was having heart palpitations. 'Plus, how embarrassed would he be to come forward, now he knows that we've seen his dirty sex secrets!' I threw my head in my hands. This trip was ruined before it had even started.

'The staff at the airline said they were going to try and contact him to tell him about the mix-up. Someone from the hotel will take this case to the airport's lost and found section for us, and then it's just a waiting game.' She shrugged, giving me a look that said I needed to control my *whoremones*. 'Unless, you want to keep this bag and the… items inside it?'

I gritted my teeth. 'No. I don't bloody want to keep some second-hand sex toys and bondage whips.'

'It's actually a paddle,' Clive piped up before looking bashfully at the floor as I glared at him.

'Georgia, calm down. I've got stuff you can borrow until tomorrow when we'll go and buy you everything you need,' Ben said slightly more softly.

I sighed and scrunched my eyes shut so no frustrated tears would fall while the camera was still rolling and nodded. 'Well, there's nothing I can do now, is there?'

Anna shrugged and gave Ben a cheeky look as if showing how innocent and available she was, compared to the stressed, grumpy and sweaty girlfriend he had chosen. I left the case in reception and snatched the room key from Ben, wanting to bury my head under my pillow and not think about what would happen if Mr Bloody Rathborne didn't return my bag. I should have known this trip would not be the answer to all my problems. I mean, what did Marie and Shelley know anyway?

CHAPTER 12

Moil (v.) – To work hard

The next morning, after a fitful sleep, I woke to find Ben at the far end of the large double bed. I watched his chest rise and fall as he slept, wrapped in the thin white sheet, lost in some deep dream, and I felt my heart contract. I'd acted like a stroppy, sulky teen last night; it wasn't his fault he picked up the wrong bag. He hadn't done it on purpose.

I needed to think positively. We had arrived safely, we were here to explore this wonderful country and spend some precious time together and that was all that mattered. Forget clothes and make-up – they were things that I could replace. I couldn't get back the time we had spent faffing or stressing or going to sleep on opposite sides of the bed with a grumpy goodnight uttered before we turned our backs on each other. I resolved to myself that I would let the bag fiasco go and focus on the things that really mattered, i.e. Ben and me.

'Morning, babe,' I said as he stirred and rubbed the sleep from his eyes.

'Hey, did I oversleep?' His voice had that adorable morning croak in it.

I shook my head. 'Nope, I've only just woken up. Listen, I'm sorry about flying off the handle last night and losing my temper. I was just knackered and wasn't expecting to see the contents of the Ann Summers bargain bin when I opened my suitcase.'

He flashed a lopsided smile and wrapped his arms around me, pulling me gently over to his side. 'I'm sorry, too. Listen, why don't we get breakfast out of the way then nip to the shops to pick you up a few things? I've got some spare stuff you can put on till then. It may drown you but I'm sure I heard Kelli say that baggy was back in,' he said planting a heavy kiss on my forehead.

'Deal.' I nodded my head firmly.

'But first, I know something we can do that doesn't have a dress code.' He nuzzled my neck making me giggle.

We were the last couple to make it to the hotel restaurant – make-up sex was the only good thing that came out of having an argument – where breakfast was being served on an endless buffet table. I physically shivered at the thought of putting back on the clothes I'd travelled in, so Ben lent me a pair of board shorts and a baggy T-shirt that I wore with my Converse trainers. Stylish I wasn't, but at least I was comfortable and clean. I was fine with my look until I stepped foot in the plum-coloured, sumptuous room where the other three women were looking super glam and ready for their close-ups. I self-consciously tugged on the hem of the T-shirt.

Jade was wearing a bright pink, tie-dyed, strapless maxi dress accessorised with heavy jewellery that clinked together as she clodded across the room in chunky wedges with her full plate of food. I was surprised that for her tiny bird-sized body she could consume so much.

'Morning, guys,' she said warmly as we walked in, not batting an eyelid at the masculine way I was dressed. Dawn, on the other hand, could barely keep a straight face as she looked up and saw me.

'Morning, Jade.' I smiled back, trying to put my dad's advice into practice by acting confident and in control, even if I didn't feel it.

Gareth was sat on a spare table, literally *on* the table with one outstretched foot on the chair opposite, looking in his element whilst chatting about something with Clive who was filming away. Damn. I thought I'd at least get to eat breakfast before having the face the cameras again. I hadn't even managed to get a cup of coffee in me yet.

'Great! You're both here,' Anna said in her perky cheerleader-style voice, stepping between Ben and me and wrapping a slender arm around us both. She steered us away from the bountiful breakfast spread to the long table everyone else was sat at. 'Now we're all here, I can let you know the plan for today.' She rubbed her hands together and called Gareth and Clive to join us.

'We're going on a bike tour of Santiago, but this is no ordinary city cycle trip. You guys will have to follow a series of clues hidden all over the city, to see which couple is the first to figure out where the tour ends and meet us in that location in the quickest time. Clive and I will wait at the meeting place to film your arrival and everyone will have a GoPro camera fitted to the top of their bike helmets so we can use footage from those, too. So, if you've all eaten enough then feel free to get changed into something suitable and meet us in the foyer in ten minutes.' She clapped her hands and grinned down the camera lens.

I raised my hand as the others got to their feet and left the room. 'I just need to nip to the shops first, to, you know, get some clothes and toiletries.'

Anna scowled for a fraction of a second before she realised that Ben had put down the milk jug he was holding and was waiting for her answer. 'I'm afraid we're on a really tight schedule here, Georgia.' She glanced at her elegant designer watch as if me losing my bags was the biggest inconvenience to her. 'To be honest, you actually look like you're dressed just fine for this activity so maybe we can factor in some shopping time later?' She said this as if I'd just asked to waltz around Beverly Hills flashing the plastic, not that I desperately needed to buy some underwear and a razor.

'Okay?' She flashed a fake smile and waited for my answer.

'Okay,' I said glumly. 'Do you know if the airline has been in touch about my bag?'

'Not yet. But I promise we can chase it when we get back later on,' she said, barely looking up from her phone screen. *Come on, try and stay positive. It isn't that bad, and as soon as this task is over you can buy what you need. Even if you do have to look like a tit in the meantime.*

*

We'd all congregated at a small, pretty park near the hotel. Out in the bright sunshine we looked a right group of misfits and amazingly my baggy outfit choice wasn't the worst of it. Despite the warm morning sun, Gareth was wearing a blazer that matched his long, salmon-coloured shorts, which perfectly matched his girlfriend's maxi dress. She'd made one concession to the fact that this challenge would be spent cycling around the city by swapping her wedges for bejewelled flip-flops. Even so, I doubted Bradley Wiggins would be quaking in his cycling shoes at the pair of them.

Dawn looked trim in a pale green, well-fitted yoga outfit that only made Simon's Hawaiian-print tank top look even more garish. I still found it hard to work the two of them out. They seemed like chalk and cheese both physically and personality wise. In fact, since meeting the 'Last Call' duo I don't think I'd heard him utter one word that wasn't either singing Dawn's praises or agreeing with whatever she was going on about.

Natalia and Tony were the most well-dressed couple, but it wasn't surprising because their bodies were so toned and seemingly designed for Lycra. Even the bright yellow cycle helmets with clunky GoPros attached looked like the latest must-have accessory on their glossy heads. Ben also fitted into this category with his grey marl tight T-shirt that made his biceps look even more lickable than normal and his navy shorts, which made his bum even peachier. I was ashamed to be stood next to him bringing down our fashion credentials. Thankfully, he didn't seem bothered about the way I was dressed in the slightest.

'Guys! Guys!' Anna was shouting and waving some purple envelopes. 'Here you go, you need to open them at the same time and try to work out the first clue. Remember, the first couple to make it to the final, secret location will win today's task. Clive and I will meet you all there and you've got our phone numbers if there are any emergencies.' I'm sure she flicked her gaze at Jade as she said that. 'So, best of luck!'

I glanced at Ben and forgot all about wardrobe malfunctions as my competitive spirit kicked in. This was going to be fun! Ben looked just as keen – we had this in the bag, surely.

'You ready, Miss Green?' he asked, winking.

'Oh yes, Mr Stevens!'

'Guys! On three, two, one, open it up and off you go!' Anna shouted as Clive whizzed around us all, trying to get our reactions on film.

'Okay. Clue number one,' Ben read out. 'Don't judge me by my cover as even though I may look beautiful from the outside I am not just a pretty face. You will find jackets and sleeves here but I am not a clothes store. I have beauty and brains; I could recite the words of scholars, historians and philosophers but my secret passion is for poetry.'

'What the?' I stared at him with a blank face. Murmurs rose from the rest of the group as we all tried to make sense of this riddle, harder to do without much sleep and chronic jet lag.

'Got it! Haha, see you later, suckers!' Gareth shouted pumping his fist in the air before awkwardly hopping onto his bike and pedalling off, leaving poor Jade to struggle to get onto the saddle in her billowing dress.

'Wait, Gareth, wait for me!' she cried as she eventually got into position and cycled off to catch her boyfriend up.

'Crap. Okay, think…' Ben tapped his forehead.

I saw Natalia and Tony high-five each other out of the corner of my eye as they effortlessly jumped on their bikes.

'Wait, does it mean…' Ben was biting his bottom lip in concentration.

'Toodle-oo!' Dawn called out, as she and Simon pedalled off. No! We were the last ones to leave, meaning Clive was in our faces with his bloody large camera, which was not helping in the slightest.

'Erm, erm, erm,' I repeated, willing my mind to think. There was no way the other couples were more intelligent than us. 'Okay, maybe we're overthinking things?' I suggested. Ben frowned.

'You need any help over here, guys?' Anna called out faux innocently.

'No, no, all good thanks!' I replied breezily, even though I felt idiotic at how long this was taking us. We were supposed to be at the top of our business game but between the pair of us we couldn't figure out this childish riddle.

'Wait!' Ben slapped his hand to his forehead. 'It's the library.' He pulled out the map and guidebook we'd been given and scanned it. 'Yep, look, Biblioteca Nacional dates back to 1813, a stunning monument that is more than just pretty architecture as it is filled with over six million publications and specialises in the works of distinguished Chilean poets.'

I grinned at him. 'You clever thing, you.' Finally, we too got on our bikes and quickly pedalled away to make up for lost time.

*

Now we were on our way and Ben was in charge of the map I relaxed and let the warming breeze rush past me. This was like something from a film, minus my awful outfit, as we made our way through the winding, dappled bike lanes of the park, past sparkling green ponds where families fed noisy ducks. It was so lovely to feel the sun on my cheeks, warming my hair that was air drying in the breeze. I kept glancing over to Ben to see if he was enjoying this as much as I was, but he had this steely look of concentration lining his usually relaxed face. Wow, I knew he liked to thrash Jimmy on video games but maybe he was more competitive than I'd thought. We stopped at the exit of the park as he pulled out the map and examined it once more.

'It's so beautiful here, isn't it?' I exclaimed, taking a sip of water. The green park behind us, we turned onto a bustling road filled with street cafés, open-air markets and shops selling trinkets and cool souvenirs.

'Mmhm,' he replied, still scowling at the paper in his hands.

'You need any help?' I offered.

He ignored me, twisting the map around before nodding to himself and flashing me a tight smile. 'Nope, all good.'

We eventually pulled up to the steps of an imposing building, which was guarded by towering palm trees, next to gleaming high-rises that were in sharp contrast to the dusty sandstone brick of the library. It resembled the Natural History Museum I once went to on a school trip where Marie got shouted at for laughing too loudly at the minuscule penis of one of the statues. The clue was right; this place was blooming impressive and ginormous. My local 1970s' style public library could not compete with this.

I was gawping up at the stone pillars when I heard Ben huff. I turned to see him jabbing his head at two other yellow bikes that were chained up outside. We clearly weren't the first couple to get here.

'Come on!' he shouted hurriedly locking our bikes up and running into the huge lobby. I raced to keep up with him, entering an ornate and bright reception area where there appeared to be only groups of students or quiet bookworms milling around.

'If their bikes are outside then someone from the show must be in here somewhere,' I said in hushed tones, scanning the floor plan of this huge building. 'Is there something more in that clue we're missing?'

Ben frowned and pulled the piece of paper out of his pocket and hurriedly reread it in a loud whisper. I trailed a finger down the list of separate rooms and sections of this huge library, not really sure what I was looking for.

'Wait – it says something about poetry, right? Well, why don't we start in that section and see if we can find a clue there?'

'Sounds as good a shot as any.'

After crossing the chequered marble floor, we turned a corner and I was sure I spotted those unforgettable auburn curls of Dawn's.

'Ben! In here!' I hissed and mouthed a quick apology to a young woman bent over a heavy tome on the table nearby who glanced up and tutted at me.

We headed over to where Dawn and Simon were hunched over a desk, both intently staring at a map they had spread out in front of them.

'Oh, hello,' I said, wishing I had a fluffy cat to stroke and a maroon Hugh Hefner style housecoat to wear as I approached them.

Dawn jumped as she saw us and a slow scowl grew on her thin lips. 'Oi! Don't be cheating!' She grabbed the map to her chest, probably papercutting poor Simon's fingertips at the same time.

'We don't need to cheat!' I replied, shocked at how seriously she was taking this, almost as seriously as Ben. 'Where's the next clue?'

Dawn looked like the last thing she wanted to do was give us any helpful information but Simon had already slid the piece of purple card across the walnut desk towards us.

'Good luck, guys, it's even harder than the first,' he said with a shrug, ignoring Dawn's angry scowl that he was fraternising with the enemy.

'Cheers, mate, you too,' Ben said and picked the card up. 'Many rooms belong to me but none so important as the ones that contained my love. Some may say cheating isn't the answer but many a man has succumbed to the wild hair and wild soul of a muse before me.'

'Eh? What the heck's that supposed to mean?'

Dawn had been staring at our faces and looked pleased at our confusion. 'Not so simple, is it?'

'You don't seem to have figured it out either,' I retorted before remembering we were all still wearing these silly yellow cycle helmets with our cameras on, and they were capturing our every move. 'I mean, best of luck to you. Come on; let's leave them to it,' I said to Ben, wanting to have some time alone to figure this one out.

We walked out of the small room and leant against the door. 'This is tougher than I'd imagined,' Ben said, rubbing his cheeks. 'I didn't think we'd be on some wild goose chase with clues more cryptic than one of Jimmy's drunken texts.'

'Wait, what was it about rooms?' I asked once more.

He passed the clue card over and shook his head. 'I literally have no idea.'

A slow grin grew on my face. 'I think we're staring it in the face…'

He turned to where I was looking and shook his head in disbelief. Etched on the glass door to the room where the second clue had been placed were the words 'Salon de lectura – Pablo Neruda'.

'Pablo Neruda's reading room. Keep it simple. There's got to be a reason the clue was plonked in here.'

I laughed. 'Yep, but now we need to find out who this guy is and where we might find other rooms that belong to him…'

Ben pulled out his guidebook. 'Okay, okay. Pablo Neruda…' he said, thumbing through the pages. 'Ah, here he is… "There are three properties linked to Pablo Neruda (1904–1973), seen as the greatest and most prolific of twentieth-century Latin American poets. A visit to all three of Neruda's homes is well worth a spot on your Chilean itinerary," blah blah blah. Wait – "probably the most famous is La Chascona, in Santiago, which was constructed in 1953 when Neruda was involved in a secret affair with Matilde Urrutia. The house gets its name in homage to his mistress with her mane of long flowing red hair. It is now a popular museum."'

'How do they say bingo in Spanish?' I giggled as we quietly scuttled down the echoing hall leaving Dawn and Simon still scratching their heads.

CHAPTER 13

Effete (adj.) – Having lost character, vitality or strength

In the time between getting the first clue and leaving the library, the sun had risen in the piercing blue sky and was beating hard on our shoulders as we cycled off. Sweat was dripping behind my knees and between my breasts into my already stinky bra. As much as I was enjoying this bizarre way to get to see the city, I was still very aware of the fact that I was in my boyfriend's baggy clothes and yesterday's underwear. Although I was enjoying myself, I did want to get to the finish line soon, in order to get the latest update on my suitcase and do a quick clothes shop.

We soon found ourselves riding through Barrio Bellavista, a quiet and bohemian neighbourhood. At the bottom of the mossy green San Cristóbal Hill that dominated the skyline, I spotted groups of tourists hanging around a set of white iron gates near a strange shaped mansion: 'La Chascona'. Strangely though I couldn't see any other bikes from our group chained up outside.

'Is this it?' I asked as we pulled to a stop and wheeled the bikes over to a post.

'Looks that way; we must be the first,' Ben said grinning, chaining our tyres together and taking my sweaty hand.

I felt a right tool being unable to take off these ridiculous cycle helmets. We'd been placed under strict orders not to remove them until we'd completed the treasure hunt, and judging by the muffled giggles and strange looks we were receiving from the staff on the main door I wasn't being paranoid.

Stepping inside the quirky house, unusual pieces of art seemed to spring from every surface. The poet's Nobel Prize in Literature took centre stage amongst curious collections that highlighted his eclectic taste.

'Ben, look.' I nudged him after stepping out of the way of an older couple who were listening intently to an audio guide. There was another purple envelope sat on a small circular table. None of the other couples from the TV show appeared to be around. Maybe we were in with a chance here, I thought, as I opened the letter and pulled out the clue that had been handwritten on thick card.

'Congratulations, you're one step away from toasting your success. I bet you're itching to get to the finish line and have a drink to celebrate?'

'God, that's even harder than the others,' Ben sighed.

'I know this one!' I said in surprise. 'Kelli had been looking at cool places we could go whilst we were here and there's a bar that's apparently *the* place to head to for an authentic Chilean drinking experience, and I'm ninety-nine per cent certain it's called Flea.' I took the guidebook from him and flicked through the pages to confirm my guess. Amazingly I was spot on, a bar called Flea existed and it wasn't too far from here. 'It's got to be that, right?'

'Perfect, let's go!' Ben said, squeezing my shoulder tight.

We cycled as fast as we could back down the hill and into the heart of Bellavista, past hipster-friendly restaurants, colourful avant-garde art galleries, and independent artisanal shops that lined the wide sun-baked streets. Hidden amongst the leafy avenues were plenty of bars and edgy nightclubs, although as they were all covered in graffiti it was hard to tell them apart. This neighbourhood seemed to hum with creativity, from bespectacled older men hunched over a chessboard in the shade, to a group of art students bending their bodies into uncomfortable-looking shapes whilst one of their mates snapped away on a long lens camera.

'This is the place,' I said to Ben, staring up at the scuzzy sign over the grated door and looking down at the map. 'I think.' I hesitated, as there was a mangy old cat sunbathing outside the faded, chipped yellow walls. A cloud of flies guarded the main door where a snoozing bald man with a newspaper half tumbling off his lap sat behind a rickety table. He was the least intimidating bouncer I'd ever seen, but still the general decay of the place gave me the creeps. I'd imagined the TV show splashing the cash on taking us to the fanciest of watering holes and classy cocktail bars, not unloved and unclean establishments. This place was probably flea-infested, as the name suggested. I shuddered.

'Do you honestly reckon that this sketchy place is where we're meant to be?' I asked Ben doubtfully. By now I was tired, my skin was tender to the touch from the scorching sun and I was beyond ravenous. Maybe I'd misunderstood the clue after all.

'Only one way to find out.'

We chained our bikes up and clasped sweaty hands to walk down the stone steps out of the warm sun to head deep into a dimly lit and grungy basement bar. Groups of men huddled around low tables littered with empty pint pots, looked us up and down as we entered what was little larger than a concrete tunnel. It was obvious that this was a local bar, for local people. Where was this Chilean hospitality I'd read so much about in the guidebooks?

Larger and busier rooms shot off from this main corridor. The sound of wheezing laughter and fast-flowing

Spanish reverberated off the bare walls. Broken chairs that looked flea-ridden were stacked in one corner and ruddy-cheeked older men, who looked as if they hadn't moved from the same spot for the past decade, sat in the other corner slapping each other on the back lost in some shared joke. My feet crunched on sawdust that had been roughly scattered to soak up beer, although it could just as easily have been intended to soak up blood, I thought as I glanced around and caught the hard scowls of the locals.

'Hey! You one of the couples in the TV show?' A smiling barmaid with dimples pierced into her sallow cheeks and murky dyed green hair asked as we made our way to the bar. Well, less of a bar and more of a picnic table piled with unusual-looking bottles and plastic cups.

'Yep, that obvious huh?' Ben pointed to our helmets and laughed. If he was as intimidated as I was in here then he was hiding it well.

The barmaid laughed back. 'Yeah you could say that. Well there are some others waiting for you next door.' She nodded towards a room opposite that had been partitioned off with heavy maroon-coloured velvet drapes.

My heart sank. So we weren't the first; we hadn't won the task.

'Cheers.' Ben nodded politely, trying and failing to hide the disappointment in his voice. 'Damn, I thought we had this in the bag. We should have been quicker off the mark to begin with,' he mumbled.

'We tried our best though,' I said, before kissing him on his cheek, our stupid helmets awkwardly slapping together.

'Guys! You found us!' Anna stood up as we walked into the smaller room that was painted in an uninviting blood red colour with candles melted into skulls and tables carved out of gnarled wood stumps. The bright welcoming sunshine of the many cheerful street cafés we had cycled past seemed a world away from the gothic crypt we were in down here. 'Second best!' she said and pointed to Natalia and Tony who were already seated on straight-backed chairs meant to look like thrones with drinks in their hands. Clive was on us with his camera filming what must have been looks of disappointment.

'Well done, guys, you must have been right behind us,' Tony said, raising his pint glass to us. 'It wasn't easy to find this place, was it?'

I smiled politely and quickly stepped out of the way of a man singing a rowdy Chilean song as someone began playing an accordion in the next room. Past the heavy curtains I noticed groups of backpackers clinking their glasses together and young Chilean couples dancing in a smaller room further down this dark corridor.

Just then a red-faced Simon and a panting Dawn almost tumbled into the grim reaper's boudoir; she took one look at us all and failed to hide her disgust that they hadn't won.

'Third? We came third!' Dawn screeched as she tugged her cycle helmet off, revealing flat, sweat-slicked helmet-hair. 'I told you we shouldn't have asked that stupid old cow at the library, Simon,' she fumed before quickly composing herself as she realised that Clive was filming her. 'Oh well, it's the taking part that counts, isn't it?' She let out a strange titter of a laugh and took a glass from a tray of murky-coloured drinks on the table in front of us. Simon just looked on, bemused by the drastic change in his wife's mood.

'So, no Gareth and Jade then I see?' Dawn added with a sly smirk. 'At least we didn't come last,' she muttered under her breath.

'Not yet,' Anna said, glancing at her wristwatch. 'So as we wait for them to appear, help yourselves to a drink and I'll get some nibbles sorted out.'

Jade and Gareth had got very lost, which meant they were very late to find the dark and dingy bar, which also meant I was on the way to getting *very* tipsy. By the time they wandered in, to be greeted by an anxious Anna who was panicking that she'd lost two of the contributors on our first full day of being here, the drinks had been flowing non-stop.

Gothic bar girl handed over another two pisco sours, served in sticky glasses, along with a chipped bowl of complimentary peanuts. I think they were peanuts; it was too dark to make out what they were but either way I decided against shoving some in my mouth.

'Now, for the classic Chilean cocktail, the *terremoto* or "earthquake" in English,' the barmaid said, grinning at the group.

'Why, does the earth move after you've made us one?' Gareth leered at her bust and snorted loudly.

'Not unless you mean slapping the floor with your face after you've had a couple – that's if you're man enough to give them a go, that is,' she replied curtly and eyeballed Gareth. She would eat him alive.

'What's in it?' Simon piped up.

The glass she was passing looked like an ice-cream float, pretty innocent actually. 'Sweet chilled white wine, pisco, sugar and pineapple ice-cream,' she reeled off as she handed a large goblet to everyone.

'Wine and…and…ice-cream?' Tony stuttered in shock, looking like he was about to pass out due to this sacrilegious act against his precious grapevine.

'Trust me, it might sound weird but they are SO good,' the barmaid said confidently, practically licking her black lipsticked lips. 'Cheers, guys, and welcome to Chile!'

We all raised our heavy-bottomed glasses that looked like they should have a flake sticking out of the top and chinked them together.

I thought my head was going to explode with the sickeningly sweet sugar rush as I took a long sip. It tasted like nothing that I'd drank before, and boy was it potent. My sweet tooth was orgasming at the hit of pure sugar, the tang of acidic pineapple and the strong alcohol.

'So…what do we think?' the barmaid asked, taking a big gulp from a sticky goblet she'd made for herself. 'Who's up for another one?'

And that was the last thing I remember.

CHAPTER 14

Invidious (adj.) – Unpleasant, objectionable or obnoxious

'Eurgh, the smell in here is making my eyes water. My mascara's going to be everywhere in a minute,' Jade moaned, covering her nose with her hand and showing off the fake tan residue that had streaked between her fingers.

The smell was doing more than making my eyes water. I was forcing myself to breathe through my mouth so as not to chuck up the remains of what was in my stomach. Over an extremely early breakfast – well, nibbling on dry toast and gulping copious amounts of coffee – I'd managed to piece together parts of last night that had ended with my head down the toilet bowl in our hotel room and Ben passed out on the bed fully clothed.

The pretty, pierced-cheeked barmaid had been telling the truth when she warned us how potent the earthquake cocktails were. We, well I especially, should have listened to her advice not to have more than two, as according to Tony I took a distinct shine to the sweet, creamy drink. He told me this fact with so much disgust on his chiselled good-looking face I felt like he'd just caught me pissing in one of his posh wine bottles.

The whole group had stayed out for most of the night, showing the locals in that dive bar that us gringos could party with the best of them. We eventually tumbled out of there and into a taxi at some ungodly hour, the bikes unfit for use due to our inebriation and they'd had to be picked up this morning by some of the hotel staff. It also meant that I still hadn't had the chance to go shopping, so was wearing another of Ben's T-shirts with the same pair of knickers that I'd hand-washed in the hotel-room sink and dried with a hairdryer whilst I was still half cut after only a couple of hours' sleep.

Breakfast was a very quiet and sombre affair, before Anna herded us all into taxis and brought us here. To a fish market. With a stinking hangover. She was fast becoming my least favourite person in this city.

We were being led through the Mercado Central, an admittedly stunning art nouveau building with sandy, terracotta walls and bright white awnings that opened onto wrought-iron gates. I just didn't have my head together enough to appreciate the pretty architecture. I was still trying to focus on only seeing one of everything. Having such little control over my senses was more of a curse than a blessing in here. I could see double of everything, including open, gaping mouths, sad, inky, black soulless eyes that stared back at us and shiny, scaly flesh that glittered under the artificial lights of the crammed fishy stalls.

It wasn't just the smell in here that made my delicate head spin but the non-stop hollering of traders wearing stained aprons and bargain hunter customers haggling for the best prices. It didn't even sound Spanish, more like ear-splitting noise and a stream of loud foreign words as locals, tourists and workers huddled around tables filled with hunks of salmon, meaty tuna and hearty portions of sea bass splayed out on beds of crushed ice.

The day had barely started outside but in here everyone was rushing around to find the best catch and pack it in large polystyrene boxes crammed full of ice as quickly and as cheaply as they could to head back to their restaurants or cafés to serve fresh. There were cockles in heart-shaped shells, chunky flat crabs, shiny black mussels with grainy barnacles suckered on, glossy lavender-coloured octopus tentacles and never-ending seafood platters as far as the eye could see.

We were led through packed alleyways, ducking as boisterous fish merchants called out their best prices whilst holding up large slippery fish in their pink hands with absolute pride, like Rafiki does to Simba in *The Lion King*. *Look at what I caught. Look!*

Around them, men and women stood at tables slicing, filleting and deboning fish on stained chopping boards at impressive lightning speed before bagging them up and weighing them out. Dotted along the edges of this fishy circus were small restaurants with eager waiters trying to tempt us in with offers of fresh fish stews, creamy baked crab and hot and spicy ceviche. I could only stomach dry toast so didn't stand a chance with anything else.

'God, there must be nothing left in the ocean,' Simon mused as we trailed past stall after stall of the fishermen's bounty.

'Hey!' Gareth almost jumped into one of the full tables as an over-enthusiasfic stallholder sprayed a powerful hose at his feet, washing away the trail of watery blood from the latest victim of his sharp knife. 'This is Versace!' he yelled, shaking his head in disgust and quickly wiping at his shorts.

'Versace? Pfft,' Tony sniggered. 'More like Primarni.'

'Okay, gather round, guys,' Anna called, interrupting Gareth's death stare reply. Clive had his camera pointed at all of us as we huddled together to let other bargain hunters push past. 'We're going to be filming some interviews with you in the market today,' she said, before puckering her lips together and nodding at Clive that she was ready.

I was seriously struggling with this hangover, which was gripping my brain as tightly as barnacles to the hull of a boat; everyone else seemed like they'd perked up, including Ben who was as focused and intent on winning the next challenge as he had been yesterday.

Anna fanned her face and switched on the TV presenter charm as she faced the camera lens. 'Today, we are in the busy and bustling Mercado Central in the heart of Santiago. Our intrepid couples will be finding out if there's something fishy going on in this plaice as they get hands-on with the help of a local stallholder, Alfonso.'

As if timed to perfection a ruddy-cheeked man with an outstanding black bushy moustache came round from the stall opposite and waved at us before clasping my hands in his, enveloping them in a mixture of slimy gloop.

'Hola! My name is Alfonso and I want to welcome you all to the best fish market in all of the world!' He grinned and continued to shake everyone else's hands with as much gusto as he had grabbed mine. I noticed Dawn pull out a bottle of antiseptic hand gel from her handbag and squirt a huge glob on her hands.

Jade nudged me. 'I thought they all spoke Chilean in Chile?' I shook my head gently.

Alfonso was as round as he was tall. The bright lights bounced off his tanned bald head, which danced about as he spoke animatedly about the hundreds of types of fish and seafood on sale here.

'I work here all my life, my father work here before me and now my son work here also!' He let out a belly-shaking laugh and called out for the young lad, who had been crouched by a red plastic bucket in his rubber boots, to stand up and say hello. As he did Jade seemingly forgot about gagging from the smell and plastered on an interested smile aimed at the young Spanish stallion, making Gareth visibly bristle. 'This is Reyes; he is the next in line to serve our famous fish to hungry Chileans!'

Reyes nodded politely at the group and busied himself with pouring a bucket of whelks onto a low-hanging scale.

'If he worked at my local Morrison's fish counter I'd be there every bloody day!' Jade whispered loudly and nudged me in the ribs. I wasn't sure if Reyes understood English but by the uncomfortable look in his dark brown eyes I guessed he could feel when he was being leered at like a piece of meat, or should that be fish steak?

'Well, you know what they say about fish oil, maybe you could do with getting some omega 3 in you to help with that one brain cell you have,' Dawn muttered under her breath. I looked to see whether Jade had heard, but either she didn't or she pretended not to have.

'Maybe, Tony and Natalia, if you two could just stand here,' Anna instructed, arranging them next to a tray of oysters that Reyes awkwardly had in one outstretched hand. 'We would love it if you could take one of these and feed the other,' Anna said, nodding at Clive to get in closer for the tight shot.

Jade loudly gagged at both the strong smell and the ugly oysters glistening in their shells and held her stomach as if trying to keep the dry heaving to a minimum.

'No problem,' Tony said, with a glint in his eye, 'the food of love is only fair to feed my one true love.' Now it was my turn to try not to vomit.

Natalia giggled and tipped her head back, actually looking excited to have a snotty bogey dribble down her throat.

'You fancy one, Georgia?' Ben asked jokingly.

I stared at him as if he'd lost the plot. 'No thanks! Who in their right mind would want to eat that gloop?' He shrugged and gave me a smile. 'Wait, do *you* want one?' He actually liked oysters? Suddenly I imagined pretty

Alice's face leant over him seductively, with her wearing nothing but a lacy negligee, feeding oysters to him. I tried to rationalise that he was soon to be proposing to me and that he loved me, but last night's drinking session had left me with a dose of morning-after, booze-blues paranoia that fanned the flames of my irrational anxieties. Why *had* he met up with his ex and not told me? I bet Alice wouldn't have made such a tit of herself on camera. *Stop it, Georgia.* This was hardly the time for finding an answer.

'Ah, excellent plan!' Anna said raising a finger, after overhearing Ben's comment. 'If all couples could circle around the lovely Reyes and on the count of three pick up an oyster and feed their partner.' I was about to scoff that this show couldn't get any cheesier when the others got into position. 'Okay, everyone ready? Clive, you got the shot?'

Clive nodded. He actually looked a little paler today than normal too.

'I usually eat half a dozen of these at least once a week, don't I, Simon?' Dawn mused, smiling at the tray of gloopy-looking lady parts.

'You got any sauce?' I asked Reyes, interrupting Simon from telling us about the local market where he sources the finest oysters from. Maybe if they were swimming in something with a bit of flavour they wouldn't be as bad as they looked, I thought.

'Like ketchup?' Reyes answered with a confused expression.

Dawn flicked her head at me horrified. 'Eurgh! You don't put sauce with an oyster. You have to eat them naked. I thought *everyone* knew that!'

I felt foolish for not knowing the correct etiquette but the thing was they didn't serve them at my local Harvester. I glanced at the others expecting them to look as gormless as I did but they seemed to be confident with their oyster-eating technique. Wait, was I the only one here who didn't know what I was doing? Great.

'God. Let me show you. I had to do this for you, too, didn't I, Simon, do you remember?' Dawn laughed and glanced down at her husband for confirmation of his former ignorance. 'Thank goodness he knows never to make those silly mistakes now.'

Simon dipped his head and smiled bashfully before passing her a small fork from a pot. 'Yes, darling.'

'Right, you take this and loosen it from the shell.'

I followed her lead, my stomach doing a small flip as I heard the squelchy, sucking noise when it broke free from the shell.

'Then simply tip it into your mouth, but don't swallow in one.'

'I've said that to many a girl before, ay Benny boy!' Gareth laughed.

Dawn flashed Gareth a look. 'You need to bite into it and release the flavour.'

'You ready, Georgia?' Ben whispered, ignoring Gareth and looking like he was struggling not to laugh at how awkwardly I was holding the rough, grey shell in one hand. 'Don't overthink it, just open your mouth and swallow.'

'That's what *she* said.' Gareth winked at Ben who once again ignored him. 'Ah come on now! Don't be shellfish, why not just do it for the halibut!' Jade was the only one who giggled at her boyfriend's awful fish puns. 'Come on now! Halibut – hell of it?' Gareth shook his head. 'Tough crowd. Ah well, when you do get the jokes don't be koi, just let minnow!'

I smiled weakly at his Christmas cracker style fish jokes and shook my head.

'I'm not sure I can do this,' was all I could manage before Anna had counted down to one and Ben had his oyster pressed against my lips. Not wanting this smidge of courage to escape me and realising that everyone else had tipped the ugly contents into their partner's mouth, I did the same.

Salty sea water mixed with the saliva that had flooded my mouth. Briny, tangy and chewy. I felt my stomach contract instantly. That final earthquake cocktail from last night would be making a sudden reappearance if I wasn't careful. *Okay, chew, chew, swallow*. But my body refused to. The offending oyster just sat in my mouth with nowhere else to go but straight back out. All over Ben's chest.

'God, Georgia!' he shouted as I sprayed him with slimy juice.

I clasped my hand to my mouth; I couldn't get rid of the lingering aftertaste. 'I'm so sorry!' I cried, realising that everyone else had stomached this delicacy, even Jade. My cheeks flamed in embarrassment as Ben was passed a napkin from Reyes to dab at the mess I'd made down his shirt.

Clive soon had his camera trained to my mouth zooming in on the strings of saliva dripping from my lips. I felt like I'd swallowed the scummy froth of the ocean.

'Cheers for that,' Ben said, less sharply but still irritated.

'Some people just don't have the palate, do they, Simon?' Dawn sniffed as she gave me a patronising pity smile.

'Excellent work! That was what we call the appetiser and now we prepare the main course!' Alfonso said, smiling at my fishy faux pas, slapping a meaty hand on my back and almost knocking me forwards into the mound of cockles. He beckoned us all over to the long white table where eight fat sea bass were waiting for us. Oh God, what now? 'They can be quite slippery, so put on a pair of gloves and hold on to them hard.'

'You want us to do what?' Jade piped up, asking what I think most of us were thinking.

'Why, you are now going to prepare your very own dinner!' Alfonso said, with a deep chuckle at the look of utter revulsion on our faces. 'Very simple, very fun and good skill to know for future romantic dinners together,' he finished with a wink.

'Uh-uh. No way. I'm not ruining my acrylics for anyone,' Jade point blank refused, flicking her head between the grinning Chilean chef and Anna, who interestingly had turned a strange shade of green herself.

'If you refuse then we will have to disqualify your team from this task,' Anna said pulling herself together, looking mighty pleased she was a presenter/producer and not a contestant.

'Fine by me.' Jade shrugged totally indifferent.

'Ah now, babe. Hang on a minute,' Gareth jumped in. 'Maybe I could do this for both of us?' he asked Anna, the fear of failure too much for him to take.

'Sorry. All tasks must be completed as a couple. They're the rules.'

Gareth clenched his jaw. 'Jade, please, baby-cakes? Dumpling pie? Snuggle kitten?' If I hadn't already chucked it up, that nasty oyster would definitely be making a reappearance now.

Jade shook her head. 'No. Way.'

Gareth let out a deep huff and kicked the table leg. 'Fine. Be like that.'

A horrible awkward silence descended on the group as Jade and Gareth stared each other out. But she wasn't backing down. I too wanted to throw my toys out of the pram and refuse to take part in pulling the innards from a gungy fish but a sense of pride stopped me, that and wanting to make amends for gozzing oyster over my boyfriend.

'Well if that's one couple down we've got an even better chance of winning this one! You up for it, babe?' Ben asked, tying on a white apron and excitedly brandishing a sharp knife.

'Course I am.' I blew out a deep breath and fixed a smile on my face.

'That's my girl. Hey, who does this remind you of?' He picked up the fish and held it at the same height as his head before pulling the identical downturned mouth and droopy-eyed expression.

I giggled; he looked ridiculous. 'Don't even think of saying my name!' I warned him.

'As if! Conrad…' He continued to pull a stupid guppy fish mouth, which made me laugh and momentarily forget about the task in front of us.

How hard could this be? I mean the workers in this market did it every day.

However, if I thought I'd lost any dignity I had remaining in the oyster incident, that was nothing compared to what happened next. It had started off so well too. We'd all washed our hands, been told to wear a jaunty white fishmonger hat and taken a space at the table as we tried to follow the instructions that Alfonso was calling out.

'Okay, so first we must trim the fins off with scissors,' he boomed.

I picked up my silvery slimy fish and hacked at the fins as instructed, which made a strange crunchy noise, like the sound of stepping on seashells – not unpleasant but slightly jarring. 'To de-scale, hold the fish by its tail and use your knife to scrape the blade against the scales to remove in a swift motion. Then use a cloth to wipe up the mess you have made.'

So far, so good.

I glanced at the other couples. Dawn was deep in concentration and checking that Simon wasn't messing up on his fish; Natalia and Tony looked as relaxed as if they were exfoliating each other in a Moroccan themed spa; and Ben was getting some inside tips from Reyes.

Alfonso's deep voice pulled me back. 'Then we must open the gills.' I looked down at the flappy part of the head. 'Inside you will see this pink fleshy piece of gristle, so trim each edge and remove.' I swallowed down the saliva that had rushed to my mouth.

Taking a deep breath I opened the gills up and made two neat incisions, brain surgeon style, before clumsily taking out what looked like pink, squelchy putty. *Imagine it's just Play-Doh,* I told myself.

'Excellent work, team. Now point the head of your fish towards you, then make a neat cut down the length of the fish, all the way to the head. Put down your knife and spread apart the flaps and pull out the slimy bag, which contains the innards. You may need to cut the membrane to really get at the guts, depending how tough your little fella is.'

This was the exact moment Clive came right close up to me and stuck his camera lens in my face. My face already felt extremely flushed from the lights, the heat, my hangover, the stink of fish and the caterwauling noises around me. Black spots started to cloud my vision. The moment Clive zoomed in was also the moment my legs gave way and I hit the deck. Literally.

'Shit! Georgia!' I could hear Ben's voice in my ear as I slumped to the cold, damp ground. 'Clive, back away from her!'

'Oh my God, is she okay?' Jade's high-pitched and worried tones filtered into my dizzy mind.

'Georgia! Georgia?' Ben was propping me up as I opened my eyes and groggily stared at him. 'Are you okay?'

I nodded as he came into focus. Amazingly, I hadn't hurt myself during the fall but I had managed to take down a bucket of fish guts with me that had slopped over my bare legs.

'We need to finish or else we'll be disqualified,' he apologised, slowly helping me to my feet. 'Are you sure you're okay to carry on?'

I nodded and gratefully accepted a soiled rag from a wide-eyed Reyes to wipe down my slimy calves. 'I'm fine, I must have slipped on something on the floor. You saw how they hose them around here,' I muttered, wishing the flame in my cheeks would die down so as not to expose my white lie.

'Are you okay, miss?' Alfonso was at our table with a worried look on his wrinkled face.

I nodded and tried to pull myself together. 'Yep. So... erm...you were saying something about membranes?' I said in a voice that didn't sound like my own, wanting to finish this bloody task and have everyone take their pity stares back to their poor fish.

Alfonso gave a tight nod and walked back to the head table to give the last few instructions on the gruesome lesson. I said a silent prayer that I could keep it together to finish the job. Which amazingly I managed to do, thanks to a lot of slow breathing and telling myself that it would soon be over.

Once we had cleaned up our work stations, Alfonso clapped his big bear paws together, telling us we were all excellent students, and came round to judge our handiwork. As I heard him give constructive feedback to the others I glanced down at my fish and actually felt a tingle of pride that I'd managed to gut a fish for the first, and hopefully last, time in my life.

'I'm dead proud of you for doing that, especially for carrying on when I know you really fainted. You've been a luminous shade of green since we got here. I'm amazed you managed to stay standing for so long, babe,' Ben whispered in my ear as Alfonso made his way over to our table. That tingle of pride grew even bigger.

'Well I know which team were the most dramatic.' He let out a chesty chuckle. 'But despite the problems you picked it back up and carried on, so for that I am going to declare you the winners of this task!'

'Yes!' I shouted without realising it. 'Oh my God. Wow. Thank you!'

I grinned at Ben who pulled me into a hug before graciously clapping the other guests. Natalia and Tony both gave me the thumbs up as congratulations; Simon was silently staring at his fish as Dawn looked like she was preparing to give him a serious tongue-lashing for having lost this task. There were going to be some cold shoulders in their bedroom tonight.

After we'd taken off our stained aprons and scrubbed our hands, Ben gave me a tight squeeze and planted a heavy kiss on my forehead. 'Go, us.' He grinned, looking genuinely ecstatic at us having a challenge win under our belt.

'I think we worked hard enough for it.' I laughed at the state of us. Me with fish innards coating my legs and him with spat-up oyster juice on his chest. I felt so unclean that I needed a thousand showers to scrub my fingertips but I'd done it! It was amazing that fish blood, actual sweat and being close to tears had meant we had won this task, putting us level pegging with Natalia and Tony and closer to the prize fund that Ben seemed so intent on bringing home with us.

We hadn't spoken about what we'd spend it on if we did win, so as not to jinx anything, but it seemed obvious to me that we would use it for the Lonely Hearts Foundation, the charity fund that we'd started after my trip to India. And now we were a step closer to making that happen.

CHAPTER 15

Jackleg (adj.) – Lacking skill or training; amateurish

I swear I still had a faint *odour de fish guts* clinging to my skin no matter how much I scrubbed myself. Any sexy time with Ben had been firmly out of the question for both of us last night as we took it in turns to spray air freshener around our hotel room and scour our fingertips until they were red raw. It felt like we hadn't had any proper time together since arriving here, with our mini row the first night over my stupid bag, us both getting paralytic drunk the second night and then stinking the room with fish guts last night. I was hoping that this next destination would allow us to have some quality couple-time away from the rest of the group and Clive's camera.

Things had been so full on since arriving. It had been hectic, fun, but also refreshingly nice to have a break from discussing work. Instead of throwing around ideas on new ways to connect with our customers, how we could improve on the less popular tour packages and even listening to him bring up the possibility of the London expansion, we had been busy following Anna's full-on schedule and, in a way, that was probably good for us.

Another piece of good news was that I'd managed to track down my suitcase. Apparently, Mr Rathborne wasn't in the least embarrassed about his sex stash and had come forward to retrieve it and swap our bags back over. Luckily, this had all taken place at the airport so I never got to see the sex perve himself; all that mattered was that my things had been delivered to the hotel in one piece so I could dress like me again.

Our short stay in Santiago had been a whirlwind, with less romance and more embarrassing social faux pas, although our success in the fish challenge had reminded me what a great team we were. Now we were taking a short flight up to the very north of the country, to the Atacama desert, and I was desperately hoping that the change in climate would mean that things would heat up between Ben and me, too.

We had congregated in the main square of the local town, San Pedro de Atacama, as Anna gave us instructions for what was to come next. It was a magical oasis slap bang in the middle of a desert. Arid heat seemed to bounce off the parched pavements; in fact, the desert surrounding this small town was one of the driest places in the world. Adorable, white-washed houses and souvenir shops lined the dusty, cobbled streets. A pack of llamas were being led down the main street, their hooves scuffing up clouds of dust into their shaggy coats as they lazily blocked the path of a group of cyclists.

'Did you know that the world's most powerful telescope is based around here?' Simon piped up. 'Apparently it is so strong it can pick up some of the most ancient galaxies ever seen. And the observatory can focus in on a golf ball that's over nine miles away.' He shook his head in disbelief.

'Fascinating,' Dawn said, dripping with sarcasm, as Gareth let out a loud yawn that made her scoff with laughter.

'Hopefully we'll get to see it, Simon,' I said kindly, before shooting a look at his bitch of a wife. I know people say that you never know what goes on behind closed doors in relationships but she acted like his presence was the most irritating thing to her. It was strange, as he came across like he had more common sense than to stay with someone who was so mean to him, but there must be some sort of attraction, surely? I was cut off from saying any more as a battered old jeep did a severe handbrake turn in front of the group, spraying us with a fine coating of churned up dust that made us all cough and stumble back from the kerbside.

Within seconds of the 4x4 vehicle coming to a dramatic stop, a guy wearing a faded tank top that showed off his tanned biceps jumped out. He must have been in his late fifties, judging by the obvious sun damage on his leathery face, but the way he leapt from the car and bounded over to the group he could have been an excitable backpacker in his twenties.

'All right there, folks!' He grinned, his crooked teeth seemed to glow against his deep mahogany skin. He spoke in a country yee-haw kinda twang, but it sounded pretty fake and could easily have been hiding the fact he was clearly more Tottenham than Texas. 'I'm Dwayne but you can all call me D-Dawg. I'll be your desert guide today!'

D-Dawg appeared to visit the same hairdresser as Rod Stewart and Peter Stringfellow. His beaming face was framed by strands of grey, wispy hair that had escaped the tight clutches of the low ponytail that the rest of the mullet had been scraped into. An unidentified animal's tooth hung from his right earlobe, one of his eyebrows had a gleaming silver bar pierced through it and more wiry hair poked out from the neckline of his naff vest top.

'I hope we've got some adrenaline junkies in the gang as we've got a mighty fine treat lined up for you!' He rubbed his hands together in glee, ignoring the horrified reaction of Dawn who had physically taken a step back the moment D-Dawg bounded into our lives. Maybe the original

D-Dawg felt threatened. I wondered if Simon ever used that as a pet name for her.

'You there.' Dwayne pointed a hammy finger at me. 'What's your name?'

I stopped laughing and blinked at him. 'Georgia.'

'Ah, well now, Miss Georgia, you're the lucky one as you get to ride up front with me.' I visibly gulped. 'The rest of you get yourselves in the back of the vehicle and remember to keep hands and feet inside at all times. I can't be held responsible for any loss of limbs now, can I?' He swept the pale faces of the group before us. 'Come on now! Whatcha all waitin' for?'

I nervously glanced at Anna who nodded and nudged Clive to take some arty shots of us all clambering into this converted jeep/truck thing, before she did a quick piece to camera explaining what was going on. The front looked like a dune buggy with red chipped metal bars over our heads instead of a roof and doors, the back where everyone else was shuffling into was more of an extended open-air trailer that you'd use to transport livestock to a country fair. Amazingly, seat belts had been fitted and thin padded cushions attempted to bring a touch of comfort to this bizarre vehicle. It would never pass road safety tests back home, and judging by the strange looks people at nearby café tables were giving us, I'm not sure it was fit for use here either.

Once everyone was in position, D-Dawg lit up a rollie, revved up his truck, and shouted something inaudible over the metallic, scraping noise the engine had begun making. He accelerated faster than I was prepared for, and I clunked my head against one of the metal bars.

D-Dawg's wide-boy driving skills forced me to shut my eyes for most of the fast and bumpy journey. When I eventually did peel them open I panicked that I'd damaged my corneas as bright sunlight bounced off a large metal road sign that seemed to be pointing us in the direction of the worryingly named 'Death Valley'.

'Is that where we're headed?' I asked through juddering teeth as we flew over unpaved roads and narrowly avoided large, crater-sized holes that seemed to have been melted away by the force of the sun.

'Sure is!' D-Dawg took a final, long drag of his cigarette and flicked the glowing butt onto the ground in one smooth movement. My stomach clenched. So long, picturesque sand dunes...hello, vultures and gnawed skulls.

Twenty minutes and two mini heart palpitations later we eventually came to a stop. I hobbled out of the front seat, too busy rubbing my coccyx, which I was convinced would have a giant bruise on it this time tomorrow, to notice the spectacular view ahead of us.

'Wow, that was actually worth that nightmare ride,' Natalia mused, pulling me from rubbing my backside to look at where she had fixed her gaze.

One hundred-metre-high sand dunes were nestled in amongst crazy-shaped rock formations and craters. The sand glowed a buttery yellow as it peaked and sloped against the clear, royal-blue sky under the high sun. It wasn't like the desert I'd imagined, not the one that you see in films with camel footprints being the only mark in an endless expanse of arid uniform sand. Here the jaggedy peaks seemed to be in some competition to touch the sun. A soft breeze swept glittering grains across the dunes, making it appear like they were gently rippling in front of our eyes and across the impressive landscape.

Even more striking than this were the towering, snow-capped volcanos dominating the rest of the horizon. Oven-like heat bounced off the vast canvas in front of us and sweat was already beading down the temples of most of the group. The only downside of this impressive other-worldly view was that D-Dawg had decided to blast out Guns'N'Roses from the jeep's stereo system, complete with subwoofers and heavy bass.

'Erm, Dwayne, can you just turn that down a minute, please?' Anna asked nicely whilst fanning her face with her hands. D-Dawg gave her a quick salute and dropped the volume a touch so we could hear ourselves think.

'Thanks. Okay. Clive, are you ready?' Anna tried to concentrate less on the make-up sliding down her face and more on the task at hand. Clive nodded and heaved his camera in her direction as we formed a semi-circle around her, all of us eagerly anticipating what today's task would be.

'So, guys, we are now in the impressive Death Valley where we want you to try your hand at sandboarding!' She paused with a manic expression on her face, waiting for our reactions. I'd never been skiing or snowboarding and had the balance of a drunk trying to walk in a straight line but I was actually excited about this task. It couldn't be so hard, could it? The general consensus amongst the others seemed to mirror my enthusiasm. 'The challenge is simple. All you have to do is trek to the top then come down in the quickest time, and the couple with the fastest combined speed will win! So, Dwayne, I mean, D-Dawg will run through the practicalities and hand you all a board. Good luck!'

She clapped and then retreated to the jeep to grab a bottle of water and wipe the dripping foundation from her flushed cheeks.

'You confident on this one?' Ben asked me, with his hands on his hips peering up at the giant peak we had to both scale and soar down. I followed his gaze and felt my stomach do a funny flip. It was so high.

'Course,' I said, lying slightly.

I was spared from hearing Ben's tactics that he had begun explaining to me as D-Dawg told us we had to head up the 2,400-metre-high dune in this never subsiding heat, before cranking up his music once more and leading the way. It was a real slog, trying to find your footing in the steep hot sand, and each heavy step felt like ten. But the heart-clenching hike to the summit was completely worth it when you took in the full beauty of Death Valley. Not a living soul for miles. The sheer isolation and natural beauty of this place was simply breathtaking. Not that I could seem to catch my breath after scrambling up here, and taking one look down to the valley below where I could spot D-Dawg's converted jeep as a tiny spec didn't help. I suddenly realised that what goes up must come down.

Walking further along the precarious ridge, D-Dawg handed us each a plank of wood to strap our boots into and made sure we covered the base in wax so we would 'glide 'n' ride' the whole way down. We each took our start positions. I foolishly peered over the edge and within a millisecond my body clenched in terror at the sheer drop below.

'Oh, my holy everything!' Simon whimpered under his breath. Dawn had her jaw clenched and was blinking back tears, but refused to let her tough woman façade slip.

'Bloody hell! This is going to be epic,' Tony cheered along with Ben who high-fived him. Natalia shook her head laughing at the pair of them and seemed utterly chilled herself. I was shitting myself, and it appeared Gareth and Jade felt the same way. I'd never heard the pair of them be so quiet.

'Guys, remember you can use your bums to brake if it gets too fast! Okay, on three, two, one – GO!' Dwayne screamed.

I yelped and somehow managed to go against my natural instincts and push myself off the ridge, desperately trying to keep my balance with the subtle movements of leaning forwards and backwards.

I quickly started picking up speed, sand was blasting at my face, my adrenaline was pumping, and my breath caught in my throat as the sand dune became one dusty blur. I couldn't even focus on how the others were doing or where I was in the running. Then I don't know what happened but I lost my balance and began to tumble, my body crumbled from the strong form that D-Dawg had taught us into this flailing mess as the world rushed past, sand flew up my nose, down my ears and into my mouth that was open wide and screaming in fear.

I don't know how but somehow I got back on track and although I wasn't standing any more – more hunched in this uncomfortable squat position – I was still flying down the slope. I landed in a crumpled heap in an explosion of dust at the bottom of the valley feeling my body ache all over. I ripped my feet out of the straps of the board and wobbled to stand up. That's when I realised I was the first one to land!

Clive instantly raced over to me and began flicking his lens between my wind-whipped and sand-blasted shocked face, to the others sailing down the side of the dune. I could just make out Ben's T-shirt and dark hair. He seemed to be neck and neck with someone who could have been Gareth, judging by the bright yellow shorts that were flying down the side.

'Come on, Ben, come on!' I willed, and began bouncing on the spot, instantly forgetting the ride of terror I'd just been on and the super fine sand that had gathered in all exposed crevices, and that I'd be washing out for the next few days.

'Arghhhh!!' A girlish squeal pulled my attention from urging Ben on. Jade had appeared behind me; she had obviously gone slightly off-piste judging by her tangled hair and the look of absolute terror on her smudged face.

'Never, ever, ever again am I doing that!' she yelled and threw her board as far as it would go, but because she had the upper body strength of a newborn baby it pathetically bounced and then slid to a stop.

Anna had composed herself, reapplied her make-up and was by our side within moments. 'And it looks like we are now neck and neck to find out which couple will win this challenge. With Georgia and Jade making it down in record time we need their partners not to let the side down and reach the finish line,' she said breathlessly to the camera.

Now my feet were firmly back on solid ground I was staring up at Ben and realising just how scary and dangerous this was. The sand dune was more of a sheer drop than a pillowy, welcoming slope. I bit my lip and crossed everything that he would make it down in one piece. I was worried for his safety but I knew how annoyed he would be if Gareth beat him, especially when they were so close.

'Come on, Ben!' I screamed. He appeared to be in control of his board and was whizzing down, making it look so easy, not the death trap that I knew it really was. Gareth, on the other hand, looked like he was following my style of kamikaze tumbles. The others were slowly making their way down behind them, stopping and starting, pushing themselves off their bums and adding more wax to get some friction.

'And we have the next contestant down the dune… It's…it's…Gareth!' Anna said excitedly as Jade broke into a high-pitched squeal. Moments later Ben effortlessly glided to a halt with an extremely pissed look on his sandy face at being so close to winning.

He unstrapped his feet and shook Gareth's hand. 'You did well there, mate, thought I almost had you.'

Gareth looked slightly shell-shocked but tried to pull himself together. 'Yeah, yeah. You too.'

'Congrats, guys! You're today's winners,' Anna said to Gareth and Jade as Ben placed a hot arm around my waist.

'Sorry, babe, I tried my best. You were freaking amazing though!' He kissed my forehead before shaking his head at these extreme sports skills I'd apparently been hiding from him.

'I have no idea how I made it down in one piece,' I said, still feeling a little shaky from the adrenaline pumping through my body. 'Don't worry, we're all equal now. That prize money could still be ours,' I offered as he shrugged, mentally berating himself for letting the team down.

Eventually the others all made it down safely and were greeted with Gareth and Jade's immodest victory dance and 'in your face' jibes. He looked as smug as a middle-class mum picking up the last box of organic baby food in Waitrose. Dawn had her fists clenched to her sides to stop herself from either punching Jade's smug face or punching Simon as they were the only couple who hadn't won a single task yet.

'Who wants to go again?' D-Dawg yelled. No one replied. I was exhausted and couldn't face the thought of doing all that again. 'Right then, let's head to the next stop on D-Dawg's magical mystery road trip!'

I let out a deep sigh and hoped it wouldn't involve any more near-death experiences.

CHAPTER 16

Colligate (v.) – To bind, unite or group together

We didn't have long to wait until the drama kicked off again. We had left the sandboarding site with everyone in surprisingly high spirits and were racing across uneven rocks at full speed. D-Dawg was blatantly loving making the women scream as he soared over high mounds. I swear I saw him licking his lips at Jade's breasts that jiggled over every bump in his rear-view mirror. Then, out of nowhere and with a noisy bang D-Dawg's jeep spluttered to a stop.

'Uh-oh,' he muttered.

'Uh-oh? What do you mean, uh-oh?' A prickly sensation shot down my spine as I looked around at where we were. There wasn't a living thing as far as the eye could see. I glanced over my shoulder at the back of the truck but everyone else appeared oblivious to our situation as they chatted away and took selfies of each other's sand-blasted faces.

Dwayne was twisting the key in the ignition with as much force as he could without it snapping.

'Dwayne...have we broken down?' I asked, terrified of the answer he was going to give.

He turned to face me. His previous grin had blown away into a pale and pinched frown. 'Ah. Well.' He scratched his head bashfully. 'Yeah, it looks that way.'

'What?' I hissed. 'We are in the middle of the flipping desert and we've broken down!'

Okay, maybe I hadn't said this as quietly as I thought I had.

'What's going on?' Tony shouted from the back.

'Everything okay, Georgia?' Ben called.

I glanced at Dwayne who had leapt out of the driver's seat and was struggling to get the bonnet open. 'I think we've broken down.'

'Whaaaaaat?' Cries rang from the back of the truck mimicking my own shocked outburst. Clive had put his camera down and was wiping a sheen of sweat from his face with his T-shirt, Jade thirstily chugged on a bottle of water, Gareth wrung his hands together, and Anna's face had paled under all her make-up.

Ben and Tony were the only ones to instantly jump down onto the rocky ground and race over to help Dwayne figure out the problem. I nervously bit my fingernails as we waited for their verdict.

'Oh my God, we're screwed. We're going to die!' Jade wailed, unable to keep a lid on her emotions. Although we were probably all thinking the same thing, this wasn't helping.

'Shut up,' Dawn hissed as she fanned her flushed cheeks.

'I won't shut up! Look around! There ain't nobody for miles. Oh my God this is a disaster. I never even got to own a pug puppy or pass my driving test.' Jade continued to cry before shoving her head in Gareth's chest looking for some form of comfort. He awkwardly patted her skinny back that was shaking with the heavy sobs.

'I'd try and calm down if I were you. We probably don't have that much water left and you'll only make yourself even more dehydrated,' Natalia whispered.

I spotted Anna nudge Clive and hiss that he needed to be capturing all of this on camera. A nervous-looking Clive nodded, wiped his sweating hands on his shorts and started filming once more.

'The guys will sort out the problem, won't they?' Gareth asked, suddenly looking like he wished he'd spent less time studying marketing crap and more time at the university of life getting his hands dirty so he could help the real men out.

'Tony is a total petrol head, he'll sort it,' Natalia said with a confident wave of her hand.

'How about Ben? Does he know anything about cars?' Gareth asked, as the others fixed their eyes on me. I didn't have a bloody clue. Is this the sort of thing girlfriends should know about? I let out a stupidly simpering tinkle of a laugh.

'Err, yeah, course, he's...erm...very handy, always fixing things with his...erm...hands...' I trailed off. How did I not know if he knew his way around the workings of a motor vehicle? I hoped he was better with an engine than a measuring tape.

'Any luck?' I called out to the huddle of Dwayne, Ben, Tony, and Simon who admittedly appeared to be more of a spare part floundering in the background.

Ben shot me a look that said 'we're in trouble', and wiped his face leaving a smear of oil across his cheeks. 'Still trying to figure it out,' he said in a measured voice that I'd only heard once before when he hadn't wanted to stress Kelli out with those problems we'd had with Serena, the con artist ex-employee who had shafted us big time last year.

Tony was waist-deep in the bonnet and was calling out things to Dwayne who was lying under the car. It was really starting to heat up now. Without the motion of the car the winds that had cooled us down as we sailed through the sandy desert had dropped off. It was like sticking your head in an oven. My mouth was parched and the sweat dried off me before it could form a single droplet, leaving a sticky, salty residue. My skin felt too tight and warm to the touch. I was desperate to gulp at the half empty bottle of water at my feet but with no way of knowing how much longer until the men fixed the problem, we needed to ration things.

'How the hell are we going to get out of here?' Jade said, through heaving sobs, clinging more tightly to Gareth.

'Now, now, babe, I'm sure it won't be much longer,' he murmured, frowning at Clive and his camera who was circling the lone jeep like a vulture trying to get all the best shots of this drama.

'Ah, got it!' Tony shouted, making us all look up in anticipation. 'The bloody spinder has slipped off.'

Dwayne pulled himself back to his feet and peered at where a scowling Tony was pointing. 'Oh,' he mumbled in embarrassment.

'This should never have got loose enough for it to come off. Don't you get these things regularly checked over?' Tony asked, looking like he wanted to either thump Dwayne or whack him in the face with whatever a spinder was.

Dwayne looked sheepish and pulled his mobile phone out. 'Well, it's not actually part of my job to get the vehicles tested.' Tony's face turned a darker shade of puce. 'But, I'll get on the phone to the lads at the office now and see what they can do.'

'*What they can do?*' Tony echoed in shock. 'We're miles away out here and unless we find shade, like pronto, we're all going to be cooked like burgers on a BBQ. We need to fix this now,' he seethed.

'What can we do?' D-Dawg asked pathetically.

'We just need something to hook it out of the gap it's fallen down into and screw it back on, but there's no chance we'll get it by just using our fingers,' Ben said, stepping between the two men and the rising testosterone levels. 'That hole is way too tight.'

'That's what she said,' Gareth piped up, then immediately looked like he wished he'd kept his mouth shut at the way Tony squared up to him.

'Not the time, Gareth mate,' Ben said through gritted teeth, trying to keep his cool. 'Have we got anything we can use to grab it?'

D-Dawg shook his head. The Crocodile Dundee bravado had puddled out of him. Now he was just plain Dwayne from London hoping not to get his lights punched out by an angry Italian.

Just then a thought struck me.

'Wait – I know! What about a wire, like the under wiring of a bra? We could twist them together to create a hook?' I offered.

Ben shook his head in astonishment and then flashed me a smile. 'Perfect.'

I turned round to the others, pleased to have something to do to help get us out of this situation. 'Right, girls, do you remember the *Friends* episode when they're locked out of the car on their way to a ski trip?' I asked excitedly. Looking at the blank faces in front of me, they must have missed this episode. 'Well, not to worry. The thing is they use the under wiring of their bras to force open a lock and I guess this could work in the same way.' I knew all those hours spent watching and rewatching the Central Perk crew would come in handy one day. 'So, we need to pull out the wire from our bras and fasten them together.'

'You what?' Jade sprang up from crying on Gareth's chest.

'We can use the under wiring from our bras,' I repeated, unclasping mine from under my top.

Natalia was already unhooking hers and pulling it out of her sleeve in one swift movement; Anna had turned her back to the car to take hers off and shouted at Clive to not even think about filming this part; Dawn who had remained surprisingly quiet throughout this whole experience duly followed orders, but Jade had folded her arms across her perky chest and flat out refused.

'This is a Victoria's Secret Angels limited collection bra. There ain't no way I'm hacking it to pieces.'

'There is if it means we can get out of here,' Gareth growled making Jade jump. 'Now take it off.'

Jade stared him out for a few seconds until she let out a dramatic sigh and rummaged under her top to take it off. 'Fine, but you owe me a new one!'

'Fine.' Gareth nodded and ripped the seam with his teeth to pull out the wire, making Jade yelp at the sight of her extremely padded bra being defaced in such a heartless way. 'Got it! Here you go.'

I grabbed the collection of wires and handed them to Ben. Using the base of his heel he bent the edge of one over another to create a long and strange-shaped stick to hook the missing part up.

'Here we go,' he said, sticking his tongue to one side of his mouth and inching the wire into the bonnet; sweat was sliding down his cheeks. Dwayne and Simon peered in as intently as if there was a naked woman inside. Tony said a quick prayer in Italian and began kissing his collection of rings and looking up at the blazing sun beating down on us.

Please work, please work, please work.

'Gah,' Ben sighed, loudly banging a fist against the metal of the car. 'I almost had it.'

God, this was worse than waiting to find out who was being voted off *The X Factor*. No one spoke.

'Easy does it, mate, easy...' Tony said supportively, with his fist pressed to his mouth, nervously peering over Ben's shoulder. All we could do was wait and hope he was some kind of secret hook-a-duck champion. It wasn't beyond the realms of possibility. After all, I'd discovered there was a lot I didn't know about him.

'Bingo!' he eventually yelled, pulling the mashed-up wire back up. 'Quick, Dwayne, try the ignition again,' he panted, wiping his face that was wet with sweat.

Dwayne jumped into the driving seat and did as he was told. Within moments the engine purred to life, which was quickly drowned out by all of us whooping and cheering.

'We're saved! Thank God, we're saved!' Jade's celebration made her loose breasts jiggle alarmingly.

'Right, let's get going quick. We need to head to the nearest town as I'm not sure how long that's going to hold,' Ben called out as Tony slammed the bonnet shut and jumped in the back.

Ben took my hand and kissed it as he ran past to get in. I smiled at him in awe. My hero. I felt this strange rush inside of me. I loved him so much at that moment. I suddenly thought about the beautiful engagement ring probably waiting back at the hotel in his bag, at how foolish I'd been in questioning whether I wanted to marry this incredible man when he was exactly the type of husband any girl would be lucky to call her own. Of course I wanted to become Mrs Stevens. Hell, at this precise moment he could probably tell me we would be expanding Lonely Hearts to London, Paris and New York and I'd be on board with the idea.

It dawned on me that maybe my fears over expanding the business were linked to my doubts over getting married. Change can be scary but right now all those worries and what ifs had vanished as I beamed at him and marvelled at how he had handled this pretty terrifying moment in such a cool, collected way.

'I never knew you knew about cars,' I said in disbelief, turning round in my seat, not giving a crap about the spine-shattering bumps that Dwayne was ragging the jeep over in his bid to get us away from here.

Ben shrugged bashfully and gulped at the rest of the water I'd saved. 'Learnt it all from my dad.'

I smiled at him and shook my head trying to imagine his alcoholic-chain-smoking-gambling father hunched over the bonnet of a banged up car giving a young fresh-faced Ben lessons on how to get the motor running.

'Well, remind me to thank him next time I see him,' I said.

'Next time?' He raised an eyebrow. A look of surprise and genuine amazement crossed Ben's face. Did he actually think I'd not want to see his dad again just because of some slightly awkward – okay, really fucking awkward – first meeting?

'Of course, next time.' I smiled back at him. *Probably that next time would be at our wedding!* I wanted to add but instead I turned back around in my seat and smiled to myself.

CHAPTER 17

Sidereal (adj.) – Measured by the apparent motion of the stars

'You were amazing yesterday; you know that?' Ben said for the third time today as he raised my hand and held it up to his lips.

I blushed. '*You* were the amazing one. I knew you were calm under pressure but that was still so bloody impressive.'

Our brush with death had been the only thing anyone could talk about since arriving back to civilisation. Jade had been embellishing the tale of our dramatic desert disaster, like a confused version of Chinese Whispers, even though we'd all been there with her at the time.

'I swear when I saw that eagle soaring nearby, oh no wait, it was definitely a vulture. Defo. Anyway, I thought to meself that's it we're done for.' She'd nodded sagely before going on about her ruined bra.

Rationally, I knew we probably would have been okay, but the whole drama had reinforced just how incredible Ben was under pressure, how well we worked together in a crisis and basically how he was the type of person you wanted by your side. I'd been thinking more and more about our impending nuptials, convincing myself that he would pop the question any moment now, and how I was so ready for it.

I mean, to marry Ben would just further cement what we were working on building together. A business, a future, life goals and even a mini empire with my best friend and lover. Why wouldn't I want that? We had been through enough challenges already on this trip – some intentional, some less so – and it just proved how even in tough times we could laugh about it and grow stronger from it.

I glanced over at the face I already knew so well, realising that this was the face I wanted to look at every day for the rest of my life, and smiled to myself. This trip really was the best idea for us. I kept thinking about something Shelley had said, that the older you get the less time you have to wait and mess around, when you know you're onto something good then why wouldn't you just act on it? Maybe it was still early days in my relationship with Ben but we weren't kids in our early twenties, and as Marie liked to remind me, my biological clock was ticking. Here was an amazing man offering to choose me over any other woman in the world. I'd be a fool not to reciprocate this.

Once I knew the plan for this evening's filming, I was even more convinced that tonight would be the night. We were going to watch the most dramatic sunset in the world, as Tony had read from his guidebook, and tomorrow I'd be posting photos on Facebook with the stunning diamond ring on my hand, sharing the news with our family and friends, I just knew it. I hugged myself with glee.

This conviction was further reinforced by the day's filming. At lunch Anna had asked us all to congregate in one of the restaurants lining the pretty town bandstand in the centre of a tree-lined square, so Clive could get some natural shots of us enjoying our food. The topic of conversation had quickly moved on to how we all made our relationships work whilst running businesses together, something I was keen to hear about from the other couples.

'I do think it's amazing that you spend so much time with each other without wanting to strangle your partner,' Anna had said, shaking her head at the thought.

'When you're in love you don't want to be apart,' Tony murmured gently kissing Natalia's cheek before topping up their glasses of red wine.

I saw Dawn roll her eyes at their constant PDAs. 'But it's also about compromise and having boundaries.'

'What do you mean?' Anna asked tucking into her barbecued beef steak.

'Well, take Simon and me as an example. We have been married for nearly twenty years, so I can tell you that it takes a lot of bloody hard work, and I'm not just talking about my business, sorry, *our* business with Last Call.'

I tried not to catch Ben's eye. There was no way I wanted us to end up like those two in twenty years' time. I was actually surprised at how open and honest Dawn was being as she began explaining about the sacrifices they'd both made – well apparently mainly her, as by the sounds of it, she had become a martyr in a bid to make a success of her new business. Simon just nodded along blandly.

Natalia leant forward. 'We too have had some problems.'

I clocked Anna nodding at Clive to focus his lens on the pretty Italian. 'Oh, please share. I really think we could all learn from this.'

Natalia took a deep breath and glanced at Tony as if getting his approval to reveal all. He nodded his shiny black head and took a large gulp of his wine, quickly topping his glass back up.

'Well, like every business we had some money troubles at first. I mean it is totally common but when you're starting out and have no idea how it all works it can be quite scary being threatened with ever-growing bills and invoices with plenty of zeros on them.'

I nodded along with her. As well as Lonely Hearts was doing, this was the very reason I was so nervous about expanding faster than we were ready for. The move to London would cost a hell of a lot of money and pretty much strip our bank balance back to where it had been at the beginning. Something that didn't seem to worry Ben as much as it did me.

'So, how did you resolve this?' Anna asked.

'We…well, we remortgaged our home, begged, borrowed and practically stole from family members until we could get on our feet. It was pretty scary though.' Natalia winced at the memory. Tony remained silent. 'I am so happy that we made it through and now Vineopolis is doing better than ever, but at times it was pretty hairy.'

'But it was at these times when you discovered just how well you work together. Literally sink or swim, I guess?' Ben asked.

Natalia nodded. 'Exactly.' She placed her slim tanned arm over Tony's hunched shoulders. 'Sometimes you need to go through the dark days to come out on the other side and realise how bright the light can be. I guess if you can't work with the person you love then who can you work with? I've had enough nightmare bosses to realise that even during the hard times it is so much better than working with people you hate.'

'I'll drink to that!' Gareth raised his bottle of lager. I still hadn't figured out exactly how he and Jade worked together; so far it seemed that she was just freeloading on his success, acting as this trophy girlfriend, success that I couldn't quite understand from his wanky jargon-filled job title.

'Georgia, what advice would you give?' Anna asked, turning the attention of the table over to me.

I thought about it for a minute. 'I guess I agree with Dawn.' I noticed Dawn do a double take as I said this. 'It is about setting boundaries and trying to leave work in the office, as hard as that can be. This is something we're working on.' I let out a tinkle of a laugh.

Ben grinned and nodded along. 'It's also about playing to your strengths, for example Georgia here is a natural with the customers, helping them to grow in confidence to book a trip with us, knowing that travel will help heal their broken heart.'

'Whereas Ben is more suited to number crunching and charming clients.' I smiled at him, spotting a strange look flash across his face at this. 'It's true, you do!'

The way Ben nodded his head I wasn't sure if he was being bashful or if there was something more he wasn't letting on.

'Good on you, mate. Money, finances, investment, whatever you want to call it, isn't easy,' Tony mumbled into his glass.

'That's why I take control of all our assets, don't I, Simon?' Dawn piped up. 'None of this crap about worrying about the man's bruised ego if he doesn't provide the hard cash for the business, or acts the breadwinner. None of that matters if you're focused on the task in hand.'

I noticed Tony grumble under his breath and Natalia self-consciously rubbing his rigid arms. Was this how Ben felt at me putting my foot down over investment opportunities? That he felt threatened that I'd crushed his alpha male persona? I hadn't even thought about it like that. Judging by the way Tony was silently brooding in the corner, reminiscing over how he'd failed to provide for Natalia and keep their business afloat in the early days, I may have stumbled across the real reason Ben was so adamant about making the London move happen – to prove himself and his worth in this partnership. I had to speak up.

'Things are different nowadays; men aren't expected to do the heavy lifting while their wife sits at home. You can work together for the same end goal, no matter which way you go about getting there,' I said, taking Ben's hand that had been gripping his glass. 'As long as you're both on the same page and having fun with it, then that's all that matters.'

'Well, this cash prize would certainly help!' Gareth piped up.

The others laughed and nodded in agreement before the conversation turned to the food we were eating, the weather report for the next few days and what the next challenge could be.

*

We'd been driven out to Valle de la Luna, or Valley of the Moon, which lived up to its dramatic name. The lunar-like landscape of this rocky valley made it feel like we were extras on a science fiction film set. It was crowned on all sides by jagged peaks and bizarrely shaped rocks eroded over time by fierce desert winds as far as you could see. The other-worldly look and complete silence of this place was beyond eerie. Even more surreal were the peaks of the Andes visible in the background, as if someone had deliberately designed a huge backdrop for this space-themed production. The harsh and uninhabitable terrain was exactly what I'd imagine walking on the surface of the moon to feel like, as dried out salt lakes had left a greyish crust on the uneven ground. It was spectacular, and a stunning place for a proposal.

'Did you know that those volcanos are nineteen thousand feet tall, and that this inhospitable terrain is the driest place on earth?' Simon explained animatedly. 'Parts of this desert haven't had a single drop of rain in over a hundred years because it evaporates long before it even reaches the ground.' He was in his element, going on to tell us how NASA tested space probes out here because the conditions mimic those on Mars.

'I assume you all know that at the most basic form, humans are made up of the same matter and complex cells as everything around us, from the sand in the deserts to the sun in the sky. So, technically, when we observe the universe we are observing ourselves.' His face became boyish as he smiled. 'Cosmology is a branch of physics and astrophysics that studies the evolution of the universe. It is all truly fascinating stuff and I don't know why you find this so hilarious, Jade.'

For once he didn't have to stop to check with Dawn if he could continue and revelled in having the whole group's attention trained on him. It turned out that both Gareth and Dawn had been struck down with heatstroke after all of us had baked in the desert yesterday. I realised that Simon hadn't complained that his wife was bedridden and missing out on this; instead he looked positively pumped up for the ride out to the desert without being constantly nagged.

'Go on, Dr Boffin, tell us more,' Jade sniggered and looked at D-Dawg who didn't have a clue what was going on.

Simon wasn't sure whether to be insulted or buoyed with confidence. He chose the latter. 'I've always had an interest in space, which started in astronomy when I was younger, and has since developed into a keen hobby of mine. I want to develop my knowledge as much as I possibly can.'

He was probably the most intelligent man I'd ever met, which begged the question what was he doing being some sort of lapdog manservant to Dawn all the time?

'I ain't got a frigging clue what you're on about, man, but you carry on!' Jade cackled, not doing her bit in helping blondes the world over move away from the Barbie bimbo airhead reputation they've been lumped with for so long.

I prepared myself for Gareth to add in some lewd comment about probes or looking at Uranus, forgetting that he'd stayed back at the guest house. It was strange as both he and Dawn had seemed their usual selves at lunch.

D-Dawg had driven us over the rocky paths to a high vantage point, promising us the best views for nature's nightly show. I was already shivering in the thin cotton pale pink dress I'd eventually decided on wearing, as it seemed to be the most 'bridal' look I'd brought with me to Chile. I'd spent longer than normal doing my hair although now the desert wind was picking up I wished I'd gone for a classic ballerina bun rather than the half up-half down style that was whipping my cheeks. I hoped that my eye make-up would remain in place for the big moment and had even borrowed a thick waterproof mascara from Jade's well-stocked make-up bag, without telling her why of course. She'd seemed a little crushed when I'd politely turned down her offer of us having matching makeovers and ignored the look she gave me when I declined her offer of heavy bronzer and sparkling glitter eyeshadow.

'Is this another challenge?' Ben asked Anna.

'No, tonight is just about watching one of the most famous and romantic sunsets in the world,' she said flashing a bright smile at my boyfriend.

'Ah, okay.' With that Ben seemed to relax a little. He hadn't commented on my more polished look but I put that down to nerves about popping the question. I wanted to whisper that he didn't need to worry, I was ready to say yes, but couldn't ruin the speech he must be rehearsing in his mind, ready for the big moment.

I didn't know if this was an extra special treat or an apology for yesterday's desert drama but D-Dawg had gone all out with the evening's preparations, including laying out handcrafted Chilean woollen blankets on the hard ground and setting out a pre-packed picnic hamper. Well, it was a bottle of cheap fizz, some plastic cups and a bag of cheesy puffs for each couple. But still, it was the thought that counted.

Dwayne then quickly made sure that the blanket he'd reserved for Jade was sufficiently comfortable with an extra inflatable neck pillow he'd picked up from under one of the jeep seats. Anna sat with Simon who was still giving a detailed rundown on the type of testing that it was believed NASA had done here; Natalia and Tony chose the rug at the far end and despite rolling their eyes at the cheap champers, they were soon entwined around each other and giggling like teens dry humping before their parents returned home. Clive was buzzing around everyone looking torn between setting up arty sunset shots and wanting to capture this attractive couple making out, possibly to add to his home movie collection.

Ben and I took the last spare blanket.

'Come here, you.' He pulled me to sit in front of him between his legs as he wrapped his arms round my waist. I leant my head back against his chest feeling the relaxing thrum of his heartbeat – was it beating faster than usual? – and looked out at the dramatic landscape ahead of us.

'Beats spooning on the sofa watching Netflix, huh?' His breath tickled my ear as he laughed softly. 'Give me this over *Game of Thrones* any day.'

As the sun streaked across the increasingly twilit sky, the mountain peaks seemed to be alight, glowing with the fierceness of flaming embers before settling down to a warming soft blush pink. A respectful silence descended on the group as we watched the kaleidoscope of colours and shadows forming on the craggy volcanic peaks.

I nuzzled closer into Ben's broad chest and watched as the sun slowly set. My breathing calmed, my smile grew and this overriding sense of peace and happiness spread over me, like the same warming and comforting sensation I used to feel as a kid in the winter lying tucked up in bed with a hot water bottle. This was perfect. I wanted to savour every moment of the sun going to sleep as the sky changed with an array of dramatic spectacular colours. The reds, golds and oranges were as bright and vivid as the paint I'd thrown around at the Holi festival in India.

How lucky were we to get to experience this in our lifetime? I felt incredibly hashtag blessed. This was surely going to be a moment I'd savour for ever. Although, as each second passed I was feeling more and more confused about when Ben would utter the words he must be running through in his mind. Was he nervous? Was he changing his mind? I turned my head to look him in the eye and smile encouragingly, but he remained silent.

In all of the loveliness I barely registered Clive creeping past getting low on his haunches to capture these intimate shots. I imagined that they would use this scene of us all, well most of us, wrapped in the arms of our loved ones wearing a soppy grin surrounded by such an intense backdrop in the opening credits to the show.

It would be our turn for the one-on-one interviews tomorrow and I was desperate to know the sorts of questions we were going to be asked. They'd probably focus on our soon-to-take-place engagement, and plans for the wedding. Anna had instructed us all at breakfast that there was to be no conferring between those who had already been filmed as we needed to keep our answers fresh, which made me think it would just be a set of generic questions they asked each couple. No biggie. Hopefully.

The night sky drew in, slowly at first, and then the fiery ball of the sun seemed to disappear in an instant. Without the light pollution we were used to back home it felt like you had telescopic eyesight as the pale mist of the Milky

Way shone against the cloudless desert sky. Stars gleamed against the inky indigo blanket above our heads. I had never felt so tiny and humbled by nature's beauty before, like I did now. It all made sense suddenly: this must be what Ben had been waiting for.

'God, I still can't believe that we're really here,' I mused, entwining my fingers between Ben's so I couldn't tell where I ended and where he began. 'I mean, if you'd have told me I'd be sat on a blanket in a desert in Chile watching this jaw-dropping sunset with you a year ago, I'd never have believed you.'

Ben laughed softly in agreement. 'I know. We've come a long way, you and I, haven't we?'

'From the Blue Butterfly to this… I still have to pinch myself,' I admitted.

'Yeah, who knew that fit girl in a bikini would be lying in my arms on the other side of the world all this time later? You know I don't believe in fate and all that nonsense but there were a fair few coincidences in bringing us together.' He smiled and squeezed me tighter.

'You can say that again. What if I'd never gone travelling, or never left that nightmare tour group to head to Blue Butterfly?'

'What if I'd met Jimmy in another country, rather than being on the exact same Thai island, at the exact time as you?' He shook his head trying to understand the millions of ways our paths may never have crossed. Something I couldn't even bear to think about.

Hearing him reminisce about the two strangers we had once been compared to how we now knew each other inside and out, my heart floated with happiness. I suddenly didn't care about why he'd met his ex without telling me, why he'd not mentioned Jimmy and Shelley leaving to me, or that we weren't quite on the same page with the London expansion. All those things would get ironed out in time. Travel gave you a fresh perspective on things; the niggles and anxieties back home just didn't seem as important out here. Right now it was about us, the people we had become, and how amazing we were together.

'So, what do you think it's all about then?' Ben whispered in my ear, sending even more goosebumps across my body.

'What do you mean? Us meeting?'

'Well that, but also this.' He raised my palm to the heavens. 'Our purpose of being here, this short time we have on this planet in this vast spectacular universe.'

'God.' I laughed. 'That's getting a little deep, isn't it? You're starting to sound like Simon, going on about the wonders of the solar system!'

'If there's a time to get deep and meaningful then it's here, surely?' He smiled bashfully.

I shifted slightly and pulled back to stare at him. The bright light of the stars illuminated his face with a soft white glow. I wondered if Instagram had a starlit filter. It would kick Amaro and X-Pro's ass.

'I think your head could explode if you think too hard about things like this, about how it all came about, what's our purpose and what happens when we're gone.' I took a deep breath. 'I guess all you can do is be grateful for what you have and make the most of the time you do have here. Whether that's by savouring and taking mental photographs of big moments like this, or just recognising and appreciating the small things in life.' I shrugged as he brushed a fallen strand of hair from my face.

He nodded slowly, thinking about what I'd said. 'I think you're exactly right. It's the small things, the moments that make up life that so many people ignore or undervalue. It's also about being with people who make you happy during these big and little moments…' He paused. 'So…'

Oh my God! This was it. The big proposal. In the walk down memory lane I'd almost forgotten the real reason we were here.

'Yes?' I whispered, not taking my eyes off his face. My heart was beating so loud I thought it would echo off the mountains. He was staring at me so intently. His lips were poised to say something, something super important. My mouth went dry, my breath caught in my throat, my whole body clenched in anticipation of the line he was going to utter next. Shit, I needed to remain poised and collected but I was so excited to hear the words that would change everything and take us to that next level. I was ready. I was so ready.

But he was cut off from finishing this sentence as the moment was shattered by Natalia's high-pitched squealing.

'SHE SAID YES!!' Tony cried with joy.

What the? I flicked my head to the Italian couple.

'She said yes!' Tony repeated standing up and punching the air Rocky style. 'We're getting married!'

The previously calm stargazing set-up became a hive of activity as everyone got to their feet to congratulate the newly engaged couple. Anna was beside herself with excitement, probably thinking this would make TV gold. Natalia was sobbing tears of happiness, Jade was acting as the unofficial engagement photographer and Simon was looking on, bemused.

'Noooo!' Everyone turned to look at me. I hadn't realised that I'd let that slip from my mouth. 'I mean, noooo way! Congrats, guys.' I blushed, heaving myself up to hug them both.

I glanced at Ben who was shaking Tony's hand and giving Natalia a kiss on the cheek. He seemed genuinely pleased for them and not the least bit annoyed that they'd ruined what should have been our moment. I couldn't help thinking, *What about my proposal? It should have been me!* Inside, Ben must have been crushed that he had been pipped at the post. I knew I was.

Finally, the excitement died down as Natalia and Tony were snogging each other's faces off, blatantly wanting us all to bugger off so they could do the no pants dance to really celebrate their news. I resettled myself on the woven rug, trying to get comfy leaning against Ben once more, although his frame seemed more rigid than before.

'You looked like you were going to say something, earlier?' I asked him, innocently, silently seething that our moment had been overshadowed.

He shook his head distractedly. 'It doesn't matter, some other time, hey.' He pressed his lips heavily against my crown. The heaviness I felt in my heart increased when Anna called out that it was time to head back to celebrate this exciting news. With Ben getting to his feet and picking up our blanket came the brutal realisation that our chance of joining the newly engaged crew had faded as fast as the setting sun.

As the daylight vanished so did the desert heat, and I found myself shivering under the darkening sky. I wasn't sure if it was the drop in temperature or going back to base camp without the ring on my finger that was making me feel so cold.

CHAPTER 18

Declension (n.) – A falling off or away; deterioration

'I'll catch you up!' I called out to Ben and the others as they wandered into a lively small bar back in the town centre. 'Just want to go and put my camera on charge – I think I drained the battery with all the star photos.'

'I'll come with you and see how Dawn's doing,' Simon said pulling himself up, looking like it took all the effort in the world. Jade hadn't mentioned her boyfriend's name once after D-Dawg's blatantly obvious attempts at getting into her knickers.

'I can check on them, if you want? I'm sure they're probably fast asleep and it's not fair for you to miss the chance to let your hair down,' I suggested, smiling at how Simon's face lit up.

'You sure?'

'Course. Grab us a drink though?'

'First round is on Si then?' Ben laughed, turning round to kiss me. 'Don't be too long.'

I gave him the Brownie Guide salute and rushed off, leaving the newly engaged couple and the rest of the group to toast their happy news. Truth be told I wasn't bothered about charging my camera; I just needed a moment alone to compose myself after such a crushing disappointment.

I felt guilty at being such a miserable cow when I was genuinely pleased for Natalia and Tony. Although I didn't know them very well, they seemed great together. I was just sulking that it wasn't Ben and me clinking our champagne flutes together and examining the beautiful ring. I almost wanted to laugh at the silliness of the situation. Just a few weeks ago marriage to Ben hadn't even crossed my mind, but after discovering that engagement ring and having time to think about the next step we blatantly should take as a couple, I now knew that I wanted to become Mrs Stevens. I just wondered how long I'd have to wait until the time was right again.

I hurried back to the guesthouse we were staying in and rummaged in my bag for my room key. I was too busy with one hand burrowing in its depths, feeling past empty bottles of water and scrunched up tissue to notice the comings and goings of the other guests around me. Until I heard a giggle that was remarkably like Dawn's – apart from the fact she rarely giggled. I'd said I'd go and check on them, I thought, giving up the search for my key that had probably fallen into a hole in the inner lining of my bag.

I began to make my way to reception to see if they had a spare key to my room and could tell me which room Dawn or Gareth were staying in. Stepping into the open-air courtyard that was filled with hammocks and squishy beanbags, I smiled to myself at the pretty night scene – someone had lit tea lights and strung them in antique teacups hanging from the beams of the mini garden. In the few seconds that I was admiring the décor and lost in slushy thoughts about my boyfriend, the door to the room opposite me opened up and out walked Dawn.

I was just about to raise my hand and call out to see how she was feeling when I noticed that her auburn hair was even more unruly than normal; she was wearing a loose black halter-neck beach dress that hadn't been correctly tied up and her feet were bare. She looked as if she was searching for something or someone.

'Dawn?' I called out. She spun around as if she'd been electrocuted.

'Oh, Georgia, hi!' she said in a strange high-pitched voice as she rushed over to me. 'What…what are you doing here? Are the…um…the others with you?' Her words tumbled out as she glanced around the empty courtyard.

I shook my head. 'No, just me.'

'Ah okay.' She was touching her earlobes, as if massaging earrings that weren't there. 'So, what's up?'

What's up! Now I knew something fishy was going on, either that or the heat had made her delirious.

'Not much. Is everything okay, Dawn?'

Her forehead tightened. There was a hesitation in her voice. 'Oh yep, fine actually. Feeling a lot better now that you mention –'

'Dawn't make me come out there and get you, tiger,' the nasally tones of Gareth bellowed out from somewhere. 'Ha ha, do you geddit? Dawn't as in don't?'

I froze. Was that voice coming from…? No it couldn't be…

I flicked my eyes to Dawn, who was wringing her hands and staring off into the distance, as if she hadn't heard Gareth bellow for sex from one of the rooms. Her face was red and flustered, and I couldn't tell how much was from the sunburn, how much from the shagging, and how much was from the embarrassment at being caught out.

As if to prove my suspicions, a bare-chested Gareth, wearing sagging grey boxer shorts, the elastic almost gone around his paunch of a belly, wandered out of the room Dawn had just come out of as bold as brass. Until he saw me.

'Georgia!' he cried and half leapt back.

Dawn let out a deep sigh and flung her head in her hands.

'What's going on?' I asked, feeling a little burp of sick rise up to my mouth. They weren't poorly at all. Poor Simon, poor Jade.

'Okay, it's not what it looks like!' Dawn pleaded as she barked at Gareth to cover himself up and put some bloody clothes on. He duly obeyed. I could see her chest rising and falling sharply, like a trapped animal looking for a way out.

'Georgia,' she said firmly, then softened her tone and placed a clammy hand on my shoulder, pressing my delicate sunburn and making me flinch. 'Georgia. I don't know what you think you saw, but nothing happened. Gareth was simply coming to check on me.'

Lying bitch. I just gawped at her and pulled back from her grip.

'I wasn't born yesterday, Dawn,' I spat.

I knew Simon was too good for her and now I had the evidence to prove it.

Dawn put her hands up defensively, 'Okay, okay, you're right. But you know what it's like, surely? When you've been with someone a while and they just don't look at you in the same way that they used to? It's only natural for a woman to want to feel desired,' she said, then glanced over at Gareth who had put his T-shirt on the wrong way round and was now struggling to take it off again. I widened my eyes at her. 'Yeah, I know, I know. He's not George Clooney, but when you get to a certain age you take what you can.' She winced.

'You are disgusting. The pair of you.' I turned on my heel, wanting to get out of this sordid sex spot. I knew the pain of being cheated on; Simon was going to be crushed. Jade, to be fair, wasn't as devoted to Gareth – judging by how she had been draped over D-Dawg most of the evening – but still it was below the belt.

'Georgia – wait!' Dawn hollered then hissed at Gareth to zip up his flies and do something.

'Simon adores you; you can do no wrong in his eyes. Maybe you feel the spark has faded but that doesn't make it okay to cheat on him and treat him like this.'

Dawn bristled for a moment then sighed. 'There's a difference between affection and desire. I know he puts me on a pedestal – he has been very good to me – but there isn't any lust left there. I mean we've been married for twenty years for God's sake. You'll soon learn that the lust fizzles out eventually. The animal urge to rip off his clothes has long gone.' She self-consciously glanced over to Gareth and a flicker of embarrassment crossed her flushed face. 'Yes, Simon is a nice man but who wants nice? I can get loyalty and caring from our golden retriever. There's no passion any more, for either of us.'

I thought about how passionate her husband had been as he explained the different star constellations and shook my head. 'But then you work hard to fix things; you don't give up. Simon is a good man who deserves more than this. More than you.'

'Please don't say anything…' She dropped her voice and clasped her hands together. The fiery scowl that I was used to seeing on her face had paled into a desperate plea.

My legs felt wobbly, my head was spinning and the heat from my sunburn was scorching my skin.

'Please, Georgia, it won't happen again,' Gareth added, having finally managed to correctly dress himself. 'Anna and Clive will be really pissed off. Think of the hours of filming they'll have to edit. We could both be kicked out of the competition if you do,' he mumbled and Dawn nodded in agreement.

That was it. The shred of compassion I had, which said I wasn't going to be the one to wreck two relationships by getting involved, vanished as fast as front row seats at a Beyoncé concert. They were more concerned about winning this prize money and how they would come across on the telly than about the feelings of their other halves.

'I won't say anything,' I eventually said through gritted teeth, finding it hard to look at either of them. They both breathed a heavy sigh of relief.

'Cheers, Georgia; see I told you, Dawn, she's not as flaky as you said she was,' Gareth said with a laugh. Dawn flashed an apologetic smile.

'I won't, but you will,' I finished.

'What?' He gawped at me.

'You'll do the right thing and come clean to Simon and Jade. This is a show about relationships surviving the highs and lows of business, not about cheaters abroad.'

'Ah now, let's not be hasty here.' Gareth tried to place a hand on my shoulder before pulling his arm back at the way I growled at him.

'If I were you I'd put some bloody clothes on and think about what you've both done.' I turned on my heel, wanting to get as far away from them as possible.

Practically running back to the bar to meet the others, suddenly desperate for a stiff drink, I tried to process what I'd just witnessed. I knew I couldn't be the bearer of bad news to Simon or Jade, and I couldn't ruin Natalia and Tony's night with this news either. I felt so torn, sick to my stomach and conflicted. But then, I couldn't just sit there drinking with everyone after knowing what had been going on at our accommodation during our stargazing trip.

'Ah, here she is!' Ben got up from his seat to kiss me as I wandered over to the table that was cluttered with glasses and bowls of nuts. 'I was worried you'd been sold for a llama or something.'

I smiled weakly and gratefully took a seat at the end of the table. 'No, you've got me for a little longer,' I joked, knowing my smile didn't quite meet my eyes.

'Good. I hope you're not going anywhere,' Ben said, rubbing my thigh. It looked like the drinks had been free-flowing since I'd left, judging by the alcohol on his breath and his hazy eyes. There wasn't any chance I could tell him what I'd just seen, to ask his advice on what to do, not with him in this merry drunken state.

Someone passed me a glass of champagne that I almost necked in one, although the fizz of the bubbles just tasted bitter in my mouth. I don't know how I did it but I tried to put what had just happened out of my mind and not give anything away. The rest of the group were half cut so I didn't think anyone noticed I was a little quieter than usual and not as involved as they swapped amusing work stories. The alcohol must have been strong as neither Simon nor Jade asked me how their respective partners were.

That evening I held Ben a little tighter in bed and felt grateful for what we had, my disappointment about our thwarted engagement lost in the night's revelations.

CHAPTER 19

Fulsome (adj.) – Excessively flattering or complimentary; effusive

I appeared to be the only one not battling a slight hangover this morning I noticed, as I looked down the long picnic table at the emergency breakfast meeting that we'd been called to. Everyone else was quiet, even Ben was clinging on to his cup of coffee waiting for the caffeine hit to bring him back to life.

I couldn't even look at Dawn and Gareth, as we waited in the dappled sunlight that streaked through the overhanging palm trees. I noticed that Jade had her arms folded over her chest and a seriously pissed off expression on her heavily made-up face. Simon was playing with an unlit tea light, picking at the wax, and seemed to be avoiding everyone's gaze. My stomach did a funny flip. Maybe the terrible twosome had actually come clean about their infidelity after all. I didn't think they actually would, if I was honest.

I sat at the end of the picnic bench and nuzzled up to Ben; he was all warm and sleepy, and I wondered how he was going to take the bombshell that was about to be dropped. Anna stood up and attempted to do her best impression of a sympathetic TV host, when you know they probably don't actually give a shit, as Clive counted her down from three.

'So, as you know, both Dawn and Gareth fell ill yesterday after the desert experience,' Anna said, looking down at her feet for a second before pulling her gaze to the camera lens. Was she willing a tear to appear? 'Unfortunately, Dawn has been to see a doctor this morning and has been advised to pull out of the rest of the filming, which means we are going to lose two wonderful contestants.'

Natalia let out a loud gasp. I clenched my jaw. So they hadn't come clean. Dawn was cowardly heading home rather than risk delivering the truth and coming clean to poor Simon. Quitter. She had obviously made out her 'heatstroke' was worse than it was – amazing given there seemed little sign of any sunburn, unless the burn of shame counted – and Gareth on the other hand had made a miraculous recovery.

'Ben and Georgia, Natalia and Tony, Gareth and Jade.' Anna looked at us in turn. 'We will all continue as planned with our journey down to the south of the country but sadly it is time to say goodbye to two excellent contributors.' Anna dabbed her eye with a tissue that was purely for the camera, then proceeded to gently and awkwardly hug Simon and Dawn. Ben, Natalia and Tony did the same, shaking hands and giving well wishes for Dawn to get better soon.

Knowing that Clive had his camera trained on us all I got to my feet, plastered on a smile that I knew didn't meet my eyes and silently hugged Dawn. I had nothing left to say to her without exploding in anger at her cowardliness.

'See you, Dawn,' Jade said, pulling her phone out and taking a sad-face selfie with the woman that was just hours ago riding Gareth, her *snugglebum*.

'Bye, Jade, good luck with it all,' Dawn said hurriedly.

With Dawn's back turned I heard Jade huff that she was sad for them leaving and all, but when were we going to get to eat as she was starving. So she hadn't found out that she had been cheated on; she was just hangry. Gareth hissed at her to stop being so childish and that they would get some breakfast soon, which only made Jade pout even more. I didn't know where to put myself. I'd never felt so conflicted.

I turned to Simon who'd come over and uncomfortably patted me on the back. 'Bye, Si, keep up with the cosmology stuff.'

'Thanks, Georgia, don't you worry about that. I think this trip, although shorter than I'd imagined, has relit my passion for it.'

I smiled sadly. If only he knew what passions this trip had ignited in his cheating other half too.

'Right, we'd better be off then,' Dawn interrupted and stepped between me and her husband before letting out a totally fake whooping cough, something I was sure wasn't even a symptom of heatstroke. 'Thanks for everything,' she said to me insincerely, and then snapped at Simon for dawdling with taking her bags to the waiting taxi.

Clive rushed after them to get some parting shots that I imagined would be accompanied with a classic Coldplay song, all strings and melodic guitar riffs, and Anna slipped off to make a call, no doubt telling Jerry and the crew back in London what had gone on and that they needed to cover their backs in case they received a claim for liability. But, at least it made exciting telly, I guess.

'You okay, babe?' Ben asked me.

I realised I was gripping the edge of the table so hard my fingernails left half-moon ridges in the wood. Gareth flicked his head up to meet my eye for a split second, a look of fear – or was he taunting me to say something? – flashed across his face, before I coughed and nodded to Ben. 'Yeah, fine, just gasping for a brew.'

'Oh, right. I thought you might be thinking how this works in our favour.'

I looked at him blankly.

He rubbed his neck. 'I mean, I don't want to seem heartless but it's one of the competition out the way.' He shrugged.

'Oh yeah, I guess.' I hated myself for pretending to be so laissez faire about it all, but was it really any of my business? It's not like they were friends, right?

'They must be gutted they didn't get to complete the trip,' Ben said, shaking his head as he watched them leave.

'Mmm.' Was all I could muster through pursed lips. Should I have said something? Should I have forced them to come clean?

'Oh well. More chance for one of us to scoop that prize.' Jade let out a cackle and rubbed her hands in glee.

Gareth shuffled on his seat uncomfortably. 'Babe, I'm not sure that now is the time.'

'What?! What's got into you? You're always telling me we have to play this game to win and now we've got through to the final three. It's like we've made it to judges' houses or somethin'. Thought you'd be over the bloody moon,' Jade huffed.

'She's right though,' Tony piped up, rubbing his hand on Natalia's thigh. 'We should all celebrate that we've got more chance of winning this thing!'

'See.' Jade stuck her tongue out at her boyfriend and smiled at Tony. I noticed Natalia bristle and wrap a tanned arm protectively around Tony's broad shoulders.

'Earth to Georgia, come in, Georgia?' Ben's voice startled me from my thoughts. 'You okay, babe? You've not got heatstroke too, have you?'

I shook my head. 'Sorry, I was miles away. What were you saying?'

'Anna has told us to get ready for our interviews. I think you're up first.'

'Oh. Yep, fine.' I smiled and stood up from the table to head off and get changed. As I walked into reception to ask for a fresh towel I spotted Gareth loitering near a large palm tree, scrolling down his phone.

'So, when are you telling Jade then?' I hissed.

Even stood behind him I could see his jaw clench at the question. He put his phone in his shorts pocket and darted his eyes around to see if Jade was in hearing range, before composing himself and turning to look at me. God, he had such a smarmy face. I'd never met someone so obnoxious and up themselves before. How the hell had he got two women to fall for whatever charms he must keep hidden in his boxer shorts? It wasn't his personality that had them flocking.

'I've been thinking, Georgia, that actually it has nothing to do with you. Not one bit.'

'I got involved in this when I had to see the sight of your pasty body coming out of Dawn's bedroom.' I shuddered at a memory of his podgy white flesh and the smattering of back hairs, acne scars and a football team crest tattooed at the base of his spine like a tramp stamp. 'And you promised me that you'd do the decent thing.'

Gareth's lips curled into a sneer as if reminiscing. 'Normally I'd say that making money is better than sex, but I may need to rethink that after Dawn,' he boasted. 'It's a shame she's gone as it's true what they say about a cougar being a beast in the bedroom, but it was only ever going to be one night of fun. Nothing more.'

I shuddered. 'You're both cowards. You not admitting what you did to poor Jade – and Dawn by leaving.'

He laughed, and it sliced through me. 'They hadn't won one single task; she left because she knew they weren't in with a chance of winning the prize money. What happened, or what you think you saw happen between the two of us, had nothing to do with why she and her snivelling husband left. She was just so competitive and threw her toys out of her pram when she didn't get her own way. I'm not saying I don't like that feisty streak in a woman...' He trailed off, lost in some memory.

'There were some things that she had managed to get her own way with,' I snarled, shaking my head at him. 'Believe what you want, not all of us are here just for the cash prize. Some of us actually want to be here to travel, learn about new cultures and experience different things. Not to cheat on our partners and keep up some pathetic pretence that you're loved up for the cameras.'

'Like you and your boyfriend are so perfect?' Gareth let out a bark of a laugh in surprise. 'I remember what you told me the night of the bike scavenger hunt in that bar.'

An icy chill tickled the back of my neck even in the roasting morning heat.

'What?' What was he going on about and why did he look even more smug than normal?

'You don't remember? God, that fit barmaid was right: those disgusting cocktails were strong. You were chatting my ear off for bloody ages about how you had only come here as some sort of test between you and Ben before you got engaged, about how you prayed he'd never turn into his father, and how you hated the name Roy. But the hilarious thing is that as you were so drunk you didn't notice that Ben spent ages talking to Jade. She told me later how Ben had been going on about money problems.'

'What?'

He let out a laugh. 'Oh come on, you can't tell me you haven't realised that I'm not the only competitive man here? Ben is worse than I am at wanting to win the prize money. Not that that's going to happen.'

Money problems – what was he going on about? I clenched my fists at my sides. I wasn't sure if I was stopping myself from punching him in the face or giving myself a much-needed slap for having told this perfect stranger the inner and drunken workings of my mind. Angry tears pricked my eyes but no words came.

Gareth folded his arms before plastering on a fake smile at the pretty receptionist who had wandered past. 'So, you see, Georgia, no one's perfect.'

I turned on my heel so I wouldn't have to look at his smarmy face any longer and stalked to my room hoping that Ben wouldn't see me in this state and ask what the problem was. As I crossed the courtyard I spotted Clive setting up his camera in the shade of a violet flowered tree. If I hadn't been in such a state I may have noticed that his prized camera was trained in the direction of where Gareth and I had just been stood, or that the little red light was flashing showing that he'd been filming the entire thing. Instead, I flounced into my room and tried to put the last five minutes out of my mind. At least these interviews would be a distraction.

*

'Okay, Georgia. Now, if you could just inch your head back a tiny bit. Yep. That's it. Oh, and try not to look at the camera but at me instead. Clive, does this shot work for you?' Anna was flicking between the pile of papers resting on her bare legs and checking the lighting on the camera angle was okay for my solo interview. I hadn't been on my own in front of the lens since my disaster in the airport before we left. Though it was less than a week ago it felt a lot longer. I was still a little apprehensive about whether my brain and mouth were going to work in perfect harmony or not this time.

Clive grunted and fiddled with a microphone clipped to my neckline that he had passed me to put under my top.

'Excellent. So as you know this isn't live, meaning that if you make a mistake we can just re-record. No pressure at all,' Anna said in a bored tone, not looking up at me.

'Okay, I'll try my best.' I laughed lightly and shuffled on my seat. They wanted to record all of the individual interviews in different places to add a 'bit of colour' to the show. I had hoped they would choose glamorous locations, but instead of a Chilean wine bar or rustic restaurant they had got permission from a local llama breeder to set up the shot in his large garden.

They had driven me out to a tiny village called Machuca that hugs the side of a volcano – thankfully in a taxi and not D-Dawg's jeep thing, as with only thirty people living here they'd probably never seen such a monstrosity and would have been scarred for life. A row of mud houses with thatched roofs and chipped blue doors lined an unpaved road, a gleaming white church shone high on a nearby hill and a couple of outdoor barbecues cooking gristly meat made up this small and remote village, which felt like it had been plonked haphazardly in the middle of the desert.

A short and round woman, who must have been in her late seventies and wore a multicoloured poncho with her grey hair braided into plaits that almost reach her dimpled elbows, waved as we wandered around trying to find the right place for the interview.

'Catch that. A bit of the local flavour will be great,' Anna ordered Clive, pointing at the woman.

The woman scrunched up her wrinkled face in glee at having Clive and his camera head over in her direction.

'Georgia, if you could go over and maybe have some fun bartering with her,' Anna encouraged.

I nodded and walked over to the beautiful woven rug she had laid on the dry ground with a selection of handcrafted ornaments scattered across. It was only when I got closer did I work out what those shiny objects were that she was trading. Tiny llamas had been sculpted and polished out of some sort of rock that looked quite cute until you saw the gigantic phallic penises that were part of the design.

'Oh!' I gasped and almost dropped one in surprise. Clive and Anna had crumpled into fits of giggles and the old woman gave me a wink and chucked her head back to laugh along with the joke I wasn't sure she fully got.

What was it with me attracting penis-shaped objects into my life during this trip?

Originally I'd imagined the villagers' lives here were simple but I bet there were as many kinky goings on behind the scenes as I imagined there were in chocolate-box English villages – well, if *Midsomer Murders* was to be believed. Despite being so cut off from the rest of the world, I bet they still had dramas, such as who had the fanciest clay daubed on their walls or maybe Barbara at number seven didn't like the way the Chilean flag was strung between the many gnarled wood posts. I bet they all still had some beef going on. People were people after all.

Thankfully, a large man wearing khaki shorts and a polo shirt, who was bounding halfway down the dirt track waving his hands in the air, saved me from buying these phallic sculptures.

'Hola! Hello!' he called out in good English. 'My name is Señor Lopez, but you can call me Luis. Welcome to our village! Can I help you?' Clive pulled himself together and went to discuss potential shots they could use for my interview.

Moments later Luis Lopez quickly led us down a small passage by one of the houses after shouting something at the old woman who swiped him away with her dimpled arm and gave him an annoyed glare at missing out on a sale.

'We are very glad to have you. We like tourists here in our town so please spend time and money with us.' He broke into a raucous belly laugh. 'Although you need to watch those old-timers; they speak the old Inca language and think that those who don't understand Kunza deserve to pay double!' He pushed open a gate to his garden. Garden didn't really do it justice. The rocky dried-out field with tufts of hairy parched plants sparsely lumped over the ground had a fence made from cactus wood, to keep in a couple of llamas. He had the biggest plot, he told us proudly, sticking his round belly out even further.

This other-worldly landscape may be pretty inhospitable but these people made it work. Luis explained how his family had lived here since the dawn of time. This was their life; they didn't know anything else. Mining was how they used to make their money but now they had jumped on the coat tails of adventure tours and tourist visits that passed through the village on their way to see some spectacular geysers. Hence grandma's side business in willy llamas.

I was soon sat on an uncomfortable stool in the sunshine with my back to the animals, who were probably looking on in amusement at the strange foreigners. Luis was stood watching Clive set up with a look of wonder.

'So, do you like your job, man?' he asked.

Clive shrugged. 'The best part of my job is that my chair swivels and the coffee is free.'

'Ah. Okay.' I'd quickly learnt on meeting Clive that he was a man of few words, and when he did speak it was more than likely to be pessimistic grunts. Luis Lopez did not get this and continued to chatter on about the exciting world of television and how he had once starred in a milk advert, aged seven.

'Best days of my life, those,' he'd chuckled, using this as an excuse to head inside and get some refreshments. Most probably a glass of chilled milk.

'Are you sure you want me here? Is it not going to be quite bright?' I asked, swatting a fly and squinting into the sun.

'The shot looks great, trust us. Clive here is an absolute pro; plus, we shouldn't be very long anyway,' Anna said. I noticed that she had positioned herself in a small spot of shade that a nearby tree gave her. *Trust the experts, Georgia,* I told myself. 'Are you ready?'

I took a deep breath before nodding. 'Yep.'

Anna cleared her throat, leant forward a fraction and tilted her head. 'Georgia, could you tell us a bit about how you find working alongside your boyfriend whilst running your own successful business?'

I smiled before realising it and nodded. 'It's a lot of fun.'

'What are the best bits?'

'Well, I guess it's being able to share the highs and lows with the person I love.'

It's true, it was. I knew that at times it felt like I was rushing through life always wanting to know what was going to happen next, and having concrete plans within my control. But the one constant through all of this was Ben. I still couldn't shrug the heavy feeling of disappointment that he hadn't popped the question under the stars. I could laugh at how just a few weeks ago marriage hadn't been on my mind when now it was all I could think about.

'It can't all be fun all the time though, surely?'

I laughed. 'Well, no. Not all the time. There are times when he drives me mad, just as I imagine I drive him mad.'

Anna laughed along with me. 'Can you give us an example?'

I shifted in my seat. 'Erm, well because it's a demanding job with lots to juggle it can be stressful at times. Oh and he sometimes leaves teabags in cups when he does a tea round.'

'I think most blokes are like that,' she whispered behind her hand and nodded at Clive. 'So, how do you cope with the stress of running a business and the pressure that puts on your relationship?'

'Well, it's hard in the sense that you can't just leave your work at the office. We rarely both just switch off one hundred per cent.' As I said this I realised that since being in Chile, we'd actually rarely spoken about work, or been glued to our phones or our emails. Having this digital detox had actually been really nice.

'Who is in charge? Who's the real boss?' she asked scrunching up her nose.

I shook my head laughing. 'We both are.'

Anna narrowed her eyes a fraction. 'Oh come on, one of you must have the bigger ego and be in charge of having the final say?'

'No, I'd say it was fifty-fifty, an even partnership.'

She kept her eyes on mine as if not believing me then looked down at her papers and continued.

'What tips would you give for others who want to go into business with their partner?'

'Well, being in a relationship and working together can actually be an asset. I mean, you trust the other so much and you already complement each other in many ways, or else why would you be dating!' I laughed, trying to ignore the ache in my bum cheeks that felt like they were about to seize up. My eyes were beginning to water from trying not to squint. I was sure I was going to look like I had been on the verge of sneezing for this entire interview. The noise of a llama chewing on something kept growing louder.

It was slightly off-putting. Anna gave me a tight smile as she flicked to the last sheet of paper on her lap and scanned down her list of questions.

'Just a few more and we're done. You're doing great, Georgia,' she said encouragingly as Clive faffed with the camera lens.

'Ah good. I was really worried I'd come across as a bit of a tit to be honest.' I clamped my hand to my mouth. 'Oops sorry!'

'That won't make the final piece,' Clive said gruffly and got back behind the viewfinder. He indicated to Anna to continue.

'Something I think viewers will be keen to know more about is how your business came about. I think you have a really remarkable story here.'

I blushed. 'Oh, wow.' Remarkable, was I remarkable?

'You were jilted before your big extravagant white wedding, isn't that right?' Anna read from her notes. 'This must have been utterly devastating.' She titled her head to one side.

'Yes, it…it was.' Alex's face rushed into my mind making my stomach tighten.

'You poor thing. No woman deserves to be dumped before her big day. So can you tell me *exactly* what happened?'

'Oh, well, I'm not really comfortable with this,' I replied looking between her and Clive.

Anna waved her hand for him to pause the filming. 'Oh don't worry, it's just to add a bit of background to the piece. You don't have to go into loads of detail, we just think that the viewers would *love* to know more, as some of them might be in the same position and could benefit from the advice you share? I imagine it was such a difficult time, but just think if you could help someone who's going through a similar thing then wouldn't that be amazing? After all, isn't that the foundation of your whole business idea?'

Well, when she put it like that. I nodded and she instructed Clive to start filming again. I didn't know if it was the setting, the sun warming me into a relaxed state or her clever argument but I began talking. 'It's hard to think back as it was so painful, realising that this man I was about to spend the rest of my life with, that I adored and thought I knew inside and out could do this to me. I found out that he'd been cheating on me; at the time we all thought he had actually got this woman pregnant too, but it turns out that wasn't the case.' I sniffed.

'Gosh! What a horrible piece of work. You must have been utterly devastated.' She slowly shook her head in disbelief.

I nodded. 'I was. But I also felt like I couldn't let this define me and ruin my life. I was determined to make something good come out of such a horrible, heartbreaking situation'

'Wow. That's so brave. So, what did you do?'

'I went travelling, well, backpacking. I joined a tour group in Thailand but that was not the fun experience I'd imagined so I found the confidence to head off on my own to one of the Thai islands, and that's where I met Ben.' I smiled for the first time since reliving this time, thinking back to how far we'd come since then. 'It was like fate meeting him and his godmother, this wonderful woman called Trisha, as since then we decided to go into business together and create The Lonely Hearts Travel Club.'

Anna was acting like she really was entranced by our story. 'Amazing stuff. So really, this nasty ex of yours did you a favour?'

I let out a light laugh. 'I guess you're right.'

'But, how does being so humiliated before your wedding, a day that every woman dreams about since being a little girl, make you feel now? Surely you must find it hard to trust men again?'

I swallowed a lump that had formed in my throat. I really could do with a drink of water. 'It's hard. You're worried it will happen again, I guess. Always slightly paranoid that this feeling of happiness won't last long. That something bad will happen, like it did last time. Although, the only upside, I guess, is that it makes you cherish the good times in a way, as you never know what is around the corner to ruin everything you have built.' This conversation was a million miles from the relaxed and comfortable way I'd felt yesterday under the stars with Ben, but Gareth had sown the seeds of doubt in my mind again, and now I wasn't sure exactly what I was saying.

'Well, Ben must be one lucky man for you to feel like you can open up this heart that has been so damaged.'

'Yeah, I guess,' I said quietly.

'Oh, you don't sound convinced?' She leant forward at the whiff of drama.

I laughed awkwardly. 'I think he's just one of those people with lots of layers.' That sun was really starting to blind me now and I could feel the start of a headache throbbing against my temples.

'Well, good luck to you. To both of you.' Anna smiled and shuffled her papers indicating that we were done. 'So, what do you feel about Natalia and Tony getting engaged? Is it hard to be around all of that after what happened to you?'

'No, it's okay.' Anna nodded distractedly. 'Well, it's not okay, okay. If you know what I mean?' I took a deep breath and clasped my hands to my warm face to shade my eyes. 'I actually thought Ben was going to propose to me.'

'Oh. Really?' Her eyes widened.

What was I doing? Why was I spilling my guts to a woman I didn't know and didn't like that much? But I just couldn't stop. It was as if having the chance to talk about this stuff had opened the floodgates and I couldn't close them again. Luckily Clive wasn't filming this.

'God, that is hard, so once again your moment of glory was snatched away from you.' My chest tightened at this. 'So, I'm guessing that you also feel a little jealous?'

I shrugged nonchalantly, trying but failing to brush it off. 'It will happen eventually, I guess.'

Anna nodded and began unhooking her microphone. 'Well, Ben seems such a lovely guy. I doubt he would do that to you.'

'I thought exactly the same about my ex.' I half joked. 'So, how was that?'

'You were great, a natural!' Anna beamed as Clive headed over and untangled the microphone from me. I sighed in relief at being able to squeeze my bum cheeks off that hard stool. I felt exhausted, my skin felt pink from the sun, and my mouth was as parched as the dusty ground.

We wandered back to the taxi that was waiting for us. My stomach rumbled as I breathed in the chargrilled smell of the barbecues cooking outside one of the houses.

'You know those llamas we were just with?' Clive nodded at the juicy-looking meat on a stick. I nodded and tried not to dribble. 'Luis breeds them just for that reason, so tourists can eat their meat.'

'What? Really?'

His face gave nothing away. 'Makes you think, doesn't it?'

I suddenly lost my appetite, but I wasn't sure if it was thinking of those shaggy, gurning animals who'd been innocently prancing around the field behind me or the flashes of anxiety at how much I'd let out through my floodgates during the interview. Anna had said to trust her and I hadn't said anything too controversial, had I. Had I?

CHAPTER 20

Underwhelm (v.) – To fail to impress or stimulate

Chile is this long and spindly-looking country, which becomes blindingly obvious when travelling down the full length of it. Looking out of the aeroplane window at the scorching desert, as it melted into lush pine forests, endless lakes and jagged mountainous peaks, truly showed how diverse this country is. We left San Pedro de Atacama early to board the teeny tiny, slightly terrifying-looking plane that was going to take us from the very north of the country right down to the very south. Patagonia was the next and final leg on this tour, a dramatic wide expanse filled with raw isolated beauty and severe, almost inhospitable living conditions that crosses two countries – Chile and Argentina – and drops to the end of the world.

Although, after landing, my first thoughts weren't how breathtaking this part of the world was but that I was ruddy freezing. The dramatic difference in scenery was only matched by the dramatic plunge in the temperature levels outside. There was no chance of getting sunstroke here, it was practically a winter wonderland – minus the snow and Christmas presents. To add to this glacial wilderness that we'd found ourselves in, Anna had instructed us to get some sleep on the flight here, something I didn't manage to do thanks to Gareth's throaty snoring behind me, as apparently we would hit the ground running once we landed.

She wasn't joking. After picking up our bags from the small and draughty airport we were herded into a large minibus to start the next and final challenge. This quick turnaround made the shock of leaving the scorching sun of the Atacama for drizzly, dull Patagonia even harder to adjust to.

Instead of cobbled and dusty roads with herds of llamas lazily trundling past, the view from the taxi window was a high-definition technicolour of rugged and raw beauty. On one side of the busy road full of pick-up trucks and jeeps were towering dense forests in every shade of green imaginable, with glassy slate-coloured lakes on the other side.

Tony had his guidebook out and was reading aloud as we drove down the tarmacked roads. 'Patagonia is famed for having four seasons in one day; isn't that some naff song title?'

'Well, let's hope this is winter and spring is next,' Gareth grumbled.

'I thought you'd be glad of a break from the sun?' Tony asked innocently. I saw Gareth's chest tense and his gaze flick from mine and then to the window.

'Yeah, yeah, it'll be good to have a break,' Gareth muttered, not giving anything away.

'Speak for yourself. I'm freezing my tits off here and we ain't even left the bloody car yet,' Jade moaned, although having her jacket unzipped and breasts spilling out of her low-cut top probably meant she wasn't quite getting the benefits of the down padding. 'We nearly there yet, Anna?'

Anna turned round from the front with a strange look on her face; her lips were curled into a sly smile as she listened to our conversation. 'Yeah, nearly.'

Eventually, as the landscape grew more lush and the road became a dirt track, the minibus pulled to a stop at a rocky outcrop. A couple of tourists decked out in hiking gear were stood in what looked like a bus shelter, hunched over a stupidly large map.

'Here we are!' Anna grinned and nodded at Clive to get out and start filming us.

'What the hell?' Tony muttered, glancing out of the steamed up windows onto a patch of crumbling road, a knackered-looking bus stop and a small cabin with posters of hiking boots, soaring birds of prey, and inspirational quotes in the windows.

'Get out and I'll explain all.' Anna was positively gleeful as she threw open her door and stepped out.

'Any guesses, guys?' I asked the others who looked as clueless as I felt.

Natalia shrugged her shoulders. 'Nope, but I hope we're not here long, as I think it's going to start to rain.'

'Eurgh,' Jade sighed. 'Let's get this over with and then we can finally go and check in at some nice five-star hotel, and not some scuzzy layby in the middle of nowhere.' She pushed open her door with all the effort she could muster and muttered under her breath about how she wasn't cut out to survive in these Arctic conditions. I didn't have the heart to tell her that we could hardly be further from the Arctic than we were right now.

I followed her and stepped out of the car, flinching as a cold gust of air took my breath away. I had a bad feeling about this next challenge. From the way Anna was acting and how we seemed to have been taken to the middle of nowhere I was guessing this grand finale was about to be upon us. The air smelt like real life pine air freshener, heavy with moisture from the threat of rain. The group of backpackers had obviously found what they'd been searching for and had set off in an excited babble to be one of the many groups who came to Patagonia to complete the hikers' pilgrimage.

I couldn't see any signs indicating where we were, but peering across the road I thought I made out a large notice tacked to one of the windows of the Portakabin. 'Signing in is mandatory for ALL.'

Sign in? What were we signing in for and why?

We were all huddled up and shivering by a huge boulder that had dropped from God knows where, our breath visible as tiny clouds, when one of us spoke, waiting for Anna to return from the cabin she had quickly legged into, to give us some much needed information. I glanced skywards, convinced that I could feel the first drops of rain; maybe Natalia was right, and we had been spoilt with bright blue skies when we were in Santiago and Atacama. Here it felt like a heavy curtain of grey was suffocating us.

Through a patch of the forest surrounding us I could make out some strange, skinny pale trees that had been bent backwards almost horizontally by the ferocious and never-ceasing wind that must have deformed them over the centuries. This place really was harsh. It was like another world, cut off from the rest of the country by huge stonking ice caps. Apparently the people who lived here saw themselves as Patagonians first and Chileans or Argentinians second. I was just amazed that people could survive living here at all.

Anna eventually padded over to us and clapped for our attention. 'Guys, listen up.' She flashed a look at Clive to check he had her best side in the shot. The light from his camera made her look almost ethereal against the dramatic rugged backdrop.

'This is your last challenge of the trip, but also the biggest and most adventurous.' I felt a strange jolt in my stomach as she spoke, as if I was subconsciously preparing myself for what she was going to say next. I glanced nervously at the others who were rubbing their arms or slowly bouncing on the spot for some warmth. Sweating on that stool in the desert felt like months ago.

Ben had his eyes fixed on Anna, a steely determination in his gaze. I thought back to what Gareth had said about Ben being desperate to win the prize fund for some apparent money problem he was having. I'd tried my hardest to convince myself it was utter bollocks and Gareth was just winding me up; Ben was always on point with our finances and would have told me if there was some sort of problem.

'The challenges we have set you so far were all in preparation for this one. From the bicycle scavenger hunt where you had to use a map, and teamwork, to get to the finish line, to gutting a fish at the Santiago fish market – so you could eat in the wild, to coping with extreme temperatures in the desert as we went sandboarding – although the car breaking down was just an ironic coincidence.'

Anna let out a tinkle of a laugh. 'All these skills you've demonstrated during this trip will, hopefully, aid you to victory. You're soon going to be heading off armed with a map. All you have to do is figure out how to get to the end point, in Torres del Paine, Chile's National Park, in the quickest time. And, as you know, you're all neck and neck with each other, so the couple who gets back to the cabin where Clive and I will be waiting will be crowned the Wanderlust Warriors and win that all-important cash prize!' she said in an overexcited Davina McCall way.

Camping. In what felt like sub-zero temperatures. Crap bags.

The slight competitiveness I'd felt on the other tasks puddled out of me. I'd never been camping before. Fishing trips with my dad were the closest I'd been to the great outdoors for any real length of time, and even then I only went to get out of helping mum clean the house over the summer holidays and I'd played with my Tamagotchi for most of it. But this, in the middle of the Patagonian wilderness with just a map, a compass and a tent, this was going to be interesting. I glanced at Ben, convinced he would be buzzing with excitement and confidence for the both of us. Seeing him chew his bottom lip as Anna began handing out pre-packed survival kits from the van did not fill me with the comfort that I'd hoped for.

Thinking back to how eager and excited that group previously waiting in the bus stop had been, I suddenly felt way out of my depth. Natalia and Tony seemed as ready to take on this task as they had all the others, a matching steely look of determination in each of their almond-shaped eyes. To be fair, Jade wasn't moaning as much as I'd expected, and I couldn't work out whether that was because she didn't realise that her five-star hotel was disappearing as fast as her mascara was running in this icy drizzle or because she was secretly some kind of Girl Guide. Gareth had the map open as soon as Anna had passed him one and was telling Jade to hold one edge and lie it flat against the side of the van so he could concentrate. He had this quiet confidence, knowing how close he was to winning that prize money. I didn't know who were our biggest rivals.

'You been camping much as a kid?' I turned to ask Ben who was intently going over the contents of the rucksacks – a well-stocked first aid kit, a mobile phone and a list of emergency numbers to call if we had any problems. Not that I was convinced we would pick up a decent signal in the depths of the forest but after Dawn being sent home sick I think Anna was super paranoid that this task had to have the right balance of danger and excitement, as well as covering her back in case someone tried to sue the production company.

'Nope. You?'

I shook my head. 'Balls.'

'It's fine, babe, it can't be that hard. Chuck us that map will you? I reckon the others will be heading off any moment and the quicker we leave, the more ground we can cover before night falls,' he said, glancing at the ominously low sky.

But Tony's guidebook had been right. By the time we'd each figured out our separate routes, double-checked we had everything we needed for the al fresco night and scribbled down our details in the giant sign-in book the sun had come out. It was actually quite pleasant when Ben and I finally set off. The stupid yellow helmets with fitted GoPros had been rigged up on our heads once more and with a final shake of hands to wish the other teams the best of luck, Ben and I were off.

On our own.

The first hour or so went by quickly. Now the weather had lifted I actually felt quite pumped up with the warming sun on my shoulders and the excitement of wandering this vast expanse of forest. Ben had nominated himself to be in charge of reading the map and I was in charge of the lols and light relief.

'Wow, Ben! Look!' I called through a mouthful of granola bar, catching sight of what looked like a majestic eagle soaring overhead.

He craned his neck, luckily avoiding me spitting crumbs in my excitement. 'Ah yeah, I've heard about those birds.' He sucked air through his teeth and winced. 'Worse than vultures apparently. They swoop in and pick on the carcasses of backpackers who didn't manage to make it out alive,' he said, with a worried expression.

I gulped and flicked my head between him and the backpacker killer bird of prey. 'Really?'

When I glanced back at Ben he was creased up in silent mirth. 'God, Georgia, you're so gullible. That's a condor, not a human-flesh-eating monster.'

I gently thumped him on his arm. 'Hey! I'm not used to this nature stuff.' I jutted my bottom lip out then laughed along with him.

Although we were having a laugh it was hard work walking solidly in the rising heat with a heavy backpack on. To keep my energy up I'd been grazing on nuts, seeds and sugary snacks that I'd found in one of the bags and gulped at fresh water we had collected in our water bottles by pressing them into a stream of crystal clear mountain water. I felt like Katniss in *The Hunger Games* and spent a good twenty minutes wondering whether Ben was more like Peeta or Gale.

But we had been lucky. Too lucky. Tony's guidebook had predicted that the weather could change with little warning here and soon the previously boiling hot sky had clouded over and felt a lot closer.

'I'm not sure about those clouds,' Ben said, looking up anxiously. 'Maybe we should try and find somewhere to bunker down for the night? We've actually covered good ground already, according to this.' He pointed to his trusted map. 'Although, I don't fancy our chances putting up our tent if the heavens open.'

I shuddered at the thought. 'Fine by me, I'm pretty knackered.'

Ben flashed me a smile. 'I hope you're not too tired…'

I raised my eyebrows. 'Ben Stevens, are you suggesting some forest fornication?'

'That I am, Miss Green, that I am.' He winked and pulled me in for a kiss. His lips tasted salty against mine from the sweat and sunburn.

'Come on then, let's get this tent shizz sorted out!' I laughed, once we came up for air. We'd been wearing the helmets and cameras for so long now that we kept forgetting we were being filmed.

If you've ever tried to put up a tent in the middle of nowhere on rocky uneven ground as an icy wind is whipping up around you then you will understand it is the worst aphrodisiac ever. The flirty banter vanished as quickly as the leaves were being blown across the ground. With neither of us exactly skilled in the art of putting up tents and the weather quickly deteriorating, it was, quite frankly, a recipe for disaster.

'I said push it in more!' Ben shouted, running a hand across his wet forehead. His curls had slicked to his head and were spraying raindrops that had formed on the tips.

'I did!' I shouted back. My hands were stinging from the cold and my patience was wearing as thin as the sheet of canvas we were seriously struggling with.

'Well then why has it popped up again?'

'I don't fucking know! Maybe you didn't do your side tight enough.'

He let out a frustrated groan and muttered something under his breath.

'What?' I barked.

'Nothing, Georgia. Nothing.' He sighed and clenched his eyes shut for a moment before looking like he was counting to ten. 'Right, pass me that blue cord. Nope, not that – yep, that's it. Okay, and now hold that as tight as you can, pull it really, really taut...' He walked me through the rest of the directions for this stupid thing in a more measured but short-tempered way. Why the hell did people do this for fun?

Eventually, and thankfully with no more bickering, the blasted thing was put up. I stepped back hoping to feel a deep sense of pride wash over me at what we had just achieved but instead I felt exhausted, grumpy, wet and desperate for a proper bed in a warm, clean room.

'Well, that was harder than I thought,' Ben said rubbing his neck. 'Right, I'm starving. I reckon we should be able to get a fire going if we crack on soonish.' He looked up at the darkening sky once more. It was as if the weather had changed to match this heavy atmosphere between the two of us.

'Finally, a plan I can get on board with,' I replied.

The only problem was that as I'd been so busy chatting about everything and nothing with him, as well as admiring the stunning scenery, on our way here I hadn't noticed I'd been slowly making my way through all the snacks and treats that we'd been given. I'd eaten all the food. Well, all the nice food.

'For God's sake, Georgia,' Ben groaned, rubbing his tired face with his hands as he glanced in the almost empty bag. All that remained was a large packet of prawn-flavoured instant noodles and two cereal bars crushed flat. We would have to go without dinner if we were to save the rest for breakfast, and then hope we were closer than we thought in order to get to the finale point by lunch tomorrow.

'It's not my fault, I didn't realise that we had rations! Nuts, cereal bars and crackers do not a substantial dinner make. It's bloody hard work all this walking!' I said, folding my arms in front of my chest and trying to deflect that I did feel a little guilty and embarrassed about snaffling all the scran.

'You didn't think to check whether this was all the food we had?'

'I'm sorry. It was a mistake. Okay?' I said in the most unapologetic way ever. I forced myself to take a deep breath. 'Do you want to try and make something with what's left?' I softened slightly, realising that I had been selfish. It wasn't Ben's fault we had only been given rabbit food or that because we were in one of the windiest parts of the world it made it harder to put up a tent, but I couldn't admit that I was in the wrong. I was too tired and grumpy to think rationally, when all I wanted was for this stupid challenge to be over. I mean, as nice as winning would be, and helping out our charity, I wasn't as obsessed as he was to get the grand prize.

'It's fine. It's probably too late to try and spark up the gas cooker in this light anyway,' he sighed.

'Is that because you don't know how it works?' I said, rolling my eyes at his incompetence. Gah, why was I being so spiteful?

Hurt flashed on Ben's face for a millisecond before he threw his arms in the air. 'Okay, Georgia. Whatever. I get that you're tired, I get that you're not used to all this.' He waved his arm at the tent billowing ahead of us. 'But you're in the wrong and it would be nice, for a change, if you could admit it. You know, just the once.'

I clenched my teeth and tried to deepen my breathing that was coming out in shallow bursts. 'And what's that supposed to mean?'

'Nothing. Forget it.'

'Fine. Whatever.' I threw back the opening to the tent and angrily unzipped my sleeping bag. I got in fully clothed, clodhopping hiking boots and all, before turning my back on Ben, too pissed off to even speak to him any more. If he had been planning to propose to me here, there was no chance it was happening now. At that moment, I was too tired to care. At least, that's what I told myself.

CHAPTER 21

Fulminate (v.) – To complain loudly or angrily

As well as barely talking to each other and going to sleep on an empty stomach, the roof of the tent leaked. I would just about force my mind to stop believing every single damn noise I heard was an axe murderer roaming the woods and begin to doze off before an icy drop would fall on my forehead and wake me back up. It was without doubt one of the worst night's sleep of my life. As I rolled over for the umpteenth time, trying to find some sort of comfort on this lumpy mat and sleeping bag that smelt of moths and wood fires and BO, I heard Ben let out a deep sigh.

'We should probably just get up. Seeing as neither of us can sleep any more.'

'Fine by me,' I mumbled, not letting on how grateful I felt at being able to get out of this stifling canvas. My whole body ached, my teeth had this disgusting furry coating on them and I was very conscious of how crumpled and dishevelled I was. Stealing a look at my boyfriend who was letting out a deep yawn and rubbing his eyes just annoyed me; he did not look like he had been sharing this awful experience with me. His near-perfect morning appearance just irritated me even more.

Amazingly the rain had stopped sometime during the early morning and as I zipped back the tent opening, bright streaks of dawn sunlight beamed through the trees. The air was still bitterly cold, but in the soft light it felt refreshing rather than freezing. *Come on, Georgia, a new day means a new start,* I told myself. *Every couple has arguments, maybe you just need to admit you were in the wrong for eating the food and enjoy the rest of this experience.*

I tried to keep our spirits up and grabbed the rest of the food bag to concoct something, anything, that we could eat for breakfast before we packed up and headed off. Maybe an apologetic serving of prawn noodles could be my white flag to Ben for being such a greedy cow yesterday. My upbeat and positive plan lasted for a whole five seconds.

I awkwardly plodded out into the fresh and bright light, remembering to put on my stupid yellow GoPro-rigged helmet, and tried to stretch out my back that had become one giant knot. I was trying to work out just how easy it would be to light this stove without Ben's help, when my stomach clenched. This tight squeeze wasn't just hunger pangs but because the food carrier bag that we'd been given was now a collection of tatty shreds and wet empty wrappers. Some creatures must have had themselves a wonderful midnight feast at our expense.

'Fuck!' I shouted and flung the tatters in frustration. Why was everything going so epically wrong?

'What?' Ben poked his head out as he fastened on his own ridiculous helmet.

'There's no more food.' I pointed to the mess at my feet and felt tears prick my stinging, tired eyes.

'What! Nothing?' He flicked his head in disbelief at the remains of the carrier bag and my miserable expression. 'We've got another God knows how many hours of hiking to do on an empty stomach, made worse by the fact we've had no dinner, because *someone* decided they were a little peckish yesterday. Well, that's fucking great.'

Seems like I wasn't the only one struggling to call a truce and wake up in a better mood this morning. My hackles rose as he continued to glare at me.

'It's not my fault some wild animals got into our food bag.'

He widened his eyes and tilted his head. 'Wait – you did hang it up, didn't you?'

I stared blankly at him. What was he on about?

He sighed loudly. 'Georgia, you always hang up food to make it harder for any animals to get to it. *Everyone* knows that!' He shook his head in disbelief at what a moronic idiot he was dating.

'How the frig was I supposed to know stuff like that? I told you I've never been camping before. I'm not bloody Bear Grylls!' I lashed out.

I was wet, cold and completely miserable. Even the sunlight was irritating me now and stinging my sleep-deprived eyes.

'No, but you do have some sort of common sense don't you?' He spat back then rubbed his face with his hands, the fight in him gone. 'Fuck it. It doesn't matter.'

'It *does* matter! No, seriously. I'm sorry about eating the food, okay? I know I was in the wrong but I didn't do it on purpose!'

'Wow. Well I maybe I should get that in writing to prove it's actually happened.'

'What are you going on about?' My voice was growing higher in pitch with every syllable.

'I mean that you don't always know best.'

'Oh, really!'

'Yes. Really. For example, our business is just that. *Ours!* A *joint* partnership, remember?'

Well that had escalated quickly.

I let out a fake laugh. 'Oh, I get it. This isn't about me eating all the cereal bars without offering you one – it's about

London, isn't it!' From the look on his face I knew I'd hit the nail on the head. With that I was off. No one could stop me. I wasn't even aware of what I was saying; it just kept spilling out like word vomit. My exhausted mind and disappointed heart had obviously decided that this was the ideal time to tell my boyfriend some long overdue home truths.

'Yeah, as it happens it is, but it's about more than that.' He crossed his arms in front of his chest. 'It's about you being too scared to trust me. London can work for us, I know it can. I've done the maths –'

'The maths! Funny that, because I've heard you've been having money problems, so maybe it's better that I stick to my gut instinct.'

'Money troubles?' The colour dropped from his face. 'Who told you that?'

'Gareth, well Jade. She told Gareth and Gareth... What does it matter who told me? Nice one on sharing whatever problems you've had with complete strangers instead of coming to talk to me about it – you know, your girlfriend!'

'Oh, like you don't hide stuff too,' he snapped. 'Like trying to get the low-down on Alice?'

I felt like I'd been slapped.

'Yeah, I know about you snooping around. You could have just asked me rather than Facebook stalked her, liking her old photographs.'

'Well go on then, why *have* you been seeing your ex-girlfriend behind my back?'

'Is that what this is about? You really don't trust me, do you?' I was sure I saw a flicker of hurt – or was that anger? – cross his darkened eyes.

'I do trust you, I just...' I sighed. Everything was coming out wrong. 'What did Gareth mean about money troubles? You're okay, aren't you?'

His jaw clenched. 'Yeah. I'm fine.'

'And the business is fine?'

'Yeah. The business is fine.'

'Then, what?'

He sighed, as if uttering the next sentence was going to change everything. 'The reason why I've been in contact with Alice is that she's a financial advisor.'

'Right…' I tried to follow along.

He rubbed his face with his hands. 'I've agreed to a deal on an office in London.'

'What?' I swear my screech made birds abandon their perches in the tops of fir trees up to a mile away. 'Ben! I hope you're fucking joking! I said I wasn't ready to expand!'

'Yes, but you're wrong. This is what we need, to grow and shape the business we need to be moving forward and not staying static.'

I was beyond livid.

'Wait – where have you got the money from if it's not the business account?'

'I'm banking on us winning this competition…' He trailed off looking like he realised how risky this was, especially in the light of our current situation.

'Oh brilliant, just fucking brilliant!' I said sarcastically. 'Is this the only reason you've come here? Not to travel with me, not to prop –' I managed to stop myself from uttering the marriage word just in time. 'But to get your hands on a wodge of cash to invest in something I don't even want to invest in!' From the sheepish look he was giving me I knew I was right. No wonder he'd been so competitive, he *had* to get that cash. 'I can't believe this!' My heart was racing, my fists were balled at my sides and my breathing was erratic. Spittle had formed on my bottom lip but I was so enraged I didn't stop to wipe it off. 'When did you do this?'

'When I was last down in London. The social media meeting was a front,' he sheepishly admitted. 'But just hang on, before you go all banshee on me, hear me out. I've loved this trip with you, getting to hang out without the pressure of Lonely Hearts, just like I love living with you, but I couldn't see a way that you'd let me show you just how wrong you are on this business decision, unless I *literally* proved it to you.'

So, this was suddenly all my fault! I took a step back, crunching the empty food wrappers under my hiking boots.

'If you think I'm so wrong, then why the hell are you going to propose to me?' I screeched.

'Propose?' He almost fell over at the suggestion. 'What the hell are you on about?'

I desperately tried to control my breathing that was escaping in short sharp bursts. 'I found the ring, Ben.'

It was his turn to laugh. A laugh of utter disbelief and incredulity. 'The ring? Oh right, so now you've been snooping through my things? Well, again, if you'd bothered to ask me then you'd know it wasn't for you.'

'What?' I felt like I'd been punched in the gut.

'I'm keeping it safe for Jimmy. He's the one who's about to ask Shelley. Not me. Do you really think we're ready to get engaged? We've only just moved in together for God's sake!'

The reality hit me hard in the pit of my stomach. He didn't want to get engaged, he'd been making major decisions about the business behind my back and had lied to me about his reasons for coming here. Feelings of embarrassment and confusion at how presumptuous I'd been swirled around my furious mind.

I felt as hurt as when Alex had ended it with me, the same startling realisation clouded me back then as it did now – that I didn't know the person I'd been living with at all. This was worse. This time I'd had two men – two men who I'd once thought the world of – admit that I wasn't worthy to take up the aisle. What was wrong with me? No. What was wrong with him? I scuffed my heavy hiking boots into the damp ground, hoping the flame in my cheeks wasn't that visible in this early morning light.

'Well, I don't know! I…' I paused. So he didn't think we were *there*, wherever *there* was. It was all such a mess.

Ben was staring at me as if trying to work out how I could be so idiotic to even begin to imagine we were ready to utter marriage vows.

'What the fuck, Georgia?' he said shaking his head as if the prospect was totally ludicrous. Before I could attempt any form of redeeming myself from this mortifying situation he sighed heavily. 'Listen, let's just get out of here. We've got a lot of ground to cover and this isn't getting us anywhere.'

'We'd better bloody race to the finish line if you so desperately need the cash,' I hissed, watching him angrily dismantling the tent and roughly packing it all away, deciding that, although feeling ashamed at getting the wrong end of a jewel-encrusted stick, I was not going to let him get away with this.

I stood and stared at him in disbelief before kicking a large rock near my backpack, blinking back the tears as my toes struck it. Just as he shoved the tent back in his backpack and began to stomp off, not seeming to care if I was following, it started to rain. Well that was just fucking great.

*

Apparently this National Park was home to an iconic trio of mountains that loomed over the well-trodden trekking route but I couldn't see chuff all thanks to the gritty pellets of sleet falling. A fine fog-like mist had dropped around us, so I couldn't even make out the supposedly stunning surroundings. Despite the many layers I had on, hailstones were savagely pummelling my exposed areas, as if I didn't feel attacked enough out here.

I couldn't speak to Ben. I couldn't look at him.

Since leaving our campsite a few hours ago, I'd been trailing him silently; I had nothing left to say and apparently he didn't either. He was in charge of the map and planning our quickest route out of here and back to meet the others. Well, he'd said he could read a map but I knew full well that we were completely lost.

'Do you even know where we are?' I demanded. I'd gone past breaking point and just wanted to get the hell out of here.

'For the last time, I know where we're going. You have to trust me, Georgia, although I know how hard that is for you to do,' he muttered without a hint of humour.

I seethed and muttered loudly under my breath that I wasn't the only one with trust issues. We were lost, literally and figuratively. I realised that no map in the world would help us find our way out of this.

My boots trudged over rocks and flattened moss and with each heavy step I thought about what had just happened. I deserved more, after what Alex had done to me and after the struggle I'd been through to let someone back into my heart. I'd promised myself that I would never ever be hurt like that again. Yes, I knew I had my own set of problems and insecurities. I wasn't a perfect girlfriend, but then who was? If I could open up and let Ben in after what had happened to me, then surely he could do the same.

'You know what your problem is?' Ben suddenly stopped walking and spun round to face me, breaking up my bleak thoughts. His tired face was pinched and his body language mildly threatening. 'You've changed.'

I gawped at him, waiting for him to explain this absurd point.

'Yeah. That's it. The Georgia I met in Thailand, the one I fell for long before I came out and had the courage to tell you.' He rolled his eyes as if it was such a madman idea that he could ever have felt those feelings for me. This only infuriated me more. 'That Georgia had this amazing, vulnerable innocence about her. I wanted to make sure that nothing bad ever happened to her. But that Georgia certainly never made the flight to Chile. You've become so tough, like you're on this stupid one-woman mission to achieve everything by yourself. It's like I'm just your lapdog. I mean, you heard what that Blaise said when we went to the TV studios – that you're the famous jilted bride businesswoman and I'm just holding onto your coat tails. I knew that a few people saw us that way after all the press last year, but I never expected you to see it that way too. It's like my ideas and business suggestions aren't ever good enough or worth listening to, as you're only ever going to go with what you think anyway!'

I gaped at him open-mouthed. 'I *don't* think like that and I *do* listen to you!'

'What? Think back to when we went to Ikea, a stupid example, but do you not remember how everything I put in the basket you replaced with the items you wanted?'

What? I hadn't done that, had I?

'I let you furnish our flat with a million fucking candles and crap we don't need because I want you to be happy. I know it must be hard for you living with a man again but I am not Alex.' He rubbed his tired face. 'I mean you've never even let me properly explain why I think the London move would be good for us; it's just been a blanket no. Because Georgia always bloody knows best.'

Had I been like that? The past few months swirled in my mind as he continued talking. Now it was Ben's turn to be on a roll.

'You know that saying of walking in someone else's shoes? Well, you might want to try it every so often rather than forging on ahead regardless as if you're the only one whose opinion matters.'

That did it. I finally found my voice. 'Maybe I am a little more guarded, but I have every right to be after what happened to me. But then *you* never tell me *any*thing! You didn't tell me about Jimmy and Shelley leaving, you didn't tell me that this so-called old friend of yours was your fucking ex-girlfriend, and you certainly didn't tell me about signing contracts on a London office behind my back! And don't get me started on your past. I mean you've never once opened up about why your mum left. Do you have any idea how awkward that was at your dad's when I didn't have a clue what he was going on about? How you didn't even introduce me as your girlfriend and seemed so desperate for us not to get to know each other?'

That hit a nerve. At the mention of his mum he flinched, as if my words had actually done some physical damage. 'I didn't think you needed to know every single effing detail of my life,' he seethed and shook his head in disbelief. 'You know what? We obviously want different things here.' His jaw was clenched so tightly I thought his teeth were going to break through the skin. 'Let's just call it a day, yeah.'

That wasn't a question.

I had blisters rubbing at my stupid ugly hiking boots that felt a size too small, my knees ached from the steep climbs up sodding hills and I was beyond ravenous, but not one of these pains matched hearing him break up with me. I felt like I'd been slapped in the face, his words hurting far more than the icy wind currently stinging my cheeks.

'Seriously?' I let out a laugh that sounded like it should have come out of the mouth of a mental patient, trying to hide how shocked and hurt I felt. 'We're over. Just like that?'

'I don't know. I mean, we obviously see this going in completely different directions…' He trailed out, thinking about each word carefully, his chest rising and falling dramatically.

'So, you want to go on a break? Like, fucking Ross and Rachel? We both know how that ends up.'

I couldn't even bear to look at him. If he didn't have hold of the map that was our only way out of this nightmare, then I would have stormed off to get as far away from him as possible. As it was, I just turned my back and let the tears run silently down my cheeks.

CHAPTER 22

Bumptious (adj.) – Obtusely and noisily self-assertive; obtrusive

'There!' I gasped, more to myself than to Ben, and picked up my pace. Neither of us had spoken since him announcing he wanted to end it with me, or go on a break, or whatever the hell he'd said. All I knew was that I needed space away from him to try and get my head around all that had been said.

The refuge we had been looking for during the past few hours was now just metres ahead. Pine Trees Cabin Park Lodge. I could have cried with happiness. Soft plumes of smoke were gently fluttering out of the chimney. A warming glow emanated from the windows that had slightly steamed up with condensation. The pretty-as-a-picture wooden cabin was tucked away neatly behind towering emerald pines and bent skinny excuses of trees. Our haven. Ha!

I stumbled through the main door as a blast of heat from an open fire hit me full in the face. I could have sunk to my knees and kissed the stone floor but was stopped from being so melodramatic when I heard a round of applause. Looking up I saw Anna clapping with a clear look of relief on her face.

'You're here! We were starting to get worried about the pair of you,' she said rushing over and pulling me into a bony hug.

'Never, ever again.' I pulled back, wondering why she was greeting me like I'd just survived some epic mission – well it did feel like that I guess. 'Did we win?' I asked, *please tell me all of this was worth it*, just as Ben flung the door open and trailed in behind me, looking as relieved as I did to be around other human beings.

Anna was too busy using this opportunity to drape herself over Ben and welcome him back to civilisation to answer me. I glanced round and finally took in the stunning cabin. It was larger than it appeared from the outside. We were in a spacious lounge with squishy sofas covered in tartan blankets placed around the roaring fire; a small open-plan kitchen was at the far end of the room and then four closed doors, which I guessed were the bedrooms, led off from the centre.

My stomach sank when I saw Natalia and Tony sat on the plaid squishy sofas. Coming second meant we'd lost the task. In fact, we had lost the whole competition. More than that, we had lost ourselves. It had all been for nothing.

'We lost!' I squeaked, as the colour slowly came back to my cheeks.

It must have been only ten minutes or so later that a soggy-looking Jade and Gareth tumbled into the cabin, wearing matching pissed off expressions because they hadn't won either.

'Now that we're all together I want to say well done to all of our super contestants. It has been a very fun trip and one that we won't forget in a long time!' Anna said, passing out glasses of fizz and toasting us.

'You can say that again,' I muttered under my breath, downing my glass in one, desperate to feel that numbing glow of alcohol.

'A huge congratulations to our winners Natalia and Tony – if you could both please stand and accept your prize!' Anna encouraged the rest of us to start a round of applause as she handed over a ginormous cheque to the blushing and graceful winners as Clive filmed it all. Seeing him move his camera around I realised that every minute of mine and Ben's big fight had been filmed with the stupid GoPros on our heads. But instead of feeling mortified and wondering how I could break the tiny camera to ruin the footage, I didn't even care. Let them broadcast what a stupid idiot Ben was. It hardly mattered now.

'Wow. Thank you so much!' Natalia squeaked as she kissed Anna on the cheek.

'This is just the icing on the cake after Natalia agreeing to marry me. Well done to the rest of you guys and thanks to you, Anna, for being such a great host!' Tony said to a simpering Anna; he really did know how to charm the ladies.

I just let out a snort of indignation. At least someone on this stupid trip was happy. Well good for them.

'We have a little time before we eat, so you can head off to get much needed showers, then relax and enjoy your last evening in Chile,' Anna said clapping her hands and getting up to instruct Clive to set up the last few shots of us all and her final piece to camera to close the show.

I must have smelled horrendous, but instead of rushing to the showers I went and sat on a separate sofa and pulled my phone out, desperate to speak to Marie, or Shelley, or even my parents, anyone who would tell me that it was all going to be okay. All the emotion must have made me lose my mind as I realised that we were in the middle of flipping nowhere so trying to connect to a phone or Wi-Fi signal was as impossible as coming to terms with what had just happened. After much huffing and puffing and contorted body movements I gave up.

In fact, I'd given up on it all anyway.

CHAPTER 23

Exasperate (v.) – To cause irritation or annoyance to

The last supper in Chile was the longest dinner of my life. I'd just wanted to get out of there, to make it back to Manchester and be surrounded by people who actually loved me for me. Ben and I didn't utter another word to each other, but luckily, as everyone else was in such high spirits, the impromptu vow of silence between us went unnoticed. We sat at opposite ends of the table as we were served a warming dinner of stew and homemade sugary cake, despite hardly eating for the last forty-eight hours I couldn't stomach much of it. The owners of the cabin had also joined us to eat and were thankfully dominating most of the conversation with tales of hikers who had passed through here over the years, so I could sneak off to bed early and undetected.

Ben clearly hadn't been in our bedroom when I woke after a deep but dreamless sleep the following morning. I had no idea where he'd slept, but it was no longer my problem.

After a rushed breakfast and bumpy ride to the airport we were finally on the long flight headed home. Now that the filming was over it was like Anna had given up on being nice and trying to organise us as we all scattered across the half-empty flight, luckily meaning I didn't have to sit next to Ben. Moments after we'd boarded I'd snapped my seat belt on, closed my eyes and willed myself to sleep for what was going to be the longest journey of my life.

It was only when Jade nudged me did I attempt any form of human interaction.

'You done with that?' she asked looking down at my untouched tray of food.

'Sure, you can have it if you like,' I offered, rubbing my tired eyes.

'Thanks, Georgia.' She took the food like a starved orphan, not someone who had already eaten breakfast and got a burger and chips down her in the airport. 'So, can you believe that we're actually going home?' she said through a mouthful of food.

I gave a half shrug and a half nod. 'Mmm.'

'It feels like we only just got here. I'm nowhere near as tanned as I thought I'd be and I'm gutted we didn't win, especially coming second to that pair of drunks,' she tutted and inspected her slim arm for freckles.

'What?'

'Look, I'm pasty!' she moaned.

I shook my head. 'No, what did you mean about the drunks?'

'Natalia and Tony, you know, the wine guys?' She gave me a confused look, like I'd never met the other contestants.

'Yeah, I know who you mean. But what were you saying about them drinking?'

She pursed her lips in the same way that Marie did when she was about to share some juicy gossip. 'They have, like, a *serious* drinking problem. Have you not noticed?' Her eyes widened as I shook my head and glanced over at the winners in the row opposite. They did both have a glass of wine in their hands.

'See.' She nodded, as if proving her point.

'Jade, that's just their drink with the meal; that doesn't make them alcoholics.'

'I'm telling you, they have been constantly pissed during this whole trip. When have you not seen them with a glass of booze in their hands?' She raised an eyebrow. Now she mentioned it, they did seem to like being around alcohol, but I'd just thought that was a side effect of the jobs they did. 'Even before they got engaged, which is *totally* a scam to win this thing and get more airtime, if you ask me,' she whispered behind her hand, 'even before then they were always drinking.'

'Wow, maybe you're right.'

'I see everything, I do.' She tapped her nose proudly. I wanted to laugh that she obviously hadn't seen her boyfriend humping Dawn but I just nodded along. 'Cheers for this.' She nodded at the food tray. 'You must have been knackered; you've been asleep for ages.'

'Yeah, probably all that walking,' I said, trying to put on a brave face and attempt a normal conversation that didn't involve slagging off Ben in my mind.

'It was tough, wasn't it? I almost gave up at a few points but just kept thinking about all the calories we were burning. You should see the score on my Fitbit!' She laughed revealing several shiny fillings.

'I bet,' I replied. Watching her tuck into the tiny pot of fresh fruit and flicking through a glossy magazine she had brought with her, looking so pleased with herself for completing what had been a really hard final task, I felt a pang of sympathy for her. I took a deep breath. It wasn't fair that she had been nothing but nice to me on this trip and I knew this awful secret about her cheating boyfriend. Yeah, she was a bit ditzy but she had a heart of gold and deserved to hear the truth. It was obvious that Gareth wasn't going to man up enough to tell her.

'Jade.' I took another deep breath and shifted in my seat.

'Mmm.'

'I need to tell you something.'

'Yeah?' She was absorbed in a how-to tutorial on replicating Kim Kardashian's selfie style.

'It might come as a bit of a shock.'

'Mmm…' She flicked over the page of the magazine and eventually looked up at me.

'Well, the thing is…' I began wringing my headphone wire through my fingertips. 'Gareth has been cheating on you.' The words finally tumbled out. I winced, waiting for her reaction. Then I panicked – maybe telling someone that they were sharing a flying tin can with their cheater, scumbag boyfriend, with no escape for either of them, wasn't the best idea.

I don't know what reaction I was expecting but not that she would just give a little shrug.

'Yeah, I know.'

It was my turn to look incredulous. 'What? You know?'

Jade sighed and licked her finger to turn the page of the magazine. 'Yeah. Been going on for ages. Can't trust him with anyone that's got a vagina and a pulse.'

I gawped at her for a few seconds, trying to take this in. She knew and she was okay with it?

'Jade, why do you stay with him if you don't trust him? If you…you knowingly let him cheat on you?' I stuttered.

'Georgia, sometimes you just don't rock the boat. I get a sweet deal out of it too. I mean all these nice things I get, I never pay for. He's very generous is my Gareth.' She pointed at her flash watch and her designer handbag tucked by her feet.

Sometimes you just don't rock the boat. Was that what I'd done? Or was I the captain of my own ship, and it was Ben who'd decided to jump overboard?

Jade closed her magazine and placed it in the seat pocket, passed me back the empty pots of aeroplane food for my tray table and nuzzled into her scarf – probably cashmere and probably paid for by her love rat boyfriend – indicating she was going to have a nap. 'It's fine. I get mine and he gets his. Not every relationship is black and white; there are loads of grey areas.' She patted my wrist and then snuggled up and shut her eyes.

I stared out of the window thinking about what she had just said. I was still so angry with Ben, at what he had said and at what he hadn't said, as well as having this ingrained stubborn streak in me meaning there was no way I would forgive and forget so easily.

But, maybe I was overreacting slightly? No relationship was perfect just like no person was perfect. They demanded hard work, sacrifice and compromise and good communication to make sure you were heading in the same direction, a tiny voice in my head tried to rationalise.

Out of the other couples on this trip maybe we were the only ones who had an actual relationship instead of a *relationshit*. Who knew if Simon was as unbothered as Jade was with his partner's indiscretions. And by the sound of it, Natalia and Tony, who looked like soulmates from the outside, were actually just a pair of lushes managing to bumble through life pulling the wool over people's eyes, including their own.

Don't be ridiculous, Georgia. No, Ben had totally blown it between us. We were broken beyond repair.

*

The taxi dropped me off at our empty flat. I'd been spared from explaining what had happened to the others as we all waited for our bags at Manchester Airport and said our groggy, sleep-deprived goodbyes. Everyone looked slightly relieved to be making their way to their own beds, even if it did mean leaving Chile and returning to the normality of home. Ben had finally come and spoken to me, just to curtly tell me he would crash at Jimmy's, so I jumped in the first available cab and didn't look back.

I struggled in with my case, heaving it in through the door, pushing post to one side and feeling the chill of our home that had been left in a state of disarray when we'd hurriedly left to get to the airport on time. God, so much had changed since that morning at the start of the trip. I felt like I'd been punched in the stomach, taking it all in.

Walking slowly through each room and seeing our things in this dull morning light only highlighted how miserable I felt. I flinched at seeing our half-finished mugs of cold tea that had a layer of fuzzy skin on the top, as we hadn't had time to wash before we'd left. I'm sure he'd said he was going to take care of that whilst I'd chased up finding out where the taxi was to take us to the airport. I sighed and chucked the tea down the drain before letting the gross mugs soak.

The light on our answerphone was flashing. I glared at it realising that it wasn't *ours* any more. Although my expression softened when I realised that the only people who left messages on the landline were my parents.

'Hola!' My mum's shrill voice filled the silent room. 'Wait – is that Spanish or Italian?' I heard her whisper to my dad, who took the phone off her. 'Hello, love, just checking that you got back okay? We've just docked and managed to get a decent phone signal. Anyway, just checking that you've both got back safely and had a great time. You and Ben would both love it here, maybe a place to add to your travel to-do list? I could see you both on a cruise, and no, it's not just for old people.'

My dad chuckled. My chest smartened at the sound of my boyfriend's name, sorry, my ex-boyfriend's name. 'Give us a call when you get a minute. We miss you and love you.'

I took a deep breath as I replayed the message. My parents would be crushed when they heard what had happened between us; they'd really liked Ben. I didn't have the energy to unpack so left my case slumped on the floor of the hall and picked up the post and began flicking through it while waiting for the kettle to boil. Amongst bills, flyers for a deep carpet clean and a takeaway menu was a handwritten envelope addressed to me and Ben. I tore it open. It was an invitation to a party, to Jimmy and Shelley's leaving party. As soon as I saw the jaunty font, colourful images and my best friend's handwriting I forced myself to blink back the tears.

It suddenly felt very real that they were leaving, leaving me alone and single and miserable whilst they lived it up on the other side of the world. Whilst they got engaged – the pain of realising it was Shelley's ring I had admired on my finger suddenly hit me square in the chest. I scrunched the card into a ball and chucked it in the overflowing bin. Suddenly I forgot about making a cuppa and just wanted to get under my bed covers to block everything out.

CHAPTER 24

Gruntle (v.) – To put in good humour

I woke up in the foulest mood after sleeping through my alarm, not helped by burning the tips of my ears on my hair straighteners, snapping a nail and splashing toothpaste on my top, all before I'd even left the flat. Today was going to be a hundred times worse knowing that I would be forced to speak to Ben and try and keep up some sort of level of normality in front of our employees.

As I made my way to our shop, a heavy dull ache seeped through me. It wasn't just the fact that my holiday was over and real life was about to begin again, plus all the emails and messages I'd no doubt be busy with. I was actually ready to get back to work; in a weird way I'd missed being at the centre of everything at Lonely Hearts Travels, but seeing as I'd had no contact with Ben for over twenty-four hours, I felt sick at this new reality I faced.

Taking a deep breath, I pushed open the door and walked into what looked like a bombsite with dust cloths covering the floor, ladders propped up against walls and some tinny version of an Elton John song playing from a radio that had been propped on a decorator's table.

What the…?

'Conrad?' I called out, making a young lad who was flicking a paintbrush across the back wall jump.

'He's just nipped out to get some coffee. The machine isn't working, you see. Can I help?' The man, who must have been in his early twenties, stood up.

'What is going on in here?' I snapped.

'All right, love? Who are you?' An older-looking man, who I hadn't spotted crouching behind the decorator's table propped in the centre of the room, also stood up and went to stand next to the baby-faced guy.

'I'm the owner of this business! What the hell are you doing?'

Just then Conrad walked through the front door holding a tray of drinks and laughing with Kelli. They both stopped abruptly as they saw me.

'Georgia? We didn't think you'd be back until tomorrow!' Kelli said, stepping over an unopened tin of paint.

I spun on my heel to face her. 'Can someone tell me why my shop looks like an extra on *Sixty-Minute Makeover*?'

'Ben hasn't told you then?' Conrad asked in a low voice, flicking his eyes between mine and Kelli's.

'Told me what!' I screeched.

'He wanted to give this place a lick of paint, to freshen it up, you know how you were saying the other day how tired it was looking in here? Well he'd arranged a surprise to get the work done whilst you were both away!' Conrad beamed before dropping his smile at my angry expression. 'I thought he would have broken the news to you in Chile, so it wouldn't have been such a shock, as it probably is now.'

'No,' I said through gritted teeth, wishing someone would turn off Elton bloody John. 'He didn't tell me.'

Kelli's eyes widened; luckily she picked up on my less than impressed mood and turned to the two men. 'Give us a minute will you?' They obediently shuffled out of the shop and lit up a fag, relieved to be given an impromptu smoking break.

Conrad put the cups down, spilling tea onto the dust cloths. I watched the brown stain spread across the floor and tried to calm my breathing down, as he pulled out a chair for me.

'Georgia, are you okay?' Kelli asked nervously.

I willed my heart to stop hammering. 'Fine. I just wasn't expecting to walk in to this chaos.'

Okay, I was probably overreacting, it was a mess in here but it was only superficial. But in light of our argument this just felt like another secret he'd kept from me about the business.

'I take it Ben's not here yet?' I snapped.

'No.' She gave me an odd look. 'Let me speak to the guys and get them to finish up as quickly as possible. They should be almost done.'

I nodded and tried to ignore the looks that passed between her and Conrad.

'Good. We have a lot of work to be getting on with and there is no way customers can come in here with it looking like this.'

*

The decorators had finished up and moved their equipment out so at least we could properly open our doors again, which also helped with the smell of fresh paint lingering in the air. I'd been silently working at my desk, letting the other two deal with phone calls and customers milling about, for the past few hours. Leaning back in my chair to massage my neck I caught Conrad flick his eyes over to me, nervously.

I sighed. I shouldn't be taking it out on either of them. 'Listen, I'm sorry about before. I think I've got a bit of jet lag. It was just a shock walking into my shop and seeing it looking such a state, that's all.'

'I bet it was, and don't worry about it! We're glad to have you back no matter what mood you're in,' he said kindly.

'So, apart from this place getting a lick of paint –' I glanced around at the room that did look pretty amazing '– fill me in on all I've missed,' I suggested gently.

Conrad kept his worried gaze on me for a second longer. 'Well, that thing is still knackered.' He pointed his head over to the coffee machine. 'I've been onto the manufacturers but they're hiding behind some ridiculous trading standards loophole.'

I needed this. I needed my mind to be kept busy with the normal day-to-day office politics and hearing him moan about inanimate objects.

'Ah, come off it! Just tell her the truth,' Kelli called out, listening to our conversation.

I spotted a blush dance on Conrad's round cheeks as he hurriedly messed about with shoving a gnawed biro into a pen pot on his desk.

'Don't know what you're talking about,' he muttered.

'Georgia – the coffee machine is knackered but this one –' she nodded to Conrad '– won't get another one as that would mean missing out on his daily visits to see Val.'

'Who?'

'Val, the barista.'

'She's not *just* a barista. She's the owner, *actually*.' Conrad sniffed, unable to help himself.

'Oh, well, either way, this one has got it baaaaad.' Kelli rolled her eyes as she told me, and I couldn't help but smile. The Conrad I knew couldn't have been further from your stereotypical lovesick puppy, although he was wearing the look pretty well.

Conrad hesitated for a moment and then let out a deep sigh. 'Okay, it's true. I fancy her!'

Kelli smiled smugly. 'I knew it!'

'Yeah, but I'm not going to do anything about it,' he mumbled under his breath.

'What?' I asked. Okay, so my love life was going down the shitter but I'd never seen him look so fragile and vulnerable as he did now. 'Why not?'

He shuffled uncomfortably in his seat, glancing round to check no new customers had wandered in without us realising. 'I don't know how,' he said so quietly I almost missed it.

'How to ask a woman out?' I asked to make sure I'd heard him right.

He nodded forcefully and then threw his big paw-sized hands to his reddened face. 'It's flaming embarrassing, and you can stop giggling over there,' he warned Kelli who sat up straighter and forced her lips to stop twitching into a smile.

'Well.' I leant forward, pleased to have the distraction from my own thoughts. 'Have you spoken to her yet? Other than placing your order?'

Conrad nodded slowly. 'Yeah, but only about the weather and the difference between soya and normal milk.' He shut his eyes, wincing. 'That wasn't my finest moment.'

At this Kelli couldn't contain herself. 'You used milk as a chat-up line? Oh my God, that is tragic. How dairy-ing of you; that is an udder mess.' She cracked herself up with her awful puns, ignoring his death stare.

'Okay, yeah, maybe that's not the quickest way to a woman's heart,' I said softly, trying to defuse the situation before Conrad started firing staples at Kelli. 'But, it's a start. Well, the next time just come out and ask her if she'd like to go for a drink.'

'A glass of milk, maybe?' Kelli said, before ducking under her desk to avoid the ball of paper Conrad launched at her.

'What's the worst that can happen? If she says no, then we'll just get our coffee machine properly fixed and you never have to see her again?'

He thought for a minute. 'Yeah, maybe. I think I'll hold off on getting that repaired, just in case,' he said, nodding to the forlorn coffee maker.

I smiled at him. Throughout the whole conversation I'd been keeping one eye on the door waiting for Ben's arrival, unsure whether he was going to show up or not.

'So, you didn't come in with Ben this morning?' Conrad asked, reading my mind and trying to take the pressure away from his awful pick-up techniques before Kelli started making mooing noises.

I blinked rapidly and buried my head into the stack of papers that I needed to sign for our next ad campaign. 'No. I didn't see him this morning.' I gave Conrad a look that said please don't push me on this; I'm too fragile and exhausted to explain it all.

'Ah, okay.'

I nodded and let out a small cough before getting back to work.

The thing was, Ben didn't show up. The afternoon had crept up on us and there was still no sign of him. I tried to bite down the worry that this was so unlike him and focus on the more pressing emotions of feeling pissed off that he had obviously just decided to take an unplanned duvet day. Conrad didn't push the matter again but I overhead him and Kelli talking in hushed whispers trying to figure out what was going on. I was too tired and drained to fill them in, and there was no way I was going to ring Ben and ask him where he was and what he was playing at. It was probably for the best that I was saved from being in this shop with him today, when everything still felt too raw between us.

'Oh. Erm hi…' Kelli's posh phone voice made me look up from my desk. She'd stood up and was holding her phone in a strange way, pointing to it dramatically as she mouthed something that I couldn't quite work out. 'Yep. It's all fine here. Busy.'

Conrad let out a gasp and turned to me as he cracked her code. 'Ben. She's talking to Ben.'

I felt my whole body tense up. I swallowed down saliva that had rushed to my mouth and kept my eyes trained on Kelli, who had also gone a little pale under her heavy blusher.

'All right then. I'll let everyone know. Yep. Okay. Bye.' The call must not have lasted more than a minute but she placed the receiver back and flopped onto her chair as if she had just won some vicious bidding war on eBay.

'That was Ben.' She turned to face me.

I nodded. Conrad's eyes were flicking between the pair of us.

'Well, what did he say?' he asked, not able to bear the tension any longer.

'He said that he was taking some time off for personal reasons and that he hoped everything was okay here.'

I slowly exhaled. 'And?'

'And, he said he would see us all soon.' She bit her lip at the awkwardness of being the messenger.

'Well, at least we know he's safe and alive, I guess,' Conrad said getting up to flick the kettle on. 'Saves us an extra job of ringing round the hospitals.'

'Conrad!' Kelli rolled her eyes and then turned to face me. 'Are you sure you're all right, Georgia?'

I nodded and plastered on a smile that I knew didn't reach my eyes. 'Fine. Well let's crack on, otherwise these invoices will never get completed.'

She bobbed her head and turned back to her computer screen. The atmosphere felt as flat and limp as my hair.

I could sense the concerned glances bouncing between the two of them and over to me but I just had to carry on as if everything was normal. Maybe Conrad was right, it was at least something that he'd bothered to call and update us at all.

Except I couldn't concentrate on the paperwork in my hands; the numbers seemed to bounce around the page like scurrying ants. I couldn't believe that Ben couldn't bear the thought of seeing me this much, that he would prefer to just disappear than face up to reality. How long was this going to last? And when were we going to talk about the lease for the London office, which we now couldn't afford? I mentally shook myself and tried to get through my to-do list so I could leave here on time. Even if the thought of heading to an empty flat that was in desperate need of a clean filled me with as much joy as trudging through these finances did.

I closed my eyes to try and gather my thoughts. Maybe it was for the best that we had some time apart.

He didn't show up for work the next day. Or the day after that either. And by day three I was at risk of developing a permanent crick in my neck from keeping one eye on the door and one eye on my ever-growing workload. The worry I'd first felt had quickly dissipated into a burning rage that he'd left us in the lurch, made me look like a right tit in front of our staff and obviously couldn't care less about us or the business. Trying hard not to think about someone when you're staring at their empty desk all day, and sleeping in their empty bed all night, is easier said than done. I was furious with him for treating me and the business with so little respect.

I was barely sleeping, torturing myself as I lay with my eyes open and mind racing, running through everything we'd said and hadn't said when we were in the middle of the Patagonian wilderness. Every time my phone buzzed, the sick feeling in my stomach that it would be him had built to breaking point. But it never was him, just my parents sending blurry photos from the cruise they were on.

I'd left work early and made my way down Market Street, preparing myself to head over to Marie's for the evening. I wasn't in the mood to socialise but the prospect of another evening alone in our flat made me agree to see her for a few hours. I was so busy running through things in my head that I almost missed someone shouting out my name.

'Georgia!' a female voice called down the busy street. Straining my neck, I couldn't help but smile as I saw Shelley frantically waving, almost taking out the eye of a dawdling pensioner, as she jogged over to me. 'You were off in your own little world then!' She laughed before pulling me into a hug. 'I was getting worried as I've not heard from you since you got back! Did you get the invite to our leaving do?' The words tumbled out of her excited mouth.

I pulled back and nodded. 'Yeah.'

'Wait!' She grabbed my left hand before her face dropped. 'Oh.'

I pulled it back and tugged at my sleeve. 'Yeah, we didn't get engaged.' I could hardly tell her that in actual fact it would soon be *her* wearing the stunning ring I'd tried on.

'Oh, right…' Shelley trailed off, examining my face as if trying to follow.

'In fact, we broke up. But then I guess he's already told you that himself.' I'd actually been a little annoyed that she hadn't bothered to get in touch about it all.

She stared at me blank-faced. 'You broke up!' She gasped. 'Wait, why would Ben tell me that?'

'Because he's staying at yours and Jimmy's?' I said slowly as she shook her head in confusion.

'No he's not. I've not seen or heard from either of you since you left.'

I felt tears prick my stupid tired eyes. 'He's not staying with you?'

She shook her head. 'Maybe he's at Trisha's?'

I nodded absently. Yeah, he was probably staying with his godmother. Why did it even matter? He'd called to tell us he was okay and not lying dead in a ditch, so the details of exactly where he was were insignificant. 'Anyway, I don't really want to talk about him. How are you?'

She nodded slowly, desperate to know the details but understanding I didn't feel like talking. 'Fine, busy, actually it's so good to see you. I thought I'd done something to upset you, you know, with us moving,' Shelley said in a sad voice that pulled at my heart. I needed to get over sulking that she was leaving and start being a proper friend to her.

'I'm still gutted, but that's just me being selfish.' I smiled sadly at her relieved face and squeezed her arm. 'I'm going to miss you loads.'

'Well think about the holidays you can have on the other side of the world! When you and Ben, you know, sort it out.'

I shook my head. 'I don't know if we will. It was one hell of a fight we had.'

It was her turn to rub my arm. 'You'll figure it out, you always do. Anyway, I need you both to make up because I'm not sure how I'll cope with it being just me and Jimmy for all that time!'

'You getting nervous?'

'It's a big move, a big step forward, for both of us. I just hope we can make it work.' She caught herself. 'Sorry, you don't need to hear me wittering on about this sort of stuff.'

'It's fine, just as you two will be fine.' I had to bite my tongue to stop myself telling her that she was soon to be celebrating her engagement, that Jimmy was in this for the long haul.

'Thank you, same to you. Argh, I'm so sorry, hon, but I need to be off. I'm already ten minutes late!' She winced, looking at her watch. 'Call me soon and chin up, okay?'

I nodded and watched her get lost in the crowd before quickly pulling my mobile out of my pocket to ring Trisha. If Ben wasn't at Jimmy's, then he must be with her. I hesitated before pressing the call button, as I didn't want him to think I was checking up on him when he so obviously wanted some space. I hung up before it rang through and trudged over to Marie's house, suddenly desperate for a strong drink.

CHAPTER 25

Obstreperous (adj.) – Stubbornly resistant to control; unruly

'So, when's Mike back?' I asked, ripping open a bag of Kettle Chips. I couldn't remember the last time I'd eaten a vegetable, let alone a substantial meal, since getting back from Chile. Marie had told me off for getting too scrawny and told me that I also needed to sort my eyebrows out. I'd explained that plucking a few stray straggly hairs wasn't high on my to-do list, and what was the point anyway? She'd scoffed that it was turning into a monobrow and that no man would fancy me with one of those.

'God knows. The last time he went out with his work mates he called me from some random B&B in Wales as they'd decided it would be hilarious to just jump on the next train to somewhere and party there. Not so funny when they all fell asleep and ended up at the last stop on the line in the middle of nowhere. Every pub was shut, not a kebab in sight, and only one chintzy bed and breakfast who let the three of them stay as long as they shared a room and didn't mind cats. He soon found out that the cat allergy he thought he'd grown out of as a kid was still with him. Serves him right though!' She shook her head laughing.

'He'll behave himself tonight though? With you being so close to your due date surely?' I asked worriedly. I knew how much Mike liked a drink and if he felt like he had been relieved of his paternal duties for a night who knew what rock'n'roll things he could get up to.

Marie rubbed her tummy protectively. 'Yeah. He's only down the local. I had to kick him out of the house to go. You're here, and he is literally a ten-minute walk away. Plus, this baby has shown no signs of budging at all.'

I nodded worriedly and said a silent prayer that the baby would stay put whilst I was around or else Mike would be yanked back from the pub faster than you could say Llanfair-pwllgwyngyll-gogery-chwyrn-drobwll-llan-tysilio-gogo-goch.

'So, tell me all!' Marie said brightly as she tried to get comfy on the sofa and handed me a glass of wine to chink with her glass of pineapple juice.

I rolled my eyes. 'Where to begin…'

'Well, I don't want to speak out of turn here but you look like shit and I've not seen any bling on your finger so I'm guessing the proposal didn't happen?'

'Full marks, detective,' I said dryly. I sighed. I was desperate for a night, or even a few hours, when Ben wasn't on my mind. 'There is no engagement ring and no happy ending.'

'Well, maybe he just didn't find the right spot or the right time?'

'Marie, we split up. At least, I think we did. I've not seen him for a few days; he hasn't been in at work or back to our flat since we came back.'

Her face was the exact same shocked picture that Shelley's had been.

'What do you mean?'

'I mean that my taste in men has once again proved to be as reliable as loaning your money to the son of a Nigerian prince.' I shook my head. She narrowed her eyes trying to understand what I was going on about. 'He has been seeing his ex, that pretty Alice girl. She is a financial advisor slash investment queen and he wanted her advice in moving forward with some place in London he's found for the next Lonely Hearts office.'

She took a quick intake of breath. 'He's going ahead on the London move even though you said you didn't want to?'

'Bingo.' I took a big gulp of my wine, enjoying the chilled tang of sauvignon blanc slipping down my throat. 'Apparently he'd agreed on a deal, but it was based on us winning the prize money from the TV show. Which we didn't. So it was all for nothing. Then he was going on about how I was wrong, how I never let him make decisions with the business and was suffocating him.'

'Wow. What did you say?'

'I said he was talking bollocks.'

'But he was going to propose for God's sake?!'

'Oh, that's the best part. The engagement ring was never for me. Jimmy had asked him to keep it safe before he asks Shelley.'

'No!'

'Yup.'

'Oh, Georgia, I'm sorry,' she kept repeating, shaking her head and rubbing her tummy.

'Me too. But do you know what the real issue is here?' I called out as she waddled back in from the toilet for the umpteenth time.

'What's that?'

'Well if he couldn't handle a successful powerful woman then more fool him. I mean, him going on about me not letting him make business decisions – which is utter bullshit – he just needs to realise that I am living large and in charge, and if he doesn't like that then he can lump it,' I said jutting my chin out and finishing my glass.

I saw Marie flinch.

'What?'

'Nothing, it's just…' She paused as if choosing her words carefully. 'It's just that this isn't you. It's just an act.'

'What? Yeah it is me!' I was gobsmacked.

'Yes,' she sighed. 'This is you in a business sense, this tough and powerful take-no-prisoners woman. I mean, I guess you need to be when dealing with clients and tour operators and complaints and whatever else, but that's not the real you. And Ben knows that too.'

I stared at her feeling like someone was squeezing the air out of me. My previously pumped out chest caved in as she continued.

'The real Georgia is just like every other woman: insecure, trying her goddam best but deep down is terrified that it's all going to be snatched away. That's why you put on this bolshie, nothing-can-hurt-me attitude.'

When Ben had said that I'd just figured he was lashing out. I was shocked to think that's how people saw me. That's how *she* saw me.

'You're not Beyoncé, I mean I bet even Queen Bey has her down days. It's okay to be vulnerable, to let others in, Georgia. Yes, Ben has been a complete dick about the way he has handled things but deep down he's done the London thing to impress you, to help you and to show you that you can trust him. Not everyone is going to let you down like Alex did.' *She* sat back on the sofa watching me as her words sunk in.

'I…I…' I stuttered, not sure what to say. 'It still doesn't make it right what he did.' I grabbed my glass and accidently spilt quite a bit of wine on the table and into the half empty bowl of crisps we'd placed on a magazine.

'Bugger.' Maybe I'd drunk more than I thought. I leant forward to mop it up with a couple of napkins as Marie groaned. 'Okay, so maybe you're right, but I'm just trying to do the best that I can. I don't want to stay the same Georgia that I was a few years ago, the one too scared to say boo to a goose, to stand up to Alex's horrible, snobby mum. Surely, everyone should be pleased that I've developed a backbone?' I continued to babble on as the strong scent of sauvignon blanc hit my nostrils, making me sneeze. Just then Marie groaned again but louder this time.

'All right, you can stop judging me…' I trailed off when I turned around and saw the normally bronzed face of my best friend contorted in pain and the colour of a squeezed plum. 'Marie!'

I leapt up, spilling even more wine, not sure where to go or what to do but hating seeing her looking like she was being stabbed with a rusty knitting needle in her pelvis.

'Owwwww,' she moaned as she let out the breath she had been dangerously holding in.

'Oh my God! Is it happening? Is it happening?' I began fanning her face and hurriedly zapped the television off so I could concentrate on the real-life medical emergency that was playing out before me.

'No, I don't think so. It's probably just Braxton Hicks.'

'The what now? Toni Braxton? What's she got to do with anything?'

She uncomfortably shifted on the sofa and started pushing out low pants of breath as she shook her head.

'No, you muppet. Braxton Hicks, it's like this phantom labour where your body gets ready for the big show.'

'What? So you have like two labours?' I asked, horrified.

She had her eyes squeezed tight and stayed silent, focusing on her breathing.

'Shit! What shall we do?' I stood up and started circling around the carpet.

After a moment, as the contraction or whatever the hell it was subsided, her breathing calmed down. 'It's fine, I'm fine.'

'Fine? You don't look fine!'

'Georgia, calm down. I had them with Cole, it's perfectly natural, well that was the biggest one I've ever had but, look, I'm okay now.'

I kept my eyes trained on her. 'Are you sure? Maybe we should call the midwife to, you know, check.'

She nodded. 'Yeah, you're probably right.'

After a short phone call the colour had come back in Marie's face. 'She said if I get another one then I need to go in, but not to panic, like I said it's perfectly normal.'

I let out a sigh of relief. 'Thank God. You scared me!' I wrapped my arms around her.

'Hey, not too tight, you'll squish the baby!'

'Oops, sorry! Shall I call Mike, to get him to come home?'

She nodded. 'Yeah, if you don't mind? Sorry to be so dramatic and ruin our night.'

'You don't need to apologise and you're not being dramatic. If that was me I'd be wheeled out in an ambulance by now.'

Neither of us mentioned the fact that after what had happened with Cole's birth it was totally reasonable and she was probably right to be on edge more.

With Mike safely back home, albeit a little squiffy, I left the two of them to it and caught a taxi straight home. I felt this strange pang of jealousy watching her loyal and loving boyfriend race through to hug her, the look of worry etched on his face when she explained about the dramatic 'pre-labour' signs she'd experienced. Watching the two of them only made my chest ache for Ben. It was a stupid feeling I tried hard to ignore. For the entire journey back through the darkened streets I let myself think about what she'd said.

Maybe Marie was right about me putting on a front and having a #girlboss attitude now, but that was only because I needed to. I'd never been in charge of a successful business before, paying people's wages and the pressure that brings. I wasn't about to change, just because it made Ben feel he had to prove something, to wave his willy about and assert some stupid male ego when it wasn't needed.

Not even bothering to get undressed, eat anything for dinner or even turn on the light, I crawled under the covers and squeezed my eyes tightly shut, feeling like the whole weight of the world was resting on our Ikea duvet cover. The duvet that still had a faint smell of Ben's aftershave lingering on it, I thought, before I drifted into a restless sleep.

CHAPTER 26

Ruly (adj.) – Obedient, orderly

'Is Ben not coming back then?' Conrad finally came out and asked the question that I knew had been burning on his lips since I'd returned from Chile. It was the end of another day, another day without Ben showing his face, and it was just the two of us in the empty shop about to close up. I'd been working late the last few nights not only to catch up as I was trying to do the work of two people in Ben's absence, but also because it was better than the alternative of going back to our flat that still smelled of him, being surrounded by his things, and being alone with memories of us that clouded my exhausted mind.

'I'm surprised it's taken you this long to ask,' I said dryly.

Conrad let out a deep laugh. 'I was trying to be tactful. My mum always says I needed to work on letting people talk when they were ready, rather than sticking my two penneth worth in. But it's been a fair few days now and you don't seem like you're going to talk any time soon, so thought I may as well come out and ask.' He shrugged, making me smile.

'Yeah, well, I don't know where he is or when he'll be back.' It was my turn to shrug, my shoulders feeling heavier than they ever had.

'Did something happen in Chile, then?'

I nodded.

'You honestly don't have to talk if you don't want, although I am an excellent listener.' He said more softly, 'It's these big wide shoulders I have, perfect for placing your worries on.' He gave me a goofy smile before pulling himself up. 'As well as carrying heavy items such as knackered pieces of furniture.'

'Yep, that too.' I couldn't help but smile. I sighed and took a deep breath. 'Yes, something happened in Chile. I guess that saying is true: you never fully know someone until you travel with them.'

Conrad gave me a look, encouraging me to continue.

'I guess we just want different things. It had been going so well too. But then this last task they had us in this freezing, middle-of-nowhere crazy wilderness and we had to get from A to B. Only we got very lost somewhere in the middle.' I could laugh at how ironic this was.

Conrad stayed silent thinking this over. 'So, that's it then?'

'What do you mean?'

'Well, you have one fight and it's all over.'

'It's not that simple.'

He bobbed his head. 'Yeah, because it's not like you two work twenty-four hours a day running a stressful but successful business as well as try to find time to be a couple, is it? Fights happen all the time in relationships but it doesn't mean it is the end. To be honest, Georgia, and I don't want to speak out of line here, but I'm amazed you two aren't at each other's throats more often considering how closely you work and play together.'

I rolled my eyes at his attempt at reverse psychology. 'It's not like that, Conrad. This wasn't just a petty little argument about leaving the loo seat up. It…it…was bigger than that.' I felt my stomach flip as my mind was filled with our big fight, leaving me feeling as worthless as when Alex left me. No, this was worse, much worse than when my wedding had been called off. This time I had willingly gone into this, knowing I'd been so hurt before but hoping it would never happen again and trusting that Ben would take care of the piece of my heart I'd offered him. Fool me once shame on you, fool me twice shame on me and all that.

'I bet it was. But that doesn't mean you're both just walking away. Taking the coward's way out.'

I seethed. 'There is only one coward in this situation. I've been the one turning up for work every day. Imagine if I had just decided I wanted to go AWOL too? We could have at least been civil, but by leaving us all in the lurch like this, that's unacceptable and cowardly behaviour.' I took a deep breath. 'Sorry, this is really not professional of me to be spilling my guts like this.'

'It's fine, me and professional don't always mix.' He chortled. 'We're just concerned about you, about both of you.'

I nodded sadly. 'Thank you. Right, so I completely forgot – what happened with Val in the coffee shop?'

He dipped his head to try and hide the blush spreading across his grinning face. 'Well, there may be some developments in that area…'

'Oh, don't be coy!'

'We're going out tomorrow night, and no, not for a glass of milk!' He threw his head back and laughed. 'I'm taking her to this concert on the lost works of Beethoven, kind of a speciality subject for me.'

My eyes widened. 'Well, you are a man of mystery.'

'Sometimes us men can just surprise you, you know.'

I was saved from having to reply by my phone ringing.

'Georgia?' a man's voice in a soft Scottish accent asked.

'Yes, speaking.'

'Oh hi, it's Jerry from See Me TV Productions.'

That's why I recognised the voice but what was he doing calling me? 'Oh, hi, how are things?'

There was a deep sigh down the line. 'A little hectic to be honest. Listen, I can't give too much away over the phone but we really need you and Ben to come down to the studios tomorrow. I'm so sorry about the short notice – we will sort all the transport arrangements, it's just very urgent that we see you.'

'Is everything okay, Jerry?'

'Like I said, I don't want to give too much away, but yes it's fine, just a few loose ends we need to tie up before the show is aired.' I hardly recognised the relaxed man I'd met in the harassed tones on the other end of the line. 'Is that going to be okay?'

'Oh, right, yep.' I flicked my eyes over my diary; there was nothing I couldn't rearrange. 'Have you managed to speak to Ben, because, he's…he's not in the office at the moment.'

'We're on it. I think Blaise has made contact.'

I felt my stomach tighten, and not in a good way. 'Oh, okay.'

'So, we're on? I'll email you the timings and see you tomorrow?' He seemed pretty keen at getting me off the phone.

'Yeah, fine.'

We hung up and I stared at the receiver, unsure what the hell was going on.

*

'Ben not with you?' Dana, the dog lover, asked as she met me at the reception of the chaotic TV production offices.

'He's not here yet?' I asked, feeling a chill run down my spine. I'd been so worked up during the whole train journey down to London at seeing him again. I'd spent ages getting ready this morning hoping make-up and a well-ironed pretty top would be the armour I needed to see him again.

She shook her head, dramatically making her long dangly ceramic paw-print earrings clang together. 'Maybe he's stuck on the Tube.'

I nodded along with her as she herded me down the corridor. 'Yeah, maybe.'

I wasn't being taken to the small room with the relaxing sofas like last time; instead she opened the door on a bright and airy boardroom. Sat at a long Perspex table with funky coloured chairs lining each side was a stressed out looking Jerry and a slightly frazzled Anna. They both jumped from their seats where they had previously been poring over stacks of papers.

'Georgia! Come in, come in!' Jerry plastered on a smile that didn't quite meet his tired-looking eyes.

As I hesitantly walked in I noticed that they weren't alone. Partially hidden behind flourishing spider plants sat Gareth, Jade, Simon and Dawn.

'Oh, hi guys,' I said, feeling more confused with every step I took.

'Georgia, nice to see you again.' Simon smiled kindly as he half got up from his seat. Gareth and Dawn both had strange looks on their faces as Jade waved a hand before going back to her phone screen.

'Erm, yeah you too,' I mumbled before Anna pulled me into a cursory hug.

'Hi, nice to see you again,' she said before ordering Dana to get me a drink. 'So, no Ben with you?' She looked behind me to the closed door.

'No, did you not manage to speak to him?'

Jerry shook his head. 'We couldn't make contact and I wasn't sure if he would have travelled down with you?'

I shook my head trying to get a grip of my emotions. 'Nope, just me.'

'Ah okay, well never mind, at least you're here. You can let him know what we've got to tell you the next time you see him, right?'

'Right.' I nodded absently.

'Well, sit down, sit down.' He pulled a chair out for me that was as uncomfortable as you'd imagine a plastic bucket to be. 'I'm so sorry for being a little guarded when we all spoke on the phone yesterday. There have been some *developments*.' He glanced at Anna as he said that last word. 'Jade, if you could maybe put your phone down for this?'

Jade sighed dramatically and tucked her phone into her blinged-up handbag resting on the chair next to her. A chair that was probably set out for Ben, I thought, before forcing myself together.

Jerry clasped his hands together. 'We really wanted to let you all know in person.'

'Know what?' Gareth asked, leaning back in his chair. He was wearing a garish lemon-coloured shirt and what I was sure was fake tan, judging by the watery streaks up his neck. I then realised that this impromptu get-together was down two members – the winning pair – where were Natalia and Tony?

'Ah, cheers, Dana.' Jerry was interrupted from revealing all as he glanced over my shoulder to the door while Dana wheeled in a trolley laden with coffee, tea, juice and pastries. I'd not had anything to eat yet and felt my stomach rumbling just looking at the food. 'If you'd all like to help yourselves?' Everyone else dived into the artfully arranged spread but me. 'Georgia, what can we get you?'

'Oh just a tea, thanks, and maybe a small croissant?' I said, quietly.

I was sure Anna flicked her eyes to my tummy as I said that but the wait was killing me. I needed to have something to line my stomach with. A few moments later, after Dana had left us alone and I had daintily nibbled on the flaky, buttery pastry, Jerry cleared his throat.

'So, as you know we are currently editing *Wanderlust Warriors…*'

I nodded as if I had some idea of how this industry worked.

'Mhmm.'

'Well, during the edits we uncovered some uncomfortable truths.'

A piece of pastry caught at the back of my throat. I gulped at my glass of water to wash it down. My eyes instinctively flicked between Dawn and Gareth. Was their dirty secret about to come to light? They both shuffled uncomfortably in their seats. Jade was pouring sugar into her full cup of tea and Simon was dabbing at a splodge of apricot jam that had fallen from a cronut onto his lap, missing their guilty expressions.

I realised that Anna was staring at me. Was it something to do with Ben and I? Had our argument been *that* bad?

'Well, the eagle-eyed amongst you will have worked out that Natalia and Tony aren't here today.'

Jade gawped around as if only just realising this.

'The reason for their absence is that they have been stripped of their winning title.' The room fell silent, processing this information. 'We found out during the edits that they had cheated during the last task. They pulled the wool over all of our eyes.' Anna finished with a deep sigh.

'No! Really?!' Dawn whipped her head around to face Anna and Jerry, whose expressions showed they weren't joking.

'So.' Jerry cleared his throat. 'We wanted to be upfront with all of you and bring you here today to let you know that because of this...' he paused '...we are going to announce Georgia and Ben as the winners because they came second on that final task,' Jerry said giving me a bright smile.

Thank God I'd put my croissant down or else I really would have choked on it. 'What? We've won?'

He nodded brightly. 'Yes! Congratulations, the prize money is all yours!'

'No fucking way!' Gareth bellowed and banged his fist on the table making tea spill out of Jade's cup and pool dangerously close to her designer handbag. 'We have just as much right as they do to that prize!'

Jerry sat up straight in his seat. 'Well, you had both completed a task each but they beat you in arriving to the log cabin.' He shrugged. 'I'm sorry we can't announce you all as winners but fair's fair.' He ignored Gareth mumbling some less than savoury words under his breath. 'We needed you to all come here today to film some reaction pieces with you and tie up the loose ends this has caused us. It is a headache, and trust me, one we could do without, but the show is so close to being aired that we have to do them today.'

'But Ben ain't even here?' Jade piped up.

Anna pursed her lips. 'We don't have any time to waste.'

I sat back in my hard chair trying to take this in when Gareth shot up from his seat.

'No. This is bullshit. That prize money is just as much ours as it is *hers*,' he spat glaring at me.

'Hey now, there's no need for that aggressive attitude. By the sounds of it Georgia and Ben won fair and square.' Simon kindly stuck up for me.

'Pipe down, grandad. Don't even get me started on what's right when you're married to that slut.'

Dawn visibly tensed; Jade immediately shot her gaze to her phone that was back in her petite hands. She'd heard all of this before. Simon, and Jerry and Anna for that matter, had not.

'What did you call my wife?' Simon growled. A vein on the side of his mole-peppered forehead was threatening to break through the hard scowl he was giving Gareth.

'Ignore him, darling.' Dawn meekly patted her husband's tense forearm. It appeared like their relationship roles were truly reversed.

'No,' Simon snapped. 'I will not ignore him. The whole time in Chile he acted as if he was the cock of the town. When in fact he is just a cock.'

The whole room fell silent in shock at hearing Simon swear. Anna's and Jerry's heads were flicking between the two men who had their hands planted on the table and upper bodies poised for a fight as if watching a thrilling game of tennis. This seemed to disarm Gareth for a moment before he squared up once more.

'At least I know how to use my cock. Had your wife screaming for more,' he boasted before realising that his ridiculously patient girlfriend was sat right next to him.

'Oh for fuck's sake, Gareth!' Jade screeched.

At this exact moment she got out of her seat and flounced out of the door, calling Gareth a granny shagger and that she didn't need to put up with his shit any longer, Simon lunged at the smarmy salesman.

'Stop it!' Dawn squealed as her usually reserved husband began laying into Gareth's tubby tummy. The two men were soon embroiled in a genuine fist fight. Jerry was trying to get in between them to break it up, Anna had bellowed down the corridor for security, Dawn was pleading with her man that Gareth wasn't worth it, that it was all lies, and I didn't know where to put myself.

Two burly men dressed head to toe in black with matching earpieces barged into the room and pulled the two men, now heavily wheezing and sweating, off each other before frogmarching Gareth out of the room.

'He started it!' he yelled as he was led off.

Jerry glared at Simon. 'You going to calm down or do we need to send you off too?'

Simon's chest was rising and falling faster than recommended for a man of his age and fitness. 'I'm so sorry. I'm calm now. I promise.' He couldn't look at anyone else except Jerry who bobbed his head and sighed.

Dawn was softly crying and Anna hadn't returned since calling for security. I just stared gobsmacked at Simon, at this man who had developed a backbone. I then realised that everyone involved in this show, which was meant to celebrate the success of working relationships, was besieged with problems. Ben and I weren't the only casualties.

Eventually, Jerry pulled his head up from in between his hands. 'It was about time that prick got his comeuppance, to be fair. We also discovered that Gareth may have been embellishing his actual role in the travel industry.'

Anna sauntered into the room and let out a snort at this. 'Yeah, and the rest.' She turned to face me, looking as shocked as I did at the turn of events. 'He's not some hotshot social media travel guru or whatever it was that he claimed; instead he can barely make a living and blags his way around on freebies.'

Wow. 'Oh, right.'

Jerry rubbed at his beard. 'So, as you can see, this is why we wanted you all to come here. It is quite an embarrassing situation for us. We should have picked up on this ages ago and chosen different contributors.' He took his glasses off and rubbed his eyes. He looked like he'd aged ten years since I last saw him. 'By the looks of it Gareth has been escorted from the premises and Jade has gone AWOL so no final interviews will be taking place today. We can assure you that there will be an addition to the end of the show explaining to viewers that you and Ben were the deserving winners.'

'We can still take part?' Simon interjected, obviously wanting to make amends for his out of character behaviour.

'I think maybe we should leave for the day,' Dawn said, beginning to get her coat and handbag ready. 'In fact, I need to nip to the powder room. I'll meet you at reception.' She jumped from her chair and was out of that room before Simon or anyone else had the chance to say a thing.

The atmosphere lay between us like the heavy odour after an all-night party. An air of regret, sweat and unresolved tensions.

'It's true isn't it?' Simon asked me in a voice that didn't sound like his, ignoring Anna who was shuffling through some paperwork we all had to sign. I lifted my gaze to be met with the wide eyes of a man who has just realised his twenty years of marriage was all a sham. I noticed Jerry cough, embarrassed to be caught up in this moment.

'Yes,' I admitted, quietly. 'I'm so sorry, Si.'

His chest expanded with the deepest of sighs. The fight had completely gone out of him. Then he gave a short, sharp nod. 'Thought so. I'm not a fool. Well, that's that then.'

I winced seeing him heave himself out of his seat and calmly shake Anna's and Jerry's hands, apologising for his outburst.

'Simon, are you going to be okay?' I asked, already knowing the answer but hating seeing a man look so broken.

He turned to face me and sighed. 'I will be. I'd had my suspicions for years. Maybe this will be the kick up the bum I need to start doing what I want for a change. Never bloody liked those Last Call products anyway.' He shrugged as if he had been waiting for this moment to happen.

'Well, we are always looking for experienced science boffins for some of our techy shows,' Anna said, raising a half smile in Simon. I knew he would be just fine.

'So, here is the cheque.' Jerry rummaged through the papers in front of him and passed over the money as soon as we were alone. 'If we could ask for you to be discreet about this, at least until the show airs next week?'

I nodded.

'If you don't mind me saying, you don't seem that excited about winning.'

I looked up from the large cheque, trying to make sense of all those zeros at the end, into Jerry's kind eyes. 'I'm just in shock, I guess.'

He nodded and began sorting out papers I need to sign to say I'd received the cash, unaware of the internal battle my head and my heart were going through. I tried to blink back the tears as I signed my name with a flourish; this had gone on long enough now. I needed to speak to Ben and tell him that the cash he so desperately wanted was ours. I just had to track him down first.

CHAPTER 27

Hidebound (adj.) – Having an inflexible character

Ben's mobile went straight to answerphone. I called Trisha but she hadn't heard from him since before we'd gone to Chile. I didn't want to share the worry that was growing in my stomach at not knowing where Ben was, so I kept the call brief and details sparse. However, if he wasn't staying at Jimmy's or his godmother's then where was he? I only had one person left to ask. I gave the taxi driver the address, hoping that I'd remembered it properly. He looked at me as if figuring out what a northerner, so completely out of her depth in a place like this, was doing asking to be taken there, but he flicked on his meter and continued to make his way through the busy streets nonetheless. As we left the buzz of the capital behind, the reality of what I was about to do kicked in.

I had nowhere else to look.

Throughout the journey I had been preparing myself to see him again, to be stood inches from his face, the face I knew so well, the face I'd thought I knew so well. I tried to control my breathing that had become a sort of panting as the taxi slowed, and the driver nodded his head towards the estate. Thankfully, there weren't any intimidating-looking youths hanging around the block of flats this time, only two teenage mums walking past pushing matching pink pushchairs laden down with Primark bags.

'Here you go, love. Belvedere Crescent.' The driver eyed me warily as I paid and got out. I glanced up at the high-rise ahead of me and took a deep breath. *Well, here goes nothing.*

I found the right flat on the third attempt after being shouted at in what sounded like incomprehensible Iranian the first time, and then berated by an old woman who was adamant that she didn't want to buy anything I was selling. Anything.

'Yeah?' a gruff voice asked, through the buzzing line.

'Oh, hi. Is that Ben's dad?' I cringed as I asked. I didn't even remember what his dad's name was.

'Yeah.' The split second of hesitation in his voice made my stomach lurch that maybe I'd got this all wrong.

'This is Georgia. Erm, we met a few weeks ago. I don't know if you remember me but...' I was cut off from explaining any more as the front door buzzed open. I took that as my cue to stop blabbering over the intercom and headed inside. The stairwell didn't seem as bad as I'd remembered it, but nevertheless, I quickened my pace and took the stairs two at a time all the way up to his flat, trying to ignore the growing sense of trepidation at what I was going to walk into. The smell of cigarettes welcomed me as it had done last time.

I gingerly pushed open the front door that had been left on the latch and made my way into the lounge. His dad stood up as I entered and gave me a broad, genuine smile before wrapping me up in his arms like some long-lost family member. He was dressed in a pair of baggy navy tracksuit bottoms and a 'We Are Runners' T-shirt that, judging from the beer belly protruding through, I guessed he wore ironically. It was a step up from the tatty dressing gown and posed less of a flashing risk, for which I was grateful.

'Gracie, right?' he asked.

'Georgia,' I corrected him quietly, as he slapped a hand against his forehead at his mistake.

'Ah sorry, Georgia.' I smiled at him kindly – I was hardly one to judge – and was about to ask where Ben was when he beat me to it. 'Is Ben sorting out the taxi then?' He peered around behind me with an expectant look on his stubbly cheeks as if waiting for his son to wander in after me. My stomach dropped.

'He's not here?' I asked in a voice that didn't sound like my own.

His dad pulled himself back and looked at me as if I'd lost the plot. 'Here? Nah, darlin', he ain't been here since the last time you two popped in. Wait – are you all right, love?'

I'd started to cry. Jeez, what was with me and my emotions at the moment? From the incredible hulk to the incredible mess. I nodded pathetically through loud sniffs. He was clearly uncomfortable, but tried to guide me to the sagging sofa.

'Sit down,' he ordered, finally finding his voice and taking control of this strange woman who'd turned up on his doorstep and proceeded to spill tears onto his sticky lino.

He wandered to the kitchen and handed me a cold can of lager. 'I'm out of milk.' He shrugged embarrassedly. I didn't care. I needed a drink, despite it being the middle of the afternoon.

'It's okay. Thank you.' I took it gratefully, cracked open the ring pull and took a long sip. So, if Ben wasn't here then where the hell was he? 'You said you haven't seen Ben since we came here last but have you heard from him at all?'

He shook his head. 'We're not that good at keeping in touch with each other. I'm here when he needs me and he knows where to find me but I'm not one for all this technology stuff. Don't even own a mobile phone; don't see the point. My landline gets me by but even that only ever rings with these foreigners calling to sell some crap.' He pointed to the brown phone on the work surface. It was probably classed as an antique. 'You going to tell me what's gone on with you two?'

I'd caught my breath and was trying to get a grip on my emotions, taking deep glugs of cheap lager as I did so.

'We've been away, to Chile, doing some stupid TV show thing.' I shook my head. 'When we were out there we had a massive fight and, well, now I don't know where he is and I need to talk to him.'

'Don't you two work together?'

I nodded. 'Yeah, we're business partners but he hasn't been in for over a week now.'

His dad gripped his can tighter. 'If there's one thing I made sure I got into his head during everything that went on, it was the importance of working hard.' He must have sensed me glancing around at the flat he was in, in the middle of the day. 'I had to quit it all because of my dodgy ticker.' He self-consciously placed a hand against his chest. 'But before then I was never afraid of a day of good, solid labour. So, where the hell is he?' He paused and took another mouthful of beer. 'Should I be worried?'

I shrugged. 'I don't think so. He called the office and spoke to one of our colleagues saying he was taking some personal time but he didn't say where he was or what he was going to be doing. I figured he might have come down here.' As soon as I said it I felt guilty; his dad would have obviously loved to have had his son around for a few days but Ben must have thought otherwise.

'Nope, not here. I guess with the pair of you about to be big celebrities I'll see even less of him.' I stared blankly at him. 'I've heard that you're going to be on the telly.' He nodded to his large and dusty TV in the corner.

'You did?' I asked incredulously. He hadn't struck me as a parent who was bothered about their kid's achievements and unless they had a telly in the pub I couldn't picture him settled in on his sofa for a night of binge watching.

'Yeah. I follow everything my Ben does. Always have done.' He got up and rummaged in a chest of drawers for a few moments before pulling out a scrapbook crammed with sheets of coloured paper and photographs sticking out of the pages. 'Best thing that ever happened to me, that lad,' he said proudly, placing the heavy book on my lap and beginning to turn the large pages.

My breath caught in my throat. Ben's life was here on every page. From a lock of hair that had been sellotaped to the rough pages that had yellowed over time, to newspaper articles of him in his school days ripped out from the local paper. I stared at this book in wonderment; this was what I'd been waiting to see for so long. A glimpse into Ben's past. I just hadn't expected to be shown this by his alcoholic but kind-hearted father in some scuzzy London flat once we had broken up.

My eyes pricked with tears, I just couldn't work out if they were angry or sad, for what had gone so wrong between us. I blinked them back and couldn't help but smile at the candid shots of a cheeky-faced young boy with unruly dark curls and birthday cake around his mouth; at the tanned, skinny toddler playing in the sea with a much younger and healthier-looking dad in some sunny destination. My heart contracted at the sight of Ben sleeping in his pushchair on what must have been the same holiday, his face relaxed into a peaceful sleep as his dad and a pretty brunette woman raised their lurid cocktails to the camera.

'That's Maggie.' He placed a finger on the attractive woman's face. 'Ben's mother and the love of my life. He used to find it hilarious when I'd sing that Rod Stewart song to her; he thought that I'd made it up and used to jump on her in bed singing the chorus as loud as he could to get her up in the mornings.' His face relaxed, lost in some cherished memory before he shook himself, cleared his throat and turned the page.

I gently placed my hand on his. 'What happened, with Maggie?' I asked in a quiet voice, looking into his grey glassy eyes.

'Just like the song, I couldn't have tried any harder but she still left,' he joked, before his smile faded and he sheepishly looked down at his off white sports socks. 'Well, that's actually the reason Ben and I have never managed to be as close as we once were. I've always been one for the ladies and as much as I loved my Maggie I acted the lad more times than I care to remember. Maggie eventually got sick of my indiscretions and left. Lord knows she gave me enough chances to change my behaviour but I was young and immature, so foolishly let the best thing I ever had walk out on me.' He looked skywards seemingly trying to keep it together.

I suddenly felt like I'd imposed too much. Here I was in bloody London in this man's flat who I'd only met once before and I was now interrogating him about his failed relationship.

'I'm sorry, you don't need to explain it to me,' I said softly. I should just leave; this had been a crazy idea to begin with.

He shook his head forcefully. 'No. I do. I need to – I've kept it bottled up for so long.'

I nodded but he wasn't looking at me any more. He gripped his can and began speaking directly at it, as if imagining someone's face plastered on the metal.

'When she left she told me that she would come back for Ben when she'd set herself up in a new town, away from any bad memories.' He sighed. 'Well, I never told Ben this. I was too distraught at what I'd done to push her away that I foolishly tried to turn her son against her. To him she was this evil witch who had abandoned him.'

I didn't say a word, couldn't say a thing.

'So, when she did come back to see him he told her in no uncertain terms that he didn't want to ever see her again. She must have realised how upset this was making him so she respected his wishes and stayed away for evermore.'

'Wow,' I breathed.

His dad let out a deep sigh and leant back on the sofa. 'I made sure he was always fed, washed and watered but I should've made him talk to me about how his mum leaving made him feel, how it made me feel too, but I couldn't. I always felt so guilty that it was my fault she'd left.' He paused. 'The thing was, my lies caught up with me and he learnt about my affairs years later. When he was a teen he used to go out to the pubs before he was old enough. The lads where we used to live were big talkers, especially after they'd had a drink or two, so it was only a matter of time that he'd pick up on the rumours about his mum's disappearance, that she'd come back for him, but because of me twisting the truth he'd lost the chance to have a mother. When he found out he packed up, moved out and got on with his own life.'

'Wow. I never knew,' I whispered.

His dad nodded sagely. 'He hated me for years. I never knew where he was living. It was like he just vanished overnight, even though I tried to search for him – even if only to send a birthday gift or a Christmas card – but he wanted me out of his life.'

I felt like saying that I knew the feeling of being cut off so dramatically by him but kept my mouth shut.

'He'd give Harry Houdini a run for his money that lad. Then one day, out of the blue, he came back. Things were never the same between us, not like they used to be when I could do no wrong in his eyes. He is much closer to Trisha than me, and that's something I'll always be grateful to that woman for, the way she stepped in and acted like a mother to him. I mean, you're a smart girl, you saw the last time he was here how ashamed he is of me.'

His eyes filled with tears that he choked back and tried to cover up with a gravelly smoker's cough.

I shook my head. 'He was proud of you though.' I remembered the way Ben had told me how his dad used to teach him all about fixing up cars, the look on his face as it lit up remembering a happier time.

'I know, and I know I can't sit here all woe is me but it still hurt. I lost everything too, and I dealt with it in the wrong way, which I'm still paying for now.'

'So, where did Ben go? That time when he vanished?' Maybe this would shine some light on where he was now.

'Jimmy's, crashing on couches, and then he went to find his mum.'

My eyes widened. 'And, did he? Find her?'

His dad shrugged. 'I don't know, love. He never said. I only learnt that he'd been trying to track her down because some lads at the bookies let on they'd overheard him and Jimmy talking about it in the boozer one night. He never said a word to me and I was so grateful to have him back in my life that I wasn't about to pry.'

I sat back letting it all sink in. 'Do you know where Maggie is?'

His dad let out a laugh that jarred with the sombre atmosphere in the dingy flat. 'Me? Ha no. I've not heard a thing of her since she walked out. She could be dead for all I know.' At the thought of this his smile dropped and his bottom lip tightened.

He took a long last glug of his lager and crushed the can in his shaking hands. 'I'm going to get another; you want one?'

I shook my head. I needed to stay as level-headed as I could. Maybe Ben had gone to see his mum once more, but if his dad didn't know where she was then how was I going to track her down? I felt exhausted. My brain was struggling to compute all the new information it had been fed, from understanding home truths to winning the prize money, and still not knowing where Ben was, it all swirled around my tired mind.

The cab his dad had called for me, from his dusty landline, was waiting outside the block of flats when I emerged out into the fresh air. As I headed back to the city to catch the next train back to Manchester I felt even more confused than when I had arrived, with one thought filling my mind. Where the hell was Ben?

CHAPTER 28

Unctuous (adj.) – Insincerely smooth in speech and manner

Managing to nab a seat on the busy train, I hurriedly flicked open the Facebook app. I might not be able to trace Ben's mum but I knew someone who would possibly be able to help. I typed a quick message then crossed everything that this was going to work. It was my last shot at finding him. And she was looking like the only one who might know where Ben was.

*

I was even beginning to annoy myself with the constant drumming of my fingers on the table. I'd been nervously waiting near the door of a French café where we had agreed to meet for what felt like a lifetime when Alice eventually wandered in. She was as pretty in real life as she was in her profile picture. Her glossy brown hair had been pulled into a high bun with loose tendrils framing her heart-shaped face. Her eyebrow game was strong and she had an expertly applied pop of deep berry lipstick staining her full lips. I shifted uncomfortably in my seat and self-consciously tucked a strand of hair behind my ears, wishing I'd made more of an effort to meet the ex-girlfriend of my ex-boyfriend.

Wow, that was weird.

I waved my arm uncertainly in the air, which she spotted, flashing me a brief smile before coming to join me.

'Georgia?'

'Alice! Hi, please, sit down; thank you so much for meeting me. I know this is a bit strange.'

'No problem,' she said in a voice that was squeakier than I'd imagined and pulled out the seat opposite but kept her leather jacket on. 'I wasn't sure what was going on but you sounded quite stressed out in your message, so…' She trailed out.

Thankfully a waiter appeared to take our drinks order, giving us a moment to gather our thoughts.

'I like your handbag,' she said, once we were on our own again.

'Thanks, it's only Primark.' I blushed and pulled myself together. 'So, Alice. I know this is out of the blue but you're the only person I can think of who might be able to help me. I have no idea where Ben is. We had this stupid fight and now I can't find him to talk to him. I don't know if he is coming back to work, if he even wants to see me again or what is going on but I…I really miss him, and…'

The words just tumbled from my mouth as I admitted my true feelings for the first time. I didn't just need him in my life, I *wanted* him to be there. He had become my partner in crime and I hadn't realised just how hard it was coping without him there to bounce ideas off, joke with, snuggle up to, eat dinner with, hear about his day and talk crap at silly o'clock in the morning with, wrapped up in our duvet.

She held a small hand up. 'He's at mine.'

My stomach flipped. I thought I was going to be sick. Was he staying at hers because they had got back together?

Had I totally got the wrong end of the stick? Oh. My. God. This was worse than I had imagined.

She must have caught my expression as her hand flew to her open mouth. 'Oh no! Not like that! God, that must have sounded awful. I mean he's been staying in the spare room. There is nothing going on with us, Georgia. I have a boyfriend, that's who I live with and to be honest I was so glad when you messaged me. Eliot, that's my boyfriend, has practically given me an ultimatum to kick Ben out as he won't stop going on about you or the business and Eliot's had enough. To be honest, Ben's a mess.' The words tumbled out of her perfectly made-up mouth.

It felt wrong but a strange flush of relief spread across my body hearing that he was in as much of a bad way as I was when it came to hiding how I really felt.

'Really?'

'Really.' She rolled her eyes. 'You two need to sort out whatever has gone on between you as otherwise I'll be joining the single crowd when Eliot leaves me. I know he is only joking at the moment but Ben has definitely outstayed his welcome.'

'It was like he'd fallen off the face of the earth. I couldn't find him anywhere.'

'Yeah, Ben does that,' she said, then took a slow sip of her vanilla latte, using a straw so as not to smudge her lipstick.

'He did that to you too?' I asked, thinking back to what his dad had told me about his Harry Houdini act.

Alice nodded. 'Only once. We'd had a row over something so silly I can't remember now. But basically he went missing for a few days and only resurfaced when Jimmy bought the latest PlayStation game or something.' She rolled her eyes at the immaturity of them. 'I'm sure you know he is a hard nut to crack; he doesn't open up easily.'

I nodded.

'Yeah, it's all after his mum left him, blah blah blah.' She wafted her hand around as if she was talking about something else.

'I know about him seeing you recently…'

She sighed, looking as if she wished that he hadn't. 'He got in touch with me randomly out of the blue. I mean, we'd stayed friends on Facebook but apart from annual and brief happy birthday messages there was never any other contact between us. So when he asked to meet for a drink I thought it was strange but went along for old time's sake. It was all about work – I'm a financial advisor, you see.'

I nodded. 'Yeah, he said.' I thought about the cheque burning a hole in my pocket.

'I know you're not keen, but the place he's found in London is a cracking deal. It's just a shame about not being able to afford it now.'

'Not having the prize money, you mean?'

Alice wafted her teaspoon at me. 'Exactly that.' She nodded. 'Because you couldn't raise the capital needed for the investment.'

I took a deep breath. 'The thing is, we did win.'

She stared at me. 'What? But Ben said –'

'I only found out today. That's another reason I need to see him. There was a big mix-up with the other contestants and we have actually been crowned the winners.' I tried to smile but it still felt so weird. Neither of us had won, not really.

'Oh wow. So, what are you going to do with the money?' She picked up her mobile phone. 'I can probably get in touch with the vendors and…'

I raised my hand and shook my head. 'I think I need to speak to Ben first.'

She placed her phone back on the table and blushed. 'Oh, yeah, sure.'

'Sorry, it's all just been a lot to take in.' I fiddled with a sachet of brown sugar, suddenly feeling like I didn't know what to do with myself.

She placed a hand, which looked like a four-year-old's, against my fleshy upper arm, and patted me daintily. 'You two need to get together and work this out.'

I nodded and sniffed loudly.

'He needs you to look him the eye and tell him everything is okay.'

'But how am I going to do that if he won't see me?'

She tilted her head, giving it some thought. I noticed that her eyeliner wasn't exactly perfectly applied on her right eye. Small victories. 'Wait – isn't there some party happening soon? Yeah!' She sat up straight as if an idea had just struck her. 'I've not been invited – Jimmy and I never really saw eye to eye when I was dating Ben as I think he thought I stole him from those stupid never-ending computer game marathons he wanted them to play together. But Ben told me that Jimmy's moving to Australia?'

My stomach clenched and I nodded. 'Yeah, he's emigrating with my best friend Shelley.'

It was going to be hard enough saying goodbye to them without having it out with Ben on the same night.

'Perfect, you're going. And I'm going to make Ben go too,' Alice said firmly, whilst raising her finger in the air to ask a lingering waiter for our bill.

'I was just going to have my own goodbye with Jimmy and Shelley,' I mumbled getting my purse out. The idea of celebrating anything felt as alien as actually saying goodbye to them. I still couldn't believe they were really leaving.

'No. You're going to fix this.' Alice stood up and placed a fiver on the table indicating that our impromptu meet up was over. 'And then let me know how I can help you with the London move.'

CHAPTER 29

Eloquent (adj.) – Vividly or movingly expressive or revealing

I remembered this thing that Astrid had told me back at the Blue Butterfly one evening about how in times of a crisis of confidence you needed to give yourself a good talking-to. She was the queen of crazy suggestions that actually seemed to work. As much as I hated to admit it, it still felt like the universe had aligned at just the right moment for Ben to enter my life following an evening spent moon chanting. Coincidence? Who knows.

I purposefully strode towards the bathroom mirror and tried not to cringe at the layer of dust and fluff stuck to the glass. I leant forward and eyeballed myself. Astrid said you had to say something to yourself in a loud and authoritative voice whilst never breaking eye contact. Okay, here goes. Oh God, I needed to invest in some proper eye-bag cream rather than eke out the last remnants of the free sample I was given when I treated my mum to some posh foot cream for Mother's Day last year.

Focus, Georgia.

'You're a grown-up. As much as you might not want this to be true, you are. Georgia, enough with the self-pity. Get some perspective on this problem. Yes, Ben was a muppet but he didn't do anything so bad that it can't be fixed. You have to at least try.'

I slicked on some more lipstick and half growled at my reflection. Bring it on.

*

The party was aptly being held in an Australian themed bar in the centre of town. Blow-up kangaroos and hats with corks dangling from wide sandy rims took up most of the low ceiling space. Table legs were made out of didgeridoos and Aboriginal music was only just audible over the bustling din of the large crowd packed in the OTT room.

I took a deep breath and hung back at the main doorway, watching the scene play out before me. I ignored the strange look the beefed-up bouncer was giving me as I pulled out my phone. Marie had promised me that she would meet me so we could walk in together. I still wasn't sure I had the courage to head in by myself.

'I'm here!' she called as she struggled out of the taxi.

I jogged down the steps to help her. 'Hey, you look gorgeous,' I said, giving her a kiss on the cheek.

She wiped her clammy forehead. 'Gorgeous is not how I would describe myself, more like bloated, pregnant whale.'

'Are you sure you're okay to come tonight? I wouldn't have minded being by myself,' I lied.

'Psssh. I am fed up with sitting at home waiting for this baby, that is obviously going to stay inside until it's eighteen years old. Mike was getting on my tits and promised to watch Cole so there was no way I'd miss being around actual people – even if I do sit in a chair in the corner all night. My bloody cankles are killing me.'

'Well, thank you. I appreciate it. And I heard that ankle bones are so last season anyway.'

I helped her up the steps as the bouncer looked us both up and down. I tugged at the hem of the royal blue chiffon dress I was wearing. It had felt strange applying make-up, blow-drying my hair and even putting on matching underwear but I needed all the help I could get to boost my failing confidence. My shoes were already pinching my toes and I was sure I was sweating in between my boobs but I tried to follow my dad's advice and act brave, hoping no one could tell that I was shitting myself inside.

'You got ID on you, ladies?' the burly bouncer asked us seriously, pulling me from my thoughts.

'Erm, baby on board.' Marie pointed to her stomach as he dipped his head and held the door open for us. 'Oh God, do you think he thought I was just fat?'

'Well if he did, he also thought you were under twenty-one, so, you know, silver linings.'

It was like stepping into a wall of noise and heat. Waiters milled around serving trays of canapés and lurid cocktails. I took one and necked it, the sickly sweet taste of amaretto hitting the back of my throat and making me cough as Marie waddled straight to the nearest toilet.

'Georgia! You made it!' Shelley appeared out of nowhere and wrapped me in a tight hug. Her familiar perfume filled my nose. I had to blink back tears because I wouldn't smell that again for a very long time. 'I wasn't sure you would come.' She held me at arm's length and gave me the once-over as if checking for something. 'You look absolutely gorgeous by the way.'

'Thank you, you too. I couldn't not come, could I?' I smiled hoping to hide how hard this actually was for me.

'Well, thank you, I really appreciate it. Here take this.' She grabbed another cocktail and placed in into my hands. 'A toast. To you.'

'I think I should be the one toasting you two!' I laughed.

She shook her head. 'No. A toast to you for being so brave. I know this must be a little weird.' She waved her hand at the room behind her. 'But you know, having to say goodbye to you isn't exactly easy for me either. Although –' she stuck a finger in the air and wobbled on her platform heels slightly; I wondered how many of those strong cocktails she had sunk already this evening '– it isn't a goodbye but a see you soon.'

'You bet,' I said, hugging her tightly then smiling for a selfie on her phone that she had pulled out of nowhere. 'So, is erm…is Ben here?' I asked nervously, glancing at the many faces around us.

Shelley pushed a strand of hair from her face. 'I've not seen him yet. But it's still early…' She trailed off as we both knew that it wasn't. I'd stayed away for as long as possible to be fashionably late, hoping Ben would already be here. What if he wasn't coming? What if Alice hadn't managed to persuade him to leave her flat and have a go at fixing things?

Right on cue, the door swung open bringing a welcome gust of cold outside air to this sweaty room and, with it, in walked Ben. My stomach leapt seeing him. He was wearing a deep maroon jumper that looked delicious on him and hugged his broad frame. His hair had been styled forward in a sort of quiff, which only made his cheekbones more defined. God, he looked fit. His eyes met mine almost instantly, forcing me to blink and avert my gaze to the floor, desperate not to give anything away. The noise of the party faded out; it was as if the DJ had directed a spotlight just on him as he slowly headed towards me.

'Here he is,' Shelley hissed and nudged me in the side.

'Crap.' All my confidence pooled out of me.

'You've got this.' She squeezed my hand and slipped away, leaving me standing alone as my past came to find me.

'Hey,' Ben said, before letting out a sigh. I couldn't work out if it was a so-this-is-awkward sigh or a here-goes-nothing sigh.

I glanced up at him, forcing myself to try and remain calm and rational even if my vagina was screaming at me for not mounting him right here and right now. The past few weeks all merged into my head, the excitement of our first trip abroad, the catastrophe in Chile, the home truths from his dad and Alice, his fierce silence and my broken heart all rushed to my mind.

'Hi,' I replied, self-consciously flattening my dress against my legs. I desperately wished I had a drink in my hand but didn't want to break this moment to try and find a nearby waiter.

'So, how are things?'

'Okay… Yeah…' I stuttered.

What were we doing? This wasn't us. Ben and Georgia were the life and soul of the party, the couple who barely stopped for air as we shared jokes and banter.

'Good.' He paused and fidgeted with the sleeve of his jumper. 'Listen, Georgia. I think I owe you an explanation.'

I had to stop myself from waving my hands as if there was nothing to discuss, as if instead of talking and digging up the past we should hit the bar and get on the shots, as if I wasn't so tired from thinking I just wanted to get drunk with the one person I had missed more than anything in the world. Instead, I nodded.

He sighed again and paused for a moment collecting his thoughts. 'I just wanted to say…you look really nice by the way.'

I blushed. 'Oh, right, thanks.'

'Well, that's not all I wanted to say but it's true, you do.' He gave me a look as if he was drinking me in, as if he wasn't just seeing the pretty dress and not bad effort at contouring that I had going on but that he saw me. The real me. Oh, fuck. *Keep it together, Georgia.*

'I also wanted to say that…'

Just at that moment the DJ decided to cut the music and bellowed down the mic for Jimmy and Shelley to join him on stage.

Ben laughed awkwardly and ran a finger under his collar. 'Hold that thought.'

I smiled but inside was cursing the DJ for his terrible timing.

'Guys! Can I have your attention?' Shelley called out, wobbling on her heels slightly as Jimmy wrapped a tree-trunk-sized arm around her slender waist and began nibbling her right ear, seemingly oblivious to the guests waiting to hear the speeches.

'Get a room!' someone called out from the back.

'Oh, we will!' Jimmy said, before planting a giant kiss on Shelley's lips. The pair of them were obviously besotted with one another. Seeing them like that made me realise that I couldn't be jealous for my best friend's happiness. There was an infinite amount of joy in this world, easily enough to go around.

Shelley had taken the mic and managed to peel Jimmy off her before she turned and addressed the crowd.

'So, I just want to say a huge thank you to everyone for coming. It means the world that so many of you made it out to say bon voyage to us as we prepare to go down under.' This was met with a mix of cheers and boos, which made Shelley laugh. 'Hey, you've all got a place to stay when you come and visit! So, as I was saying…' She paused to collect her thoughts. Her expression grew more serious and she turned to look in mine and Ben's direction.

'Jimmy and I may never have met if it wasn't for two people in this room. Our best friends, Ben and Georgia.'

She pointed to us, making many nameless faces turn around to smile at the pair of us.

'Oh God. What is she doing?' I muttered under my breath.

Ben's hand was on my shoulder and gave it a quick squeeze. The movement felt both alien and so natural that it made my head spin.

'These two are the best friends that anyone could ask for. We are going to miss you both so much it actually hurts.' Her eyes began to fill up with tears and her voice wobbled. Just watching her get so emotional made me feel like welling up too.

Jimmy gently took the microphone from Shelley and quickly nodded to Ben.

'I'd just like to say a few words.' He cleared his throat. 'I never expected to leave England, to swap football for rugby, kebabs for barbecues, or harmless house flies for poisonous spiders.'

Shelley rolled her eyes in mirth.

'But I would give up anything for you.' He stared at her so lovingly and intently it was as if the rest of the room had disappeared. 'I am ready to make this giant move across to the other side of the world as it means getting to spend every day with you.'

I spotted a single tear rolling down Shelley's flushed cheeks as she tried to keep up with what he was saying.

'I've never been good with words, failed GCSE English, and never set foot in a school since, but I can say this: I love you more than I ever knew it was possible to love someone. Shelley…' he took a deep breath and dropped down to one knee, the movement making the audience gasp dramatically '…will you –'

'Owwwww!'

Jimmy was interrupted from uttering the next few words as a torturous scream filled the air.

'Shit! Marie!' I left Ben and pushed past other people to get to my best friend who was gripping the armrest of the chair she was awkwardly spread over.

'Is she okay?' someone called out.

'Eww. She's pissed herself!' some dude with a nose piercing shouted. I glared at him.

'That's her waters breaking, you moron. Oh shit! That's her waters breaking!'

A wall of noise, confused murmurs and people chattering faded away behind us as I helped her outside. Jimmy's proposal had been ruined, but right now Marie's baby was more important.

'Georgia, wait!' Ben's voice shouted down the steps, 'I'm coming with you.'

Gone was the awkward man who had been stood next to me previously; in his place was a man who seemed focused and calm. The Ben I knew who worked so well in a crisis. He helped her get into a waiting black cab and directed the driver to the nearest hospital.

'Thanks,' I mumbled as we snapped on our seat belts.

'No problem,' Ben said quietly.

'Phone…Mike!' Marie ordered between puffs.

'Right. Yes. Okay. Shit!' I went to rummage in my handbag, remembering we weren't here to swap pleasantries with each other but had a much bigger job in hand.

'I'm on it,' Ben said, pulling his out of his pocket and calling Mike, telling him to meet us at the hospital pronto.

'I could have done that,' I muttered after he'd hung up.

'Don't you two start. Woman in labour here!' Marie uttered in a low growl.

I nodded and blushed. 'Sorry.'

As the cab careered through the streets, barely under the speed limit, I kept glancing over at Ben. It felt so strange to be in a confined space with him after such a long time apart. It was made even stranger by Marie's presence between us groaning in a way that didn't exactly sound human. He didn't look fazed one bit by her grabbing his hand and squeezing it so hard her nails left indents in his flesh.

'Call the hospital,' Marie managed to say as the driver took a corner too sharply. 'Fuck, these contractions are coming on strong.'

'You gonna hold it in till we get there, darlin?' The bald-headed cabbie asked through the intercom, more concerned for his leather seats than keeping to the speed limit.

'She's fine, just get us there as fast as you can!' I shouted back.

'Oh God, Georgia, it's really happening!' Marie gasped as another contraction subsided. Her eyes were wide and the colour had drained from her face.

'Yes, and you are totally going to nail this,' I replied more confidently than I felt. I just wished we weren't having this conversation in the back of a cab but rather in a safe, clean hospital full of qualified doctors. There was no way I knew how to deliver a baby. 'Just keep breathing through the pain, and try your hardest to keep him or her in.'

'I'm trying my best. But what if something happens, something like what happened with Cole?' Tears were falling from her terrified face. I wiped them away with the base of my thumb.

'You are going to be just fine. You've got this,' I said assertively, desperate to mask the fear in my voice. I felt Ben's eyes on mine as I gave Marie a pep talk.

'Georgia's right, you're a trooper. We've not got much further to go,' he said, jumping in.

I rolled my eyes, unable to contain myself. 'I thought you felt threatened by strong women.'

'Not the time, Georgia,' he sighed.

Marie glared at us both. Her hair was plastered to her forehead, her cheeks were rosy and a sheen of perspiration glowed on her heaving chest.

'Are you two going to sort your issues out or what? I don't want this baby to come into the world with you two acting like this. This isn't you, you're Georgia and Ben, not some nasty, bickering couple picking fights for no reason!'

'He started it,' I mumbled under my breath, cringing at how childish I was being. She gave my hand an extra hard squeeze that wasn't because of any contractions.

'Stop it. You both messed up, wires got crossed and mistakes were made,' she said preparing for another blast of pain in her uterus. Neither of us said anything; her groans of agony were the only sound that filled the back of the cab.

'Here we are!' the taxi driver called out, relieved to have made it without an extra passenger joining us.

Marie looked like she had zoned out to anything going on around her and gripped on to Ben's arm for support as he gingerly led her out of the taxi and over to the entrance doors of the maternity wing, stopping every so often for her to pant and lean onto the wall for more support.

Marie was about to have a baby! The sobering thought swirled around my disorientated mind. My various life problems suddenly paled into insignificance compared to how she was going to get through the next who knew how many hours.

I made sure the driver received his big tip as smiling and calm-faced staff were there to meet us with a wheelchair for Marie to lower herself into. The contractions were coming thick and fast now, my hand was red raw from her gripping it and my legs wobbled as we hurried to follow where they were taking her.

Thankfully it wasn't long before a pale-faced Mike raced through the double doors looking petrified.

'Marie! Are you okay?'

'Do I look okay?' she barked at him.

'That's our cue to leave. Good luck, guys!' I shouted, grabbing Ben's sleeve to leave them to it as we went to sit together in the small empty waiting room.

I couldn't stop my eyes from trailing towards the large clock on the wall and watching every second slowly click by. She must have given birth by now. God I hoped she was okay. What if there had been complications? How much longer would it be until there was news? All these thoughts swirled around my brain.

The sound of Ben clearing his throat made me glance over at him. He was sat on the opposite row of uncomfortable chairs lining the pistachio-coloured walls. In between us was a battered coffee table with dog-eared magazines and a pathetic selection of children's toys. I wasn't sure if I was grateful we were alone or not. The room suddenly felt quite claustrophobic as I realised we had no other options but to have it out with each other. We needed to, I knew that, it had gone on long enough, but at the same time I didn't want the confrontation. I half expected Clive to jump out with his camera and capture this moment.

'So, I guess we need to speak…' he said quietly, before clearing his throat.

I found it hard to look up at him. My head and my heart were so conflicted with what just being so close to him did to me.

'Yeah. If you're finally ready for that.'

He ignored my dig. 'I'm sorry for going AWOL, for agreeing to things on the London move without your express permission, and I'm sorry for not opening up about my past more,' he said, genuinely. 'But, you also need to take a share of the blame.'

I tried not to let my hackles rise too much.

'Like I said when we were in Chile, probably not in the best way, you do need to let me in more with the business and admit when you're wrong.'

'I thought that I did,' I squeaked.

He shook his head gently. 'I've known since the first time I met you that you like to have a plan, to know where you are headed and to stay on top of everything. I just hadn't realised that you needed this, not because of the control this brings but because it gives your mind some clarity. I know you, remember. I know you have a million and one thoughts fluttering around that beautiful head of yours like hyperactive butterflies, which is why you need to clear space in order for your creative genius to shine through.'

I couldn't help but let my lips curl into a smile at that. He had hit the nail on the head.

'But, at times this infuriates me. You need to make room for me in this plan, you need to allow me to suggest a new plan, to be able to divert from things at times because you don't always know best.'

I was too tired to fight back with a biting retort. I was too tired of not having him, the person who knew me inside and out, in my life where he belonged.

I nodded. He was right, annoyingly.

'I know.'

He stood up from the chair opposite, with a loud creak, and came to sit next to me. I felt my breath catch in my throat at his closeness, his familiar aftershave filling my nostrils.

'Georgia, you are the most intelligent, caring, generous, kind and genuine person I've ever met and I was the luckiest man in the world getting to call you mine. Something that I didn't realise until I lost you.'

His eyes were fixed on mine, my breath caught in my throat in anticipation of what he was going to say next. This was Ben after all. Ben didn't do soppy, public displays of affection.

'Seeing how happy Jimmy and Shelley are has only shown me how happy I was but how I chucked it away by going about things in totally the wrong way. I hope you understand why I did what I did, but I know now it wasn't my finest hour. I've never been good with words. Or showing what I mean through my actions either. Instead I have a tendency to run away and bury my head in the sand. I'm sorry for disappearing but I needed that space to get my head together. It is pretty full-on for me too, at times, with us working and living together.' Ben pulled himself taller and boldly took my trembling hand.

'I thought you wanted us to move in together?'

'I did! And I love that I get to wake up with you every morning and I feel honoured I get to share all the amazing parts of our day together. But it doesn't mean that it's easy.' He paused to get his thoughts together. 'I got used to my own company and fending for myself after my mum left and my dad went to ground. It is also a big deal for me, everything that has happened between us. I wouldn't change it for the world, I need you to know that, and I know I should open up more to you when I'm feeling a little claustrophobic but the truth is I don't want to be taken for granted. I want this to be equal and to feel wanted too.'

I couldn't breathe. My words were trapped in my throat. 'I didn't know you felt like that…'

He nodded sadly, looking bashful at having opened up so much. 'That's because I suck at telling you.'

I let out a faint laugh that seemed to echo off the bare walls. I could hear the sound of a baby screaming somewhere down the corridor. The noise made me flick my eyes back to the clock – Marie had been gone ages. Right on cue, before either of us could say another word, the waiting room doors swung open and Mike was stood there looking almost as dazed as he had when he'd raced into the hospital hours ago.

'Mike?' Ben and I both said in unison.

As Mike's eyes focused on us, you could see the enormity of what had just happened in the maternity ward come into focus on his face. Slowly, the look of shock melted into the widest grin I'd ever seen him wear.

'A girl! I've got a daughter,' he said through gulps of tears.

'Oh, Mike, congratulations! How's Marie?' I walked over and hugged him tightly.

Ben got to his feet and went to shake Mike's hand, congratulating him.

'Wow, yeah she's great; she is beyond great. I don't want to scare you, Georgia, but what she just did in that room is more than a miracle.' He shook his head in utter disbelief at what he'd witnessed.

I let out a laugh. 'So, can we see them?'

'Of course! She's been asking for you.' Mike nodded then placed a heavy hand on my shoulder. 'Thanks again, Georgia, and you too, Ben. I can't remember if I already said this but I don't know how she would have coped without you being there.'

I had to look away from the deep stare he was giving me, his red-rimmed eyes fixed on mine, full of gratitude and emotion. I noticed Ben look down at a piece of fluff on his jumper, unsure where to put himself.

'It's fine, I did what any best friend would do. Now come on, I'm desperate to meet your new princess,' I said, pecking Mike on his cheek.

I gave Ben a smile that I hoped would say our chat was to be continued.

Somehow Marie had lucked out and got a private room. A kind-faced nurse told us to wipe our hands clean with antibacterial gel before we were all allowed in to see them. I gasped stepping through the door seeing my best friend cradling this tiny bundle wrapped in a pale pink blanket; she seemed so serene and blissful it couldn't only be the result of the gas and air she'd been on.

'Ah hey, guys.' Marie beamed at us both and winced as she tried to sit up in the bed.

'Oh wow, Marie, how are you doing?' I stepped closer. I couldn't take my eyes off the baby in her arms.

'Tired, sore, but my God I feel amazing,' she said in a groggy voice. 'So, do you want to say hello to her? Her name is Lily and she is very excited to meet her Aunty Georgia, and Uncle Ben.'

'She is the smallest thing I've ever seen!' Ben shook his head in disbelief.

'Lily,' I breathed.

'Do you like it?' Marie looked up at me.

'I thought you were going to go with Beyoncé,' I teased. 'But looking at her, Lily is just perfect.'

'Cole wanted to call her Makka Pakka from *In The Night Garden*, but we managed to change his mind.'

'Who?' Ben asked blankly.

I let out a laugh and felt a warm glow watching this amazing family unit in front of my eyes.

'You look incredible. And she is the spit of you.' I placed a kiss on Marie's head and leant in to get a better look at baby Lily. She was fast asleep, eyes closed and long eyelashes fanned out into half smiles on her porcelain skin. She did not look like she had just been forced out of Marie's nether regions less than an hour ago.

'It'll be you next,' Mike piped up.

Marie gave me a look; she obviously hadn't filled Mike in on the dramas we'd been having.

'Mmm, maybe,' I mused, suddenly feeling rather warm in this room, and not wanting to catch Ben's eye.

'After your help making sure this one got here safely I reckon you're more than ready to bring a mini Georgia or Ben into the world.' Mike laughed, not picking up on the look Marie was giving him.

'Maybe one day, mate.' Ben laughed along awkwardly.

'So, have they said when you can come home?' I asked, desperate to change the subject.

'Soon I think. The staff all seem happy with the two of us and they'll be wanting the bed back, so hopefully it won't be much longer,' Marie said before turning to Mike. 'Would you mind giving your parents a call and checking how Cole is? I could murder a cuppa too.'

Mike stood to attention immediately. 'Anything for you, babe.' He leant over and kissed the two most important women in his life. 'Ben, you fancy a brew? Leave these two broody women to it?'

'Yeah, sure.' Ben seemed relieved to be out of the way of any more potential baby questions.

'Georgia, you want owt?'

I shook my head. 'All good thanks.'

Once they had gone, Marie rolled her eyes to the closed door. 'Sorry about that. I hadn't told him anything about you two as to be honest I wasn't sure it really was properly over.'

I let out a sigh and sat on the nearby chair that was comfier than it looked. 'It's fine. You've been pretty busy.' I gave her a smile.

'Soooooo, have you sorted it out?' Marie asked.

'Yeah, I think so.' I coughed. 'So, no marriage proposal yet? Considering how fast Mike jumped up to get you a hot drink, getting down on one knee and giving you a ring can't be far behind. You are wonder woman in his eyes, and mine too.' I thought back to the stress and drama of when her labour had started. She had been so brave.

'Don't be trying to change the subject, missy. Today is all about me and I can ask the questions I want to ask and you *have* to answer.'

'That's what you say when it's your birthday too,' I teased.

'Well okay then, it's Lily's day of birth and if she could talk she would be asking her Aunty Georgia the same thing.' Marié stuck her tongue out at me playfully. 'Mike's head is up his arse today; I doubt he could even string a sentence together to ask me, but it's okay. It'll happen when it will happen. Nothing can dampen how happy I am right now.'

'I think you've probably all had enough excitement for one day anyway.' I smiled then let out a yawn.

'Sooooo? You and Ben?' she pushed.

'It's like you said – I need to let people in. I don't have to do it all on my own.'

Marie looked up from cooing at Lily and raised an eyebrow on her slightly clammy face. 'Good for you. You're just like everyone else. We're all trying to figure out our way through this thing called life. Sometimes you feel like you've hit the jackpot.' She paused and looked at Lily with such a rush of love and complete adoration it made me catch my breath. 'But to get to the moments like this isn't easy, simple or pain free.'

'Wait – are we talking about childbirth or dating men?'

'Both, I guess. No one has a clue how to be an adult or *do* life, you just gotta try your best and be happy with what you get.'

'Ben has also apologised about the way he went about things, so hopefully we can just put this behind us and start again, but this time in a mature, open and honest way,' I said in a voice that didn't sound like my own. It was measured, controlled and determined.

Marie's face lit up. I'd obviously chosen the correct answer. She went to clap her hands in support but struggled with balancing Lily in her arms. It seemed weirdly normal, Marie holding this pink, bud-lipped baby girl.

'Yes! Go, go and track down that hot man, work this stupid thing out and have the best make-up sex you can!'

I tutted and rolled my eyes.

'What? Then you can get one of these too!' She kissed her daughter and laughed.

'Let's not get carried away with ourselves just yet.' I smiled.

I got up and leant over and pecked her on the cheek and Lily on her forehead, breathing in that addictive newborn baby smell. 'Try and get some rest. I'll call you later,' I ordered.

'I'll try. Oh, and Georgia, thank you so much for everything. I honestly don't know how I would have coped without you, without both of you.'

'It's nothing.' I smiled before adding, 'Maybe I'll be asking you to return the favour someday.'

I left the two of them and headed to find the hospital café where Ben and Mike were hanging out. We had a lot of making up to do.

CHAPTER 30

Delectation (n.) – Delight, enjoyment

'It's on! Georgia, hurry, it's on!' Marie yelled. I raced through to the lounge. Ben smiled up at me, patting my bum as I went past, making me spill the glass of red wine in my hand.

'You're not making one of your special cocktails?' Shelley winked at me.

I laughed. 'I thought Chilean wine would be more suitable.' I suddenly felt very flappy and stressed. I didn't know where to put myself so I began wandering around the small lounge before she shouted at me to bloody park my bum somewhere.

'Right, everyone shush, it's starting!' Marie hushed us all. I squeezed in to sit round the ginormous dining-room table that I'd covered with every snack, crisp and nut selection I could grab from the supermarket. Ben placed his hand in mine and kissed it firmly.

'You ready?' he whispered.

I shook my head. 'Let's just turn it off? I'm sure there must be some interesting wildlife documentary show we can watch instead.' Someone threw Wotsits in my direction.

'Tsk. It's staying on. You can close your eyes and shove your fingers in your ears if you don't like it. Anyway less of your moaning and pass us a choc, will you? Oooh, we should have got popcorn and dressed up like it's a film premiere!' Marie said excitedly, before triple checking that baby Lily was still fast asleep in the carrycot next to her. Mike's parents were visiting and had offered to watch Cole, meaning they could both slightly let their hair down.

I gave her a look. 'I think we're fine as we are.' I was trying to stay cool, calm and collected but I felt this flutter of butterflies as our closest friends huddled in our flat, around this stupidly large table that Conrad had already walked into twice since arriving. He was here with Val and hadn't taken his eyes off her all night. I suddenly felt this burst of happiness, mixed with nerves, at how we would come across on screen, at being able to share our experience with everyone. Everyone apart from my parents who had messaged reminding me to tape it so they could watch it when they got back from their cruise, and Trisha who had been surprisingly guarded with her reason why she couldn't come over. She'd blustered about having a prior engagement but didn't go into details. In a way it was good she hadn't made it as it was already a tight squeeze in here.

For all the drama this show had caused us I'd been adamant that I wasn't going to watch it. I didn't want to be reminded of our awful fight, but Ben had promised me that it was all in the past and we couldn't miss out. Ironically, the TV show that I thought had torn us apart had actually brought us back together. It had allowed me to see what we had almost stupidly thrown away because of mixed signals, confusion and stubborn beliefs.

The opening credits started running, the room was filled with a Spanish samba beat theme tune, and 'Wanderlust Warriors' in newspaper-type print flashed up on the screen over a backdrop of some amazing shots that Clive had taken. The starry night sky of the Atacama desert,

Dwayne's bizarre-looking jeep trundling over the rugged red sand, the myriad of greens from the Patagonian National Park and the city landscape of sunny Santiago. It looked incredible and immediately I was taken back to this wonderful country.

'Shall I turn it down? I don't want to wake Lily,' I said, reaching for the remote.

'She's fine.' Marie nodded at the baby fast asleep next to her. 'She's just like her father, sleeps through anything. Ah wow, Chile looks gorgeous.'

I nodded. 'It was.' I took a deep breath to get ready to head down memory lane.

Anna, looking uber-glam, very professional and smiley, was shown wandering down a wide pavement in the capital. Sunlight that shone through the leaves of the trees lining her path cast her in an ethereal glow. She clasped her hands together, newsreader style, and began explaining the show, the rules and a bit about each couple before Polaroid style photos of us swiped over the screen.

I instinctively let out a little scream at seeing my face glistening with sweat, hair frizzed up, fill the screen in a montage. I placed my hands over my face and peeked through my fingers. Conrad and Ben both cheered, whilst Kelli was flicking her head from the television screen to her phone screen as she live tweeted about it all.

'Oh my God, guys! This is so bizarre!' Shelley yelped along with me, pointing at the telly.

'What on earth are you wearing? Why are you dressed like a man?' Marie asked, almost snorting her drink out of her nose at the state of me. To be fair, I did look ridiculous.

'Oh my God, I forgot to tell you about my case! It got mixed up with some kinky passenger on our flight and –'

I was saved from explaining any more as the shot of me looking extremely harassed slumped on the floor of the

Santiago hotel's reception waving a rubber penis in the air was aired. The whole room erupted into laughter.

'Whoa, guys, I didn't think you were into all that *Fifty Shades of Grey* stuff!' Jimmy winked, nudging Ben in the ribs.

'Hahaha!' Marie was wiping the tears of laughter from her eyes at the state of me.

'That was not mine!' I protested and had to watch through my fingers at footage of me kicking off. We'd barely stopped laughing when we broke into new fits of giggles at how unladylike I looked spitting out oyster juice over Ben.

'I'm so sorry about that.' I faced him, and he shook his head in silent mirth.

I felt this strange ache in my chest when I saw just how happy we looked at winning the task of gutting that fish. How had the rest of the trip gone so wrong?

'Is this hard for you to watch?' Marie whispered, having calmed down slightly, using her best friend skill of reading my mind. 'You know, after everything that happened?'

I shook my head and gave a small shrug. 'It's just weird seeing us on the telly, full stop. Gawd, do I really sound like that? Why has no one ever told me I have such a mannish voice before,' I wailed, cringing at how deep and Mancunian my accent was.

Ben shushed me and turned the volume up. 'You sound perfect.'

'God, he looks like a right tool – is that that Gareth you were telling us about?' Kelli asked through a mouthful of Wotsits. 'The one that cheated on his missus?'

I pursed my lips and nodded. 'Yeah, he was shagging that one.' I pointed to the smug face of Dawn. Then I shook my head remembering what Jade told me on the flight home, how she wasn't shocked in the slightest at Gareth's indiscretions and put up with it as 'she got hers too'. I'd only remembered to fill Ben in on all this earlier this morning, and he was as shocked as I was. Nowt so queer as folk.

After the initial shock of seeing myself I began to settle into my seat and enjoy the programme. It was incredible to think that the majority of the hours of footage Clive had taken, the shots he had sweated over and the camera angles he had worked hard to get just right had been left on the cutting room floor. I'd known a lot wouldn't make it as it was only a one-hour show but I was still amazed at how much had been missed out, including, thankfully, the introductions at the airport. Anna and Jerry had been right, Natalia and Tony's appearance was briefer than the rest of ours.

The scenes of Santiago were even more stunning than I remembered. The city seemed to be buzzing with activity all around us that I hadn't picked up on as we pored over the clues and maps. It was also strange seeing Dawn and Simon again. Marie had already commented how under the thumb that fella with the dad wardrobe seemed to be. I wondered what they were up to now.

The first challenge of the scavenger hunt made us all laugh. We all looked like right plonkers in our bright yellow bike helmets riding through the city following some cryptic clues. It was amazing to get an insight into the other couples as they tried to work out what it all meant. I was starting to wonder if Jade's ditzy blonde routine was all an act as she seemed quick off the mark in solving the clues. Dawn just barked at Simon to hurry up and figure it out, while Natalia and Tony seemed more concerned with stopping off en route at a cute-looking café bar for a quick glass of crisp white wine; maybe there was something in Jade's alcoholic allegations after all.

Dawn's face was a picture in the scene where she accused us of cheating in the library, like some school swot using their arm as a barrier to hide their homework. I shuddered at the sight of that dingy bar they had us in, especially the earthquake cocktails I'd developed a taste for, and breathed a sigh of relief that the drunken heart to heart I'd had with Gareth hadn't made an appearance.

Next up was the gutting a fish challenge. I warned that they might get a little squeamish but Shelley rubbed her hands together as excited as if sitting down to watch an episode of *Casualty*. I felt this bittersweet emotion that I'd been brave enough to actually complete this task, minus a small matter of fainting. You could see on mine and Ben's faces this look of joy, happiness and excitement at being in Chile together. I may have been biased but compared to the other couples we seemed to be the only ones having a laugh and not concerned with making sure our best sides were always facing Clive and his camera.

'That was vile. Never ever again.' I winced looking at the bloody mess we'd made on the chopping boards under Alfonso and Reyes's watch. 'But we won, I guess.'

'This is so cool!' Marie said excitedly during the ad break. I leant back in my chair after unwrapping a Malteser celebration, trying to take it all in. 'It's usually you guys that watch me on the small screen. I'm loving it!'

'Haha, yeah I guess. Although none of this was acting.' I waved my hand at her television set and shuddered, thinking of the amount of Oscars I could have won if it had all been one big scripted act.

She placed a hand on my thigh and gave it a squeeze. 'You look great though, well once you'd got your suitcase back. Everyone watching will love you.'

'I've turned my phone off tonight; I know I'm not strong enough to deal with any internet trolls.'

'Well, you should turn it back on.' Kelli beamed. 'Everyone loves you two! There's even a hashtag #BenandGeorgiaToMarry and another one is #Gareththeknob!'

I shook my head in amazement. This was all so bizarre.

With everyone's glasses filled up we got ready to watch the next part. Dramatic music started up after showing Ben narrowly missing out on winning the sandboarding challenge. The desert disaster clips were shown along with me tugging the under wiring from my bra and raising my arm in the air, waving it around like some saggy-breasted suffragette.

'You're not as daft as you look, are you?' Mike whistled as I laughed.

But actually, it did look pretty cool, especially with Ben and me jumping up to get involved when the other couples sat back. We looked intent on saving the day and getting us all out of that blistering heat. A pang of pride clenched at my chest. We really were a bloody good team. I leant over and squeezed his hand tightly.

Before I could get too nostalgic the scene changed to Anna explaining about the final challenge of the forest survival task. Everyone was oohing along with the building tension about how raw and wild this part of the world is. Anna solemnly explained how this group of inexperienced and basically hapless walkers were going to be put to the ultimate test of trying to survive the rough terrain.

'Here we go,' I muttered. It was Ben's turn to squeeze my hand.

'We've got this; it's going to be fine.'

I'd already warned everyone that they would get to see the moment everything fell apart for us. They had cut out all of the individual interviews, obviously so as to avoid having to give any more airtime to the rogue couples.

The forest challenge began with an awful scene of us arguing in the woods. My stomach clenched and I gulped down a bubble of saliva that had risen in my dry throat. Anna's voiceover informed viewers what was going on as I stomped around with a face like thunder. My body language was closed off, arms folded over my chest and deep frown lines marked my pale face. I shivered, not knowing if it was remembering how bleeding freezing it was in Patagonia or at what was about to come next.

'I sound like a right bitch!' I slapped my hand to my head. I gripped my glass tighter and tried to stop clenching my jaw so hard.

'Oh God, this is awful,' I moaned, turning round to slosh some more wine into my glass.

'Babe.' Ben squeezed my hand. 'It's fine.'

Actually, it was all right. Gareth and Jade had also had a blazing row and Natalia and Tony seemed to stomp through the thick undergrowth in silence. None of the couples came across particularly well.

'I guess it shows that no relationship can stand the test of nature!' Conrad chuckled then grabbed Val's hand and gave her a look as if they would totally nail a night in the wilderness.

'See, it wasn't that bad,' Ben whispered in my ear.

It cut to the scene in the log cabin where we sat down to our final dinner together. You could see there were problems between Ben and me; there was a shot of me hunched over on one of the brown armchairs as I flicked through my phone desperately trying to get a signal so I could message Marie or Shelley and tell them what had happened.

What I hadn't realised, as I was so consumed in the moment of what I thought was my solid relationship crashing all around me, was that Clive didn't have his camera trained on Anna but on Ben. He looked pale, his hair was even more messy than usual from the windswept conditions we had battled through to get to the finish line, and purple bags marked his eyes. My heart clenched at seeing him looking so dishevelled.

'I didn't think they would actually use any of this,' Ben muttered under his breath, suddenly occupied with peeling the label off the bottle of wine in front of him.

Clive must have asked a leading question as Ben appeared to take a deep breath and run his hands through his hair before answering.

'What have I learnt?' Ben repeated and flashed a bashful smile. Probably just stalling for time as he concocted something to say, some positive spin on such a horrible experience, my brain sniffed, as my heart begged for it to shut up and just listen.

'I guess the main thing I've learnt through all this is that maybe I'm not the guy Georgia deserves.'

Wait, what? I sat up straighter in my seat and called for Marie to turn up the volume a little more. I could feel him cringing beside me. No one in the room said a word.

'I'm not going to lie; I'm gutted we didn't win. Not because I'm really competitive, although if you asked my best mate when we play FIFA he would probably say otherwise.' At the thought of Jimmy his face lit up into the boyish grin I found so attractive. 'No, I wanted us to win because I never want to let Georgia down. It might be this stupid male bravado but I want her to always feel like she can count on me and I failed at this.'

My breath caught in my chest. I was still partially in shot, huffing at my phone not working as I raised my arm as high as I could to try and find some signal, oblivious to my boyfriend and business partner finally opening up. I looked like a right tool and now hearing him say these heartfelt words I felt like one, too.

Anna was now stood next to Ben gazing up at him. 'I think Georgia, like most women out there, will understand that you did your best and that is all she can ask for.'

Ben shrugged. There was this strange flicker of emotion on his drawn face that I didn't recognise. Was he thinking about his mum, thinking that he'd let her down when he'd pushed her away? My heart ached at how hurt he looked. How he had just bared his soul on national television and I didn't have a bloody clue. As it cut to another ad break I swivelled round to face him.

His head was buried as low as it could go. He looked like he wanted to be anywhere but here.

'I thought you wanted to win because of the money?' I asked him slowly.

He eventually looked up and made eye contact. 'I did. But that wasn't the *only* reason.'

'God, you two are a right bloody pair!' Jimmy said loudly, breaking the atmosphere. I rolled my eyes and laughed softly. It's true, we were.

'Come here, you.' I wrapped my arms around Ben. 'You never let me down.'

At the end of the show, it was time for Anna's final piece to camera. She was stood in the boardroom, the place where Simon had punched Gareth, and plastered on a smile that didn't meet her heavily made-up eyes.

'We have had some new information come to light, since filming the show, that has changed everything.' She paused dramatically and even appeared to lick her lips, totally playing up to the camera one last time. 'Because of evidence of cheating by certain contestants, it means we have to look at who placed second, so, we can in fact reveal that the worthy winners are Ben and Georgia from The Lonely Hearts Travel Club! Huge congrats, guys!'

'What the?' Ben turned to face me. 'Did you know this?'

I smiled coyly and nodded. I may have been a bit sneaky here and kept our winnings from him. I didn't want to ruin the surprise after all.

'Wait – you won?' Conrad boomed in shock.

I cleared my throat and stood up as the credits rolled; everyone's eyes were on me.

'Yes. Ben and I won.'

Murmurs of confusion grew around me; Ben's face was a picture.

'What? We won…' He trailed out, his forehead knotted in a frown as he tried to piece this news together.

I nodded firmly. 'I found out a few weeks ago when Jerry and Anna called and asked us to go to the studios. Ben couldn't make it.' I saw him duck his head in embarrassment. We had tried so hard since then to put everything behind us. It wasn't relevant any more. We were both going to learn and grow from what had happened – in the least wanky sense of the sentiment.

'I can't go into the details but the prize money is ours.' I took a deep breath to announce the next part. 'I have kept this quiet as I gave it some thought. I'm sure everyone in this room knows what money can do to a relationship, even more when it is a relationship and a business entwined.' Ben's eyes were trained on my mouth, trying to follow what I was saying.

'So, because of this, I felt that I needed some expert advice, that of a financial advisor.'

Ben still looked as clueless as everyone else. 'I met a lady, who despite being the most glamorous and perfect-looking woman I've ever met – and Ben's ex-girlfriend – turned out to be very helpful and extremely savvy. So, looking at the finances, doing the maths and having her on our side has meant I was able to get my head around how we should spend the money.'

I turned to face him and picked up his hand, giving it a tight squeeze before I continued. 'I hope you don't mind me going behind your back. I know we said no more secrets between us, but I wanted to do this for you, for us.'

'Wait, you haven't….'

'Haven't what?' Kelli piped up.

I nodded at Ben and turned to the others, taking a deep breath. 'The Lonely Hearts Travel Club is expanding and we have just secured the contract on a gorgeous building in London!' I squealed, unable to keep it in.

No one seemed to mind that my excitable outburst woke up Lily, who began crying loudly, or that the ridiculous table was in the way so people couldn't get round quick enough to hug us both.

'No, really?!' Ben stood up and wrapped his arms around me. 'But you said –'

'I know what I said, but I'm not always right.' I smiled at him, those words not tasting as bitter as I had expected them to. 'I have been looking into this and Alice has been a complete star, running through all the pros and cons. I feel ready and know this is the right thing, for the business and for us.'

He planted his lips firmly on mine to passionately kiss me. 'I fucking love you! You know that?'

I pulled back laughing. 'I love you too.'

As everyone congratulated us, Marie got Lily back to sleep and another bottle of wine was opened, I leant back against Ben's chest. 'You sure you're not mad at me for not telling you?'

He shook his head firmly. 'As long as you are happy then I'm happy. Thank you. It's going to be a hell of a lot of work but we've got this. I know we have.' He kissed me firmly on my forehead. 'Wait – but what about giving the money to charity like you said you wanted to do?'

'Well, I thought of that too. Looking at the figures and if, like you said, we can work hard enough, then having an extra base and more customers will mean that the charity fund receives a massive boost.'

'I think that's a brilliant idea.' He pulled my hand to his lips and kissed it. 'I love you, Georgia Green, especially when you admit you're wrong.'

'Hey!' I gave him a friendly shove and burst out laughing. 'Don't get used to it, okay!'

CHAPTER 31

Expatriate (v.) – To move about freely or at will; wander

I hadn't had time to go through all the messages but despite the way my phone had been going mental I was surprised so many people had tuned in to the show. It felt a little overwhelming but amazing and exciting at the same time. I turned my phone to silent once more as Ben nudged me.

'There they are!'

We were stood nervously waiting at check-in. My tired eyes were still sore from all the crying I'd been doing. But this time it was happy tears, and I felt them well up again when I spotted who we'd been waiting for.

'We're here! We're here! Are we late?' Shelley cried out as she half jogged down the check-in hall, leaving Jimmy to carry their bags, which still looked like it took more effort than it should considering the size of him.

'No, you're right on time,' I said, pulling her into a hug and inhaling her scent. 'I still can't believe you're going,' I said nuzzling into her shoulder.

'I know. I still can't believe he's agreed to it. It must be love.' She glanced over at her new fiancé who was showing Ben something on his phone.

'But things won't be the same. What am I going to do without you?'

'I know things are changing and we all know how well you two deal with that.' She rolled her eyes and laughed. 'But maybe we need to create some new traditions. It doesn't mean we can't use this as a way to celebrate.'

I looked at her. 'What do you mean?'

'Well, we can meet to celebrate our awesomeness. Let's say September 19th is We Rule Day. We make the rules.'

'Sounds like a plan.' I laughed. 'So, are you nervous?'

She winced. 'A little.'

I smiled. 'It's okay to have mixed feelings, to know that something huge and amazing is coming but you are completely shitting yourself at the same time as it's so terrifying. That's the thing about freaking out, you get to ride the roller coaster of emotions whilst wolfing down a hotdog then bringing it back up again before the ride has even started. But you need to focus on the stuff that calms you down, whether that is Channing Tatum's half naked body or gifs of goats screaming.'

'Since when did you get so wise?' She grinned.

'Since I decided that I needed to grow up,' I said. 'And do you know what? It's not as scary as it first appears.'

'You're right. Plus, there's the matter of a wedding to sort out to take my mind off this momentous decision we've made,' Shelley said flashing her ring at me. Looking at the dazzling piece of jewellery I just knew it belonged nowhere else than on her finger. Mine would come one day, and I was totally okay with that.

'I know! Well as soon as you set a date, make sure we're the first to know.'

'Deal!' she said. 'Right, I'm so sorry but we need to be making a move. It's just that I know how hard it is trying to get him out of Duty Free, nah, who am I kidding? I'll be in Duty Free and he'll be in the bar. I'll make an Aussie out of him yet!'

'Gah, come here, you!' I pulled her close for a tight hug and decided to let the tears flow, happy tears for my brave best friend who had the courage to live her life the way she and Jimmy wanted.

'I love you,' she squeaked.

'You too.'

'See you, Ben,' Shelley said going to hug my boyfriend who also looked on the verge of tears.

'Just look after him, okay?' Ben nodded to his best mate who was acting as if he had something in his eye.

'I promise.'

Jimmy hugged me tight and uttered the same words in my ear too.

'God, look at the state of all of us!' I pulled back laughing, promising Jimmy that Ben would be well cared for. 'Right, go on, good luck, and call us as soon as you land!'

We watched them until we couldn't see them any more in the busy queue for security. Both Ben and I were struggling to hide how difficult this was. He placed his arm around my shoulders as we began to wander out of there.

'I can't believe they've gone,' I repeated for the umpteenth time, shaking my head and sidestepping a kid being pulled on a purple Trunki.

'I know, neither can I. It's like the end of an era,' he said in a dopey voice, making me laugh.

'But also the start of another one?'

'Exactly.' He planted a heavy kiss on my forehead.

As we dodged trolleys, businessmen striding around looking important, and large groups of families, he took my hand and pulled me to a stop.

'Being here has made me realise that I still owe you a proper holiday.'

I glanced up at him under my damp eyelashes. 'Really?'

He nodded. 'But this time no cameras, no drama and certainly no more secrets.' He smiled and shook his head at all that had brought us to this moment.

I smiled at him and looked up at the flight departure boards hanging from the high ceilings. 'Sounds amazing. Where shall we go?'

'You choose. Although can we maybe swerve the cruise option that your parents suggested?' Ben laughed.

'Deal.' I kissed him, cupping his stubbled jaw as he wrapped an arm around my waist. I guess I just discovered what the next part of our adventure would be.

ACKNOWLEDGMENTS

My dad likes to tell me the third novel is like the difficult third album, well, my dear father, I hope you enjoy the way this sounds. I don't think this book would be finished if it wasn't for you feeding me your famous curry and listening to me tear my hair out when certain characters refused to behave. Your faith that it will all work out okay, one step at a time, has helped me immensely.

To my mum who lovingly tells everyone and anyone we meet that her daughter wrote a book and they should buy it. Gavin from the Apple Store in Liverpool – sorry you got an earful! To my noisy, fun, entertaining family and especially my siblings for letting me blow off steam in impromptu dance-offs. I love you all.

Thanks, as always, to my fantastic editors Lydia Mason and Victoria Oundjian. Your words, insight and advice never fail to be spot on. This novel would not be polished to perfection if it wasn't for these two ladies. Also on Team Colins are the lovely Jennifer Porter, Hannah McMillan, agent extraordinaire Juliet Mushens and all at Carina/ HarperCollins – you all *get* Georgia, and me, and I am so grateful for that.

Thank you to one man who has been on this entire journey with me. Who can argue with fate for bringing us together? John Siddle, you inspire me to be the best version of me that I can be. I cannot imagine my life without you and your lovely family in it.

Huge virtual and real-life hugs for my bunch of wonderful and wise writing friends; you guys have been such incredible role models and supporters. To friends and followers on Twitter, Facebook, Instagram, Snapchat and my blog, you guys all deserve high fives for being so awesome.

To Jen Atkinson (ooh, fancy new married name!), you have been by my side for so long I cannot imagine (and wouldn't want) you anywhere else!

Since writing the first two novels in the Lonely Hearts Travel Club series my life has ramped up quite a lot. I would like to say a sincere and heartfelt thanks to everyone who has bought, read, reviewed and shared *Destination Thailand* and *Destination India*. If I could meet and hug you all then I would. Your support with my writing and my blog (www.notwedordead.com) means the absolute world and I don't take any of it for granted.

If you've never truly felt where your place is in this world, then this series of books is for you. One day I hope you will find what you are looking for.